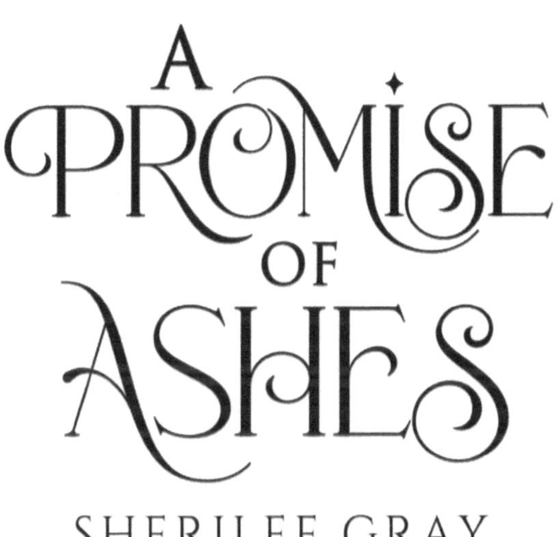

SHERILEE GRAY

*Today may seem dark, but I promise, tomorrow is worth fighting for.
You are fucking amazing, and the world is a better place with you
in it.*

Play List

- PICTURE OF YOU – The Cure
- LOVE SONG – The Cure
- ALL I WANTED – Paramore
- LAST RESORT – Papa Roach
- LAST RESORT – Falling in Reverse
- ADORE – Amy Shark
- HOW DEEP IS YOUR LOVE - Calvin Harris, Disciples
- WAITING ALL NIGHT – Rudimental, Ella Eyre
- CALL ME WHEN YOU'RE SOBER – Evanescence
- THROW YOUR ARMS AROUND ME – Hunters & Collectors

Prologue

Jasmine

Three years ago

Grumbling, I yanked up the sheet. It did nothing to stop the chill across the back of my neck. I'd shoved my lower leg out of the covers before I went to sleep, and now, with it still hanging out, goose bumps prickled over my skin. I slid my foot back under and reached for my quilt, then remembered it was mid-July and my quilt was folded on the chest at the foot of the bed—because I didn't need it.

Adrenaline spiked through my body, my heart thumping hard in my chest.

I squeezed my eyes shut tighter. Everything was fine.

Just go back to sleep because this isn't happening. It can't be.

We were traveling to Roxburgh early in the morning to help my cousins with something involving our family cemetery. I needed a good night's sleep.

Perhaps I was asleep? Maybe this was a nightmare?

A whisper. Close to my ear. I froze, terror seizing me by the throat, and I choked down my scream. *Not a nightmare.* I'd prayed to the mother every single day, ever since Zinnia received her gift. I prayed that if she gave me one, it would be different, and then I received my empathic powers—and I thought I was in the clear...

Another whisper. Closer. More urgent. Desperate. My eyes snapped open, and I cried out, recoiling until I was pressed against the wall.

My room was crowded. There were at least ten of them. Souls. All trying to tell me something. Some whispering, some shouting, others unable to do anything but show me, like a grizzly game of charades. Battered and bruised. Insides on the outside. Missing limbs. Mouths open in soundless, tortured screams.

I closed my eyes, covered my ears, but they were relentless. Wishing them away wasn't going to work. They weren't going to stop. Logically, I knew that.

Zinnia knew how to control it. She'd mastered her gift, using magic and sigils to quiet the noise, but when a soul was persistent, there was only one thing she could do—listen. Make them feel heard. But I didn't want to. I didn't want any part of this. This wasn't a gift; it was a curse. A living hell. Yet I knew, deep down to my soul, there was no escape from it. The only way to make them go away was to hear them out.

I was breathing so hard, I was on the verge of hyperventilating, and the tight band of fear around my chest wasn't going anywhere. Slowly, I lowered my hands from my ears and opened my eyes. The ghostly figures swarmed forward, crowding me. I wrapped my arms around myself, sucking down desperate breaths, trying to hear what they were saying.

They were talking over one another, but their fear and horror came through loud and clear.

"P-please, one at a time," I said, but they weren't listening. It was as if they'd been waiting for this very moment, waiting for me to acknowledge them, and they were afraid if they didn't get it out now, they'd never get the chance again.

Ren.

The name filled my mind until it became almost a chant.

Tell Ren. Tell Ren. Tell Ren.

Over and over again, amid their whispers and cries, Ren's name was said. These souls, they had a message for Ren—my cousin Willow's familiar.

Their words, the images, rolled into one, and the message became clear.

"I u-understand," I said, trying to get them to stop.

They didn't. They came at me over and over again, battering my subconscious with everything they were feeling, that they'd felt during the most horrific moment of their lives. Sharing with me on repeat their grizzly deaths.

I was right there with them. I gasped for breath. "Stop, please. You can stop now. I'll tell him."

Their screams grew louder, more urgent, more panicked. Darkness crawled in from the corners of my vision. My heart that had been racing so fast seemed to suddenly stop. I gasped and grabbed for my chest. *Thump.* My heart took a sluggish beat, followed by a long pause. *Thump.* Another pause, longer this time. *Thump.*

The blackness swam forward, my sight fading.

Darkness. Quiet pressed in.

Then there was nothing.

"Jazzy?"

I blinked at the sound of Zinnia's voice. She was on the bed, lying beside me.

She brushed my hair back from my face. "You're back."

My gaze shot around the room, but it was just the two of us here now, and it was light outside. "There were souls, Zinny." I sat up and my head spun. "So many."

"Take it easy. Don't stand yet. Passing out happens sometimes. It's the whole straddling-life-and-death thing the first time, it's a real kick in the head. It shouldn't happen again."

"It never happened to you."

"No, but you're sweet and caring and feel everything deeply."

Her gaze was steady, sympathetic, and even though I knew what this was, what it meant for me, my stomach sank. "I don't want this."

"The mother gave you this gift for a reason, Jazzy. Trust her."

I shook my head. "I already have a gift. I don't want this one."

"She sees the goodness in you, baby sister, just like I do, like everyone who meets you does, and she knows what good you can do with your gifts and how many people's lives you can touch." She brushed my hair back from my face. "I promise, Jazzy, it'll be okay. And you won't be doing this alone, you'll have me."

I wrapped my arms around my sister and clung to her because I couldn't do this without her. "There's something else I need to do when we're in Roxburgh," I said against her sweater.

She ran her hand over my hair. "What's that?"

"They gave me a message...for Ren."

We finally finished the ritual, the reason we'd made the trip here, and I could feel it, the difference. Our family's cemetery had been tainted by evil, poisoned by darkness, and it'd taken almost two hours, and the combined magic of Zinnia and me, my cousins Willow, Iris, and Magnolia, as well as my aunts Daisy and Else to remove every last drop from the soil. I stomped my numb feet to get the blood flowing again.

"All right?" Zinnia rasped, then cleared her throat.

Our voices were hoarse from chanting for so long. I nodded, though it was a lie. I was far from all right, but it wasn't like I could do anything about it. I quickly finished dressing, pulling on my shirt, and shoved on my sneakers.

"Okay, let's head back..." Iris trailed off as she looked across the cemetery.

I knew who she was looking at without having to turn around. Ren.

Zinny had given me her sigil necklace to wear so I couldn't see them, but I still felt them. The souls, they surrounded me now because he was here. The closer we'd gotten to Roxburgh, the more I'd felt their presence. They were eager for me to pass on their message.

Zinnia turned and waved at him. I took a steadying breath and turned as well. A large red fox moved out of the shadows.

"Ren?" Willow choked out when she saw her familiar. He'd been staying away from even her, and it was causing her so much pain. She missed him terribly.

She took a step in his direction, but Zinnia stopped her before she could go to him. "He's here because I asked him to come," she said gently.

Willow stared at my sister in shock. "What? Why? How?"

"I got his number from Else. I wasn't sure he'd come." Zinnia rubbed my back, trying to keep me calm. "Jazzy has a message for him." She gave me a nod.

Willow's gaze sliced to me. I could tell she wanted to say more, to ask me what it was, but she didn't.

My mouth was dry, and I swallowed repeatedly, trying to control my breathing when I felt the souls surrounding me press closer. Gathering my courage, I started across the cemetery, heading to Ren.

I hadn't seen him in at least a year. In his human form he was, well...beautiful, like model gorgeous. He'd never been conceited about it, though. He'd always been kind to me, to everyone, and funny. I hated that he was suffering, and despite how much I didn't want this "gift," I was glad that my first message was for Ren. I only hoped it helped.

He stood utterly still as I approached him. He didn't shift from his animal form, but I knew he was in there, that he'd hear me.

Not sure what else to do, I crouched in front of the large fox. Touch came naturally to me, was part of the first gift the mother gave me. Providing comfort was something that went hand in hand with my empathic power—that and the ability to soothe and heal others' emotional damage. So I ran a trembling hand across his neck. I could feel his anguish, his self-loathing, his helplessness. It rolled off him in agonizing waves. Still, he didn't move, his amber eyes remained fixed on me.

I gave him a shaky smile, hoping to put him at ease when my own heart was pounding like mad in my chest. "Hey, Ren."

He blinked at me.

I swallowed several times, sorting through the noise, narrowing everything down to what I needed to tell him. "They want me to tell you, they don't blame you."

He jerked back, but I couldn't let him retreat, not until he heard it all. I took his furry face in my hands, not letting him pull away. "Your guilt is keeping them here, Ren. They can't move on. They can't be at peace until you try to find it as well," I choked out, emotion welling inside me.

Ren shifted suddenly into his human form, stumbling several steps away from me. He looked around startled, as if he hadn't meant to shift. Tears trekked through the dirt on his cheeks.

"Ren!" Willow called.

"Ren," I whispered. "Don't go."

He backed up, then spun and ran into the woods.

Willow cursed behind me, her pain sharp, jagged.

The souls surrounding me retreated, satisfied that I'd delivered their message, but I barely noticed because all I could see was the horrified expression on Ren's face, the agony in his amber eyes. These souls were all people Ren had killed while possessed by an evil spirit, his body used, forced to commit all kinds of evil while he was taken along for the ride, witnessing every disgusting, twisted act. His guilt, that he hadn't been able to stop it from happening, was drowning him.

I forced myself to stand and walk back to Zinnia and my cousins, though it was the last thing I wanted to do.

Something new and powerful filled me, like a tether in the center of my chest was trying to tug me back, telling me to go after Ren, that he needed me.

It was hard, but I ignored it...because I didn't understand it.

Why would Ren need me?

Chapter One

Jasmine

"THIS PLACE IS the creepiest we've been to by far," I said and peered into the shadows.

"Agreed." Zinnia's fingers unconsciously slid over the hilt of the knife strapped to her hip.

The private cemetery was seriously old, the final resting place for the people who'd owned this land through the generations. Human teenagers dared one another to come here at night, trespass on the grounds, and walk through the crumbling headstones.

"I can feel them," I said. There were several spirits lingering here.

Zinnia nodded. "Me too. They're calm."

I hitched my bag higher on my shoulder. "Definitely not feeling anyone pissed off enough to try to burn a house down."

Zinny looked toward the old groundskeeper's place. "We should probably check out the cottage."

"I was afraid you'd say that." I reluctantly followed her. The old building was nestled among weeping willows, their branches swaying, making them look like bony monsters and shrouding the place in darkness. The cottage was mainly made of stone, except for what was left of the shutters on the windows and the wooden door that was currently creaking and banging against the half-rotting frame in the wind. You could guarantee if a place looked like something from a grizzly horror movie, that was the place we needed to "check out."

"Don't worry, baby sister, I'll protect you." Zinny chuckled.

I snorted and rolled my eyes, but I was glad as hell she was here.

As we got closer, a chill breeze brushed past me, lifting goose bumps across my arms. "You feel that?"

"I felt it."

Zinny had spent the last month at home, and we'd tried to cram in as much time together as we could. I'd rescheduled most of my clients needing clairvoyant help, but not those in need of emotional healing therapy. That wasn't something I could or would put off. Thankfully, I hadn't had many in need of healing this month, so I could devote every remaining hour helping Zinnia. Her time with me was almost over, though, and in a few days, she'd have to return to Limbo—to Death. We'd really been hoping she'd have found what he wanted by the time she had to return, something she could use to bargain with, since that was Death's preferred currency.

He'd asked her to find some missing souls, promising to grant her a boon if she succeeded. She'd planned to ask for more time with me. Unfortunately, so far we hadn't been successful. And it wasn't just Limbo, Hell was missing souls as well. When the reapers had shown up to collect them, they'd been gone without a trace.

We'd spent most of her month home investigating volatile spiritual activity in the city. So far, they'd been your average spooks. Souls who were stuck here for different reasons, tied to a person or place, who weren't scheduled to be reaped until whatever had them tied here was resolved. Not everyone died, then instantly headed where they were supposed to go. We were yet to find out what we were dealing with here—if it was one of the missing souls destined for Limbo or Hell or your average ghost with unfinished business.

This particular soul had been going up to the main house and scaring the fuck out of the family. The place had been empty for years, and when the aunt of the current owner died after a long stay in a nursing home, her niece, who had inherited the place, moved her family in.

There'd been the usual stuff—footsteps in the hall at night, lights going on and off, doors opening and slamming shut—but more alarming were the fires. There'd been one in the family room, when the fireplace door had opened and a burning log was tossed out, and another in the kitchen, where a wooden spoon slid across the counter and over the gas flame when the owner left the room. She was adamant none of her family were responsible. Her aunt had never said anything about any paranormal activity at the house, so either the soul was new—hopefully one of our missing friends—or it was old and having new people in the house had disrupted it.

An icy blast rushed from the cottage when I opened the door. "I think we're at the right place."

"Best we work quickly, then," Zinny said, taking the black candles from her pack and setting them out in a square around us. She grinned over at me. "Wooden floor."

"Oh, I noticed. Thank the goddess for that small win." I pulled out a can of spray paint and quickly sprayed the protection sigils on the worn planks under us. If the floor had been made of anything else, we'd be getting naked right now and covering our skin in a special oil for extra protection. Witches and nature, trees especially, were intrinsically connected, which meant they were like a conduit of power.

Zinnia lit the candles. The wax was mixed with a potion she

and Else, our great-aunt, came up with a few years ago, and it was highly effective protection against your average soul. For ones like the one we were about to tangle with, not as much, but it did provide an extra layer of protection, and layering up in these instances was always the best bet, which was why we laid out a line of salt mixed with cemetery dirt as well. Always have backup.

I turned so Zinny and I stood back-to-back.

"Ready to meet our friend?" she asked.

"As I'll ever be."

I took off the sigil charm I wore around my neck and placed it outside the square, followed by my leather cuffs inlaid with the same silver sigil. Zinny did the same, then her hands clasped mine and she started the chant, with me joining in a couple beats behind her.

It didn't take long. A rumble echoed in the distance, and the ground trembled beneath our feet. Not thunder or an earthquake, a highly pissed-off soul who didn't like us forcing them to come to us.

The wind inside the small shack whirled angrily, the door opening and crashing shut with more force. My hair whipped around my face, and my eyes watered. A high-pitched sound began, steadily growing in volume, until it was a shriek that made my ears ring.

"They're almost here!" Zinnia yelled over the noise.

I braced as the ground shook harder. The soul was old and filled with rage. "Not one of the souls we're looking for."

"No," Zinny yelled. "Way too old and powerful."

Souls were at their weakest right after a person died. If they were one of the ones we were looking for, there wouldn't have been anywhere near this much resistance. The door flew open with force, crashing against the wall, then flung back, slamming shut. A female shrieked and rushed at us, then screamed louder when she hit our protection barrier. She flew back, then rushed at us again, around and around the barrier we'd made, looking for a way in.

"We're here to help you," Zinnia said.

I watched over my shoulder as the spirit came to an abrupt halt in front of her. "You can not help me!" she shrieked.

"We can. We're not mere humans. We're more. We've helped souls just like you. Let us try."

Her hazy form flickered, her mouth opening in a soundless scream, her neck stretching in an odd way before her face snapped back into place. She flew around us again, floating to a stop in front of me. "I don't like it here," she said, her voice changing, becoming almost childlike.

"We can help you leave. I promise," I said. "What's your name?"

"Elizabeth." Her gaze darted around the room. "I don't like it here," she said again. "He'll come back. I have to leave. Let me leave."

"Who's coming back?"

"Mr. Stetson." Her form flickered again. "He'll hurt me! I don't want him to hurt me anymore. Let me leave. I want to go home!"

"Colin Stetson? He lived in the main house." We'd done some research on this place. The groundskeeper had shot Stetson, then paid for the murder with his own life. He'd been hung right here on the property.

She nodded, her gaze darting around in terror. A doll appeared in her hands. "He comes here when Papa's working. He hurts me." An image appeared in the corner—Elizabeth sitting by the fire, the way she looked now, probably seventeen or eighteen. The vision continued as the door opened and a well-dressed male walked in. She turned with a smile, but it dropped as soon as she saw who it was. She shook her head and backed up as he strode toward her, grabbed her by the throat, and shoved her against the wall.

The image dissolved and nausea hit me hard. The male who employed her father had been abusing her for years, if the doll was anything to go by. "He killed you, didn't he, Elizabeth?"

"That's why you want to burn the house? He's still here as well and you want him gone?"

She nodded again.

Her head whipped around. "He's coming!"

Zinnia's hands tightened on mine as the door flew open again and a second soul rushed in. It was Stetson. There was a gaping hole in his chest where Elizabeth's father had shot him.

He ignored us, a smile curling his lips. "There you are, Lizzy. You can't hide from me, girl."

She was trapped here by our spell and now so was Stetson. Elizabeth crumpled into a ball in the corner, shaking in terror. He'd been hurting her even now. The power of his emotion had trapped her here with him, even in death.

"Stetson!" I yelled, trying to get his attention off Elizabeth, but he was focused on his target.

"Blood," Zinnia yelled to me. "We'll call up Hadeon."

I nodded and sliced my palm. Hadeon didn't like being called, but this was an emergency. We could destroy Stetson's soul, but this monster deserved to suffer.

We joined hands again, and Zinny began the chant. "Hell, take this soul so dark, remove it from the mortal realm, never to return." I followed, oldest to youngest, always, so there was a chorus of voices, repeating the spell one over the other, an unbreakable loop of words and magic flowing from us.

We spelled faster, louder. The floor beneath Stetson shook.

The ground shuddered, and he stopped in his tracks, a look of confusion on his face. The floor glowed bright, heat and an orange-red light filled the small space. A loud rumble echoed beneath us, then the ground opened.

A second later, Hadeon, a demon and one of Hell's reapers, appeared. Seeing a reaper "on the job" was impossible unless the reaper chose it, and most didn't. Hadeon always showed himself, at least to us, although he did keep his face concealed. He looked to us, and although I couldn't see his features, I felt his displeasure. "He's one of yours," Zinnia said. "Take him."

His head tilted to the side. "Not your lapdog, witch. Being Death's consort means nothing to me," he said in a low rumbling voice.

"My association to him has nothing to do with this. I've called on you many times over the years."

He growled. "Didn't like it then, like it even fucking less now." Still, he turned to the souls, both of which stood frozen in place. Hadeon moved to Stetson and lifted a hand, power radiating from him, ascertaining if Hell was where the soul was destined to go. He growled again and both souls unfroze, then he grabbed Stetson, who screamed as soon as the demon's hand curled around his wrist in an unyielding grip, and dragged him to the glowing hole in the ground. Then, without looking at us again, they were gone.

Elizabeth stood to the side, her eyes wide as a white light, warm and welcoming, shone down beside her.

"No one can hurt you ever again," Zinnia said.

"Your father's waiting, Elizabeth."

She dropped her doll and stepped into the light.

Then she was gone.

I released the breath I was holding. "Fine. I don't mind creepy-as-hell cottages when that's the outcome."

"Truth," Zinny said. "I hope they make that asshole scream for an eternity."

I blew out the candles. "Unfortunately, Death's still missing his souls."

"We still have a couple days," Zinny said, but there was a note of defeat in her voice, and I hated it.

"Let's get out of here," I said, trying not to think how little time we had left.

Chapter Two

Jasmine

Zinnia curled her arm around my neck and bumped her hip into mine. "This is probably your best idea yet." We walked down the stairs to the main tunnel below the hellhound's clubhouse and into their underground den.

I bumped her back. "Do you really love the design?"

"It's stunning, Jazzy." Hemlock, her familiar, poked her head out of the hood of Zinny's sweatshirt to take a look around, then pressed her little face against Zinnia's.

"Hey, Hemy." She gave her head a scratch.

Hemlock was a sweet black rat and extremely shy. Most mediums had gentle familiars, and usually animal, not shifter, since they were less intimidating to the souls we communed with.

The first time Zinny went to Limbo, she'd left Hemy with me, not sure it was safe for her there. Now Hemy went with her, and I was glad she at least had the comfort of her familiar when she was away from us.

I inwardly shook myself. I couldn't even think about her leaving, not yet. Zinny didn't talk about what she did while she was away. I'd tried to ask her, and she always shut me down. Now it was an unspoken rule for me, and my cousins as well, not to bring it up unless she did.

She never did.

It'd always really just been the two of us. We'd grown up in Philadelphia with our mom, not that she'd been around all that much. Our dad left when I was a baby. Like Mom, he was a free spirit. Being in one place for any period of time wasn't something either of them handled well. We never saw Dad after that and had spent school holidays here in Roxburgh with my aunts and cousins. When Zinnia was old enough to look after me on her own, Mom had taken off to see the world. I didn't blame her for it, I knew she loved us, she just had a restless soul. But at times like this, I wished she'd put her daughters first and come home. But that just wasn't her.

She texted occasionally to let us know where she was, that she was okay, and we'd learned a long time ago not to expect more. Or anything at all.

"Do we have time to check out the nursery first?" Zinny asked, stopping outside Willow and Warrick's place. Willow's mate had dug through the wall, connecting three of the original rooms and turning it into one underground apartment. He'd also put in several skylights to let in more natural light.

"Yeah." I knocked, and my current tiny familiar, a mourning cloak butterfly who had been with me a while now, and had been resting on my shoulder, fluttered up to rest on my hair just above my ear. Wills asked me to paint a mural in Violet's nursery when she was pregnant, and now I hung out there a lot when I wasn't working. If I wasn't with her or one of my other cousins, I was usually with Relic or Roman.

Relic was my gym buddy, he'd also taught me a few self-defense moves. After what my cousins had been through the last few years, he said Thornheart females needed to be ready for anything. And Roman had become a friend—well, as much as you could be friends with a thousand-year-old hellhound with limited emotions. But being an empath, spending time with hellhounds was kind of a nice break from all the noise. The emotions they were capable of were far from complicated.

I'd asked Rome to teach me to tattoo after Zinnia left. Basic tattooing was sometimes needed in witchcraft, especially when you were dealing with souls, and I'd used my new skills several times already. That led to designing tattoos for Rome and his brothers when they asked, which they did more and more lately. In exchange, Roman gave me the ink I wanted. Both of my arms were now covered in pretty, delicate tattoos, mainly flora and fauna, animals and insects. I loved them; it was kind of an addiction.

The door swung open, and Warrick stood there, Violet nestled against his chest, holding her close with one massive arm. "Yo," he said and opened the door wider for us to come in.

Zinnia swiped Violet from her daddy as we walked in.

"I've come to show Zinny the nursery," I said to War as we headed into the new living room he'd created—and had to force my expression not to change, or to instinctively retreat, like I usually did.

Ren was on the couch beside Willow.

Our cousin jumped up, a wide smile on her face. She pulled Zinny in for a quick hug. "Hey, I didn't know Jazzy was bringing you over for a visit."

Ren stood as well. "Hey," he said, his voice deep, a raw quality to it he hadn't had before the evil spirit had possessed his body. What hadn't changed, though, was how devastatingly handsome he was. He was rougher around the edges, of course—the scars and that hardness he wore like a shield—but Ren was still utterly beautiful. Tall and muscled, that angled jaw and the sharp cheekbones —and that mouth. I'd dreamed of pressing mine against it so many times, against lips that had been sculpted by the goddess herself and designed to tempt us mere mortals with all kinds of wicked thoughts.

Zinnia smiled at Ren. "Haven't seen much of you the last few weeks. Glad I am catching you now, before I leave."

"Yeah, you two haven't been around much," he said with an easy grin, a grin that didn't reach his eyes. They never did anymore. There was a hollowness there, and I knew I couldn't be the only one who saw it.

His gaze slid to me, and he ran his fingers through his deep russet hair, making his scarred bicep bulge, not that I was looking. I didn't give a shit about his biceps, or any other...parts of him.

Yeah, right.

Fine. I was in love with the asshole. That didn't mean I liked him very much right now. We'd barely said two words since Magnolia's mating ceremony four months ago. Since I blew up at him after I saw him with one of the females he regularly fucked. He'd had the nerve to look at me the same way he'd just looked at her, like someone he wanted to go a round with between the sheets. Like I was no different than all the others, just some Band-Aid to numb his pain for a few hours. If he'd been sober, he'd never even consider taking it there with me...which had kind of made it worse.

I would've been just another distraction from the things he needed to deal with but wasn't. He'd been drunk, I should have let it go. Instead, I'd let my hurt take over, and I'd reacted. I'd called him a bunch of not very nice names. Ren's surprised expression was branded on my frontal lobe for eternity.

"Hang on a minute, I was just—"

"You were just what? Do you even know? Behaving like a slime ball comes so naturally to you now, I don't even think you're aware of it," I bit out.

The surprise vanished and his lips curled. He leaned against the wall, not taking his eyes off me. "You kind of sound like a judgmental bitch, Jasmine."

I inwardly winced, studiously not looking at the male now standing only a few feet away from me, because that hadn't been the worst of it. He'd dealt a final blow that day, and it had hit way too close to the bone.

"I don't really give a fuck how you think I sound." My voice shook. *Goddess, my heart was eviscerated in my chest.*

"Really? You look like you're about to cry." He straightened from the wall and stepped close, too close.

I could smell the wolf's perfume on his clothes and bourbon on his breath. He dipped his head, his face an inch from mine.

"Or maybe you wish it was you I was kissing, that it was you I was taking home to fuck?"

The rough way he'd said it sent tingles down my spine even now.

"How you been, Jaz?" he asked.

Embarrassingly, I jumped, not expecting him to actually speak to me directly. I tucked my hair behind my ear, then hovered my fingers above the mourning cloak butterfly in my hair, feeling her wings flutter, trying to cover my reaction and calm myself down. "Um...yeah, fine." I turned back to Wills. "Zinny wants to see Violet's mural before we get our tattoos. Rome said he could do them today."

Ren straightened. I wasn't looking his way, but still I noticed the movement. I ignored that as well.

Violet let out a cry in Zinnia's arms, and before Willow could reach for her, Ren was easing her out of Zinny's arms and laying her carefully over his shoulder. "I got you, Vi," he said in a low, rumbling voice that made my heart do all kinds of flips and flops in my chest.

Wills watched them, her heart in her eyes, then turned back to us. "I love that idea." We followed her through the living room and along the short hall to the bedrooms. "So what tattoos are you getting?"

The tension in my spine eased the farther away from Ren we

got, even though the feeling of longing that hit me when he was in the same vicinity had increased to painful levels.

"Our flowers together. Jaz designed it. Wait until you see it," Zinnia said when I didn't respond. My sister raised a brow, not missing how distracted I suddenly was. I grabbed her hand, ignoring the look, and led her to Violet's room. I hadn't told her how I felt about Ren. I didn't want her worrying about me when she had her own stuff to deal with. I had a bruised ego and a broken heart, both of which I'd given myself. There wasn't anything anyone could do about that but me.

"Holy shit, Jaz, this is amazing," Zinnia said when we reached Violet's room.

She stood at the door, and I watched as she stepped inside, taking it all in. Pride filled me. I'd put my heart and soul into every inch of wall I'd painted. I wanted Violet to look around and find something new every day. An insect or an animal, a flower or herb she hadn't noticed before. There were animals sitting, sunning themselves with their families, others hidden behind trees and flowers and shrubs, a tail, an ear, a paw peeking out if you studied the walls hard enough. A tiny family of mice you really had to search for.

"It's so beautiful," Willow said. "The amount of time Jazzy spent making this room magical for our baby girl...I'll never be able to repay her."

"I told you I don't want anything. I loved every minute of it." I glanced to a spot in the corner and wondered if Willow had noticed the golden amber eyes glowing gently among the leaves and the tip of one pointed, orange ear. I hadn't meant to do it, it just...happened. It was kind of humiliating, but I couldn't bring myself to paint over it.

Had Ren seen it? There was no missing how much he adored Violet. He was Willow's familiar, he was here all the time. He could have seen it.

I fought against the heat that traveled up my neck.

When we walked back into the living room, Vi still over Ren's shoulder, with one of his scarred, rough-skinned hands supporting her little booty, the other on her back. He was swaying side to side as he talked to Warrick. My belly swooshed as he pressed his nose to her head, kissed her softly, and breathed in her scent.

He turned when we walked in, his gaze coming straight to me and lingering before it slid to Wills. During our argument, I told him to never look at me again. He hadn't taken the note. Was he messing with me? I wasn't sure what else to think because I still felt his eyes on me all the damn time.

I studiously ignored him as we walked back through the living room.

"Don't forget movie night tonight," Warrick said when I opened the door.

"We'll be there," Zinny said as we walked out.

"Catch," Relic called and tossed me a bag of Peanut M&M's.

I snatched them up. "Sweet, thanks."

Once a week, the common room down in the den was made into a makeshift theater. Every Monday night the hounds rearranged the couches and chairs and set up the projector Willow got for them. She was trying to teach them about emotion and the right and wrong way to behave in different situations. The hounds felt loyalty, anger, lust, but tender emotions were a mystery to them, at least until they mated. I came most Mondays. The hounds' commentary was worth it, even if some of the movie picks weren't my fav. It had been Relic's turn to choose last week, and he picked a gory '70s flick, *The Texas Chainsaw Massacre*. I was hoping for less blood this time.

"Don't say I don't do anything for you," he said and plonked down on one of the recliners.

"I would never." I grinned at him as I opened the bag and shoved a handful in my mouth.

Zinny scooted down and opened her bag of Skittles. Hemlock was curled around her neck, getting comfy. "What are we watching?"

I bumped Roman with my elbow. "Do you know what movie we're watching?"

He rested his beer on his massive thigh. "*Romance is a Stone* or some such bullshit."

"*Romancing the Stone?*"

He shrugged.

"Yeah, that's the one," Relic said and tossed a pretzel in his mouth. "It's Wills's pick this week. She said we'll like it."

Zinny snickered beside me.

I glanced around the room. Warrick, Wills, and Violet were snuggled up on a couch. All of the hounds were here except those on security detail, and there were a few others here as well, wolves, mainly females.

My wee mourning cloak settled in my hair, her love still strong even in her weakened state. I sent love back, my heart aching. She wouldn't have much longer now.

The mother had given me not one familiar but infinite—the catch was they only lived a short time—some a couple of weeks, others a month. In the case of this little sweetheart, roughly a year. I wasn't like Iris, I couldn't communicate with animals, but I felt my familiars deeply, communicating with them through emotion.

The door opened and I glanced over as Ren walked in. He strode to a spare seat on one of the couches. Relic tossed him a beer. He caught it and sat back. One of the wolf shifters, Breanne, got up from her seat and strode over to sit beside him. His gaze sliced to me, and I quickly looked away. He'd made his way through almost every female in Draven's pack. Okay, maybe that was an exaggeration, but that's how it felt. I'd threatened to knee him in the nuts so hard he'd black the fuck out if he looked at me again. Sadly, I'd just been running my mouth, making threats I wasn't capable of backing up, which gave me one choice—go back to pretending I didn't notice when he looked at me.

The lights went off and the movie started. Relief filled me. In the dark, I could pretend he wasn't right there, that I couldn't hear Breanne giggle and whisper. Zinny pulled a fluffy blanket over us, and I held it up to Rome. "Want some?"

He shrugged. I tossed it over his lap as well. Zinnia leaned into me, and we settled in with our snacks to watch.

I finished my M&M's and tried to keep my eyes open, but it'd been a long day, not to mention night, sending that creep Stetson to Hell where he belonged. Zinnia relaxed deeper against me, giving me all of her weight, her breathing coming slow and even. I glanced at her. She and Hemlock were both asleep. I tried to stay awake a little longer, but I was so warm pressed against Rome, snuggled between him and Zinny, the fluffy blanket over all of us, that it was a losing battle.

I jolted awake when Violet let out a little cry. Wills quickly fed her, and she instantly calmed, drifting back off—that's when I realized I was lying down, my head on Roman's massive thigh, and he was playing with my hair. I started to sit up.

"You're good, Jaz," he rumbled.

Rome and I were buds, and hellhounds were tactile and protective of females, especially when they were in their territory, emotions or not, mate or not. Nothing about what he was doing meant anything more than he liked the way my hair felt. He'd never tried anything before, and he wasn't now, but for some reason, my eyes shot to Ren like I'd been caught doing something wrong.

He was looking right at me, and his eyes were narrowed. As soon as I caught him out, his gaze sliced back to the movie. I quickly sat up, wiping the side of my mouth. "Sorry I drooled on you," I said to Roman.

"Not worried about a little drool, Jazzy girl," he said, his gaze still on the movie. "You want to keep using me as a pillow, have at it."

I smiled up at him. "Thanks, but I'm good." I sat up and looked down at my sister. She was still fast asleep. I tried not to jostle her. She'd been exhausted the last week. I knew she was sleeping even less than me.

The movie ended a short time later, and while the credits rolled, a hellhound in one of the seats behind us piped up. "So the takeaway from this one is besides good orgasms, a female likes her male to protect her, but also treat her as an equal?"

"Well, yeah," Wills said and elbowed Warrick. "The caveman routine gets old fast."

"Bullshit," her mate muttered. "You love it when I go all caveman in the bedroom, Dove, and don't even fucking try to tell my brothers otherwise."

Laughter rumbled around the room.

Her eyes narrowed, and I saw the moment Warrick realized he'd said the wrong thing.

"Now, Dove..."

"Yes, sometimes a female likes a male to be dominant in bed, as you all know."

Noises of agreement rumbled around us.

"*But* you can't tell me some of you don't like it the other way around from time to time." She winked. "I know War does, don't you, alpha?" There was more laughter, and Warrick scowled. "What you need to remember is, there's nothing you can give us that we can't do for ourselves. When you find your mates, don't assume they'll fall all over you because you have big muscles and sharp teeth."

"We don't just have big muscles, Wills. And I assure you there is one thing they can't do for themselves," Relic said with a wink.

"Oh, I assure you we can," Zinnia said as Hemlock scurried back into her hood and she sat up. "And that way we don't even have to make small talk or stroke your giant...egos."

The females in the room burst out laughing, and there was more grumbling from the males.

"Right, I need to put Vi to bed," Wills said before looking at us. "Catch you both tomorrow?"

"Absolutely," Zinny said, then gave me a nudge. "You ready to head home?"

"Yeah."

Zinny got up with a yawn.

I tried to get up as well, but the blanket was tangled around my legs. Rome obviously felt me struggle beside him because he hooked me around the waist, tugged me forward, then gripped my hips and lifted me to my feet.

I grinned. "Thanks."

"No problem."

"And thanks for the new ink, we love it."

"We do," Zinnia said. "Thanks, Rome."

He shrugged one of his big shoulders. "Anytime. No hardship having a couple hot babes in my chair."

"Idiot." I gave him a shove. "Later."

He flashed his teeth. "Later."

I turned, and *bam*, I was instantly caught in Ren's sights again. I felt his gaze like a lightning strike. I refused to react. What the hell was his problem, anyway? I rolled my eyes, even as my heart pounded like mad. Turning away, I hooked my arm through Zinnia's, and we headed out.

Chapter Three

Jasmine

Zɪɴɴʏ and I walked out of the clubhouse and onto the parking lot. It was early autumn, and there was a chill in the air. We weaved our way through the bikes lined up along the front of the building, and I waved to Brick, who got the short straw that was patrol duty on movie night. The hounds looked like a human motorcycle club to anyone paying attention, which worked for them perfectly. If they weren't running in the forest in their hellhound forms, they were on bikes.

Reaching up carefully, I helped the weakened mourning cloak butterfly onto the palm of my hand. After hibernating through the summer, something unique the mourning cloak did in certain areas, she'd ventured out late last month and found me again. We'd spent months together before she'd found a place to hide away during the hotter months, but now she'd reached the end of her life cycle.

My tiny familiars poured every bit of love and comfort they

were capable of into me while I had them. I loved them just as much, and it hurt every time I lost one of them. From spring through to autumn, I lost at least one of my tiny friends every week, and in winter, while they lay dormant, hibernating or waiting to emerge when it warmed up, I missed them terribly. I wasn't sure why the mother did this, to them or me, but it seriously sucked.

"Thank you," I whispered to her as she lay on my palm. She gave one last gentle flutter of her wings. "I'll miss you." Then she was gone. A tear streaked down my face, the pain sharp, like it always was.

Zinnia wrapped her arm around my shoulders. "I'm sorry."

"I thought I had another day." I closed my eyes, gathering control, and used my power to soothe the jagged edges of my pain. It helped, which I guess was why the mother had given me this empathic gift in the first place. The weight of their loss would be too heavy otherwise.

The door opened behind us, and Ren walked out, Bree at his side barking out a laugh that had me jolting. I gritted my teeth as they strode past. "Night, *witches*," she called, waving without looking back, and the way she said witches, she totally meant bitches.

I hated her. Zinnia scowled after her.

Ren glanced back right as I swiped the tear from my cheek and stopped in his tracks. He said something to Breanne, and she looked pissed but headed to his hearse parked on the other side of the lot. He strode toward me, and I knew my eyes were huge in my head.

"Jaz...you okay?" he said in that husky voice of his that lifted gooseflesh all over me.

"She's good, Ren, thanks," Zinny said.

He ignored my sister, his pretty amber eyes locked on me. "You're crying."

A million replies ran through my mind. *Your wolf's waiting.*

Remember what I said I'd do if you ever looked at me again. But I didn't have it in me to start something with him, and honestly, there was no reason to. I was in love with a part of him he'd buried so deep, I wasn't sure that male even existed anymore. It was as if the evil spirit who'd possessed him had broken our Ren beyond all recognition, but when he looked at me now, I was positive I saw him. I saw the old Ren, and goddess, it took everything not to rock back.

I felt like an asshole for giving him a hard time at Mags's mating ceremony now. He'd acted like a dick, yes, but that hadn't been him. The male who'd said that shit to me hadn't been the Ren I knew and loved. He was Willow's familiar, part of the family, and he'd be in my life in some capacity for the rest of it.

So instead of the other replies flying around my head, I held up my hand where my butterfly lay and offered an olive branch. "One of my familiars died."

His chest expanded, hands curling into fists, and his intense gaze dipped briefly to my mouth before coming back to mine. No false smiles. Not this time. "Fuck, I'm sorry, Jaz," he said, deeper, rougher than before.

I nodded, expecting him to walk away, but he didn't. His jaw worked like he was about to say something else—

The hearse's horn blasted, and the Ren I'd seen in his eyes retreated, the barrier coming up. He took a step back. "I'm sorry, again, about your familiar, Jaz. Night," he said and walked off.

With my sigils on, I couldn't see them, but I felt them, the souls of the people he'd been forced to kill while possessed. Waiting, always waiting for him to do what he needed for them, to set them free. My heart hurt for Ren and those poor souls.

We headed toward my car.

"So, Jaz, um…what the hell was *that*?" Zinnia said. "There were like sparks flying, and waves crashing, and angels singing." She stopped by the passenger side. "Is there something going on there? Like did you two hook up or something?"

"Nope, we had a fight," I said and opened the driver's door. "Besides our stilted and awkward greeting at Willow's earlier, that was the first time we've talked since."

We both got in. Zinny looked concerned, and that's exactly what I didn't want.

"What did you fight about?"

"He was drunk and being a dick. I told him so. I think he was embarrassed. But we've talked now, so it's all good. No harm done." I opened the glove compartment and pulled out an empty Nerds candy box and carefully placed my familiar inside, then tucked her in the pocket of my hoodie.

I started the car and drove toward the exit. There was no way I was telling my sister what we really fought about. I didn't want her last few days spent worrying that she was leaving me alone to nurse a broken heart.

I felt Zinnia's eyes on me. "I'm glad you're moving past it." She glanced in the rearview mirror, and I did as well. The hearse was behind us. "He needs all the friends he can get."

"Oh, he has friends." I wasn't sure he spent a night alone. Ren lived just down the street from my aunt Daisy's house, in an apartment under Foxglove Funeral Home, his family business. Ren worked there as a mortician.

I glanced in the rearview again. He was obviously taking the wolf home with him. Cool. Whatever, right? He could fuck whoever he wanted. It had nothing to do with me. We reached the house, and I couldn't stop myself from watching his brake lights flash before he turned into the driveway a few houses down.

"Is Mags here tonight or with the crows?" Zinny asked. "I wanted to check if she'd heard anything."

My sister didn't like to talk about Death when she was home, but Mags was now one of his reapers, so she knew what we'd been doing the last month and why. "I think her and Bram are with the crows, but when I spoke to her this morning, they still didn't know anything."

Since Death couldn't leave Limbo, not in his physical form, anyway, he needed someone else to find the souls. Reapers would seem the obvious choice, but they weren't mediums and only saw a soul here on Earth when they were sent to collect them, which meant his reapers couldn't help.

Would he be angry with Zinnia when she went back? Furious that she hadn't found his souls? I'd always respected Zinnia's wishes when it came to him, but I couldn't swallow down my next words. "Does he hurt you, Zinny? Is he cruel?"

She swallowed several times before she turned to me and shook her head. "No, he hasn't hurt me." She squeezed my hand. "I promise."

We went inside and Zinnia headed straight up to bed, but I wasn't tired—not after falling asleep and drooling all over Rome, and not with my emotions so raw after losing my familiar—so I headed to the kitchen to make a hot chocolate.

Stanley smiled when I walked in. His green feline eyes filled with warmth. He was sitting at the kitchen table reading a book.

"Hey, Stan, how's it going?" Stan had been around so long, my and Zinnia's sigils didn't work on him anymore and hadn't for a long time.

"Not bad. We went to the Coven Elders Assembly tonight." He chuckled. "Else was in fine form."

Zinny and I were the only ones who could see Stanley, and that's the way he liked it. He'd made us swear never to tell anyone about him, not even Else. He'd been her familiar and soul mate until he'd been tortured and murdered by Else's evil cousin Edward, when Stan was twenty-one. He didn't want Else to change how she lived her life, something that could happen if she knew he was always with her.

Else had only been nineteen at the time, and losing Stanley had left her heartbroken. She was now seventy-five and had started dating again, like a year ago. Connor was a good guy. He made her happy and thought her grumbling was cute. It made Stan happy that Else was happy, but he was waiting for her, for the time when they could be together again.

To add to the twisted tale, Else's cousin Edward was the one who had possessed Ren, making the whole situation, that was already utterly horrific, that much more awful for everyone.

Nothing was black and white when it came to souls. Some instantly went where they belonged after death—Heaven, Hell, or Limbo—and some, like the ones that surrounded Ren, were trapped here by the person who caused them harm, or by unfinished business, or for a multitude of other reasons. Emotions were a powerful thing, strong enough to send ripples through the spirit world, which is why Edward's victims wouldn't leave Ren. They were trapped until he forgave himself. And some, like Stanley, went to the other side and came back, reassigned as spirit guides or guardian angels rather than being reincarnated so they could stay with the person they loved, which was another reason our sigils didn't work on him.

"Else is always in fine form," I said and grabbed a thermos mug.

Stanley chuckled and came to stand beside me. "She is," he said fondly. "So, you look kind of queasy. What's the skinny?"

"I saw Ren tonight. He spoke to me."

"Far out. Did he apologize?" He sat up on the counter beside me.

"No, the whole thing was kind of weird, honestly." I glanced over at him. "He took one of the wolves back to his place."

He winced. "I'm sorry. That boy is blind to everything but his own pain right now. You can't take it to heart."

Stanley was the only person I could talk to about how I felt. He was also a great listener. "I know, and I get it. But being in love with someone who will never love you back seriously sucks. I wish there was a way..."

"A way to what?"

"Take it all away, these feelings I have for him. To rip them out of me."

"Don't wish that, Jazzy. Love, heartbreak, it's how you know you're alive, and life is a beautiful thing."

I shook my head. "I can't imagine you and Else together. You're such a romantic and she's—"

"Fierce."

"Yep."

He grinned and hopped down from the counter. "I wasn't all sunshine and roses when I was alive, Jaz. I just see things differently now, you know? I don't need to fight or rage. I just need to be here, for Else. Speaking of..." He held his finger to his lips and turned to the door.

A few seconds later, Else limped in. Her soft, silver hair was disheveled, and she was in her fuzzy yellow slippers that made her feet look like giant baby chicks and a matching robe.

"Hey, pumpkin. You and Zinny have a good night? What was the movie?"

"We did. *Romancing the Stone.*"

She cackled. "The hounds would've loved that."

"I'm not entirely sure what they thought of it, though the consensus was orgasms are good. I'm sure they had more to say during it, but I fell asleep early on."

She laughed. "I'm not surprised. You and Zinny have been burning the candle at both ends." She motioned to my mug. "You want one of my elixirs to help you sleep?"

"Thanks, Else, but I'm fine. I think I'll read for a bit."

"Okay, pumpkin." She filled her glass. "See you in the morning."

She walked out and Stan waved to me before he shifted into a beautiful black cat and followed her. He only really left her side when she was asleep, and even then he didn't go far.

I finished making my hot chocolate, pressed the lid on the

mug, and despite what I told Else, I had no intention of going to bed, not yet.

It may only be early autumn, but it was already chilly, so I tugged on a coat and slipped out the door, grabbing the small gardening shovel sticking out of the veggie patch as I passed.

I tucked the shovel under my arm and sipped my cocoa as I headed down the street. Sliding my hand in the pocket of my hoodie, I wrapped my hand around the Nerds box. She'd been a joyous one, my little mourning cloak, filled with light and warmth. They all had their own personalities and this sweet girl had sent a constant flow of loving energy my way the last month. I was going to miss her so much.

I tried to stop myself from turning toward Ren's place as I passed. The mortuary was closed, obviously, but lights were on in his apartment below. The curtains were drawn, but I saw someone move behind them, then stop. And I realized I had as well, my feet just ceasing to carry me forward. It was Ren. His broad shoulders and tapered waist were perfectly outlined.

Then there was another outline right there with him, so close they'd morphed into one.

I quickly turned away. I didn't want to see, didn't want to know what they did together. I didn't need that in my head, and I forced my feet to keep moving. It was like my heart was constantly being hit by aftershocks, opening new wounds with every one. I'd tried to use my power to heal it, but when it came to Ren, it couldn't even come close. As soon as I smoothed one painful, jagged wound, another opened.

Shoving him from my mind, I focused on what I was doing out here.

The field was just ahead. In a couple of months, all the wildflowers would be gone, and the oak trees dotted around would drop their leaves. We had a field similar to this behind the house, beside our cemetery, but that one didn't have as many trees, and butterflies seemed to love it here.

This was where most of my familiars lived and where I was drawn the first time I lost one of them. I'd been coming here ever since. The moon wasn't completely obscured by clouds, thankfully, helping me see where I was going since my only flashlight was the one on my phone. I made my way to a small clearing, got down on the ground, and dug a little hole, then carefully placed the small box inside and covered it over, returning her to the earth like the others.

Laying my hand on the soil, I closed my eyes and thanked her for all the love she'd given me. Exhaustion overcame me, and I lay down and wrapped my arms around myself, letting the chill breeze drift over me, listening to the night.

I woke with a start and sat up, quickly checking my phone. I'd been asleep for an hour and was chilled to the bone. I dragged myself to my feet, picked up the hand shovel, and headed for home.

Everything was quiet in Ren's place as I approached, the light off now.

"You stalking us, *witch*?" a female voice said.

The glow of a cigarette told me where she was in the shadows a moment before Breanne stepped forward. She was in the shirt Ren had been wearing earlier, her legs bare.

"Nope. I had something I needed to do."

She smirked. "Something that has you skulking past Ren's place late at night?"

"Yes, as a matter of fact, and I wasn't skulking, I was walking."

She stubbed out the cigarette against the wall and tossed it on the ground. "I see you watching us. It's embarrassing. I'm embarrassed for you."

I curled my fingers tight. This female was stronger than me, faster. She could shift into a wolf and use her sharp teeth and claws to kill me easily if she wanted to, but as hard as I tried, I couldn't swallow down my anger. Okay, yeah, maybe there was some jealousy behind it, but right then I was too tired and cold and I didn't care. "As riveting as your sex life is, my walk tonight had absolutely nothing to do with you or Ren. And what's embarrassing is that you think you and he are an *us*. You're one of many, *wolf*, and not even in his top five. Have a good night." I walked away, giving her my back, which was highly stupid, but I was too emotional after burying my familiar and pissed off to think clearly right then.

A growl erupted behind me, and I braced for impact.

"Don't even fucking think about it, Bree," a deep voice said behind me. "Go back inside."

Ren.

Awesome.

Had he heard what I said? I cringed. He had to have heard me. I tried to resist, but I couldn't stop myself from turning back. *Fuck.*

He stood on the road in only a pair of jeans, his hands on his hips, moonlight highlighting every muscle and the thick scars on his chest and arms. I opened my mouth to say something, but nothing came.

What the hell could I say?

I turned my back on him and quickly walked away.

Chapter Four

Ren

I WOKE WITH A JOLT, covered in sweat.

Blood and screams filled with horror and pain, noises a being shouldn't be able to make, filled my head. Their eyes, wide with terror, locked with mine, my roars muffled, trapped, unheard as I watched my own hands slice and cut and tear at their flesh, unable to stop it—to stop *him*.

His voice in my head, like it had been then, telling me to stop fighting him, to enjoy it, that deep down I wanted it. His sick thoughts had been a nightmare on constant loop in my head.

I shoved back the covers and stood, thrusting my fingers through my hair. Breanne stirred. I looked down at her, surprised. What the fuck was she doing here?

I couldn't deal with her right then.

Striding from the room, still naked, I walked out the front door, shifted, and ran. I ran through the field that often had Jasmine's scent drifting through it. It was stronger now, but she wasn't here. She'd gone home.

I shook my head as I ran, trying to shake her image from my

mind. I didn't want her in there, not with everything else, not with his voice ringing through my head and the grotesque images of what he'd made me do.

My fox burst into the forest, running hard, trees flying past as the churning in my gut grew deeper, yawning wider until it was unbearable, until I was gasping for breath as I raced through the forest. I'd lived out here for nearly two years after it all happened. There was a small cave close by, and every morning I crawled out of the dark and ran to the same spot.

The red cliffs. When I finally reached them now, I shifted back into my human form and walked up to the edge, gasping, drawing in one desperate breath after the other. I could make it all end. I could stop this feeling, this awful, unbearable fucking torment inside me. No more nightmares, no more blood and screams and horror. No more guilt that I couldn't stop him, no matter how hard I fought.

All I had to do was take another step, just one more, and the four-hundred-foot drop would take it all away. I stared down the cliff face to the rocks at the bottom so sharp they'd tear flesh from bone, reducing a body to pulp.

My fox clawed at the ground, trying to make me step back, before he filled my head with a pair of bright green eyes, like he always did, right before I took the final step. *She needs us*, my usually tight-lipped fox growled through my mind.

She didn't, but it stopped me every time. This unexpected kernel of hope filled me, like a starburst breaking through the darkest night.

He didn't let up, showing me Jasmine and the way she'd looked that day striding across the cemetery, the way she'd crouched down in front of us. *"They want me to tell you, they don't blame you."*

The way she'd taken my fox's face in her hands when I'd tried to retreat and trapped us in place with that unwavering gentle gaze, holding us captive as she'd delivered her message. *"Your guilt is keeping them here, Ren. They can't move on. They can't be at peace until you try to find it as well."*

I stumbled back from the cliff's edge with a roar.

It was impossible, what she asked of me. How did you move past that? I couldn't, and I couldn't jump, not today, so I did the only thing that helped.

You're too weak and pathetic to even kill yourself, Edward's voice echoed through my skull.

I ignored the voice that my own fucked-up mind fed me. Edward's voice. Willow had exorcized him, casting him from me, almost three years ago. He was gone, but my mind didn't give a fuck. I strode to the rotting tree a few yards away, pulled out the blade I'd hidden inside it, and held the tip to my flesh. "Chest to rib." I gritted my teeth as I cut through barely healed scar tissue. "Midsection to hip." Another slice. "Right thigh."

The panic began to ease as the scent of my blood filled the air, as I said aloud and reenacted each precise slice. It was how he started each torture session, those cuts, in that order. My hands and this knife had carved them into innocent strangers. But now, it silenced their screams in my head for a little while. "Collarbone to shoulder." Blood dripped from the cuts to the forest floor. And when I made the final slice, "bicep to forearm," I could finally breathe again.

I dropped the knife and stumbled back, leaning against a boulder, its rough surface cool against my overheated flesh. I was a shifter, I healed fast, but my skin still scarred, and I deserved to wear every one of them. When I caught my breath, I scooped up the knife and tossed it back in the hole under the tree. Suddenly feeling fucking exhausted, I shifted back and ran for home, stopping by a creek when I got close to wash off the blood.

When I finally walked back into my apartment, it was seven in the morning. I frowned at Bree still asleep in my bed, then quickly dressed, shutting a drawer harder than I needed to, and she jolted awake. I'd told her to leave last night after the shit she said to Jasmine, but she'd obviously let herself back in when I was asleep.

"Hey…where'd you go?" Her gaze roamed over me. "I woke and you weren't here."

I pulled on my boots, lacing them up. "Thought I told you to leave last night."

She smiled. "You didn't mean it, so I came back. Why don't you come back to bed?"

"I don't say shit I don't mean."

She sat up. "Did you run off to be with that fucking witch?" she said with a lot of growl in her voice and shoved back the covers.

Jasmine had been coming back from that field last night, after doing fuck knows what. It was dark and she'd been unprotected. My stomach twisted remembering what she'd said before I walked out and stopped Bree from going after her. *You're one of many, wolf, and not even in his top five.*

Jasmine was the only one who'd called me out on my shit, who didn't walk around me on eggshells. *Yeah, and now she just avoids you completely.*

Not surprising after the shit I'd pulled. I knew exactly what she thought of me, how she saw me, and I fucking hated it.

I shoved my phone in my back pocket. "She's got a name, and where I go and what I do is none of your business." Why the fuck was Breanne still here? She knew what this was. She'd made it crystal clear she wanted nothing more from me than sex, and sleepovers weren't part of the deal, and sneaking back into my place was seriously fucked up. I shoved my fingers through my hair. "We got a problem here?"

She made a show of sliding on her panties, a sly smile on her lips.

I scanned her body, searching inside myself for something, any emotion at all, but found nothing. My cock didn't even stir. After my visit to the cliffs, I was back to the way I needed to be—cold, numb, detached. I'd had to find a way to shut everything down, because if I hadn't, I wouldn't be here. I'd still be living wild, my fox in control, letting animal instinct override everything else—or I'd be dead.

Numb worked most of the time, thank fuck, or there'd be no getting through the day.

And when it stopped working, I fucked and I fought to shove back the demons in my head, the self-loathing, to drown out that fucking monster's voice that was so clear sometimes I thought he was still there, and when that didn't work anymore, I went back to the cliffs. A fucked-up cycle that, for now, kept me breathing.

Only the females and the alcohol hadn't really been working, anymore, had they? Not like they used to.

"No problem," she said, her smile dropping, replaced by a scowl. "I just don't want you coming back to me, if you've been fucking that wit...*Jasmine*." She smiled, flashing her fangs. "I don't do sloppy seconds."

I didn't like hearing her say Jasmine's name.

"Again, what I do and where I go is none of your business. You need to leave." I strode out and down toward the mortuary door at the end of the hall. No, if I was honest, the sex, getting wasted, it hadn't really been working for a long time. But I'd kept it up because the truth was far too fucking terrifying.

Only one thing had been truly working lately.

A pair of jade eyes filled my mind, and my gut clenched so tight I sucked in a breath. Maybe I was a masochist now, because the images my fox kept throwing at me of Jasmine felt like pure fucking torture. Wanting what I could never have, a female I shouldn't even be thinking about but did anyway because just the thought of her was a lifeline, and a seriously fucked-up torment.

I might think my unsuspecting lifeline hated me, but Jasmine wasn't capable of the emotion. She did think I was a "fucking creep" though, and a "slimeball"...oh, and let's not forget the way I made her "skin crawl." Can't forget that part. I'd been drunk when she'd laid that on me, surprising the fuck out of me. I had no idea little Jazzy Thornheart had it in her. I'd never seen her so pissed.

But I'd more than deserved her anger, and I fucking cringed when I thought about the shit I said to her.

She sure as hell wouldn't want my slimy hands on her, and I'd never touch her, not in a million years. All I needed from her were her eyes on me.

It didn't matter if those gorgeous eyes were filled with disgust or anger—or disappointment. I just needed her to look at me, so that late at night I could close my eyes and see them, see her. So I could fall so deep into her eyes that the blood and the pain couldn't reach me.

And I was ashamed to admit I had a fucking entire file of photos of her on my phone, like the fucking creeper she thought I was. While she thought I was texting or watching something on my phone, I took pictures of her. If I wasn't too far gone, like I was this morning, I scrolled through them, and they helped me regain control. Yes, it was fucked up. No, I had no idea what it was about her that soothed the horror inside me, and I realized when I walked in and found Breanne still in my bed, I didn't want random hookups anymore. I didn't want any of it. Besides running to the cliffs and cutting, Jasmine was the only thing that truly helped.

What the fuck did I do with that?

I unlocked the door and walked into the cold room. The only reason I could think of was that she was the one sent to deliver the message to me three years ago, that those souls had chosen her. I didn't know exactly what they'd shared with Jasmine, but I knew enough about her power and how it worked, to know they'd shown her what happened to them, how they'd died—how I'd killed them.

The thought turned my stomach, but it also connected us in some fucked-up way.

Because she knew more about what I did, what that evil fuck

had made me do, than anyone else. I hadn't even shared it with Willow. I didn't want that in her head.

No wonder I disgusted Jasmine.

Shoving it all from my mind, I turned on my music and put on my rubber apron. The still healing slices in my skin pulled as I moved and helped keep my mind clear.

I drew back the white sheet covering Mr. Fulton. The witch was in his eighties. He'd died suddenly yesterday night in his sleep. The family was coming to view his body tomorrow, so I needed to get him ready.

"Let's get you dressed and looking good, Mr. Fulton," I muttered and got to work.

A couple hours later, I'd finished touching up his face and had him in his suit—

Something cold, like icy fingers, brushed across the back of my neck. I froze. It definitely wasn't the first time, but this shit was getting more and more frequent. I looked behind me, but, of course, there was nothing there. Gritting my teeth and fighting down the anxiety, I finished getting Mr. Fulton ready, ignoring the cold touches that kept coming.

"Go," I ground out. "Just follow the fucking light already."

Spirits weren't new here. This place got its fair share, but they were transient. They were passing through, if they ended up here at all. I wasn't a medium, but I'd felt them, had seen things all my life living here and so had my parents, it was part of dealing with death every day.

But this, what had been happening to me more and more lately, was something else, and after what happened to me, even with the rune Willow had inked on me to stop a soul from possessing me again, that fear was always there. It didn't help that things were getting worse and I didn't know why. I jolted when invisible, cold hands pressed against my back again, the iciness soaking through my clothes.

No. I shook my head when the thought filled my mind. It wasn't them.

It couldn't be one of the souls Jaz spoke to three years ago, because they were gone. I did what they asked, right? I somehow found the strength to come home, I left the forest. That was as close to peace as I'd ever get. No, this was someone, something else, it had to be. Those souls, they were just on my mind because the anniversary of that fucking nightmare was fast approaching.

It was hard, but I forced myself to continue to ignore it. I turned the music up and got back to work, telling myself over and over I was safe. Possession wasn't possible.

Maybe it was just Mr. Fulton? Maybe he was fucking with me? I hoped like hell it was, the alternative wasn't something I could stomach.

❧

I pulled up to the clubhouse. I hadn't been by last night. After preparing Mr. Fulton, I'd shifted and left. I hadn't been in the mood to be around anyone and spent the night in the forest—running, hunting, letting the fox lead and my animal instinct take over, keeping me firmly out of my own head.

But I couldn't be away from Willow and Violet for long. We were witch and familiar. Being away from her all that time when I'd been struggling so bad had only added to the pain. It was early evening, and as I strode toward the clubhouse, I heard the music, nineties dance, the kind of stuff Asher played if the wolf shifter wasn't listening to death metal. Colored lights flashed through the glass windows high along the wall.

"What's going on?" I asked Relic, who was working on his bike out front.

"Zinny's leaving tomorrow. Her cousins are here with some of the wolves. They threw her a party."

The rumble of bikes echoed behind me, and I turned as the

rest of the hounds returned from their ride, the ones not stationed around the clubhouse on security detail, anyway.

Warrick kicked down his bike stand, swung his leg over the seat, and started toward us. "Wills was waiting for Violet's daddy to get home so she could join the fun," Relic said.

Warrick was frowning when he reached us. "What's going on?"

"The females are cutting loose," Relic said. "Mags made some potion, supposed to get you wasted and no hangover."

He crossed his massive arms. "Who's in there?"

"All of 'em," Relic said.

"You been in?" War asked.

"Nope. Was told to stay the fuck out."

Grumbling, War strode to the door and yanked it open. I followed, the rest of the hounds striding in behind us. We all stopped just inside the doorway.

Fuck.

"Fuck," Relic muttered beside me.

War shook his head, cursed, then strode across the room and through the door down to the den, and his mate and pup.

Roman and Lothar moved up beside Relic and me and all three of them were grinning.

Dance music pumped through the speakers, and all the females were on the dance floor, bodies and faces decorated with glow-in-the-dark body paint, swirls and colorful designs I just knew Jaz had painted on everyone. They were all barely dressed, hair wild, and obviously fucked up on whatever Mags had given them. More than half of them were tits out, the rest in only a bra.

The Thornheart females were right in the center of it all, Asher with them. Zinnia threw up her arms, spinning, and then Jazzy was suddenly there, bursting from the crowd, her blond hair streaked with glowing pink paint, and unlike their cousins, who wore actual bras, Zinny and Jazzy had matching glowing blue ones they'd fucking painted on. It hid nothing. I was an animal, my sight was excellent, even in the dark, and I could see her tight little nipples perfectly.

I couldn't fucking look away, and I had a strong and sudden urge to tear out the eyeballs of every male watching her dance and laugh and sing, watching the pleasure on her face as she cut loose. She was right here, in this moment. What would that be like? To not think about the past or the future and just be.

I didn't want anyone else to see it. I wanted to greedily keep it all to myself, take a picture so I could look at her like this over and over again.

A hand came down on my shoulder. "Brother, you good?"

Relic's voice called over the music, and I realized I'd been growling, the sound vibrating from the center of my chest.

No, I fucking wasn't. I wasn't fucking good. Not at all.

Jasmine spun then, her blond and pink hair flying around her before she spotted us. Her gaze sliced from the hounds gathered around, then her gorgeous green eyes locked on me. She blinked several times, then she swayed a little, before she straightened her shoulders and started toward me with more than a little roll in her hips.

I couldn't move. There was a design painted on her stomach, swirling around her belly button. I tried really hard, but there was no stopping the way I ate up the sight of her.

She stopped in front of me, tilting her head back. "Ren...why—"

Breanne came out of nowhere and shoved her aside. If Rome hadn't grabbed her, Jasmine would have hit the floor. Jaz pushed away from Rome and charged Breanne, shoving her back. Bree spun on her, and I grabbed for her to hold her back, but then she was wrenched aside, and Asher was standing over her, snarling in her face.

Ash growled low, the sound coming from her chest. Breanne whined and quickly bared her throat. "You lay a hand on Jasmine again and I'll fuck you up, bitch," Ash said.

Ash was an alpha of the Silver Claw pack, and there weren't many in their pack, male or female, who would take her on. She shoved Bree away, who took off back to the dance floor, then Ash wrapped her arm around Jasmine's shoulders and pulled her into her side. "Well, aren't you a scrappy little fucker." She grinned. "But, babe, you gotta be more careful. Yes, Breanne's a screaming bitch, but she has fangs and claws and you don't."

"I don't like her," Jasmine said, still looking pissed off, and her gaze was more than a little unfocused.

"No one likes her, Jazzy," Asher said and chuckled.

Jasmine's gaze lifted, locking on me, and as soon as it did, something went wrong in my chest and my gut and I broke out in a cold sweat.

"Ren does. He likes her, don't you, Ren?" she said.

My mouth was dry, my tongue stuck to the roof of my mouth.

Asher snorted. "There isn't a female Ren doesn't like, babe."

Her lashes fluttered, shutting, locking me out before she turned away. "I need to dance."

"You go dance. I'm gonna kick these fuckers out. Females only, assholes," she said to the males gathered with me.

"You sure you're not sick of dancing?" Lothar said to her. "I got a soft bed and a bottle of whisky in my den. You want, Ash, we could have a party of our own."

"And I've got a vibrator and a bottle of bourbon back at the keep. I'm good," she said, barely sparing him a glance. "Now, all of you, fuck off." Then she strode away to join her females.

"Harsh," Relic said, grinning wide.

The door to the dens below opened and Willow ran out, a huge smile on her face as she rushed to dance, and for a moment, I almost fucking smiled. All I'd ever wanted was for her to be safe and happy, and she was. So fucking happy.

Warrick filled the doorway she'd just walked through, jabbed a finger at us, and then pointed at the exit behind us, silently telling us to get the fuck out, then he disappeared, going back down to look after Violet.

As we were filing out, the hounds grumbling all the way, a new song started. The females cheered and whooped, and I tried not to, but I couldn't stop myself from turning back to get one last look.

And if no one had been with me, I would've snapped a picture of Jasmine in that moment. Head thrown back, blond and pink-streaked hair flying everywhere. Huge smile on her beautiful face.

My memory would have to be enough, but I didn't think I'd have any trouble remembering.

Fuck, no. The sight of her was burned into my mind like another scar.

Another I never wanted to heal.

Chapter Five

Jasmine

THERE WAS STILL PINK in my hair. It wasn't as bright, but it would probably take a few more washes to get it all out. I lay on my bed and tried to calm my anxiety. Zinnia was leaving today, going back to Death, going back empty-handed. She said he hadn't hurt her, but she could be lying for my benefit.

I slid my sketchpad and charcoal aside, unable to focus. I worried about her the entire time she was there, and I wouldn't be able to talk to her, not even text or call, for a whole month. I wouldn't know if she was okay until she walked through that gateway in another month's time.

Since drawing wasn't working this morning, I snatched up my phone instead to distract myself while I waited for her to get here. She was doing the rounds, saying her goodbyes. It was self-ish, but the goodbyes and seeing my family sad all in one day was more than I could take, so I sat that part out. I clicked on Nightscape to check my notifications, then couldn't help but smile. Asher had posted pics from last night. At least her page was private, so we weren't flashing our boobs to all of Roxburgh.

I flicked through them, then stopped. Breanne with her arms around two other wolves, smiling, laughing. Asher had dominated her last night after she shoved me, but they were pack, family. I hated that she saw right through me to my jealous little heart. The fact that she got to be close to Ren, to touch him, kiss him, talk to him in his room at night, yeah, it ate at me.

I'd never know what that was like, and I hated that I still thought about it, that I still wanted to know. Asher had tagged her, and I clicked on her name like some saddo stalker. Of course, her page wasn't private. She'd love to flash her boobs to all of Roxburgh.

I cringed, hating how bitchy I was being. That wasn't me, and I didn't like feeling this way.

Still, I scrolled through a few pictures, then a few more.

Don't be such a tragic loser, Jasmine.

But I couldn't stop myself. She was gorgeous, her body was perfect. She had all these friends, and the Silver Claw pack gatherings looked like so much fun. My cousin Iris, her familiar, Nia, the sweetest dog in existence, and her mate, Draven, their alpha, were featured in quite a few photos. I'd been to pack land, of course, but I'd never stuck around for one of their parties.

I flicked to the next picture. It was of Draven and Warrick, and Ren was with them. They looked deep in conversation. The next one was a selfie, and she was on Ren's lap. She was grinning, and he was talking to someone beside him.

The next was a photo of a male's bare, ripped stomach, obviously on a bed. There was a scar on his side, and she'd captioned it with a hot face and raindrop emojis. Shifters had their shirts off a lot, and I recognized the scar instantly.

Ash told me that after we'd had our little shoving contest, Bree had warned the other females in their pack to stay away from Ren,

that he was hers. Nausea curdled in my belly, and I scrolled away—
so quickly that I didn't look where I put my finger.

I froze.

NO!

The like button glowed up at me. *I'd liked it!*

I quickly unliked, but it was too late. She would've gotten a notification. I tossed my phone aside like it was made of lava and jumped off the bed. I wanted to hide under the bed and never come out.

Maybe she wasn't just sleeping with Ren anymore? Maybe they'd started dating? She'd posted pics of him, that wasn't something you'd do if you were just casual, right? I'd been busy with Zinny the last few weeks. I was out of the loop. Maybe...they were exclusive?

In which case, I was the one who was in the wrong. I was the one pining after her male, staring at him like a lovesick idiot. I'd walked by his place late at night, it didn't matter that he wasn't the reason, Breanne saw me, what else would she think? Then I'd walked right up to him last night, under the influence of Mags's potion, so far gone I'd actually been about to ask him *why not me?* The words had been right there on the tip of my tongue before she pushed me aside.

I was the problem, not her.

Me.

My phone dinged from the bed, and I walked toward it like it was a rattlesnake about to strike. I had a DM request in Nightscape. I felt sick as I clicked it open, because of course it was from Breanne.

Hey, stalker, feel free to add that pic to your wank bank. That's the closest you'll ever get to the real thing.

Then there were a whole lot of laughing emojis.

I clicked back out and shoved my phone in my pocket. Would she tell Ren? Of course she would.

"Jazzy?" Zinnia tapped on the door before she eased it open.

I tried to look normal and not like I was going to die of shame and humiliation. "Can I walk you to the gate?" I blurted. I wasn't ready to say goodbye, and I needed to get away from here. "I mean, if it'll be safe for me to walk back out on my own?"

Zinnia usually insisted on going alone. Death made sure she was protected on her hike through the demon-infested forest, but I wasn't sure he'd cover me on the way back. She studied me. "I mean, I can make sure you're safe on the way out, but I'm not sure..."

"Please," I said.

She mulled it over for several seconds. "Okay, fine, but I've got one condition. You tell me what put that look on your face."

"What look?" I said, trying to deny what was obviously plain to see.

She crossed her arms. "Like you crapped your pants in a room full of people."

I opened my mouth to protest.

"And before you even think about lying to me or telling me you don't want to worry me or burden me with your problems right before I go back, don't. This isn't my first rodeo. I've been going to Limbo for a while now, and I come back every time unscathed, don't I? No, I don't like going there or talking about it, because when I'm here, I want to enjoy every moment I have with you, with my family. It's boring there, honestly, so talk to me."

She was lying. I could tell. "Zinny..."

"Talk to me, Jazzy. Don't shut me out. I'm your big sister, so let me do my job." She grinned. "Distract me."

I shoved my feet in my boots and snatched up my jacket. "Fine. I'll fill you in on our hike." I'd do whatever Zinny needed, even if that meant telling her what a dick I'd been the last few months and what a massive idiot I'd just made of myself.

We pulled up to the entrance of Oldwood Forest thirty minutes later. It was at the southernmost end of the larger Roxburgh State Forest, and infested with a whole bunch of demons. Zinnia grabbed her large pack from the back, filled with a few more books, some of her favorite moisturizer and other toiletries, and some more clothes as well. Limbo didn't exactly cater to the living. I'd slipped in some of her favorite treats as well. Skittles, of course, and sometimes a girl just needed chocolate.

She lifted Hemlock off the car seat. "Hop up, Hemy," she said. Hemlock scurried up her arm and into the pack, his little head popping out the top to look around before disappearing inside, to nap.

I locked the car, and we headed into the forest. A lot of the forests around Roxburgh were inhabited by demons, the kinds that couldn't pass as human. Thankfully, humans were naturally repelled by the evil that flowed from the most densely populated areas, and the witches in the city used wards and spells to keep them from the rest. The safe areas were safe because Draven's pack patrolled them and kept them clear.

Usually, we'd try to avoid the demons lurking here, or if I was one of my cousins or Zinny before Death gave her protection, I'd be kicking their asses and lopping off heads left and right. But for this hike, we didn't need to worry. Death kept us concealed or kept the demons away, I wasn't sure which, but they wouldn't give us any trouble. Without Death's protection, though? I'd be demon chum.

"You heard from Mom lately?" I asked after a few minutes.

"Not for months."

"I guess she's still in Paris?"

"Your guess is as good as mine." Zinnia nudged me. "Enough about Mom. Time to spill. Tell me why you looked like you'd just sharted when I walked into your room earlier."

I rolled my eyes. "We're just going right for the jugular, then, no easing into it?"

"Nope, give me the goods."

I sighed. I'd been keeping everything to myself, so she didn't worry, but I realized not telling her when she could see I was keeping shit from her would only make her worry more. "I like someone. Okay, more than like, and while I was stalking his female's Nightscape page, I accidentally liked an old picture of his naked abs."

Zinnia was quiet a second, then she winced. "Shit."

"Yeah."

"We're talking about Ren, right? And that bitch you shoved?"

I stopped in my tracks. "How did you know?"

She gave me a gentle smile. "Jaz, I've known you had a thing for Ren for years. I was hoping you'd tell me yourself, but no. So here we are, you forced me to squeeze the truth out of you."

"You knew?" I started walking again. "I'm so embarrassed."

"What's to be embarrassed about? He's an insanely good-looking guy. Is he a manwhore? Yes. Is he fucked up probably beyond repair? Also yes. But I see the appeal. Just be careful. A male like that will only cause you pain in the long run."

"You don't have to worry about him breaking my heart." Mainly because it was already broken, but there was a more obvious reason. "He's not interested in me. I'm in no danger of him seducing, then dumping me."

She gave me a look I couldn't read. "Just promise me you'll be careful, okay? The darkness surrounding him is thick and cold. The souls who visited you, are they still with him?"

"Some, not all." Some had wandered off, slowly going mad over time, searching for something they'd never find if Ren didn't forgive himself and set them free. Not all mediums saw all spirits. And for some reason, Ren's lost souls had chosen me.

She nodded. "He needs help, and if he doesn't let someone in to give that to him, he's a broken heart waiting to happen."

"I promise you have nothing to worry about, Zin. There's no chance he'll suddenly decide he desperately wants me," I said even as a pang of hurt slid through my chest. "And you're right, his emotions are...turbulent." To put it mildly. My empathic power made it hard to be around a lot of people, which was why I stayed "tuned out" unless it was needed.

She gave me a look. "Have you considered using your healing gift on him?"

"I have, but it's not like I can force him. Wills did mention it. She was going to talk to him, but she never came back to me, so I have to assume he said no."

"Idiot," Zinny muttered.

"Yep." I won't lie, it'd been another blow. I mean, what was he so against? The type of therapy I provided, or that it was me? There was a reason all my appointments were snapped up. What I did worked, and word of mouth from my clients ensured I always had work. "So what do I do about accidently liking that post? Do you have any sage advice for your younger, extremely idiotic sister?"

"Is your name on your Nightscape account?"

"Yes. And she messaged me straight after and said that looking at that picture was the closest I'd ever get to the real thing." My face flushed hot just thinking about it.

"Okay, so basically you only have one option here."

"What's that?"

"Brazen it out. You have no shits to give. It never happened."

My cereal curdled in my stomach. "What if she tells Ren?"

"Same thing. Unaffected. No fucks given." She grinned. "If nothing else, it'll confuse the hell out of them."

We were quiet for a few minutes, and I glanced over at her. I could see the change come over Zinnia the closer we got to the gates. She stood straighter, her expression growing harder, more fierce. She was bracing for whatever would happen when she walked back through that gateway.

"Does he talk to you? Like, do you have conversations?" It seemed an insane question. Did my sister chat over breakfast with Death? *Death.*

Her gaze remained focused straight ahead. "We bargain and

verbally fence. I know nothing more about Mors now than I did the first day I walked through those gates." Something moved through her eyes, something I didn't like.

"Are you scared, Zinnia? Are you scared of him?" I waited. I didn't think she'd answer or she'd feed me the same lies she always did to try to keep me from worrying.

"Yeah," she finally said. "I'm terrified of him. But so far, he hasn't hurt me. There's something, it's like...he's watching, waiting for me to do or say something, and the more time that passes, and I don't...the more volatile he becomes."

I wanted to grab her hand and drag her back the way we came, but I couldn't. She'd made a bargain and there was no going back on that. "Zinny..."

She shook her head and forced a smile. "I know after what I just told you, asking you not to worry is an impossibility, but I honestly don't think he'd physically hurt me. He rages and stomps around, but he's never raised a hand to me. If he ever had, no way would I bring Hemy with me."

"And he hasn't...he hasn't forced you to—"

"No, Jaz, I promise. He hasn't touched me."

Relief made my legs shake. *Thank the goddess.*

The small clearing appeared just ahead, a pile of unimpressive rocks and boulders sat in a mound off to the side. We strode over and Zinnia made a small slice in her palm, letting a drop of blood land on one of the stones, then she whispered the words to open the gate.

"Open sesame?"

She chuckled. "No, but so close."

The boulders started to roll, to move and reform.

Zinnia pulled me in for a tight hug. "Be good, be safe, and steer clear of fuck boys, yeah?"

I fought back my tears. She didn't need to see that. I didn't want to make this harder on her than it already was. "You got it."

"Love you, Jazzy."

"Love you, too, Zinny."

She released me, and we turned to the archway the stones and boulders had formed. Limbo was just beyond. Its dark forest was far from welcoming, and the path through it made of skulls even less so.

She didn't walk through right away, though. She waited.

"What happens now?"

"I'm waiting for him. I'm not going through until he ensures your safety home."

With the gate open and Zinnia on the other side, it didn't take long. There was a boom before something huge and black rushed through the trees.

It flew right up to the gate, so fast I stumbled back a step.

Death. He loomed at the entrance, and except for one tattooed hand curled around his long wooden staff, his entire body was concealed under his black cloak.

"Step through the gate." His voice rolled over us, deep and horrific, the sound of a million screams of terror. I wanted to cover my ears with my hands and weep. Zinnia gripped my hand, stopping me from retreating further. He thought she was going to deny him or try to renegotiate, I heard it there in that terrible voice, in the way he leaned forward as if he were waiting for an opportunity to snatch her off her feet and steal her away. His corporal form was trapped in Limbo, though he found other ways to communicate outside it. If he visited Zinnia while she was here, I didn't know.

"I will, but first I ask that you ensure Jasmine's safety out of this forest and back to her car," Zinnia said.

"Come here to me first, then I'll do as you ask."

His fingers were wrapped tightly around the staff, so tight his inked knuckles turned white. He was desperate to have her back. Death didn't like that Zinnia left him, he'd made that clear. He took another step forward and snarled when he couldn't go any further.

"You still don't trust me," Zinnia said. "I made a deal with you. I promised to come here every other month. I haven't reneged and I'm not going to now. Why do you always pull this shit? Does every fucking thing need to be some deal or a fucking bargain? Just say you'll keep my sister safe on her walk back to her car, that's it. No deal, no payment. Just do this one thing for me without a condition placed on it."

He was utterly still, silence stretching out between them.

"If you deny me, I'll have to walk her back through the forest, then come back again—"

"If she continues to search for my missing souls, she has safe passage," he said.

Zinnia blew out a breath. "Seriously? Are you fucking serious right now?" Hemy squeaked from inside the pack but stayed hidden.

Zinny said she was terrified of him, and I believed her, but she was tough and stubborn, and apparently not even Death himself could make her cower. She would keep to her end of the deal, but that didn't mean she'd make it easy on him.

"You failed to deliver the souls, which means the boon is mine," Death said. "Your sister will find them."

"It's fine. I was going to keep looking, anyway." I didn't want Zinnia dealing with a pissed-off Death because she hadn't been able to find them.

"Jazzy, I don't want you putting yourself in danger for him."

"I won't."

"If you want to leave here in a month's time, consort, then those souls need to be found," Death rumbled.

She spun on him. "You can't hold me against my will. You can't go back on the deal we made."

"If balance isn't restored, Limbo will become unstable. Chaos will ensue. Souls roaming where they shouldn't, barriers falling, gates...not opening."

Her fingers curled into fists. "You're Death, for fuck/s sake. Why can't you see them?"

"That's not how it works. Now come, do not keep me waiting."

She ignored him and pulled me in for another tight hug.

Fear had me trembling hard. How the hell was I going to do this? Yes, I'd planned to look, but I hadn't known the stakes then. What other choice did I have? "I'll find them," I said, trying to convince myself as well as Death that I was capable of doing what he asked.

"I know you can do it, Jaz. I know you can," Zinny said. "But you have to promise me you'll stay safe. That you won't do anything risky alone?"

"I promise."

"I will see you in a month, Jazzy. Even if I have to claw my way out of Limbo. I will come home."

She meant it. Nothing could stop her if she made up her mind to do something, not even breaking out of Limbo. "I'll be waiting."

Then she squared her shoulders and strode through the gate, brushing past Death as if he were of no consequence. She turned and waved, a smile on her face for my benefit, then the gate closed and she was gone, the boulders collapsing, rolling back to their pile at the edge of the clearing.

With my heart heavy and full of fear, I headed back through the forest.

At least Death kept his word.

I made it back to my car in one piece.

Chapter Six

Ren

I DRUMMED my fingers on the arm of the couch. "So...the party got a little wild the other night."

Wills sipped her tea, her lips gently curved while she watched me from the end of the couch. "Yep, though, not as wild for me. I couldn't take one of Magnolia's potions, not while I'm feeding Violet. Which was fine. I just wanted to dance and be with my sisters and cousins. I just...I wanted to be with Zinny."

I had planned to talk to Wills about the spirit I'd felt hanging around, how it was lingering longer, becoming more aggressive. I'd woken last night, the air so cold in my room that I could see it. And when it touched me, it'd burned, but seeing the sadness in Willow's eyes now, I couldn't do it. I couldn't cause her more worry, not today.

"You doing okay?" Zinnia going back to Limbo always cast a dark shadow over the family.

She nodded, but she was lying. "I've been going through our

library at home, and Rose has been spending time at the council library. So far we've found nothing that'll get Zinnia out of her bargain with Death. Iris and Mags have been talking to some of the crones in the area. Agatheena told Mags she'd look into it. Hopefully something comes of that."

The deal Zinnia made with Death was that she'd live in Limbo every other month, but that would change to staying there permanently when Jasmine turned twenty-one. That was in nine months. "How's Jasmine taking all this?" I cleared my throat. After Edward talked through me, my voice had never been the same, but when I said Jasmine's name, my already fucked voice went even rougher.

"She's not saying much." Wills shook her head. "When Zinny's here, I see the way Jaz clings to her. It's killing her. I haven't talked to her yet, but Mom said she hiked to the gateway with her this time and saw her off. She met Death—"

"The fuck!" The words exploded from me, loud and growled, and Willow actually jumped. Violet let out a cry from the other room.

Willow blinked at me and put down her tea. "It's fine. Death gave her safe passage back, apparently." She stood and went to get Violet, and I sat there breathing in through my nose and out my fucking mouth so I didn't lose my shit. I'd lived in that forest for almost two years, and the thought of Jasmine in there alone was bad enough, but standing face to face with Death? Fuck no. She was way too fragile, too breakable. So fucking vulnerable.

Willow walked back in, Violet held against her. At the sight of them both, the storm inside me increased. They had Warrick, they were both safe, protected by him, by his whole pack, but as her familiar, the desire to protect Willow and now Violet as well, was a fundamental part of me.

"Vi okay? I didn't mean to—"

"She's fine." She sat back down, and Violet drifted off in her mother's arms.

"That was a pretty big reaction," she said carefully.

I forced my muscles to relax. "You've already been through enough. You're already worried about Zinnia, last thing you need is to be worrying about Jasmine as well." That was all true, but I recognized that wasn't the reason I'd reacted the way I had.

The idea of Jasmine being hurt or put in danger—I didn't fucking like it.

"Zinnia wouldn't have let her go with her if she thought it was dangerous."

I nodded and forced myself to take a sip of my lukewarm coffee. "Yeah, of course."

Willow shook her head, a small smile curling her lips. "Jazzy's changed so much. When you first met her, pink was her favorite color, and she was so painfully shy it hurt to watch her around people who weren't family. Now?" She chuckled. "Well, two nights ago she was dancing in a room full of people in only a pair of shorts and a painted-on, glow-in-the-dark bra. She almost had a throw-down with a wolf, she's covered in tattoos, and she talks to dead people for a living."

I swallowed, my mouth weirdly fucking dry all of a sudden. Jasmine had looked...beautiful...and completely and utterly untouchable.

"She's actually consoling herself over Zinny leaving with another tattoo."

"Yeah?" I gripped the arm of the couch tighter.

Wills pressed a kiss to Vi's little head. "A bigger piece. She drew the rough outline for it a while ago. She finally got it exactly how she wants it. Rome's doing it now."

My thigh muscles clenched, and I had to fight with myself not to stand.

"So what's going on with you? You were gone a couple days."

There was worry in her eyes. I forced the tension from my shoulders and smiled. "Just busy at work." That wasn't entirely true, but I wasn't going to tell her I'd been too fucked in the head to be around anyone.

"I was worried, then I heard about you and that Silver Claw female. Breanne? So I assumed you were with her." Hurt filled her eyes. "I wish you'd told me yourself."

I stilled. Breanne? "Told you what?"

"Is she your mate, Ren? Is that it? You can tell me. I know it's scary and you might not think you're ready, but you deserve to be happy. So if you've found your female—"

"Who the fuck told you that?" The armrest groaned when I gripped it again. Bree sure as fuck wasn't my mate. I didn't have a mate. I didn't want one. I could barely function as it was; how the fuck could I protect and provide for someone else as well.

Wills studied me. "Jazzy said something to Mags. Sounds like Breanne staked some kind of claim over you."

"And she told Jasmine I was her mate?"

Willow frowned. "I mean, I don't know exactly what was said. Jaz called her your female, said she saw her at your place the other night when she was out walking. You guys seem to hook up a lot, I guess we all just assumed—"

"Well, don't. We're not mates. We aren't even friends. We fuck sometimes, but I'm done with that." I shoved my fingers through my hair and stood, pacing away.

"She was with you last week according to Jaz."

Pressure built in my chest, growing tighter and tighter. The need to fucking roar, to join the roaring already vibrating through my skull, damn near choked me. I didn't want Jasmine...fuck, anyone...thinking that shit. My reaction was extreme, even I could see it, and the only reason I was able to swallow the anger down was the sight of Violet lying against her mother, my instinct to protect them so much stronger than my outrage. "It won't be happening again."

"It's no big deal. Be with whoever you want." Willow stood.

"I don't want to be with her. I don't want to be with any

fucking one." The confession fell from my lips before I could stop it.

Willow closed the space between us. "Then why are you?"

Fuck. She knew, she knew what I was doing and why. No, she didn't know the details of my time possessed by that twisted fuck, but she knew I used that shit as an escape, because Willow knew me better than anyone. We had a connection that ran deeper than the one I had even with my own parents. "You know why," I ground out.

She cupped the side of my face, and I flinched, then forced myself to stay still when anyone I loved touching me made me want to run like fuck the other way. Holding Violet felt like the sweetest thing in the world, and it made me want to flay my own skin from my body. Hands like mine, the things they'd done, they didn't belong on someone so innocent and precious. But denying Willow, pushing her away again, pretending Violet wasn't here, would kill her, and I couldn't do that to her.

Wills brushed her thumb over my beard. "I've known you since you were fourteen years old, Renny. You knocked on the door, all gangly limbs and boundless energy, and I loved you instantly. My sweet familiar. You'd finally found me. Goddess, Ren, you're my brother, my son, my best friend...my sweet fox, you're a part of my soul, right alongside Violet and Warrick."

I couldn't do this. "Wills—"

"You've come so far...after everything you've been through. You've come such a long way. Don't stop. Promise me you won't stop trying, that you'll keep pushing. I need you. Vi needs you. Do you understand?"

She saw me, right into my very soul, and I suddenly felt as though she'd stood behind me every time I paused on that cliff's edge, every time I almost stepped off.

I nodded, and she leaned into me, her head to my chest, and I wrapped my arms around her, locking my hands together so they didn't touch her, didn't taint her.

"If you leave me, Ren, if you choose to leave me, I'll never forgive you," she said against my chest, proving just how much she saw.

I strode out of Willow and War's place a few minutes later, feeling wired as fuck. Despite my efforts, I was still hurting Wills. She was worried about me, and I didn't know how to ease her fears because I couldn't make her any promises. I'd fight it, the darkness as thick and sticky as tar, for as long as I could, but it wasn't getting easier.

As I strode along the caves, I told myself I was just walking, no destination in mind, but I knew exactly where I was going—to get my fix, my elixir, the antibiotics for the infection festering inside me.

She doesn't want to see you. Why would she want to see a pathetic piece of shit who carves himself up like a psycho? Edward's voice invaded my mind, and I forced it back down deep.

The buzz of the tattoo gun reached me first, a steady hum over low music and murmured voices, over the occasional crack of balls on the pool table. Roman did his work in an alcove off the common room and kept his gear set up there. Nothing unusual about me walking in there. I did it all the time. I hung out here more often than not. No one would think I was there because of Jasmine.

I walked in, and as hard as I tried to play it cool, to not look at her as soon as I entered the room, the pull was too strong. My fucking head swung her way as soon as I stepped foot through the doorway. The pressure in my chest I'd felt when I was talking to Willow returned tenfold as soon as I saw her.

Light flooded the large alcove where Rome was working on her. Jasmine lay on her back on the massage table, feet crossed at the ankles. She wore jeans, and her stomach and chest were fully exposed, except for a thin strip of white fabric covering her nipples. There was new ink already on her stomach and upper chest. Rome was bent over her now, one hand on the inside of her cleavage, pressing on the soft flesh to keep it taut, pulling it outward as he inked something on her breast.

Jasmine lay still, both forearms across her eyes. Her lips were relaxed, and she murmured something to Rome, making the hound grin. The pressure in my chest grew, and the roaring in my head was fucking deafening. I took a step in their direction—

"Ren, brother. Game?" Relic said, his voice having the effect of a record scratch through the noise in my head.

"Yeah."

He passed me a pool cue, and I motioned for him to go first. I'd never played so badly in my life, because all I could focus on was the buzz of that fucking tattoo machine and their murmured voices, interrupted now and then by Jasmine's soft laugher. My fox was clawing to be free, snarling and whining. He wanted to go over there. He wanted to snap and snarl at Rome even though he knew the hellhound could bite his head off with one snap of his teeth.

"You want in on the pit tonight?" Relic said absently.

My fox also knew we were faster, more agile than a hound. "Who's fighting?" Not that it mattered, I needed to blow off some steam. Badly.

"Me, Loth, Fender, Jag, Rome." Relic grinned. "Whoever else is in the mood for me to hand them their asses."

"I'm in."

"You're a glutton for punishment, but I like that about you," he said and took his shot.

The hounds had trained me several years ago, when Willow's role in the family changed and she became her coven's Keeper. She'd been in danger all the time, wasn't mated to Warrick yet, and as her familiar it had been my job to protect her. I couldn't fight my way out of a cardboard box, and because it was impossible for me to stand down, since protecting her was literally part of my DNA, she'd brought me here. It was either that or watch me die trying. The hounds had kicked my ass repeatedly. They'd been hard on me, but fair, and not without mercy. I got a few broken bones, some scars, but I left knowing how to fight really fucking well.

Fender whistled, and I lifted my head as Jasmine jumped off the table, one arm across her chest. There were four butterflies on her stomach as if they were flying down and more flying upward all from a larger one between her breasts; one just above her cleavage, one on her upper chest, one by her collarbone and another on the side of her neck, all different colors and species.

"Looks fucking awesome, Jaz," Relic said.

She grinned, blushing when the rest of the hounds howled their agreement. She checked it out in the mirror Rome had there, then spun to him, beaming, and threw her arms around him. He patted her on the back, then dipped his face into her neck and scented her.

The urge to tear his nose off his fucking face and make him eat it filled me as the roar in my chest grew so intense I had to grit my teeth so it didn't burst free. What the fuck was wrong with me? Hounds were tactile, they scented, they touched, it didn't mean shit, I knew this. Yes, I had a fucked-up obsession with her, a weird connection, but I'd never go there with Jasmine. And yes, I recognized how beautiful she was, but I thought lots of things were beautiful, that didn't mean I wanted to fuck them. She was too young, too fucking innocent, especially for someone like me.

But when Roman started swiping antiseptic cream on her fucking chest, the way he touched her, the way she looked at him —I had to turn away, *this close* to going over there and—what? What did I think I was going to do?

I finally heard her saying goodbye, and I couldn't stop myself from turning back. She had her shirt on again, and for some reason, that soothed us—my fox wasn't baring his teeth anymore, at least.

Her gaze lifted, finding me, and she froze, just for a split second. Her throat worked before she quickly looked away and started for the door.

"Jaz," Rome called.

She turned back, and he tossed something to her. She caught it, lifted it, and laughed. Peanut M&M's, her favorite.

I didn't like that either. Not at all. So much so, there was no stopping my feet from following her. "Catch you later tonight," I said to Relic and told myself I was leaving anyway, when I knew I was full of shit.

I'd tried to convince myself there was nothing going on between Jaz and Rome, but now? They were close, too fucking close. Fuck, were they...were they actually together?

I walked out and it was as if my fox was locked on to her scent like a fucking bloodhound, following her as if his life depended on it.

And I let him.

I walked out into the parking lot in time to see her drive away.

I got in the hearse and followed.

Chapter Seven

Jasmine

I STRODE into my field at the end of the street and breathed in the cool air. The scent of this place helped soothe me instantly. Walking to my favorite oak tree, I kicked off my shoes, pulled off my socks, and sat down, burying my toes in the earth. Placing my hands down beside me, I let tendrils of magic flow downward. The earth replied, sending vibrations back through my feet and hands, the oak humming softly behind me.

When I felt off-kilter, or alone, this place patched me up, stitched me back together. I'd been coming here a lot since Zinny started spending time in Limbo.

And now that I was alone again, all my fears bubbled to the surface. Somehow, I had to find those missing souls or my sister could be trapped in Limbo indefinitely. Who the hell did Death think I was? I was not my sister. Zinnia was the capable one, the powerful one. Hunting for the souls while she was here had been easy. She led, I followed. I always followed.

Breathe.

You can do this. You have to do this.

I forced myself to focus on the tender skin on my chest and stomach and the new ink Rome had just given me instead of thinking about what I had to do, or what Zinnia was doing now and if she was okay.

I took another deep breath and wriggled, getting more comfortable. The packet of peanut M&M's crackled in my pocket. I smiled and slipped it out. Relic always had them for me on movie nights. He'd started doing it after seeing Rome give them to me. I liked to snack when I was nervous, and so I brought some along when I got my first tattoo. Now it'd become a tradition between Rome and me. He always had some for me whenever I got a tattoo, even though I wasn't nervous anymore. No, getting new ink helped me get out of my own head, and after saying goodbye to Zinny, I'd needed that more than ever.

I popped a candy in my mouth and closed my eyes. *Think, Jaz.* I needed a next step. Had souls ever gone missing before? If Zinnia knew, she hadn't said. Where would I find that out? We had a library full of our histories, but Death was a god, and in his case more closely linked to demons. I'd need access to a demon library. I knew where one existed, but I'd need help to get to it. I'd need safe passage.

There was a chill in the air, but the early autumn sun was warm against the tops of my feet and ankles.

I kept my eyes closed and tried to focus on the earth and the healing energy it was giving back—but my mind kept wandering.

Ren had been at the clubhouse while I was there. I don't know for how long, but as soon as I saw him my stupid heart had filled with...elation, quickly followed by hurt. Ugh. My heart was an idiot.

I couldn't get out of the den and the clubhouse fast enough. If Ren was there, Breanne probably wasn't far behind, and the last thing I wanted right now was to see the two of them all over each other, or have her bring up that I'd liked that photo to humiliate me.

No, it wasn't Ren's fault that I was in love with him, or that he didn't love me back. It did fucking suck, though. Goddess, if I could take these feelings away, I would, in a heartbeat.

I felt a gentle push against my magic, a little rush of joy, then more, until the energy I felt was like ten overexcited puppies jumping all around me at once. Something tickled my cheek, and I opened my eyes and chuckled. At least ten mourning cloak butterflies danced and dived around me, their happiness at finding me infectious. I held out my arms, and they landed, then took flight, over and over again. Their love for me was instant, beautiful, and utterly pure. My familiars were tiny in size, but their love for me was overwhelming, all-encompassing. I often wondered how it was possible for such tiny beings to love so huge.

One fluttered around my face and landed on my head, and I giggled again, letting their happiness and excitement fill me.

Movement caught my eyes, and I looked across the field. My heart thumped hard in my chest.

Ren stood at the edge, watching me.

And instead of taking off or looking away when he realized I saw him, he strode toward me. My flight instincts kicked in, but I made myself stay sitting, even while my heart galloped faster.

Calm the fuck down.

My new little familiars sensed my unease and immediately tried to soothe me, landing on my skin as if they were giving me a hug, or trying to protect me in some way.

Ren stopped several feet from me, his gaze moving over my bare feet, my arms, where most of the butterflies had landed, then my head where at least two were sitting.

He shoved his fingers through his russet hair. "Hey."

"Hey." I tried to sound unaffected, but it wasn't easy. Being this close, and alone, with the male I loved beyond all reason was hard as hell.

"I was, ah...just going for a walk and spotted you sitting here," he said and rubbed the back of his neck.

His bicep bulged, and my gaze took in the jagged scar there. It looked raw, almost new, when I knew it wasn't. "Right." He must have left the clubhouse soon after me. I'd dropped my car off at the house and come straight here.

"You come here a lot," he said, looking around.

"I like it here."

He took another step closer. "So what kind of butterflies are those?"

"Mourning cloaks."

"They the only kind in this field?"

What was with all the questions? "There are others, but it's starting to get too cold for many of them."

He nodded slowly, his gaze sliding to my chest. "Saw your new ink." He crossed his arms, then uncrossed them. "Wills said you designed it yourself."

This was so freaking awkward. Why was he here? Had Bree told him what I'd done and now he was here to let me down easy? My face heated. "I did, yeah."

"It's cool... Really cool."

"Thanks." The silence dragged out. I couldn't take it. "Ren—"

"So are you and Rome—"

"What?"

We both stopped talking over each other, and when he said nothing more, I made myself speak. "Are me and Rome, what?"

He cleared his throat, his gaze darting around the field before he shoved his hands in his pockets. "Together? You with him now?"

He thought Roman and I were together? Together, together? I studied him. Why was he so stiff? And why was he here acting all awkward and weird? Although there was literally zero going on between Rome and me, I found myself shrugging, like an idiot, because if he thought I had feelings for someone, anyone else, then maybe he wouldn't think I was a giant loser with a crush on him when Bree told him I liked his abs pic. *Cringe.* But then maybe he already knew that I was hopelessly in love with him? As hard as I tried to hide my feelings, the guy wasn't blind. I acted like a damned fool around him, blushing and stuttering, or snapping and snarling. My cheeks felt warm all of a sudden.

His brows went up, and he crossed his arms again, the muscles flexing, his veins bulging. "You think that's a good idea, Jasmine? Rome's way too fucking old for you."

Whoa. What? So now he was going for the concerned friend approach? "You could say Rome is too old for everyone." He was a thousand years old, at least. "I, on the other hand, am twenty, and definitely old enough to decide who I spend time with." I needed to stop insinuating Rome and I were something we weren't, but Ren was starting to piss me off.

"He's gonna hurt you."

I stood, and my little crew of mourning cloaks fluttered around me, sensing my volatile emotions. "Roman's one of the best males I know," I said, telling the truth. The fact there was less than zero sexual chemistry between us was beside the point. "He'd never hurt me."

Ren flinched, but then his jaw hardened. "And when his mate shows up and he tosses you aside like yesterday's garbage? Will he still be the best male you know then?"

"How do you know he hasn't already found her?" WHAT? What the hell was I doing? *Shut up, Jasmine, now!* I mean, I didn't say *I* was his mate. I could be talking about anyone, right?

Shit.

"He's found his mate?" Ren asked, his face going utterly blank, gaze locked on me.

I shrugged again, not answering. "So where's Breanne? You two are usually joined at the..." *Lips? Genitals?* "Hip."

His expression went dark at my question. "Breanne and I are nothing and never will be."

My pulse was going mad, and my palms were sweaty. "She's saying otherwise."

"She's full of shit," he bit out.

Stop talking. "You obviously made her think you wanted more." Apparently, there was no shutting me up.

"I told her what I wanted. She said she wanted the same. We fucked a few times, but that definitely won't be happening again."

My heart slammed into the back of my ribs, stupid, dumb relief filling me. "Okay, well, thanks for the update." In trying to hide my misplaced relief and the unwarranted glee I'd suddenly felt that they weren't an actual item, I went too far the other way and ended up sounding like a sarcastic brat instead of the cool and unaffected I was going for.

He frowned. "It's just that you told Willow that Bree and I were together, and I wanted to...I don't know, clear it up."

"Oh, you did." It was as if some alternate version of me had taken over and I was watching from a distance as I opened my mouth and more venom poured out. "You don't catch feelings. Fucking is just fucking, and if someone is stupid enough to catch feelings for you, you'll dump them like a hot flaming turd? Noted."

He shifted in place, his biceps bunching again, the muscles in his jaw doing a dance as he gritted his teeth.

I felt like a giant asshole. "Ren—"

"Sounds like you got me all figured out, Jaz. I guess we're done here," he said, then strode away, back toward his house.

I inwardly screamed as I watched him go, wondering what the hell had just happened.

Ren

Fire burned in my gut as I strode through the tunnels under the clubhouse and toward the fighting pit. I could already hear the hounds, their howls and cheers at whoever was already fighting. Aggression pumped wildly through me. Images of Jasmine filled my head—the way she'd looked when I'd followed her to that field, her sitting under the oak tree, her feet bare, her blond hair still streaked with pink disheveled around her delicate face, giggling as butterflies fluttered around her.

What the fuck was wrong with me? Why had I followed her? Why did I give a fuck what she thought? But I did, and the urgency to tell her there was nothing between Breanne and I had ridden me the entire way there. I was a fucking idiot, desperate for her approval. Why? I jammed my fingers through my hair and sucked in a breath, trying to gather some control, but then my brain hit me with a greatest hits of what she'd said, and *"Roman's one of the best males I know"* was a personal favorite.

They couldn't seriously be together. She couldn't be Rome's mate. Willow would know, right? But then she'd been so busy with Violet she could have missed it.

I walked into a large cavern. The pit was in the center, dug into the ground, the walls blackened and charred. Hounds surrounded it, watching as Relic and Fender went at it. Powerful blows landed one after the other, smacking against flesh. Blood sprayed the wall as Relic slammed his fist into the other male's face. Fender grinned, spitting out a tooth, and opened his hand, flames igniting across his fingers before he sent a blast at Relic. Snarling, Relic dodged it, then delivered a final blow, knocking Fender on his ass.

The hounds stomped and howled, and Relic walked over and helped his brother up. I searched the room. Rome stood at the edge, shirtless, ready to go next. When the pit was empty, the hound jumped in. Jagger was about to follow, but something came over me, the aggression in me reaching all new heights, and I jumped in before Jag could.

Rome's head tilted to the side, taking me in, not missing what

I was giving off. He grinned, amused. "You think you can take me, fox?"

"Not in here to make out with you, hound." I wasn't as big or powerful as the hounds, and I'd never fought Rome before. I'd sparred with him, he'd been at some of my training sessions, most of the hounds here had at different times over the years, but we'd never fought in the pit, not like this. I'd watched him, though. He was brutal, relentless, and like all the hounds merciless in a fight.

I wasn't arrogant enough to think I could take Rome out easily, or at all. But I was fast, and I could shift quickly and cause a lot of damage before I was knocked on my ass. I could make him hurt. Bleed. And I didn't care how much damage was inflicted on me for that to happen.

Edward's laughter rang through my mind. *Rome can protect her. You can't even look after yourself. You make her skin crawl; she told you so herself.*

I jerked my head from side to side, shaking the voice from my head, and focused on Roman. My fox was right there with me, just below my skin, ears pointed, springing on his hind legs, going against every one of his ingrained instincts to flee. Something was driving him to fight as much as me.

Rome's eyes narrowed. "You got a problem with me, pup?"

Yeah, I wasn't hiding anything from him. The hounds used the pit to blow off steam, to keep their fighting skills sharp, and to settle scores. Kicking each other's asses amused them. Now that I was standing opposite the other male, I knew exactly why I was here.

"Yeah, I've got a problem," I said before I knew the words were coming, before I allowed myself to acknowledge what that problem was. "I have a problem with you sniffing around barely legal females."

Roman's chin jerked up. "What the fuck you talking about?"

I don't know where that came from. She was twenty years old, not some teenager; hell, I was only a few years older. I forgot sometimes that I just felt as if I were sixty despite my actual age. The rage in me, that pressure behind my chest, built to unstoppable proportions.

"Jasmine." Her name burst from me in a snarl.

His brows lowered, his amber eyes boring into me, then his lips curled up. "That female's far from a fucking pup, even by human standards. Jazzy's old enough to do whatever the fuck she wants." He grinned, taunting me. "Seems you're worried, fox, that right now...that's me."

My claws burst from the ends of my fingers, and I dove at him, using my speed to my advantage, tearing into his side before swinging and slamming my fist into his jaw. His head jerked back, his lip splitting. I'd taken him by surprise, but I wouldn't get that opportunity again.

He grinned at me, blood smearing his fangs, and punched me in the gut, throwing me across the pit like he was swatting a fly. I flew off the ground, and back at him, punching, kicking, clawing wherever I could get him. He hissed and growled, his fists like anvils smashing into my body every time I came at him.

I spun, punching him in the kidney, grabbed the fist coming at me, and spun back around behind him, slamming my foot into the back of his leg. He dropped to one knee, but only for a moment, before he tossed me like a football across the pit and into the wall, cracking at least two of my ribs.

I ignored the pain radiating through my body, the taste of my own blood, and ran back, time and again. Returning blow for blow. The hound's healing was a lot faster than mine, and his cuts and bruises were already fading. Our fighting techniques were different. I was relying on speed, dodging, spinning, kicking. Roman was all about brute force, using his fists like sledge-hammers.

If we both shifted, I'd already be dead. He did use his claws, though, and I hissed when he dug them into my side. Black spots danced in front of my eyes, and I shook my head, trying to clear it, then slammed my fist into his nose. Blood sprayed me before he tossed me aside again.

I staggered back to my feet, about to charge him again—

Warrick was suddenly in front of me, shoving me back. "Enough."

"Not done," I snarled and tried to push past him.

"You're fucking done," he said and all but tossed me out of the pit.

He followed, and when I tried to get back in, he planted a hand to my chest. "You proved your point, you can fight. You fucked up Rome, you made him bleed. But he heals a fuck of a lot faster than you, and if you don't get your wounds looked at now, you'll bleed out and die. Wills will be sad and fucked off at me for not doing what I am now. So go get that shit taken care of."

Rome jumped out of the pit and grinned at me, barely a scratch on him now. "Here for round two when you are, pup," he said, then turned his back, dismissing me.

I took a step toward him. If I had a knife—

My brain screeched to a halt, the rage draining away instantly. The fucked-up direction of my thoughts was enough to stop me from charging after him. I got the fuck out of there.

Chapter Eight

Ren

I STUMBLED DOWN THE TUNNEL. I just needed to stay conscious long enough to get home.

The door opened ahead of me, and Willow rushed out, her eyes widening when she saw me. Fucking Warrick ratted me out.

"What the hell were you thinking? War said you wouldn't stop." She helped me into their place.

I scowled, while my fox whined, happy to see her, wanting her comfort. "Your mate has a big fucking mouth."

"He was worried you'd bleed out." She shoved me down the hall. "Spare room. Now." Then she rushed off.

Violet's door was open, and I leaned against the jamb. She was in her bed, her little chest rising and falling, so vulnerable, so precious. I'd do anything to protect her, to stop anyone from hurting her—even make her mate, whoever they turned out to be, bleed if I didn't think he was good enough for her. That's why I fought with Rome, right? Because he wasn't good enough for Jasmine, because she was Willow's family and she deserved better.

I looked at the mural she'd painted for Vi. Jaz was kind, caring, and so incredibly talented. Her dad had nothing to do with his daughters, her mom had fucking left her when she was still a kid. She needed people to look out for her, especially while Zinnia was in Limbo.

Something orange caught my eye. It was the tip of a pointed ear, and below it, amber eyes glowed among the leaves.

It was me.

My heart thumped behind my ribs. Is that how she saw me? Hiding, watching? Always at a distance?

I mean, it made sense, that she'd paint me, right? This was Violet's room and I was her mother's familiar.

Wills took my arm and all but dragged me to the spare room. She had a bunch of towels and tossed several over the bed. "Now lie down before you fall down." She handed me another towel. "Hold this to your side. We need to stop the bleeding."

Willow took off again and was back a minute later with her supplies. She winced as she carefully lifted the towel. "He got you deep."

"I'm fine."

"You're not fucking fine. Look at you!" Her gaze moved over me, lingering on the scar across my chest. Pain filled her eyes, but she quickly looked away. Did she suspect? Did she know that self-mutilation was my thing now? The thing that kept me as close to sane as I was capable of getting. She'd never said anything.

"You've fought in the pit before, but you've never let things go this far. Why did you do this?" Her green eyes latched on to mine. "Tell me."

I couldn't. I barely comprehended it myself. I thought I was already as far past sanity as I could go, but it turned out I was wrong. "I just wanted to fight, Wills, it's not that deep."

"Bullshit," she said as she cleaned the deep gouges. "Something's bothering you, I can tell."

"Apart from the *savagely murdering a bunch of people* thing, you mean?" I said, then tried to crack a smile like a fucking psycho.

She didn't smile, she looked pissed. "Would you just fucking talk to me?"

This whole thing with Jasmine, yeah, I wasn't getting into it with Willow. How would I ever explain it? She was Willow's younger cousin, so of course I was feeling...protective, and then there was the connection between us, because of the message she'd given me—and that she knew...she knew what I'd been forced to do to those people because they'd shown her everything. Oh, and yeah, I had pictures of her on my phone that I obsessed over because even when I couldn't have the real thing, her eyes on me stopped me from killing myself—but I'd never touch her in a million years because I was stained with death and blood.

Not that she would ever be mine, because she was Rome's.

Fuck.

I thought about the mural, the way she'd painted me, summing me up so easily. Jasmine saw me, like no one else.

"Ren?"

"I've been feeling a spirit around me...not the normal shit at work. They're not moving along as quickly," I blurted, telling her something I'd already planned to, just not yet. But it was either this or tell her about Jasmine and all the shit with her that even I didn't understand.

She straightened. "How long have you felt them?"

I shrugged. "A couple months, I guess. I don't know why they're lingering, but it's getting worse." I lifted my arm, showing her where one of them had touched me. There was a handprint burned into my skin. "Wouldn't mind some help sorting it out."

"A spirit did that?" Wills asked, worry in her gaze but also a small amount of relief. This was something she could actually help me with.

"Yeah."

"Why didn't you tell me?"

"I wasn't sure it was anything to worry about at first."

"We'll sort it out, I promise. We'll get whoever it is to move along." She swiped some numbing balm over my side and pinched my skin together. "I'll need to sew up these larger slices to stop the bleeding."

I nodded and closed my eyes. Once the soul moved on, things would go back to the way they were. My fox pressed against my skin and whined, telling me I was full of shit.

"We'll get it sorted tonight," Wills said.

Jasmine

Aunt Daisy and Arthur were out for date night somewhere. Else was in her workroom, which meant so was Stan. And I was curled up on a chair, watching TV and chatting with Mags, who was cuddled up with her crow-shifter mate, Bram.

I just needed a moment to chill after a full day of seeing clients, and fruitlessly searching for Death's missing souls. Unfortunately, there'd been no mention of any recent hauntings or ghost activity in the Roxburgh area on any of the human ghost hunting websites or online groups I'd found.

"Mags?"

"Yeah?"

"When you deliver a soul to Limbo, do you ever see Zinny?" I'd wondered, but I'd never asked before. I don't know why, maybe fear that she might have seen something...bad.

She shook her head, her eyes softening, and held out the bowl of popcorn to me. "I'm usually in and out pretty fast. I always look for her, but that's not really how it works. When I'm there, I'm in that soul's own "personal" limbo. Like the space they occupy there is created from something in their memories. I'm there, but I'm not *there.* Once I pass through the forest and reach the end of the skull path, I'm in that spirit's eternal resting place. Not in Zinny and Death's world, or Limbo as they see it."

I wasn't sure if I was relieved or disappointed. "So I take it you have no leads on the missing souls you want to share?"

Mags shook her head. "No, dammit. The other reapers have been looking as well. Hadeon's had no luck either. You'd have a better chance than us, though. I only see a soul here on Earth when they're ready to move on, same for Hadeon and the rest of Lucifer's reapers. We're not like you, we're not mediums."

"Me and Zinny found nothing. I have a few ideas, though." How I was going to execute those ideas, I still didn't have a freaking clue. "Can we keep Death's warning between us for now? No reason to freak everyone out just yet." My family had tried to help us find the souls when Zinnia first came home, and like us, for an entire month, the whole family had turned over every single stone, searched every bit of information at our disposal, and had come up with nothing. Telling them what was at stake, the possibility of Zinnia being trapped there if I failed, would only freak everyone out when there was nothing more they could do.

"You got it. Mom and Else would lose their minds. You're the expert here, Jazzy. I'm at your disposal. We all are. You need help, say the word."

I didn't feel like an expert, far from it, but I did have a place to start. One that wasn't quite as horrifying as going to the head demon's place of residence, an old, decommissioned asylum, and poking around his bookshelves. "Well, actually I will take you up on that—"

"What's up?" Willow said, walking into the living room.

"Wills, hey, what are you doing here?" Mags asked, as surprised as I was that she was here this time of night.

I couldn't decipher the look on her face. Her green eyes came to me. "I need to speak with Jazzy, actually. Got a minute?"

"Yeah, of course."

I followed her from the room, and the vibe coming off my cousin was seriously tense. She was worried. Maybe even scared. "Everything okay?"

"Not exactly." Her hands were shaking.

"Wills?"

She looked down at her hands, at the way they trembled, and shook them out. "Don't mind me, I'm kinda freaking out, probably for no good reason. It's Ren. He fought in the pit earlier. The way Warrick describes it, he was blinded by rage and didn't care if he got hurt."

I gripped the back of the chair so I didn't react in a way that gave my feelings for Ren away because instant panic filled me as well. "Is he okay?"

She nodded. "Physically, he'll heal quickly, but he's struggling and keeping it to himself again. I finally got out of him that there's a soul hanging around him. He said it's getting closer. It touched him. It marked him, Jaz, burned him. I tried not to let him see how terrified I am. But I'm so scared he'll go fox and run away and I'll lose him all over again. He needs you, your gift. Anything I do will only be temporary, and Ren needs a more permanent solution. We need to know what's really going on. Do you think you can help him?"

Whatever was going on between Ren and I, none of it mattered, not when it came to this. This was serious. The last few years, Zinny had taught me all she knew. This was my specialty. Whether or not I'd wanted this gift, I had it, and I'd learned all I could to master it. "I'll need to assess the situation, but I'm confident I can help him."

Her tense shoulders lost some of their stiffness. "I told him I'd be by tonight."

Nerves zipped around my belly. "Let me grab a few things and we can go."

"It's one of them, isn't it?" she said stopping me. "One of the people he was forced to kill."

"I think so, yes," I said as gently as I could.

She nodded, and I rushed upstairs and gathered everything I thought I'd need, then we told Mags we were heading off for a bit and left for Ren's place. The last time I'd walked past there at night, Breanne had been outside, wearing one of Ren's shirts. Would she be here now?

Wills strode up to his door and knocked before opening it and walking in without waiting. "Renny? We're here."

I looked around. His place was tidy but not overly homey. There was a shirt tossed over the back of the couch and a couple empty beer cans on the coffee table and not much else.

"Hey," he said, distracted as he walked in, and I had to stop my gasp when I saw the damage to his face. His gaze sliced to me. "Jaz...I didn't know...Willow never said..."

Willow's gaze slid from Ren to me and back, worry crossing her face. "Zinny and Jaz are the only witches in the family who have the gifts you need."

He thrust his fingers through his chestnut hair. His knuckles were split, still healing, and his battered and bruised face darkened. "Yeah, of course."

Willow noticed as well. "Jasmine won't say anything to anyone about what she sees or hears here. This is just between us, yeah?"

He nodded, and that muscle in his jaw jumped. He was clenching his teeth again. He did that a lot around me, as if he were constantly biting something back, holding something in.

Willow's phone rang and she quickly answered. "What's up?"

Warrick's voice filled the room, Violet's wail right after. She'd hit speaker. "Dove, Vi's messed all through the bed, and I can't find the clean stuff. There's...fuck, there's shit everywhere, and I'm trying to fill her little tub, but every time I put her down, she cries harder."

Wills looked up at us. "Is Relic at the clubhouse? Can he help you?"

Relic was also good with Vi. She liked him.

"He's on patrol."

"I've got this," I said to Wills, because I could tell she was feeling torn. "We'll be fine." Just Ren and me, alone, that won't be awkward at all. I inwardly cringed, thinking about our conversation in the field and what I'd implied. And let's not forget the fact that I'd liked a photo of his bare abs on his girlfriend's Nightscape page.

"You sure?" Her gaze was on Ren.

"I'm fine, Wills. Jaz will sort it out," he said, not looking at me.

He walked her to the door and opened it. Willow stopped, and she studied his face. "You're looking a bit better. Your healing's kicked in."

"I've had worse. Stop fussing."

Her mouth twisted to the side. "I'm still gonna kick Rome's ass when I see him next."

I froze, and Ren stiffened, his shoulders squaring. "No, you're going to say nothing and leave it alone."

She grumbled. "Fine, but I'm pissed off with him."

"I challenged him, not the other way around. And he was just as fucked up; he just heals faster."

I'd lied to Ren, implied Rome and me were an item, then he went to the clubhouse and challenged him?

Wills nodded, but she still didn't look happy. She finally said goodbye to both of us and left. Ren shut the door, and his shoulders were stiff as hell as he turned to face me. There were several questions on the tip of my tongue. Why did you fight Rome? Was top of the list. I swallowed it down, though. I was here for a reason, and that needed to be my main focus.

"So what happens now?" he said, pretending that entire

conversation didn't happen in front of me, like the one we'd had in the field was a figment of my imagination.

"You tell me what's been going on and I fix it," I said, doing the same.

I listened while he explained how spirits came and went through the funeral home. "There's always someone here, but in the distance, you know, and it's never bothered me, well, not until..." He rubbed his hands on his jean-covered thighs. "But lately, they're closer."

"You feel more than one?"

"I'm not sure. You can't see them?"

I shook my head. "Right now I'm blocking them." It was as if someone were calling, and I could choose to pick up the call or not. "I can feel them, though. There's definitely more than one." I felt them around Ren all the time. I'd assumed he didn't. But I couldn't decide how much of a risk they were to Ren or to me until I let them reach me again, which meant I'd have to take some extra safety measures. "So you're more aware of...a presence around you?"

"Yeah, they've touched me, a cold hand on my skin, bumping up against me. Then last night..." He lifted his arm, showing me a burn in the outline of a hand. "This happened."

Seriously not good. I schooled my features so I didn't freak him out. They were getting desperate.

He cleared his throat. "Is there a chance they could..." He clenched his fists. "Do more?"

Like possess him? That's what he was asking. I kept all traces of the alarm I was feeling off my face. He was worried enough as it was. I saw the question in his eyes, the question he didn't want to ask, and we both knew the answer, whether he would admit it to himself or not. He knew who was haunting him, just like I did. "Wills inked you with the same rune as the hounds?"

He nodded.

"Can I see it?"

"Yeah." He paused for a second, his gaze going flat, then he reached back and tugged his shirt off, tossing it on the couch.

I gasped, unable to hold it in this time. He was bruised and battered, and going by the darker color at his ribs, he had to have broken at least a couple of them. Wills had obviously stitched the deeper cuts at his side. "Jesus, Ren."

His eyes flashed, gold bursting through amber, his fox staring back at me as well. "It's nothing."

"It doesn't look like nothing." I stepped closer, lifting a hand to touch him before I realized what I was about to do. I quickly dropped it.

"I'm a shifter. I'll be back to normal in a day or two."

"And you did this for fun? You males beat the shit out of each other for the hell of it?" I just didn't get it.

"Yeah," he said, his voice impossibly rough. "That's it. For fun."

I shut my mouth, not saying anymore, not asking what I wanted to. He didn't want to talk about it? Fine. The rune was on his chest, just above a vicious scar. One of several scars on his upper body. "This is good, and for most beings, enough, but I think it's best we go a little more heavy duty with you. First, though, I need to see who we're dealing with." I knew, but the question was how far into madness they'd gone.

He studied me. "Okay."

"Can we move the couch?"

A few minutes later, the couch was against the wall, leaving plenty of room for me to set up. Usually it was as simple as answering the spiritual "call" and letting them through, but I needed to try a few things with Ren at the same time, while I gauged the soul's responses and made sure I was using the correct sigil configuration. He stood to the side and watched as I took four black candles from my bag and placed them at each corner of the large rug he had in the middle of the room, then I lit them. Next, I got my salt mixed with dirt from our cemetery.

"When we're ready, I'll need you to lie in the middle."

He nodded, prepared to do whatever I asked without question. Ren had been around witches and witchcraft since he was fourteen. He might not have seen this exact ritual, but he would've seen a lot of others that involved the items I was using.

"So you have the same runes tattooed on you?" he asked.

I poured the salt and cemetery dirt mix around the candles, forming a barrier. "No, I wear sigils. They're stronger, and that's what I'll be tattooing on you." I lifted the one hanging around my neck and held out my wrists, showing him the symbols on my cuffs. "If I had permanent sigils like you will, I wouldn't be able to use my gift."

"So if you take them off…"

I removed my boots and socks. "If I take them off and don't at least hold them, I'm at risk of possession from certain souls. Though I can usually feel if there's that kind of risk. I can feel if a soul is truly evil or wants to do harm before I let them come through."

"And the ones around me?"

I bit the side of my lip. "They don't feel evil as such, but there is an energy that I don't like, so I'll need to take extra precautions when I let them through to speak to them, just in case."

His hands were clenching and unclenching at his side. We were still dancing around the truth, pretending we didn't know exactly who we were dealing with. Maybe he was hoping he was wrong.

"So is your whole place carpeted? No wooden flooring?"

"No, it's all carpet on concrete."

Fucking wonderful. "I can still work with that." I didn't have any other choice. This was where all the activity was happening. Here it had to be. I pulled the mortar and pestle from my bag, herbs, the oils, and more cemetery dirt.

Ren watched me intently.

"To stay safe while I do this, I'll need to coat my skin with a barrier." I'd wanted to get naked with Ren for years but not like this. At least it was warm in here. "Is there somewhere I can prepare?" I did my best to sound unaffected, as if this was nothing, something I did all the time.

"Ah...yeah." He led me down the hall. "You can use my room."

"Thanks."

He left and I quickly mixed the oil, infusing it with the rest of the ingredients. When it was ready, I set the mortar on his dresser and looked around. The navy duvet was pulled up and smoothed out, everything in the room in its place. There were bedside tables on either side, but only one had a lamp. There was a phone charging cord there as well. Ren's side of the bed, which meant the other side was where...Breanne slept, where all the other females had slept. He said he and Bree weren't together, but that wasn't what she was telling everyone who'd listen.

I shoved those thoughts from my mind, and with shaky hands stripped off my clothes, placed them on the end of the bed, and started smearing my skin with the oil. It acted as a barrier, stopping any souls from possessing me, if they tried, when I removed my sigil charms. This wasn't needed very often, most souls weren't a danger, they just wanted to be heard before they moved on, following the light in most cases.

At least I wasn't at risk of blacking out. If I was right, and I was positive I was, I'd met these souls before. I was prepared for what they'd fire at me. Unfortunately, that first time I'd lost consciousness when confronted by souls wasn't the last. Thankfully, I only passed out now if a soul was putting out incredibly strong and volatile emotions and I hadn't prepared for it.

I quickly finished up and then stood there, trying to gather the courage to walk back into the living room completely naked in every possible way. Nakedness wasn't new to me. Witches often had to strip to work certain spells. We worshipped Mother Nature, so it came with the territory. I'd just never done this in front of a male I was deeply in love with, a male who wanted to fuck everyone but me. To say I was self-conscious was a freaking understatement.

Shoulders back, tits up.

Zinnia's voice filled my head—my fearless-as-fuck sister. The way she'd confronted Death, her courage and attitude. She amazed me. I'd always been painfully shy. Yes, I'd been conquering that part of myself more and more over the last couple years, but that didn't mean it wasn't still there. Ren was counting on me, though. He needed me. I could do this. I had to.

I'd wanted to be like Zinnia my whole life, and if she were me, she'd walk into that room with all the confidence in the world. She wouldn't try to cover herself, and she sure as hell wouldn't blush.

I straightened my spine, opened the door, and strode down the hall. Without pausing, I walked into the living room.

Ren turned. "Fuck," he bit out, startled, then froze completely. Well, except for his gaze that sliced down my body and back before quickly darting away.

"I should've warned you," I said. "I thought you knew what I was doing."

"No, I'm sorry. I didn't mean to, uh..." He rubbed the back of his neck. "Look."

I took a steadying breath. "Lie on the rug, Ren."

Chapter Nine

Jasmine

"So how does this whole thing work? You want to talk to a soul and you just summon them to you?"

"It depends. All spirits are called to one of three places—Heaven, Limbo, or Hell. Once a soul's in Heaven, they can stay there or choose to become spirit guides or 'guardian angels,' and yeah, most can be called on to commune with. Limbo, however, is a little like Hotel California—you can never leave. Spirits in Limbo can't be guides, and they can't be reached by someone like me. Hell, well, that's a little fuzzy. We can speak to *some* of those spirits, but I have no idea how or why that is." I had to assume they had different levels of evil, and access was denied or granted on those grounds. None of the hounds or Willow could tell me, so I assumed it was on a need-to-know basis. "Most souls are greeted with a light, though, that leads them to Heaven. The rest are collected by reapers like Magnolia and taken to either Limbo or Hell." I pulled the rest of what I'd need from my bag. "But some linger, tied to a person or a location. This can be for a lot of different reasons." I held his gaze. "I think that's what we're dealing with here—"

"You don't know, though," he said roughly. "Not until you talk to them."

I shook my head, but inside I was certain these were the first souls who came to me, the ones with a message for Ren, something we'd never talked about since.

Taking a roll of twine and some sprigs of rosemary from my bag, I laid the twine around Ren in a wide circle just outside the salt line, layering up the protection, always, and then muttered a powerful protection spell as I wrapped the twine around each of the four sprigs of rosemary lying at the midpoints between each candle. The herb had many uses, but in this instance I was using it for its cleansing, purification, and, most importantly, its protection properties.

Ren was breathing heavily, his fists clenched at his sides, body so tense that he looked close to snapping, to jumping up and running out of here. I got it; I used to be terrified as well. Now, I refused to let what I was rule my life in a negative way. What he faced was different, of course, but I knew how to ease his fears and help start his healing. Hopefully he'd let me this time.

"It's going to be okay, Ren, I promise," I said as I walked over and kneeled just above his head. Sitting back on my heels, I placed my hands on the sides of his face, my palms on his cheeks, my fingers against his beard.

He looked up at me, into my eyes, purposely not at my nakedness. "What are you doing?" he rasped.

I sent a healing rush into him. The more contact the better, but this was a start and would ease his fears for now. "Calming you down. The calmer you are, the calmer they'll be."

He nodded stiffly.

I smiled, projecting as much warmth and comfort as I could, and gently sent more power through my hands. "Breathe in for me, nice and slow. That's it, now let it out, slowly. Slow it all down. You're safe in this circle. They won't cross over the line; the salt, the rosemary, and candles are warding them off." His eyes hadn't left mine. "Another deep breath for me," I whispered as I slid a hand higher, working my way to his third eye, right between his eyebrows, and massaged there with two fingers while I cupped his jaw with the other hand, giving him a sense of being held, cocooned in warmth and comfort. "How you doing?"

He released a shuddery breath, but his breathing had slowed, his fingers no longer curled in tight fists. "Yeah…" He cleared his throat. "I'm good."

"Awesome." I smiled and slowly slid my hand from his bristled jaw and stood. "No matter what happens, I need you to stay where you are, okay?"

His gaze came to me. "What if they come after you."

"I'm safe. I promise."

He nodded, but he was clearly worried.

There was nothing else I could say to reassure him. I just needed to do what I was here for. So, kneeling outside the circle, I removed the first sigil charm, the one around my neck. "If you see me move in an odd way, don't be alarmed. When souls are unable to pass over, they learn to move things, or touch, which is why you're feeling them. They can get angry, and they can become physical."

"I don't like this," he said and looked as if he were about to stand.

"This is what I do, Ren. Do you trust me?"

He stared at me, his fox swirling in his eyes. "I trust you, but—"

"I've done this before, many times." I undid one of my cuffs and set it on the ground with my necklace. "My eyes will look strange; that's normal as well."

He nodded again, but his entire body was tense.

I took off the second sigil cuff and placed it with the other two.

As soon as I did, they were there. The souls rushed forward, faces contorted with anger, the injuries that caused their deaths gaping, festering. Flesh rotting, bones exposed. Their souls were decomposing the same way their physical bodies had...and they were scared and confused and filled with rage.

They shoved at me, yelling, roaring, begging me to help them, to make Ren set them free. Ren may have found the strength to come home, to live in his human form again, but he'd far from forgiven himself. These tortured souls, still stuck here with him, told me that.

They screamed louder, shoved harder. There was nothing I could say, nothing I could do to help them, only Ren could do that, he had to make the choice, but I tried anyway. They were in pain, afraid, going insane. They desperately needed help. They pushed and pulled, yanked my hair, roared in my face. I let them, focusing on remaining calm in the face of their fury.

"I'm sorry," I said. "I'm so sorry you can't leave."

They slapped and punched me, screaming in agony.

"I'll do whatever I can to help you," I said. "I promise." They weren't listening, and the longer I sat with them, the angrier and more violent they became. "I'm sorry," I said again and snatched up my necklace and cuffs. The moment they were in my hand, the souls receded. Their energy was still there, violent and twisted, but they couldn't do as much damage. Although I wasn't sure how much longer that would be true. Their anger had reached a point that finally allowed them to break through, which was why they were able to touch Ren now. Left like this much longer and they'd become even more dangerous.

"Jasmine?" Ren snarled.

He sat up, about to get off the mat. "Don't move."

"Fuck that. You're hurt." He got to his feet.

"Stay where you are," I snapped.

He paused, breathing heavily, his face lined with concern.

"They're stronger right now, and you're their number one target. So sit down until I say you can move."

There was a bruise already showing on my shoulder and one on my hip, red handprints all over my body from their slaps and my scalp stung from the hair pulling, but I was okay.

"It's them, isn't it?" Ren said. "The people I...I tortured and murdered. It's them."

"You didn't do anything to them. It was Edward who did those things. Only him. You were the vessel he occupied, nothing more, and the sooner you believe that, the sooner you can forgive yourself, and they can move on."

He shoved his fingers in his hair. "I can't. I can't fucking do that."

"You have to try. All that you're feeling, the guilt you carry, the intensity of it, is making it impossible for them to go where they need to. And right now, they've never been more drawn to you."

He lifted his head. "Why?"

I didn't want to scare him, but he needed to know. "They've been with you for so long, Ren, but their anger has reached a new level, and the angrier they get at being trapped here, the deeper they slip into insanity, and the more desperate they become, the more harm they want to cause you. It's tipping them into darkness. You've been a vessel before, and those scars are still on your soul. It makes you a target. They've reached a point that if they're given the chance, they will possess you."

"And the scars on my...on my soul, that'll make it easier for them to do that?" he asked, voice raw.

"Yes. If they can't leave, that's the next best thing." I slipped my necklace over my head and secured my cuffs. I motioned to his shirt. "Can I?"

"Yeah...of course."

I quickly pulled his shirt on to cover my nakedness, and when I looked up, he was watching me intently, his fox back in his eyes, the amber and gold swirling as he took me in. I pretended I didn't notice.

He cleared his throat. "So what can I do?"

"You have two options. The first is a kind of exorcism. It's what we do when we have no other recourse. When a spirit won't or can't pass over and has become a danger to the living, the soul must essentially be destroyed."

His brows lowered. "No afterlife, no reincarnation, nothing?"

I nodded.

"No, not that. They've suffered enough. What else?"

I held his gaze. "You have to set them free, Ren. You have to forgive yourself."

Ren

I stared back at her, into her soft fucking eyes, feeling vulnerable in a way I hadn't with anyone else, not even Willow. "I don't know how."

Somehow, her eyes softened even more. "Let me help you."

"You've seen them, what I...what *he*...did to them, Jaz. You saw. How the fuck do I let that go?"

She shook her head, tucking her long, blond hair behind her ear. "You need to heal. We may not be able to heal the scars on your soul, or on your body, but the emotional ones? I can help you with those. Right now, with that mess of emotion swirling inside you, especially the guilt, it's stopping you from moving forward... of them moving forward. Punishing yourself over and over again for something you had no control over isn't working. It's time we find another way. It's time you let me help you do that."

"I don't expect you to—"

"It's what I do, Ren. It's my gift." She stood and walked to her bag, and despite how fucked up this entire situation was, I couldn't help but eat up the sight of her in my shirt and nothing else. I'd tried not to look, but she'd been fucking naked, her smooth inked skin slick with oil. The sight of her like that would be burned into my mind for the rest of my life.

She pulled out a small book, a marker, and a battery-powered hair trimmer. "For the next few nights, I'll need to come back here to work on your healing and tattoo your sigils. There's also a ritual to keep the souls calm while we're doing that. Then I'll need to come once a week for a while to perform the ritual and repeat a healing session to make sure it sticks." She held up the marker. "But tonight, drawing them on with a tattoo marker will have to do."

Jaz stepped over the string and salt line and back to safety. My relief was instant. My fox calmed as well, no longer whining and growling and pacing restlessly. Seeing Jasmine being attacked by invisible hands was fucking horrific. I'd just been about to leave my spot when she finally stopped it.

She motioned for me to sit again and she kneeled beside me. "So, the scars the possession left you with aren't something that can heal." Sympathy filled her eyes. "But the sigils will hide them and prevent you from being a target for any souls searching for a vessel."

I was broken, marked by what happened in a way that would never leave me, and I was making the souls of the people I had a part in murdering suffer, torturing them even in death. Fucking awesome.

There was one way to stop all of this, though.

It was simple. I just had to take one step, one more step, the next time I was at my cliff, and the pain would be all over—for them, and for me.

"You're going to need quite a few," she said.

"Sorry?"

"Sigils. You'll need a lot of them."

I nodded as her scent washed over me. *Fuck*. It was mixed with mine, while she was still in my shirt. Christ, I barely stopped myself from leaning forward and pressing my nose to her shoulder and breathing her in. Now my fucking fox was whining again, pawing at the ground to get closer to her.

"They'll go along here." She ran her finger across my shoulder, causing tingles to dance all over my skin. "Both sides. One on either side of your throat, here and here. Down your spine, and from the top of your ribs, here..." She pressed a finger to the point just below the center of my chest, and goose bumps lifted all over me. Could she see them? "Down to, well...all the way down." Her face turned pink, and she glanced at the trimmers. "I'll need you to uh...shave."

"And you can do it? The ink?" I asked, my voice weirdly deep, even rougher than usual.

"I can. It's part of my job. Zinny was teaching me before she had to..." She stopped herself, her throat working. "Before she had to leave that first time. Rome finished training me, so I know what I'm doing."

My fox growled at the mention of that male's name, the sound rumbling through my chest. Jaz paused, her gaze darting to mine. I quickly cleared my throat. "And it'll take a few nights?"

"Three or four. The sigils are powerful and your body, and your soul, will need to realign with each session." She licked her lips, and my dick stirred. "One person has to ink all of them, once we start, there's no changing who does it. I know you two fought, but if you're uncomfortable with me doing it, I could bring Rome. He could—"

"No!" The word burst from me in a snarl. "You can do it." My skin felt hot all of a sudden, my muscles tight as hell, and I had to fight not to jump to my feet and pace. I did not want Jaz here with him. I didn't want to see them together. Again, my fox and I were in agreement on that point.

Jasmine ignored my outburst and my fucking odd behavior and popped the lid off the marker. "Okay, then. You ready to get started?"

I nodded, and she opened the book beside her, running her finger down one page, then the next, and seeing her do that had me thinking of how it felt when she did the same to my shoulder. I fucking shivered, more goose bumps lifting all over me. My dick felt heavy and hot as fuck, which was not okay. This was Jasmine. Willow's sweet, little cousin. How the fuck was I hard when I was sitting in a circle surrounded by the souls of the people I'd fucking murdered? How was that possible?

I quickly reached down and adjusted myself when she slid the book out of the way. Yes, she was beautiful and sweet and funny and at times feisty. Yes, there was this fucking weird connection between us, but still, this was messed up even for me.

Then shit only got worse when she placed her hand on my shoulder and started drawing the sigils on my skin. I could feel the heat of her body, where she touched my shoulder was searing hot, and her breath, warm and sweet, brushed the side of my neck as she whispered a spell. The usual urge to pull away, to not let anyone touch me, reared up, but a different, stronger urge to rub against her, to nuzzle, to curl up with her in a confined space and share body heat, was even stronger.

My fox wanted to herd her to our den, to my room, I could feel it. He wanted to press against her and protect her. I breathed deep as she moved to the next shoulder, telling him to calm the fuck down, but his tail just wagged harder, and he pressed closer. I needed to get my dick under control before she started on the sigils that would run down my chest.

She touched my jaw. I jumped.

"Sorry. I just need you to tilt your head to the side."

I did, and she drew a sigil on the side of my neck, then on the other. Her breath tickled my ear as she whispered that same spell over and over, and I bit back a fucking moan. I was in sensation overload.

No one had touched me this much since before I was possessed. When I fucked, I made it clear I didn't want them touching me or I just made them grip the headboard or lifted their arms above them to make sure of it. Every touch from Jasmine was fucking unravelling me, it was pleasure-pain. Agony and ecstasy. The fox wanted more; the male whose hands had held people down, who'd cut and tore and tortured, whose face and chest and arms had been sprayed with their blood and gore wanted to push her away in horror, in shame and guilt.

I gritted my teeth and stayed where I was.

"Can you lie on your stomach?" Jaz asked.

I quickly did as she said and squeezed my eyes closed, letting the images I tried to lock away come forward. My dick went soft in an instant, and I released a shuddery breath. I heard the rustle of pages as she referred to her book again, then she carried on drawing, working her way down my spine.

"Can you...I'll need you to lower your jeans a bit for me, so I can do the last two."

"Right." I rolled to my side, undid my jeans, and rolled back.

Jasmine tugged them down, and I dragged in a shaky-as-fuck breath, all the gruesome images in my head washed away again in an instant as every bit of my focus went to her hands on my lower back as she drew a sigil right above my ass crack.

"Just the chest sigils to go," she said, her voice overly bright. "I'll need you to roll to your back."

Fuck. I wasn't hard, hard, but I sure as fuck wasn't soft either. I rolled over and she handed me the clippers.

"How far down are we talking?" I asked.

She bit her lip and motioned to my groin. "To the top of your... I'll need to do one on...uh, your..." She motioned to my dick. "On the base."

"And I can't do it?" I asked desperately.

She shook her head, her face growing darker. "I'm sorry. It has to be my voice, my spell, and since it's me you want inking the rest of the sigils, then it will have to be me who does them all, or the barrier I've created will have a broken link."

I nodded, and my heart was hammering in my fucking chest. Plenty of females had seen my dick. What was my problem? Having a semi wasn't ideal, but I was a shifter, I wasn't exactly shy. Still, my breath was shaky as fuck as I shoved my jeans lower and quickly used the clippers to manscape. I just kind of shaved to the base of my cock, then tried to gather the hair and shove it in my pocket because this had to be bad enough for Jasmine without her getting one of my pubes in her eye or mouth or fucking breathing one down her throat while she was bent over me.

I handed the clippers to her and lay back, trying to think about anything but Jasmine's hands on me, the sound of her voice as she spelled, the warmth of her breath on my abs as she made her way down my body.

I thought about Mrs. Baumé in the cold room. She needed embalming in the morning. Her family was coming in to dress her in the afternoon, her daughter wanted to do her mom's makeup. The viewing was the next day.

Jaz's hand touched the skin below my belly button, and I stilled, all thoughts of Mrs. Baumé flying from my head as every one of my instincts zoned back on Jasmine and what she was doing, the sound of her voice, her breath. Goddammit, her breath on my skin was fucking with me the most.

My dick wasn't semi-hard anymore, it was hard as steel. I'd angled it down, and now it hurt like a motherfucker. I didn't dare look. I knew what I'd see, a clear outline of my hard-on along my thigh, trying to burst through my jeans.

She drew the sigil just above the base. I breathed deeply. She already thought I was a slimeball, and I was lying here, reaffirming that for her right now. I winced.

"Ren?"

Her voice softly calling my name had me jolting. "Yeah?"

"Like I said earlier, placement is um, really important." There was a pause. "You're ah...angled to the side, this last sigil needs to be in the center."

Could this get any worse? I didn't think so. We were at peak worst, this had to be the summit. There was nothing else I could do but reach down, shove my hand in my jeans, grip my hard cock, and reposition it. "I'm so fucking sorry, Jaz. You must think I'm the biggest fucking creep." She made a sound of denial, but what else could she think? I had to give her some honesty. I couldn't let her leave thinking I was some slimy fucking perv. "I...I don't do touch if I can help it, not anymore. I'm not...used to being touched like this. My senses are all over the place. I'm in stimulus overload, and it's making my body react intensely, and in a way it wouldn't usually. I normally have a fuck of a lot more control than this."

"Ren, seriously, it's okay," she said softly. "Please, don't even worry about it."

I grit my teeth, because her sweet fucking voice only made it worse. "I just don't want you thinking I'm doing this on purpose or whatever..."

Her hand went to my thigh, and then I felt the cool ink of the marker on the base of my hot-as-fuck shaft—then her hand was gone, and with it her warmth, her presence.

"All done," she said.

I opened my eyes, and she was back outside the barrier, already putting everything away in her bag.

"Let me just place these crystals around your house, and say a quick spell. It'll help to keep the souls calm while we figure things out and make those sigils permanent."

She didn't look at me, and her face was bright red. I stayed where I was while she quickly finished up, then headed back to my room. When she walked back out a short time later, she was dressed.

"It's safe for you to move around the house again," she said and hustled over to blow out the candles and gather up her string and rosemary.

"Thanks." I felt like a fucking asshole.

"No problem." She did up her bag and turned to me. "So, just one more thing before I go. If you're still game?"

I lifted a brow. "What's that?"

"Your emotional healing. We can start that now as well. You said touch is hard for you, and I'm sorry to do this now, while you're feeling so overwhelmed, but it'll only take a couple minutes, and I really think we should make a start."

I'd never wanted to do anything less, but if I was going to free the souls around me, then I had to try. "What do I have to do?"

A soft smile curled her pretty lips. "Nothing, just stand there." She walked over, and her still pink cheeks deepened in color. She tilted her head back and looked up at me. "I'm going to wrap my arms around you. You'll feel a warmth move through your body when I use my power. Like when I touched your face earlier, but more intense." She looked awkward and sweet. "Hugging me back is not mandatory. I know that's not your thing, but everyone else I've worked with says it helps."

Jesus. I hadn't had so much contact in a fucking long time. I felt twitchy and restless, and I wanted to retreat. But I also wanted to feel Jasmine's arms around me really fucking badly. I nodded.

Her skin's going to crawl. She doesn't want to touch you. She knows what a monster you really are. They showed her what you did to them. Bet she'll scrub your scent off as soon as she gets home. She thinks you're a slimy fucking creep, remember? Edward's voice filled my head, and I squeezed my eyes shut, trying to force him out.

Jasmine closed the space between us, sliding her arms around me, and pressed the side of her face to my chest. I jerked in her arms, my heart smashing against my ribs.

"It's okay," she whispered.

Warmth washed through me almost immediately, and I curled

my fingers into fists at my sides. I didn't hug her back, that would be...too much. Way too much.

"I'm not going to hurt you," she said in that soft, soothing voice.

My heart hammered faster and sweat coated my skin.

"Everything's going to be okay," she whispered next.

Why was she saying that? I jerked again. It was involuntary, but the urge to pull away, to escape this, whatever this was, filled me hard and fast. "Jasmine?" My fucking eyes stung, my emotions going haywire. What the fuck was she doing to me?

"Just a little longer, Ren. I've got you."

I was breathing harder, close to hyperventilating. "Fuck," I choked out.

"Thirty more seconds."

It was too much. I couldn't do this. I couldn't do it.

She started counting down from fifteen.

My muscles spasmed. "Jasmine." It was a plea. There was no missing it in my voice. "I couldn't stop him," I gasped, the words torn from me. "I fought, but I...I couldn't..."

"It's okay," she murmured softly.

The pain it...fuck, it slipped away in a rush, and the sudden urge to hold her back filled me along with a wave of euphoria. There was no other way to describe it. I didn't know what the fuck to do with myself. I fisted my hands tighter to stop from wrapping my arms around her, but there was no stopping my face from dipping lower, from pressing it into the side of her neck and breathing her in. My lips grazed her throat, and a jolt of something powerful slammed through me.

Fuck.

She counted down the last five seconds, then her arms fell away, releasing me. She stepped back, and I sucked in a desperate breath.

"You did amazing," she said, turning away from me. She was shaking, her cheeks damp with tears.

I wanted to ask if she was okay, but my throat was too fucking tight.

She grabbed her bag and slung it over her shoulder, still not looking at me, and I realized she was giving me privacy to get my shit together. "What time do you finish work tomorrow?" she asked, swiping the tears from her cheeks, her body still trembling, her gaze on the floor.

"Six." My voice was fucked, it was all I could manage.

"I'll see you around seven, then?" she said.

I nodded.

Then she was out the door, closing it softly behind her.

I shoved my fingers through my hair and sat heavily on the couch.

How the fuck would I do this all over again tomorrow?

Chapter Ten

Jasmine

Magnolia and Bram got in her car, and I jumped in the back.

"And she definitely knows we're coming?" I asked Mags.

"Yep, I texted Agatheena last night, and she was cool."

Bram snorted beside her. "Still can't believe she took that phone you gave her."

"Me either, honestly," Mags said and grinned. "Though I can be persuasive."

"No shit," Bram said, but I saw his lips curl.

Magnolia and the crone had struck up a kind of friendship. Agatheena Burnside was scary, powerful, and more than your average witch. She was half demon and, like Mags, walked a precarious line between dark and light magic. I guess you could say she'd become a kind of mentor for Mags.

Mags thought the old witch might be able to help me with Death's missing souls, or at least point me in the right direction. I won't lie; I was nervous as hell to meet her. My other cousin, Rose, had met her as well, and she was not in a hurry to ever go back.

Bram started the car and reversed out of the drive, then turned in the wrong direction.

"Are we going somewhere else first?" I asked, leaning around Mags's seat.

"Picking up Ren," Bram muttered. "That forest is crawling with demons. Not taking you both in there without backup."

I froze. "Ren?"

"Bram and Ren know those woods better than most. You'll be safe," Mags said, mistaking my freeze response for concern over my safety.

It wasn't. I knew Ren could kill a demon, multiple demons, on his own. I'd heard the hounds talk about him. My reaction was over the fact that last night I'd drawn sigils all over his body, including the base of his dick, followed by some intense emotion-healing therapy, where I'd been bombarded with everything he was feeling, as if those feelings were my own, and the enormity of that had left me shaken and in tears.

He'd also scented me, and his lips had touched the side of my neck. I hadn't quite recovered from either. I thought I had the rest of the day to get it together. Instead, I had to get my shit together right the hell now.

Bram pulled up outside the funeral home, and Ren jogged out. As he passed the driver's door, he bumped Bram's fist through the open window, then climbed in the back beside me.

I forced myself to act normal. It didn't totally work, though, because my face heated to painful levels. "Hey," I said when he glanced my way.

"Hey," he said and rubbed his palms on his jean-covered thighs.

"Glad you could come," Mags said as Bram headed off.

He flashed her a grin and settled back. Bram and Ren were the same age, and being familiars for the same family, they'd become extremely tight over the years. Mags, Bram, and Ren were more than friends; they were family. After what happened to Ren, he'd distanced himself, but he'd slowly been letting them back in, or at least he'd been trying.

Mags put on the stereo, and I tried to think of what the hell to say. Was I supposed to make small talk now? "Thanks for this. I hope we didn't pull you away from work?"

He shook his head. "It's all good."

"Well, I appreciate it," I said and tried not to fidget.

"I know what's in that part of the forest," Ren said without looking my way. "No fucking way I'd let you go there without me."

I stared at his profile. He made it sound like he was doing this for me, not as a favor for Bram. I didn't know what to say, so I pulled out my phone and pretended I had important shit to do. Well, I kind of did. I spent the rest of the drive replying to clients and confirming and making appointments.

We turned off the main highway and started up a dirt road that took us deeper into the forest.

"I would've thought Rome would be here," Ren said low.

"Why's that?" I asked and inwardly cringed. *Because you implied he was your mate, idiot!*

Ren frowned and opened his mouth—

"Hey, Ren?" Mags said, turning down the music, and thankfully interrupting. "Did you ever go out past Bleak River?"

They started talking, and I quietly breathed a sigh of relief. I was a dumbass for implying anything was between me and Rome, but now wasn't the time to clear the air and utterly humiliate myself.

"We'll drive as far as we can, then walk the rest of the way," Mags said a little while later, glancing at me in the rearview mirror. "You'll be fine, Jaz. We got you," she added, obviously seeing the fear on my face.

They were forced to walk because of me. Bram would usually

fly Mags to Agatheena's and avoid the danger completely. "I won't lie. I am kinda nervous." That was a complete lie, I was so nervous I wanted to puke. "Wish I had wings like Bram."

Bram's dark eyes stayed on the road. "Asked Talon. He was gonna carry you in, but he got called to a job with my brothers."

A low rough sound had me spinning to Ren. His expression hadn't changed; his gaze trained straight ahead. Had he just... growled? I'd hung out with Bram's brothers a few times—they were good guys. I mean, they were all assassins, but then so was Bram. They were no threat to me. I had to be hearing things.

The road grew bumpier the deeper we drove. Bram did his best to avoid the potholes, but it was getting harder. Finally, he pulled the car off the road—it was more a track at this point—and shut it off. "We'll walk from here."

We all got out. Mags slung her bag over her head, which was no doubt well stocked with face-melting potions, and both Ren and Bram strapped massive knives to their thighs. "Got one of those for me?" I asked, only half joking, while silently freaking the hell out.

"You know how to use one?" Bram asked, not joking in the slightest.

"Ah, no."

"Then no knife for you," Ren said and closed in, kind of crowding me. "Stay close."

I gave him a thumbs-up, even though this was very much a thumbs-down situation and I'd much prefer to get back in the car and get the hell out of this forest, but Zinnia needed me, and I'd do anything to make sure she could come home again.

We headed off in silence, and all three of them surrounded me. Their demeanors changed completely as we walked through the forest. They were on guard, scanning our surroundings, and every now and then Bram would tilt his head in an extremely birdlike manner, listening for any demons that might be coming too close.

This was my first time in this part of the forest. Where I'd gone with Zinnia was bad, but this place was next level, and the farther we went, the louder it became. Roars and screams and barks, none of them of this world, all of them demon, or some other creature.

"Why would anyone want to live out here?" I said under my breath.

"It has its moments," Ren said from his position beside and a little behind me.

I snorted. "If your idea of fun is running around a demon-infested forest, hoping they don't catch you, drain your blood, and serve it up like an aperitif before eating the rest of you for their main course, then *sure*, this place is like Disney."

His low laugh, deep and rough, slid over me. I barely stopped myself from stumbling and falling on my ass. I hadn't heard Ren laugh in a *really* long time, years, and judging by how fast Magnolia spun our way, neither had she.

"That's some imagination you got there," he said.

That low, raspy voice combined with that sexy-as-hell laugh and I was having trouble catching my breath. "A female's mind is a dangerous place."

He huffed out a breath, still with humor, just less.

"Hell, yes," Mags said.

Bram grunted his agreement and Mags poked him in the ribs, getting a sound out of him I'd never heard before, making Mags and I crack up and Ren emit a low chuckle that I felt in the pit of my stomach.

The fact we were in a demon-infested forest no longer mattered. All I wanted to know was how to make Ren laugh again. "So what's Agatheena like, Mags?" From what I'd been told, she was a recluse and had lived out here for fifty years.

Mags grinned at me over her shoulder. "I could try to describe her, but she truly has to be experienced for yourself."

"Now I'm truly terrified."

"Don't be," Mags said. "She likes me, so I'm pretty sure she won't eat you."

"What?" I stopped short.

Ren ran into me, and his arm automatically hooked around my waist, stopping me from falling on my face. He kind of lifted me, setting me on my feet a few steps ahead, and kept his hand on my lower back for a few very long seconds to make sure I kept moving.

"She's joking," Ren said. "Agatheena prefers demon meat."

"So you do know her?" Mags asked him.

"No, but I've met her."

Mags glanced back at him. "I wondered, with how long you were out here."

Ren's eyes went kind of blank, but he smiled. "She snared me in one of her traps. I talked her out of turning me into stew."

"Holy freaking shit," I whispered.

Ren's eyes lit up again, and he huffed out that sound again that wasn't a laugh, but close.

This news was not great. "So if she's half demon, and she eats demon, that kind of makes her—"

"A cannibal," Bram said.

We all went silent, and that's when I felt the low hum of power. I realized it'd been steadily growing the farther we walked. It was Agatheena, her magic, reaching out to us—

Ren grabbed me suddenly, his solid arm hooking around me again. He pulled me back, stepping in front of me so fast he was a blur. The knife he'd had strapped to his thigh was in his hand a split second later, then it went sailing. A thunk and a shriek followed before a pissed-off, seriously hideous demon burst from the trees, Ren's knife buried in one of its eye sockets.

"Watch her," Ren muttered to Bram and Mags, and then he ran at the demon.

In a blur of motion, he took the demon to the ground, pulled the knife from its skull, and with a snarl decapitated it, turning it to ash. He stood, barely puffing, slid the blade back into the sheath strapped to his thigh, and returned to us.

Bram's head was tilted again, listening for more, and Mags was scanning the trees, a vial in her hand. "Clear?" she asked her mate. Bram nodded.

We started walking again.

"Okay?" Mags asked when she looked back and saw I was close to hyperventilating.

I nodded.

"Sure?" she said.

"I mean, I've never seen anything like that in my life. A demon like that or one having its head cut off, but yeah." I took another deep breath, getting my shit together. "I'm okay."

She winked. "Good, 'cause they only get uglier the farther we go."

"Cool." I shuddered. "That gray, slimy, googly-eyed creep was barely ugly at all."

Ren muttered something under his breath, then he was chuckling again, and I felt as if I'd just won the lottery. I saw Mags and Bram exchange a look.

More demon calls echoed in the distance, noises of creatures even I couldn't imagine what they looked like, and Agatheena's power seemed to grow stronger, as if it were wrapping itself around us, checking us out, testing us. I could feel her wards, and I still hadn't even seen her cottage, but that was a given considering where she lived.

We rounded a massive oak, and then I spotted it. Her cottage was like something from one of the storybooks my mom had read me before she decided parenting wasn't her jam and left. This wasn't the soon-to-be princess's house, though. No, this was the evil witch's house. It blended in with the forest, trees growing all around it, even through it, and the moss-covered stone walls were stained with age.

A worn path came from the bottom of the porch steps and wound its way around trees to the two thick pines standing either side directly in front of us, their branches forming a leafy arch above.

Hanging from the branches, secured by thick twine, were bits of fabric, several buttons, a glove with the thumb cut off. There were also bones and skulls—demon, by the looks of things—some picked clean, some smeared with fresh blood. There were jars filled with all sorts of crap that had my gag reflex working overtime, eyeballs floating in some kind of murky liquid, what looked like fingernails in another, and yet another nearly full with matted hair in a multitude of shades, and then bigger things that I could only assume were organs.

"What the hell am I looking at?" I said as Mags moved up to stand beside me.

"Offerings." She walked around to the side of the tree. "You have your blade?"

"Yeah, of course." I followed her, and she motioned to a knot on the side of the trunk. There was an indent in the middle, and in the very center it was a deep mahogany color, a lot darker than the rest of the tree.

My cousin tilted her head to Bram and Ren, who were watching us closely. "They can't come with us—"

"You're not going in there without protection." Ren said it directly to me.

"You know she's not going to hurt Jasmine," Mags said.

"What I know is she's capable of anything. I've watched her paralyze and disembowel a demon alive for her pot."

Mags frowned. "She's my friend. I'm her guest. She doesn't hurt...or eat...her guests."

Ren turned to Bram. "You're okay with this?"

"Was nervous at first," he said, "but Mags has been here a lot. The crone likes her. Jaz is safe."

Ren's jaw clenched. "I don't want you going in there. Not without me."

I blinked over at him, taken aback. "Um...I need to go in there. She might have information that'll help find those souls. And Mags will be with me." I pulled my blade out and watched as Mags sliced her thumb and pressed it to the dark patch on the trunk, and I realized it was blood that had stained the wood.

"So she knows we're who we say we are," Mags explained before sliding her blade into her pocket.

I did the same. Ren flinched, a low growl emanating from him when I sliced the end of my thumb. He'd seen Willow, her sisters, Daisy, Else, all cut themselves, use blood magic, and I'd never, not once, seen him flinch. Did he think I needed his protection because I didn't have a familiar who could fight? I pressed my thumb to the tree trunk as well.

"You coming or what?" a voice called.

We turned. The old witch stood on her porch, her piercing green eyes boring into me.

"Be right there," Mags called back.

"I need some of your cousin's hair before you can come in," she said, then walked back into her cottage, slamming the door after her.

"My hair?"

Mags motioned to the jar of matted hair. "Yep."

"How much are we talking?" I asked, pulling my knife back out.

"Not much."

I dragged a piece from underneath, at the back, and sliced some off, then popped it in the jar Mags held open for me.

"Right, we're good to go," she said.

"I don't like this," Ren said.

I followed Mags through the opening to the path. There was a light staticky sensation, but nothing else.

"Fuck this," Ren snarled.

He strode toward us, his gaze locked on me.

"I wouldn't do that," Bram muttered at the same time Mags told him to stop.

He only made it to the trees bordering the path's opening. As soon as he reached it, he was tossed back like a pebble from a giant slingshot.

He jumped to his feet and was about to charge it again, I could see the determination on his face, but Bram planted his hand on Ren's chest and shook his head. He was talking, but I couldn't hear what he said because Mags had taken my hand and was leading me up the path.

Mags glanced back at me. "Wonder what's gotten into him?"

"No idea."

She gave me a funny look.

Then we were at the door, and it was flung open. Magic coiled around us, and we were both dragged inside.

"Come on, hurry up," the crone said as we slid to a stop in the middle of the room. I looked around and tried not to show my horror, but I was pretty sure I was failing big-time. There were more jars hanging off the ceiling and walls, and they were filled with...truly disgusting things.

"You trying to catch flies?" Agatheena said to me.

I snapped my mouth shut.

"You seem too squeamish to be a Thornheart, but that's what you are, so stop gawking like a nun in a whorehouse and get your butt over here."

I jumped like I'd been plugged into an electrical socket, but my feet wouldn't move me in her direction. She stood in a small kitchen off to the side, a raven perched on her shoulder, the bird eyeing me with terrifying black eyes.

"She need my blue smoke?" Agatheena asked Mags, flashing yellow, pointed teeth.

"No, she'll be fine." Mags's hand touched my back, and she gently but firmly pushed me forward.

"If you say so." Agatheena's gray hair was wiry and pulled tight in a thick braid, her skin wrinkled and saggy, but her eyes were sharp as they looked me up and down. She huffed, seeming highly unimpressed.

I needed to snap the hell out of it. I was embarrassing Mags and myself. "Sorry, I'm not normally...I just...I don't usually..."

"Stutter like an imbecile?"

My face went up in flames. "Sorry."

"Stop apologizing. And stop looking at Dolores like she's going to peck your eyeballs out." She grabbed three teacups and banged them down on the table. "She only does that if I ask her to."

Jesus. "Right."

"Sit," she said.

We both sat.

"So why are you in such a foul mood?" Mags asked, bravely but unwisely in my opinion.

She filled her teapot with steaming water and banged that on the table as well. "I'm having trouble with a feral shifter. Keeps getting to my traps before I can. Can't make a living if that cockwaffle keeps stealing my demons."

Cockwaffle? "You sell them?" I blurted before I could stop myself. Demons turned to ash when they were killed. Did that mean she sold them alive?

Agatheena took her chair. "Yep. I bind them so they don't lash out, then harvest their organs and bones, mainly."

Jesus, that was grim.

"So what do you want?" she said, pouring the tea.

"Well, we were hoping—"

"Not you," she said, cutting Mags off and pointing a bony finger at me. "This one needs the help, she can do the asking."

Mags stared at her for several seconds. "You really are pissed off, huh?"

She scowled, and Mags gave me a nudge.

I jumped again and ground my teeth. I needed to stop doing that. "Right, well, this is the thing..." Agatheena stared right at me, as if she could see through skin and bone, right to my soul. Mags gave me another nudge, and I barely stopped myself from jumping again and forced myself to talk. "Um, so my sister is Death's consort."

"I know."

"You do?"

"I know everything."

Mags snorted. "I told her."

Agatheena turned her scowl on Mags, and I was glad of the reprieve and quickly rushed on. "Okay, so Limbo and Hell are both missing souls. Death wants me to find them, only I have no idea where to look, and I was hoping you might have an idea where to start?"

"You're right. I do," she said and took a sip of her tea.

"You do?"

"Yep."

I waited for her to continue. She did not.

"Oh, you think you should have that information for free, do you?" she said. "Well, that's not how this works." Agatheena sat back in her chair. "Get rid of the feral, I'll give you the information."

"You want me to kill a feral shifter?" I asked in disbelief.

Her eyes darkened. "Not you. As if you, who probably jumps at her own damn reflection, could kill a feral. No, princess, I meant for your fox to do it. I know him. I've seen what he can do. Get it done. I'll give you what you want."

I frowned. "My fox?"

She rolled her eyes, shook her head, and turned to Mags. "I can't deal with you clueless goddamned Thornhearts today. When you come back to see me, come alone."

Magic snapped around us, and we were lifted out of our seats and, feet hovering above the ground, were thrown with force toward the door. Thankfully, it flung open before I could crash face-first into it.

"When the feral's dead, come back. I'll leave what you need on the tree," Agatheena said.

Then the door slammed behind us, and we were dragged back down the path. Ren and Bram watched, eyes wide, as we were thrust toward them, then dumped outside the wards. I landed on my butt in the dirt. A burst of power followed, letting us know her ward that had allowed Mags and I to pass was back in place.

Ren hooked me under the arms and hoisted me to my feet.

Mags turned to me. "I don't think she liked you."

"What gave it away?" I said, brushing dirt off my ass.

"What happened?" Bram's gaze slid over his mate, making sure she was okay.

"She'll give Jaz what she needs." Her gaze shifted to Ren. "But only if you kill a feral that's been stealing from her traps."

"Me?" he said, looking confused.

Mags looked from Ren to me and back. "That's what she said."

Ren frowned. "I can do it, but I'll need a couple days to track it."

"It's way too dangerous. We don't even know if the information Agatheena has is worth it." I met Ren's amber and gold eyes. "It's too much. You don't have to do this."

His gaze moved over my face, then his nostrils flared and a strange look shifted through his eyes. "Yeah, I do."

Chapter Eleven

Ren

Jasmine had been quiet as we made our way back out of the forest, and every now and then she'd cast sidelong glances my way. I didn't blame her. The way I'd acted back there, like doing anything for her was my right, was fucking weird and pushy. But my fox had sprung to his feet and demanded we kill the feral for her, and it came through in a way that was, yeah, intense.

Maybe because her scent had lingered in my place all fucking night, mixed with mine—on my skin, and on the shirt that she'd worn—and it'd messed with us.

It didn't help that she'd just come out of the crone's cottage and I'd been tense as fuck the whole time she was in there. I didn't trust the old witch. I didn't trust many people. Add in the demon-infested forest, a forest I knew well, and I was feeling out of control and overprotective.

I was doing it for Willow. I'd do anything to protect Wills from pain, which meant protecting her young cousin. I didn't need to worry about Mags, she could take care of herself. She also had her assassin mate with her, and Jaz was helping me and I owed her. I'd felt the cold brush of a hand on my arm this morning, but just a whisper, and it'd felt more distant. What Jaz had done for me was working, and I wanted to repay her for it. That's all this was.

I glanced at Jaz now, walking a little ahead of me. She was wearing black jeans and a black, fitted long-sleeved T-shirt topped with a dark denim jacket with black leather sleeves that I knew belonged to Zinnia because I'd seen her give it to Jazzy the last time she was home. Her long blond hair was down, and there were small braids here and there. It always looked a little wild, that tousled just-out-of-bed look.

Jesus.

I quickly shut that thought down.

When she glanced at me again, I got a glimpse of the butterfly inked on the side of her throat. Similar to the live ones she usually had on her shoulder or in her hair, with colorful wings that fluttered, every now and then as she walked. Willow was right, Jaz was different now, not the female I'd first met years ago. She'd been a kid then, always in pink, painfully shy. Whenever I'd tried to talk to her, she'd ducked her head or hidden behind her sister or one of her cousins.

She wasn't that shy, little female anymore. She still liked pink sometimes—my gaze dipped to the hot-pink belt she wore—but now she was a powerful witch, one who wasn't afraid to call me out on my shit, who shoved wolves back and had covered herself in tattoos because they made her happy. A female who spent a lot of her time laughing and dancing and taking care of everyone else, who'd made me laugh when I thought that was impossible. A female who made anyone who got to know her fall at her fucking feet—

Unhinged cackling echoed through the forest a moment before several demons stepped out of the trees, their lizard-like eyes sliding from Bram and I to Jaz and Mags. I grabbed Jasmine's arm and pulled her against me. They were more humanoid than some. Well, they wore clothes at least. Their faces, however, yeah, not so much. Bram pulled his knife and Mags fisted several vials full with deadly potions.

"Leave the breeders, and we'll let you walk out of the forest," one of them said around the thick, drool-covered tusks protruding from either side of his mouth. "You're weak shifters, and you're outnumbered. Hand them over now, or we'll eat you."

Fury burned through me. "Don't recognize me, Husk?"

The demon eyed me, then his chin jerked back. "Fox?"

I wasn't surprised he didn't recognize me. I'd rarely taken my human form out here, only when I needed to fight, and then I'd been naked and covered in blood and dirt. "That's right, and you just threatened our females."

I saw the fear shift through his bulging eyes. I didn't care. He'd threatened Jasmine, and I couldn't let him live. My fox bared his teeth in complete agreement. He needed to die. I grabbed Jaz around the waist, and she squealed in surprise as I hoisted her up into the closest tree. She scrambled farther up as I pulled my knife free and stood under her. "You have two choices," I said. "Fight me now with honor, or show your brothers what a coward you are and run. I promise either way I will end you."

Mags and Bram had moved closer as well, all of us surrounding the tree Jaz was in.

"Come on, coward," I said to Husk. "Let's see what you can do."

He snorted like a bull and charged.

I grabbed him by the tusk as he swiped his clawed fingers at me and slammed his face into my knee, then started hacking with my knife. There was nothing but a red haze after that. All I could see was Jasmine, so soft and fragile, visions in my mind of what these pieces of shit wanted to do to her, and I was lost in my rage. I fought, punching and kicking, slicing and hacking until there were no demons left to kill.

Until the red haze cleared and I stood in a sea of gore and ash. Bram and Mags, with bloody knives of their own, demons with melted, bubbling flesh from Magnolia's potions, dissolving them into nothing, scattered on the ground around us. I looked up. Jaz stood in the tree branches, eyes wide and locked on me. I didn't know what she was thinking, but there was real fear there.

She'd seen me lose it.

And become the monster you truly are, Edward's voice hissed.

My scars itched, my gut caught in a jagged grip, the past fusing with the present. I wanted to turn the knife on myself. I needed it.

"I won't hurt you," I choked out, the words tumbling from me.

She blinked down at me. "I know...I know you won't."

I swallowed hard and watched as she tried to climb down. I lifted my arms automatically, again, like it was my right, like the action was out of my control and driven by pure instinct. And she responded in kind, gripping my shoulders and letting me lift her down.

"Thanks," she said as I lowered her to the ground.

I wanted to pull her in close to me so fucking badly right then. "No problem."

Mags and Bram quickly started off again. Staying in one spot was only asking for trouble. We were close to the car, though, and as soon as Jaz reached it and got in, I took a fucking breath, then backed up several steps.

Bram raised a brow.

"The feral." I needed to run, to work out this tension inside me. I needed some space from Jasmine because I was feeling... fuck...possessive over her in a way that was not okay.

He nodded. "Be safe."

"What are you doing?" Jasmine said through the open window and grabbing for the door handle. "You're going after the feral? Now?"

I held the door shut when she tried to open it, keeping her in the car. "Just some tracking. To find his den."

"On your own? It's too dangerous," she said, trying to shove the door open again.

Again, I stopped her. "I've dealt with ferals before."

Her lips thinned. "What about our appointment later? You can't miss a night."

"I won't miss it. I'll be there." I took a step back when Bram started the car.

"You better be," she said, trying to sound bossy, but all I heard was fear.

She was scared for me, and twisted fuck that I was, I liked it.

Jasmine

Ren hadn't missed our appointment. He also hadn't told me what happened in the forest after we drove away, and I was dying to ask. He'd been quiet when I showed up at his place. He was fresh out of the shower, smelling of soap, his hair still damp.

I cleared my throat and dipped my needle in the ink, then continued with the sigil I was working on, just below and between his shoulder blades. It was an important one. They all were, but this was a grounding sigil, one of the main anchors for the rest, and it was more intricate.

He had a really nice back, smooth, muscled, skin tan. *Jesus, focus.* It wasn't easy, not when all I could think about was the way he'd looked fighting earlier, the way he'd fought those demons. *You threatened our females.* My heart had jumped at those words. He hadn't meant *his*, of course. Just the females that were with them.

Still, my stupid heart had gone a little nuts, all the same, because I was an idiot.

Goddess, he'd killed so many of them. Mags and Bram had fought as well, but they'd been more...in control. They'd worked together, cutting through the demons coming at them. Ren had hacked and snarled. His face twisted in rage.

"Did you find the feral?" I asked as I wiped away the excess ink, unable to hold it in anymore.

He was quiet for a few seconds. "I picked up his scent. Pretty sure I know where his den is. I'll go back tomorrow."

Fear filled me. "And what will you do then?"

"I've got this, Jaz. He isn't the first feral I've faced off with."

He'd said something like that earlier. I didn't care. Why the hell did Agatheena insist on Ren doing this? "You shouldn't even be doing it in the first place. This is my thing; it has nothing to do with you. That crone is just using this whole situation to her own advantage."

"That's what she does. She's a female, alone, and she wouldn't have always been that powerful or that jaded. She's the way she is because life hasn't been easy. She doesn't ask for help because she probably doesn't think anyone will help. So she does deals. Barters for what she needs."

I huffed out a breath. "Well, now I feel like an asshole."

He chuckled. "You're not an asshole. You worry, that's your thing. But you don't need to worry about me."

I leaned in and started on the next sigil. "I'll never forgive myself or her if you get hurt because of this, because of me."

"Jaz—"

"You don't have to do it, you know. It's too much. I feel terrible." I had to find those souls, but not at Ren's expense. He didn't answer. He'd gone utterly still. I looked down and watched as my thumb stroked his skin. I realized I'd done it several times. I quickly got back to tattooing.

He cleared his throat, and his voice grew deeper. "You need the information, and this is how we get it. With all that you're doing for me, I owe you. And this is something I can do. I want to help."

"I still don't like it." At least with him on his stomach, I didn't have to worry about the fact that I was sitting there completely naked and covered in oil.

"I'm getting that," he said, and he sounded amused again.

He wasn't going to back down, so I shut up and carried on with what I was doing, working my way down his spine. The sigils were a necessity, yes, but they also looked really good on him.

"Just one more to do. Can I lower your pants a bit?" My face heated. He was wearing gray sweatpants and nothing else.

"Yeah," he said and kind of did a plank, lifting off the ground, causing his back muscles to flex.

I bit my lip and slid my thumbs under the waistband and tugged them lower. Nope. Nothing underneath. The top of his butt was also smooth and tanned like the rest of him. Ren was beautiful everywhere. "We'll just do this one, then we're done for the night," I said as I inked the outline. "This one's another anchor sigil. It's really pretty, so intricate. I'm glad I can actually do justice to something like this now."

"Pretty, huh?" he said, and he sounded like he was smiling. "Just what every male wants on his ass."

I laughed. "Better than something hideous, I guess."

He chuckled, and it was husky and sexy and made my belly flip-flop like crazy. "You got me there."

I finished up and was still smiling. "I'll just go clean up, then I'll be back. You can sit up, but stay inside the salt line until I get back." The souls had surrounded us, wailing with despair and fear and rage the entire time I'd been working. I needed to monitor them closely, gauging their reactions, to make sure each sigil was doing what it needed to, which was why I still had to take off my cuffs and necklace and do the naked, slathered-in-oil routine.

I'd done my best to tune them out. It hurt to listen to their suffering, but I didn't tell Ren how bad it was. He asked if they were there, and I said they were, but any more than that I'd kept to myself. He was already suffering enough and doing everything he could to set them free.

I put my sigil necklace and cuffs back on. The souls receded instantly, and I stepped out, over the line, and rushed to the bathroom to wipe off the oil and dress.

When I walked back out, Ren was sitting in the center, his forearms resting on his knees. Every lean muscle was taut, defined, and I had to stop myself from staring too hard.

He rose when I walked in, and I closed the space between us and tilted my head back, trying to be professional, to stop my heart from racing in my chest. "Ready?"

"You're going to…ah, do your healing thing?"

"Yep, you still good with that?"

He nodded slowly. "You think it'll help, and I trust you."

That he trusted me meant more than I could say. It meant everything. I smiled. "And I'll text you a link to an online guided mediation class that's great for beginners, to help you quiet things down and center yourself when I'm not here."

Now he looked skeptical. "Meditation, really?"

"Yes, really. It'll help, I promise. You'll love it." I took a step closer. "Right, let's—"

He brushed his thumb over my jaw, and my pulse went wild.

"You've got some"—he motioned to my jaw—"ink on your face. I was just…" He dropped his hand.

My cheeks heated. "Oh…" I laughed awkwardly and wiped where his fingers had just been, and hoped he didn't see the way mine trembled. "I'm always doing that. I was drawing earlier. Is it gone?"

He cleared his throat. "Yeah."

"Let's get started. I know it's hard, but you can't pull away, okay?"

He nodded again, and I closed the space between us, wrapping my arms around his stomach and lacing my fingers together behind his back, so every part of me that could was touching him. My face was against his chest, and I could hear, feel, his heart banging hard as I sent power into him, seeking out the damage, wrapping around it, not tight, not yet, brushing past it and smoothing it out.

His breathing grew choppy.

"It's okay, Ren," I said. "Everything's going to be okay." His exhales grew almost frantic, and I hung on to him tighter. "I've got you."

I filled him with warmth, with love and affection, as waves of guilt and horror rolled off him and into me. *Oh goddess.* It was as if, for a short time, his pain was my own. I trembled, tears springing to my eyes like the last time, the feeling too big, too over-whelming to hold them back.

"Fuck," he bit out. "Fuck."

I unlaced my fingers and rubbed his back, soothing him as best I could. Most people were calmed by this, my arms around them, and hugged me back, letting the warmth and the healing fill them. People who didn't think they deserved healing responded like Ren. Feeling good, feeling warmth, affection, it terrified them because they didn't believe they deserved it.

"I can't...Jaz. Fuck."

I pressed closer, linking my fingers again tighter, wanting to take all of his pain away so badly and fucking hating that I couldn't. "Don't fight it. Let it in."

"I don't think... I can't..." He growled, his muscles twitching, his body trembling against me.

"Hang on, just a little longer." He was rock solid, so tense it had to hurt.

Then his arms suddenly banded around me, gripping me to him tightly. He shuddered out a breath as his face went to the crook of my neck. My power had won out, for now, and the euphoria was kicking in. He groaned, his lips brushing my neck like last time, but they lingered, and the brush turned into sucking kisses across my skin.

I'd never had anyone kiss me while I healed them. They hugged me, tight like he was now, but this—

Shivers slid through me as his mouth skated along my throat to the underside of my jaw. It wasn't time to stop. I couldn't pull away from him yet. "Jasmine," he groaned, his arms an iron band around me. He trembled harder.

"It's okay," I rasped. "You're okay."

Everyone reacted differently when I healed them. I'd had people feel unexplained rage or resentment toward me, another client had professed his love for me during every session and begged me to go out with him, another had followed me around for a couple weeks, positive I was the love of his life. In all instances, these feelings had worn off when the work was done.

His hand slid up my spine, his fingers thrusting in my hair, his panted breaths against my ear.

Oh goddess.

Ren's reaction was just more...physical.

He tugged lightly, like he was trying to get me to turn to him, while he kissed along my jaw. It was wrong, but this was Ren, and there was no stopping my body from heating, from responding.

The waves of his emotions ebbed, slowly rolling back. He released his grip on my hair and lifted his head from my throat and, still breathing hard, he pressed his mouth to the top of my head.

"Ten seconds," I whispered, and counted down.

Finally, I released him and stepped away, turning away without looking back. He didn't need me staring at him when he was already feeling so utterly vulnerable. I quickly swiped away my tears, still recovering from the intensity of his emotions and of his arms around me—his mouth on me.

"You can move around now," I said, making myself busy picking up the string and rosemary line and packing away the candles.

"You're upset," he choked out, alarm in his voice.

"It happens. Not just with you but with all my clients. I get a bit of what you're feeling, and it can take me by surprise." It was the truth, but I'd never felt anything like I did when I was with Ren.

The color drained from his face.

"Don't overthink it," I said quickly. "What I feel coming from you is nothing that I haven't felt before." Another lie, but I couldn't bear to see the horror and humiliation in his eyes. He had nothing to be humiliated about. I hitched my bag over my shoulder and headed for the door.

"Jaz?"

I turned back, and he moved closer. "While you were healing me, and I..." He shoved his fingers through his hair. "I didn't mean to... I'm sorry, I crossed a line—"

"Don't be. You did nothing wrong. My magic, it's powerful. It affects everyone differently. Please, don't apologize. I promise, I'm not bothered at all." I reached for the door, but Ren reached around me before I could open it.

"I just want you to know that. I'm not...my control...this isn't..."

I turned and looked up at him, into his pained eyes, knowing exactly what he was trying to say. "You're not weak, Ren. You need to know that and believe it. I know it. I feel it, how impossibly strong you truly are."

He stared down at me as if he couldn't register my words, as if they didn't make sense or I were speaking a language he didn't understand.

"You truly mean that, don't you?" he finally said.

"I wouldn't say it if I didn't."

A few strands of my hair were stuck to my lip, and I was about to swipe it away, but Ren beat me to it, our hands bumping. "Sorry." I had no idea why I was apologizing.

"I was just..." He carefully hooked my hair around his finger, brushing it back, then quickly crossed his arms, shoving his hands under his pits and taking a step back.

My face heated, but I pretended I wasn't blushing, that Ren brushing my hair back was nothing, that the kisses he'd just given me were nothing, and I smiled. "I better get going. I have to be somewhere, so I'll see you tomorrow." I started to turn and Ren stopped me.

"Big plans?"

"Um...kind of." Why the hell was my face getting hotter? Ugh.

His lips thinned, his gaze darkening for some reason. "You have a good night."

"Thanks." I walked away and felt his eyes on me until I was out of sight.

Chapter Twelve

Jasmine

I LOOKED up as Mags walked into the kitchen. "Hey."

Thanks to my family's association with a councilor on the witches council, I'd managed to get some names of some very powerful beings in the city who *might* be able to help me. Councilor Trotman had only been able to fit in a meeting with me last night after I'd seen Ren. He'd given me the names on the condition I didn't share where I got them from. I was fine with that.

"Sorry, I hope you haven't been waiting long?" she said.

"Nope, I just got here. No Bram?"

"There's a blood-drunk vampire on the loose." Mags shuddered. "So no Bram, but we can't waste time waiting for him."

I raised a brow. "Did you tell him that?"

She grinned. "Not exactly. You know how he is about me doing shit like this alone, despite the fact that I can kick all kinds of ass. I do have several vials in my bag that can melt a face right off, though, just in case."

"Excellent."

"I mean, it's not like these people are dangerous, right?" she asked.

"Um...honestly, I have no idea."

She chewed her lip.

"I guess we could ask Relic or Rome?" I said, because walking into an unknown situation without backup wasn't smart. I'd also promised Zinnia I wouldn't take any stupid risks.

"Or maybe Hadeon. I mean, yes, the guy's weird, but he lives in Hell, so who wouldn't be?"

Um, hard pass. "Me and Zinnia aren't exactly his favorite people either, and doesn't Bram hate that guy?"

Mags winced. "Good point." She leaned against the counter. "So how many people do we need to drop in on?"

I pulled a crumpled piece of paper from my pocket. "Four."

"I think we'll be fine."

My sister's voice telling me not to do anything without backup filled my head. "What if we take two names each, ask Relic and Rome to tag along, and get it done faster?"

Her mouth twisted to the side. She didn't look happy. "Those hounds can be overbearing. They mistake backup for protection. I don't need protection."

"No, you don't, and Relic knows that. He'll let you lead. I, on the other hand, am no great kicker of ass. I could, of course, use one of those face-melting vials of yours, but I don't like my chances. Zinny's counting on me, and this way we get through the list faster and your mate won't have reason to lose his shit."

"Yeah, I suppose." She rolled her eyes. "Relic's gonna give me shit for this."

I chuckled. "Probably."

She growled under her breath. "Okay, let's do it. You call them, though. I don't want to hear the glee in his voice when you ask."

A short time later, we were in Magnolia's car and heading to the clubhouse to pick up Relic and Rome.

"Will Bram really be pissed when he finds out you did this?" I asked Mags.

She glanced over at me. "Probably. He's not just my mate, he's my familiar. Can't get much more protective and, yeah, irrational when it comes to my safety than that—or his possessiveness when I spend time with other males. But I'll deal with that later. He thinks a witch should have their familiar with them if there's even a sniff of danger." She glanced at my shoulder, then up to my head, where two mourning cloaks had landed as soon as I walked outside. "But this is the right move." She grinned. "Yours don't exactly have fangs or claws."

I laughed. "Sadly, no. Though they could probably love someone to death if given the chance."

Mags chuckled.

When we pulled into the clubhouse, Relic and Rome were already waiting. They strode over and stopped by the car. Mags rolled down the window. "Get in the back."

Relic scowled. "You can ride with us. We're not all squeezing into that tin can."

"Bram would murder you in your sleep if I rode on the back of your bike, Relic, and you know it."

"He could try," Relic said and flashed his teeth.

"I'll ride with Rome. We're going to have to split up anyway," I said.

Mags reached over into the back seat and grabbed her coat, passing it to me. "You'll need this."

I tugged the list from my pocket and tore it in half, giving her two of the names and addresses.

We'd gone over what we needed to ask on the way here.

"Give me a call if you find out anything useful and I'll come to you," I said.

"Will do."

I got out and Relic took my place, jamming himself into the passenger side. Mags did a three-point turn and tore out onto the street. Relic looked like he was hanging on for dear life. Hounds didn't love cars or letting someone else take control of the wheel.

I chuckled. "Relic looked a little green around the gills."

"Better him than me," Rome said and gave me a little nudge before he headed for his bike.

I loved Rome's bike, it was all chrome and leather, and had a metallic, gunmetal-gray gas tank with chrome skulls on either side. I pulled on Mags's jacket while he started it up.

I was about to get on when the door to the clubhouse opened and Ren strode out. He turned our way and stopped suddenly, his eyes darkening.

I froze under that hard stare, my feet rooted to the spot.

"Get up, babe," Rome said.

I jolted out of my stupor, flicked a wave in Ren's direction, and quickly climbed on. I rested my hands at Roman's hips, and he reached back, grabbed my hands, and pulled them around his waist, making sure I was hanging on tight, and because of his size, that meant my front was plastered to his back and there was nothing I could do about it. I'd ridden with him before and hadn't been worried, but now, with Ren watching, I wanted to pull away and jump right off the back of the bike for some reason.

"Where to first?" Rome asked.

I told him the address, then we were moving, rolling through the gates. As Rome checked the way was clear, I couldn't stop myself from glancing back at Ren. He was striding in our direction, a thunderous expression on his face.

We roared out onto the street, and I shivered, not from the cold air instantly soaking through me but from the look on Ren's face.

A short time later, we pulled up outside the first house on the list. I looked up. The place was tall and narrow and had two levels. It was painted pink with white trim and had wisteria creeping along the narrow veranda. In summer it'd be absolutely covered in gorgeous mauve flowers. It was quirky and cute. When I was younger, this would've been my dream home. Who was I kidding, it still kind of was.

I climbed off and Rome did as well. "You can wait here, I'm fine."

"Not happening," he muttered and swaggered up to the porch and knocked on the door.

I rushed up and muscled in front of him. "If she looks out and sees you, she'll never let us in."

"Females love me," he said with all the arrogance in the world.

I honestly hadn't met a hound who wasn't arrogant, and yes, females loved them, but outside of the clubhouse, most people, male or female, who had even a grain of self-preservation gave these guys a wide berth.

"To anyone looking, you're a seven-foot-tall, long-haired biker with bulging muscles covered in tattoos, and freaky eyes. The only females who love you guys on sight are females looking for a walk on the wild side. The rest of us need a minute."

He grunted and took a step back. "My eyes aren't freaky."

I knocked again. "Yes, they are. You're just used to them." They looked human, yes, but the color changed and sometimes got all swirly, depending on the male. When their inner hounds came closer to the surface, which happened a lot, they flashed red.

"Haven't had any complaints," he muttered.

"'Cause the females you're with aren't looking at your eyes."

He chuckled as the door opened.

A tall, slender female stood there. If I had to guess, I'd say she was in her early fifties. She was stunningly beautiful, had a mass of black curly hair streaked with gray, and dark brown skin. Her rich brown eyes sparkled as she took us in. I wasn't one hundred percent sure what she was. I thought I sensed demon, but there was more as well. Human. I was sure of it. Zara Harris was a demi-demon.

"Can I help you?" she asked in a cultured British accent.

"Hi, are you Zara?"

"Who wants to know?"

"I'm Jasmine Thornheart. You don't know me, but I was wondering if we could have a chat?"

"About?"

"Soul summoning. We were told it's your expertise. I'm hoping you can help us?"

She held my gaze and her head tilted to the side. "You're a medium as well."

Somehow, she knew what I was just by looking at me. "I am."

"Then why do you need me?"

"The souls we're looking for aren't showing themselves to me."

Her gaze slid to Rome, taking him in from head to foot. "And who's this." She liked him, there was no missing it. A lot.

"This is Roman, my friend."

She held out her hand. "Roman, nice to meet you."

He took it. "Call me Rome."

"Come on in." She opened the door wider for us to follow her inside.

Rome nudged me, and I looked up. "Told you."

I rolled my eyes, and he chuckled as he followed me in.

Zara made us tea. She was open and honest about her gift, but unfortunately wasn't able to help me.

I left the house twenty minutes later with a stash of herbs that I'd been struggling to find and one of the candles she made. Rome left with her number. She'd slipped it into his hand before we walked out.

I really liked the female. She'd told me to come by anytime, and I was actually contemplating it. She was one of those people who hid nothing, and you felt it. She was who she was, and she was extremely cool.

Rome started for the bike. "Where to next, Jazzy?"

I fished out the address as my phone dinged. I quickly checked it. A client I'd been trying to connect with could finally see me. I had a message for her that was important but sensitive, and not something I wanted to give her over the phone. Part of the job, for me at least, was being there when you delivered the kind of news I needed to deliver to her. It was irresponsible to hit someone with something potentially devastating when you had no idea where they were or if they were on their own.

"I actually have to be somewhere else. Can we pick this back up later this afternoon, if you're free?"

Rome frowned. "Something up?"

"Just a client I need to see. They don't live that far from here. I'll walk."

"I'll take you."

I hitched my bag. "I'm good. It's literally just a few blocks away."

"How long you think you'll be?"

I shrugged. "Probably a couple hours."

He flashed his teeth. "I can work with that, I'll just"—he looked back at the cute pink house we'd just left—"find something to keep me occupied until you're ready."

I shook my head and rolled my eyes. "Well, you have fun, and I'll text when I'm done."

"You need me before that, call, yeah?"

"Will do."

Rome winked and strode back up to Zara's veranda, and I headed off down the street. I realized after several blocks that I'd underestimated the distance. I texted to let my client know I'd be a little late, and they replied with an apology that something unexpected had come up and asked to reschedule again. *Dammit.*

I quickly replied and shoved my phone in my pocket. Now what was I going to do? There was no way I was going back to Zara's house. The last thing I wanted to do was interrupt her and Rome—if what I thought was happening was happening. Which meant I had at least two hours to kill.

I pulled the piece of paper from my pocket and typed the address for the next person on my list into my maps app. It was literally a block away. I headed off again. I wasn't going to go in, but no harm in doing a walk-by. I pulled the paper back out as I walked and checked the name again.

Xavier Rush. I'd met the male before at Rose and Ronan's place. He was a dhampir as well, someone Ronan had met during some business dealings. They'd become kind of friends. He was a little odd, but then Ronan had been as well when we first met him. Ronan was a good male. He wouldn't be pals with the guy if he was a homicidal maniac, right?

It started to drizzle, so I walked faster, and my two little mourning cloaks fluttered from my head and landed on my shoulder, sheltering under my hair. I zipped Magnolia's coat right up to my chin and pulled my hair forward so they were protected from the wind and rain.

I rounded the corner and rushed down the narrow street, checking numbers on mailboxes, then spotted it. Xavier's house was a massive brownstone, four levels high, with dark gray trim and a shiny black door. The rain came down harder, and I rushed across the street and up the stairs. Rome might be pissed when I told him that I'd come here, but I'd met this guy before, I'd even had a brief conversation with him.

I was about to knock when the door opened and a female walked out. There was a wide smile on her lined face, a look in her eyes as if the heaviest burden had been lifted from her shoulders.

"Whatever you're here for, you've come to the right place," she said and walked away.

I watched her go. It was impossible to miss the warmth, the happiness radiating from her. I *felt* it.

"Can I help you?"

I spun around. Xavier stood there, his lips curled up on one side, his cool lavender eyes moving over my face. "I'm not sure, but I hope so."

"We've met before. Jasmine, yes?"

"Sorry, yes. I'm Rose's cousin. We met at her and Ronan's place a few months ago."

"I remember." He smiled.

His eyes drew me in, and I momentarily forgot what I was doing. He was handsome, there was no missing it, I'd thought as much when I first met him. His hair was a deep brown and had a wave to it. It was combed back and seemed to sit perfectly around his chiseled face. He was tall and lean but muscled from what I could see. His jacket and trousers strained around his biceps and thighs.

"You said you needed my help?"

I jumped again, my face flaming hot at being caught checking him out. "Oh...right." I laughed, and it came out a weird kind of giggle. "I heard you're a specialist when it comes to metaphysical barriers?" Similar to Ronan's ability, all dhampir seemed to have some kind of metaphysical blocking ability, though not as many were as powerful as Ronan. Xavier's power was different, from what Councilor Trotman said. Apparently, he could search nooks and crannies on metaphysical planes, but couldn't create his own.

"I am, among other things. Would you like to come in?" he asked.

"Please, if you have time to talk?"

He opened the door wider and motioned me inside.

I walked in. The floors were hardwood and gleamed. Wainscoting matched the floors and the rest of the walls above were a rich cream. Twin curved staircases rose from the grand foyer on either side of the room, leading up to the second floor. There was a delicate and expensive-looking side table with a marble statue of a female looking into the distance, her body draped in silk, on top. I'd never seen anything like it. "Your home is stunning."

"Thank you. It's been in my family for several generations. I've lived here my whole life." He motioned to a door on the right.

"You collect antiques?" I asked as I walked into the beautifully furnished room.

"I do."

I guess you'd call it a formal living room. Damask silk fabric covered the couch and chairs, there were gorgeous pieces of furniture, vases, statues, and a rug that I assumed cost more than my car. "I don't know anything about antiques, but everything is just...beautiful."

"That's very kind of you. Please, take a seat."

I sat on the love seat, and Xavier sat across from me in an armchair.

"Thanks for agreeing to talk."

"Of course."

"When I asked if you were a metaphysical expert, you said among other things." I was extremely curious about the male now that I was here.

"Yes," he said and didn't elaborate.

"The female who just left, she said you helped her?" I was being nosy, but I wanted to know. The happiness that flowed from her when she left was...intense. "Can I ask how you helped her?"

"I don't usually discuss my clients with other people, Jasmine. The service I provide is...delicate. But I guess in this instance, I could share a little of what I do. I assume someone told you of my ability to travel through realms? Yes, it sounds exciting, but there isn't much call for it." He grinned, and his eyes seemed to swirl as he took me in. "If I were a great explorer, maybe it would be something I'd enjoy, but I prefer to be here."

"I don't blame you. Your home is amazing."

"I'm glad you think so." He tilted his head to the side. "To explain what I do, I'll need to give you a little backstory. Like all dhampir, or at least those not stolen and used for their powers, I was raised by my human mother. She was cold, though, held her emotions close, I assume to protect herself from her own trauma —I later found out her parents were...extremely unkind to her. Thankfully, she kept me around. Had she not, I would have ended up emotionless. But it was through my mother's cold demeanor, her neglect, that I discovered what I could do."

If a dhampir was separated from their human mothers at an early age, they lost the ability to feel emotion, which was what happened to Ronan and his sister.

"I'm sorry you went through that. It had to be tough growing up that way," I said, not sure what else to say. He seemed like a nice guy, and no one should have affection withheld or be ignored like that. My own mother had been restless and absent, but she loved us. In her own way.

"That's very kind of you to say, Jasmine," he said. "But it was a long time ago now."

He obviously didn't want to get into his emotions, we barely knew each other, but I was used to caring for people's emotional well-being. It was my job, and it came naturally. I shifted the conversation back. "So what is it you can do?"

"As you know, dhampir are born with an array of blocking powers. No two are the same, but they can be similar. As a child I learned I could block certain emotions I was feeling, put up a wall to completely protect myself from anything…unpleasant I was feeling. Compartmentalize, if you will. As it grew stronger, I could do it for others, for short periods of time, and now, after years of practice, I can locate intricate emotions, localize them and build walls, completely cutting off those feelings permanently."

I stared at him stunned. "And that's what you did for the female who just left?"

"Yes." His gaze seemed to draw me deeper. "She'd grieved her mate for a very long time. The weight of it was more than she could bear. It was stopping her from living, from moving forward. So I concealed that pain from her."

I blinked several times, trying to absorb the enormity of that, of what he'd just done. "Will she still remember him?"

"Yes. But the longer the walls are intact, the longer those feelings of grief will be starved and eventually wither and die. Now she can remember the good times without the pain. She can be happy."

"That's an impressive gift." Extreme but impressive.

Could something like that work for Ren? Possibly, but I doubted he'd go for it, and he had me. I'd heal him, it'd just take a little time. I definitely couldn't do something like that. Take away the way I felt about something or someone. Then I remembered telling Zinnia I wished I could take the way I felt for Ren out of my body. Maybe I could understand why someone would contemplate it, but that had just been words, said when I was feeling particularly low. I'd never actually do it.

"Your gift is impressive as well, Jasmine, I can feel it."

I smiled and looked away from the intensity of his lavender eyes. "I'm no slouch."

"What can you do exactly? I'd love to know."

"I'm a medium. I communicate with the dead. I also have the ability to heal emotional scars via touch, which is why my sessions usually end with a hug. Receiving messages from loved ones who've passed on can be painful. I do my best to ease that pain before they leave me."

He stilled, his gaze penetrating. "As I thought. Impressive."

I smiled. "I guess we're kind of in the same business, we just have different forms of treatment. Sadly, it doesn't help my sister, or Death with his problem."

"Death?" He frowned. "What problem is that?"

"Missing souls."

He sat forward. "Missing?"

"The body count to soul ratio there isn't adding up. Death and Lucifer are both missing souls."

He sat back, looking surprised. "That's astounding."

"I was wondering if there was something you could do to help find them. If maybe you had the ability to sense them in this realm or others?"

He shook his head. "Unfortunately, no. If only I were that powerful. And your sister's somehow involved."

"My sister is Death's consort. It's this whole messed-up situation."

"Indeed."

"Anyway, thanks, Xavier. If you think of anything, or of someone else who might be able to help, could you call me?"

"Of course."

I stood, and he did as well. He slid his phone from his pocket, typed my name into his contacts, then handed it to me. "Can I ask, the butterflies in your hair? My curiosity has gotten the better of me."

I quickly typed in my number and handed it back. "My familiars," I said and smiled.

"Really?"

"Yep."

"But their lifespan... I'm sorry," he said quickly. "I understand the relationship between a witch and their familiar, or familiars in your case, is very close."

"It's okay, and you're right. At any one time, depending on the time of year, the number of familiars I have can range from none, while some hibernate and others wait to emerge, to hundreds. That kind of loss is extremely hard." I lifted my hand to one of the sweet little souls with me, and she fluttered to my hand. "At the moment, there are only mourning cloaks around. These two have been with me for just over a week now."

"And you feel a connection to them?"

"Yes, very strongly. Their love is...overwhelming at times, especially when I have two hundred of them flying around me." I chuckled. "But yes, our connection is as strong as any other witch and her familiar, which is why it hurts so much when they go."

His mouth tipped up to the side. "If it ever becomes too much, I'd be happy to help you with that."

I shook my head. "Thanks, but they deserve to be mourned. I

love them just as fiercely. I'd be afraid that would change if I never felt their loss."

"Very wise."

"Well, thanks again, Xavier. It was fascinating talking to you."

His lips curled up and his eyes warmed. "You as well, Jasmine. Maybe we could...do it again sometime?"

I paused. "Talk?"

"Well, yes. Over dinner perhaps?"

My face heated. "Like a date?"

His smile widened, and I got a flash of fangs. A little shiver slid down my spine. "Yes, like a date."

"I'm not sure... I mean... I don't know."

"I'll let you think about it. In the meantime, if I think of anything that could help you, I'll let you know."

Chapter Thirteen

Jasmine

IT WAS LATER than I'd intended when I was finally on my way to Ren's place, but after my disappointing day, hitting wall after wall in my search for the missing souls, then meeting up with Rome, who was pissed with me for going to Xavier's alone no matter how many times I told him there was absolutely no danger, I'd been running late.

I'd asked Rome if he was going to see Zara again, and he'd looked at me like I was insane. "Was just a hookup, Jazzy," he'd said. "She's a nice female, but she was just a way to pass the time, and I was that for her as well."

Harsh but true. Now that Warrick had found his mate, a lot of the hounds, especially the really old ones, were getting restless. They wanted what their alpha had, and I didn't blame them for it.

After that, I met up with Mags for a debrief. She'd gotten the same amount of leads as me—in other words, none at all.

And now I was on my way to Ren's place, and trying to get my head in the game when all I could think about was Zinnia and how she was counting on me, and I was failing her miserably.

Hitching my bag higher, I walked the short distance to the funeral home, across the parking lot, and down the external steps to Ren's basement apartment. Music played low inside, so I knocked harder than I usually would.

The door swung open and Breanne stood there. She smelled of alcohol and cigarettes. As soon as she saw me, she scowled. "What the fuck do you want?"

So much for him and Breanne being done. He obviously couldn't stay away from the wolf, no matter what he'd said to me. Pain sharp and ugly swamped my chest. I gave myself a mental slap. *Get it the fuck together.* "I'm here to see Ren."

"Hey, I've got a better idea!" she said in an overly bright and high-pitched voice. I assumed it was her attempt to imitate me. Her eyes flashed wolf. "How about you fuck off instead?"

I so wasn't in the mood for this shit. My temper skyrocketed, but I fought it back. "I don't know what your problem is with me, and I honestly don't care. Whatever it is you think I'm here for, I can guarantee you're wrong."

"I think you're here to beg my male to fuck you like the pathetic little *bitch* you are," she snapped. "Well, you can't have him. For one, he doesn't want you. And for another, I'm here to give it to him the way he likes it."

Ouch, that fucking hurt, way more than it should. This entire thing fucking hurt, but that was my problem, not Ren's. Still, I wasn't some emotionless robot, and holding in my anger was *hard*, especially after the crappy day I'd had. "I'm so happy for you both, you deserve each other, but—"

"Jaz?" Ren moved in beside Breanne. "Ah...hey."

"Hey. I'm sorry if I'm interrupting something, but we have to do this tonight, you know, like we arranged yesterday." I sounded pissed, snappish, and seriously judgmental. I didn't want to be any of those things, and that pissed me off as well.

He smelled of alcohol as well, and I was seriously thankful they were both fully dressed, unlike the last time I saw Breanne here. "Yeah, right. Sorry, I lost track of time. Come in."

"You're asking her in?" Breanne snarled.

He turned to her. "This'll take a while."

"I'll wait."

He shook his head. "No, you'll go."

She stared at him for long seconds, her lips curling, fury burning in her eyes. "If I leave, I won't ever come back."

Ren said nothing, just stood there.

She growled so loud, I jumped. Then she disappeared back into his apartment and grabbed her jacket, bag, and a bottle of vodka. "Your loss, asshole." Then she stormed off.

Awkward silence filled the space between us.

He rubbed the back of his head. "Sorry about that."

"What the fuck, Ren?" I said before I could stop myself. "You knew we were doing this tonight. What the hell is wrong with you? I can't believe you've been drinking."

His eyes narrowed. "I wasn't aware I had to run every minute of my day by you."

I stared at him. Was he serious? Yeah, he was drunk, or at least on his way, but really? I shoved down my anger. Arguing with him was a waste of time and energy. "Let's just get this over with." I strode into the living room, dumped my bag on the couch, found my candles, and set them out on the rug.

I sensed Ren walking in behind me and ignored him, going back to my bag and getting out the salt and cemetery dirt and laying out my line, followed by the string and rosemary, and setting them out as well, while saying my protection spell. The mortar and pestle were next. I put them on his table and angrily pounded together the ingredients for my soul-repelling oil. The souls would get riled when I started tattooing his sigils again, and I needed to make sure they continued to work, which meant I still had to remove my sigil charms and protect myself with oil since they were so volatile. Ren watched all of this but still said nothing.

Yesterday, in this very room, he told me that Breanne meant nothing to him, that he was done with her. He'd also kissed my neck, which I knew had nothing to do with me and everything to do with my power, but humiliatingly, I thought about it on and off all day, and the way I'd made him laugh, because again, I was an idiot. And when he'd seen me with Rome this morning, there'd been this look on his face? He hadn't liked it. Why I didn't know, but it obviously wasn't because he wanted me for himself, something I'd secretly hoped.

He was still quiet, and I could see out of the corner of my eyes that he had his arms folded, a stubborn damn look on his face now, which was probably why instead of going to his room to strip, I did it right there.

What I was trying to achieve, I wasn't one hundred percent sure. He obviously saw me as nothing, barely a female, not desirable, not anything at all, so why hide? Did I think this would change his mind? Put a crack in that armor, make him sorry for choosing literally everyone over me, or make him feel shitty for hurting me over and over again. No. Because he didn't even know he was doing it.

Still, it made me feel better somehow.

I stripped down to my bra and panties, then without pausing took them off as well. It was hard, but I ignored his sharp indrawn breath and got busy smearing oil all over my body. He didn't avert his gaze. I felt his eyes on me the entire time, probably because he was drunk and I was throwing my naked ass in his face. "Get on the mat, Ren," I said as I smeared oil over my breasts and down my stomach.

He didn't move. "Jasmine—"

"Now," I bit out. "And take your shirt off."

He growled low under his breath but did as I said, and my stupid belly quivered at that rough sound. I covered the last of my skin with oil, grabbed my bag, and stepped into the string line with Ren.

I quickly removed my necklace and cuffs, placing them outside the barrier. I'd felt the souls pressing in as soon as I walked in the house. I was positive the sigils I'd selected for Ren were the correct combination, but I needed to know for sure. They stood around the string line, moaning and screaming, begging me for help, but it was more distant than it had been. The sigils I'd already done were definitely working. I tried to tune them out now, to not feel their pain and fear, and to focus on what I had to do. It wasn't easy.

I checked the sigils I'd drawn on his skin with my tattoo marker. They'd held up well. I took out the box with my portable tattoo machine. It was small and light but did the job.

Ren tilted his head my way. "Jasmine?"

His low, raspy voice lifted goose bumps all over me. "Eyes straight ahead," I bit out.

He did as I said and thrust his fingers through his hair. "What you walked in on—"

"I didn't walk in on anything. I arrived at a mutually agreed upon time for our appointment, since I'm providing a professional service and all. And you know, doing a favor for Willow, but instead I get insults thrown at me by your *friend*. I'd say I was sorry for interrupting your party with Bree, but I'm not. My time is important. In case you've forgotten I have souls to find."

"You didn't interrupt anything."

"No? She seemed to think so. Since, apparently, I'm a bitch, and the only reason I'm here is to beg *her male* to fuck me."

"What the fuck?" he snarled.

"Don't act so surprised. You either want her and you're denying it for some reason—while, by the way, treating her like crap—or you're using her to get off, giving the female mixed messages, and generally being a dick."

"Jaz—"

"When you invite someone over to drink vodka with you,

someone you bone on the regular, they're going to have certain expectations." I was being a bitch, like Bree accused me of, but I couldn't stop myself.

"I didn't invite her here."

Oh sure. "It's none of my business."

"You seem pretty worked up, Jasmine, throwing a lot of shit at me about it, so I should get to defend myself. No, I didn't invite her here. I've had a shitty fucking day, and she showed up with vodka and I wanted a drink." He took a steadying breath. "I shouldn't have let her in, but I...I wasn't thinking clearly. It won't happen again."

"Like I said, it's none of my business." I finished getting my tattoo machine ready, filled my little ink cup with ink and added a few drops of the potion I'd mixed before I came, and stirred it carefully. "I'll start with your shoulders. It'll be easier if you sit up straight." He was sitting on the floor with his forearms resting on his knees.

He did as I said, and I gasped. His scars looked raw, goddess, almost fresh. I reached out. "Ren, what happened to you..."

He grabbed my hand, stopping me from making contact. "Nothing." He held my gaze, his tone a demand that I don't ask him any more about it, that I ignore what was right in front of me. Our eyes stayed locked, and his fox swirled behind his. "It's nothing," he said again, breaking the silence.

I nodded and pulled my hand out from under his. "If you say so." Then I turned on the tattoo machine, dipped it in the ink cup, loading the reservoir, and angled closer. "Try not to move." Then I started tattooing while I recited the same spell I had the night before, over and over again.

An hour passed without him saying a word, and I was glad for it, then he said out of the blue, "You painted me."

I stilled.

"My fox, anyway, on Violet's wall."

He'd seen it. "Yep. You're important to her. You're Willow's familiar," I said, telling him the truth. Yes, he'd belonged there, but that wasn't the only reason I'd painted him. I'd seen his eyes in my mind and envisioned them in that leafy corner, and there'd been no stopping me. I started spelling again, killing the conversation, and thankfully he let it go.

It took me several hours to do his shoulders. It'd taken longer because this set was a lot more intricate. I'd also needed to monitor the souls closely as I went. They were furious, not at Ren but at me, which meant I was using the correct sigil configuration like I thought, and now that I was using magic ink, the souls could feel it, the distance growing between them and Ren, and not in the way they wanted. They were still stuck with him, only now they couldn't get to him quite as easily, and when I was done, not at all.

I turned off the tattoo machine and shook out my hand. "That'll do for tonight. I'll be back tomorrow and hopefully get the rest done then. If we could start earlier, that'd be good. It'll take a few more hours, but I want to get this finished." My voice was hoarse from spelling for hours.

"Right," he said and turned to me, keeping his gaze above the neck. "Thank you, Jaz, for this."

I nodded and quickly put on my necklace and cuffs. The souls drew back, then vanished from view. Calmer again now. "Stay there while I get a towel to wipe off this oil."

I went to stand, but he grabbed my arm. "I'm sorry I was an asshole."

"Are you?"

"Of course I am." His gaze searched mine.

I wondered what he saw when he looked at me. This male confused the hell out of me. I'd made Ren think I was with Rome, and he picked a fight with him. He saw me with Rome this morning, and he'd looked at me in a way that I couldn't read but had twisted my belly in knots. Then I get here tonight, and he was with Breanne, almost like he was trying to hurt me. "Why did you invite

Breanne in, Ren?" I said, finding courage I didn't know I possessed.

"Like I said, she had vodka," he said roughly.

"And that's it? No other reason?" *Like trying to make me jealous?*

As I sat there, looking into those wild eyes, his expression as closed off as it ever was, I knew I was wrong, that I'd read into things, seen things that weren't there because I wanted it to be true so badly, and my face heated.

His nostrils flared. "No other reason."

I nodded, feeling stupid. If there was another reason, it wasn't to make me jealous, it was to sleep with Bree. Goddess, I was an idiot. "If you could gather everything for me, that'd be great," I said, snatching up my clothes and leaving to clean up.

When I walked back out, he had his shirt on and the candles were sitting on the coffee table, the string and rosemary gathered beside it. He'd packed my tattoo machine as well, and it sat by my bag. I strode over and put everything inside the bag, then turned to him.

My belly was in knots, and the last thing I wanted to do was pull him into my arms and hug him. Well, I did, despite every-thing, which was why this sucked so much. *You're a goddamn professional, act like it.* I looked up at him. "I'll try to make this as painless as possible," I said, attempting a lame joke and forcing myself to relax.

"Jaz, about earlier. We made a time. I shouldn't have let Bree in."

"Let's just forget about it. I'm sorry for being a snappish shrew. I had a weird crappy day as well." I forced a smile. "Now, I just need you to stand there and think of England while I do my thing."

He frowned. "What?"

"It's a British saying. Don't worry. Let's do this." I stepped closer and wrapped my arms around him. The hot, hard wall of his chest pressed against mine. His arms stayed at his sides like last time, at the beginning anyway, and I wrapped myself around him and poured my powers into him, seeking out his emotional wounds. I gently wrapped around them, doing what I could to add to the foundation of healing I'd been building.

His body grew hotter, his muscles twitching, trembling. "I've got you, Ren," I said softly. "Everything's going to be okay. You did nothing wrong. It wasn't your fault." The words came to me again, the words his damaged emotional state told my gift he needed. He shook harder, telling me I was right.

"Fuck," he croaked. "Jaz—"

He tensed, and I knew like last time, it was a lot for him. He was moments from pulling away. "Just a little longer." A tidal wave of pain and fear, of guilt slammed into me, more powerful than last time, and I bit back my cry of agony.

I whimpered and held him tighter. "You're almost there."

"Fuck," he said again, trembling so hard it had to hurt.

My gift coiled tighter around his emotional wounds, pouring into them, smoothing over some of the jagged edges. Not enough to make a huge difference yet, and Ren might not even notice, but it was a start. A step in the right direction. I thought about the way he'd laughed in the forest. Or maybe it was already helping.

Tears swam in my eyes, my throat aching from fighting back a sob, then it happened, the agony began to recede, and like last time, Ren groaned. He was breathing harder.

"I can't...I can't stop," he said and wrapped his arms around me, one sliding into my hair and tipping my head back. "Jaz, fuck." His mouth slammed down on mine.

He kissed me.

He kissed me deep, his tongue sliding against mine hungrily. I was locked in his arms, my head held in place by his fist in my hair, so all I could do was surrender to it—give him the release he needed in that moment. This kiss, his hunger, it wasn't about me, I reminded myself. It wasn't for me. This was a reaction to the way my power made him feel and the alcohol he'd shared with Bree, that's all.

But, goddess, it was so good...and so wrong. I could taste the vodka he'd been drinking, and I wanted to shove him away and pull him closer at the same time. This was torture.

"I'm sorry," he panted against my lips. "But I need to..." He kissed me again, his arms a tight band of muscle around me.

I didn't fight it. Humiliatingly, I didn't want to.

Finally, he lifted his head, panting.

I released him and stepped back, my self-preservation instincts still intact, even if my common sense had left the building. "All d-done."

His gaze went to my lips, and without thinking, I wiped the back of my hand over them, needing the taste of him gone, needing to pull myself back together.

He flinched. "I'm sorry. I...fuck, I shouldn't have done that. I forced myself on you. I didn't mean to... I couldn't stop."

"It's...it's okay, I'm okay. My magic, is strong, things happen." I'd had more than one client become confused about their feelings for me, the ones that needed multiple sessions could sometimes grow attached.

He watched me for several long seconds, and I could tell he wasn't sure what to do or say. "I made you cry again," he rasped.

"That's all part of it as well," I said and brushed the tears from my cheeks.

His hands were trembling. "You sure you're okay?"

"Positive." I smiled up at him and hoped it wasn't as shaky as it felt. "I should get going—"

"Please, not yet. After that...I ah...can you just stay for a little longer?"

I wanted to run away, but what he was feeling after such intense emotions wasn't unusual.

"I ah...went out again earlier, tracked the feral for a few hours. He's claimed a large territory while he's been out there, and he moves fast." He rubbed the back of his neck. "I'm still working out his patrol route, but I should be able to corner him soon."

"You did?" Now I felt even more of an asshole. "Thank you. Really. You shouldn't even be doing it. Agatheena had no right to ask—"

"Don't need to keep thanking me, Jaz."

"Right."

"You have any luck today?" he asked, fidgeting, seeming unable to keep still. Not surprising after that session.

I was far from okay, but I had to show him I was because that's what he needed. "No, actually. Nothing. My next move is paying the demon leader a visit at that creepy old asylum he lives in."

"What?"

"He has a library I need access to." These were the demons who could pass as human, who didn't eat humans and who followed the rules.

"No. No fucking way. That place is too dangerous," he said.

"I wasn't asking for your permission, Ren."

He was still shaking, and he shoved his hands in his pockets. "I know. But that place, it's dangerous."

"I'm aware. I was hoping Chaos could organize something for me." Chaos was a Knight of Hell and demon hunter. He'd brokered the conditions the demons in the city lived under, and he was an ex and good friend of Willow. But since I was trying to keep Wills out of this so she wouldn't worry while her hands were full with Violet, I couldn't ask her to call Chaos for me.

"Do you have Chaos's number?" he asked, like he was reading my mind.

"Well, no, and I don't want to worry Willow right now—"

"And Warrick hates the knight, which means the other hounds aren't fans of the guy either. Not sure Rome would like you calling him."

I frowned. "It has nothing to do with Rome."

"I take it he'll be going with you? You'll need someone at your back. That asylum is a seriously fucked-up place."

"You don't need to worry about it. I have it covered."

"Right." His jaw tightened. "Your voice is wrecked from spelling. Let me get you a drink before you go?"

I just wanted to get the hell out of there. He wasn't the only one shaken by our session. The residual from his emotions was still working its way out of me, and I was struggling not to cry. Though, if I was honest, it was more than that. This whole thing was taking a toll on me, one that was getting harder by the day. "I have somewhere to be—"

"The clubhouse? Rome waiting for you?" he asked, doing more of that jaw clenching, and he pulled his hands from his pockets and crossed his arms, his forearms bulging.

I ignored his question, for reasons unknown. No, that was a lie. My reaction to seeing Bree here with him tonight had been extreme. She already thought I wanted Ren, I didn't want him thinking it as well.

The out-of-control kisses we'd just shared weren't helping my cause, but I couldn't handle the humiliation. I was already feeling too raw. So I didn't correct him. I let him believe whatever he wanted without confirming or denying it. "I'll see you tomorrow," I said, then walked out.

And didn't even jump, much, when I heard him growl viciously behind me before he closed the door.

Chapter Fourteen

Ren

I sipped my coffee and sat back. Relic was in the chair beside me, telling me about the problems he'd had with his bike and what he thought was wrong with it. I hardly heard a word. All I could think about was Jasmine and if she'd come here to the clubhouse last night after she'd been at my place. After I'd kissed her like my world was about to end and she was the only thing that could save me.

I'd fucking kissed her, and nothing could have stopped me.

She acted like it was nothing, like it was just part of the job, which had sent my possessive instincts through the fucking roof. Were her other clients kissing her, touching her? My fox snarled. No, that wasn't okay. We had to make sure that wasn't happening. We had to put a stop to that if it was.

Like I had a right to demand she do...or not do...anything.

She'd said she had big plans, and she'd been fucking blushing, her face bright red. She'd left my place, the taste of me still on her lips, and she'd come here. Where else would she be going? She'd left me standing there trembling, fucking knees weak, body on fire after she'd decimated my emotions, after she'd let me hold her, kiss her, and she hadn't looked back. She said it was her power making me feel this way—she was wrong. I'd felt this way for a long fucking time. Her power just drowned out all the noise, all reasons I couldn't have her for a few minutes, and heightened the reasons I should.

When that high had hit, Jasmine was mine. Every part of me roared she was mine.

Until she pulled her power back and left me shaken and restless and confused.

I tapped my fingers on the table, unable to keep still. Was Jasmine here every night with Roman now?

I'd almost expected him to come to my place last night, to fuck me up. He had to have scented me on her. He had to know I'd kissed her. Unless Jasmine had washed me off, washed away every trace of what we'd done.

I wouldn't blame the male if he had come for me. If I were Rome and had a female like her, I'd want her with me every night as well, but Roman wasn't right for her, no fucking way.

"Did Jaz come by the clubhouse last night?" I said before I could hold it in any longer.

Relic shrugged. "Don't think so." Then he studied me more closely. "Why? What's going on?"

"Nothing. She's been helping me with some stuff at work, was going to ask her about it, but she's not answering my text." A lie, all of it, but I was positive Relic was part bloodhound, and if the male caught the scent of weakness, like me having some weird fucking thing for Jasmine, he'd stick his nose in my business. If he knew I'd spent most of the night looking at pictures of her on my phone like a fucking psycho, he'd never let me live it down. "So you think it's the carburetor?" I asked, getting him back to the previous conversation.

He jumped straight back in, and I tried really hard to listen, but images of a naked Jasmine, coating her smooth inked skin with oil, kept slamming into the back of my skull. *Fuck*. I should never have let Bree in. She'd showed up with a bottle, and I knew she wanted more. I'd had no intention of giving it to her, but I knew what she wanted. My head hadn't been right, far fucking from it.

After I'd seen Jaz and Rome that morning on his bike, her arms around the hound, plastered to his back, something had snapped inside me. I'd walked away, straight into the woods, shifted, and ran straight to my cliff.

I'd stood at the edge, the cool air on my bare skin, the wind whistling around me as if it were telling me to take that last step, to jump, to stop the awful fucking feeling inside me. Jasmine had been mine, in my head, she'd belonged to me in some twisted, weird, fucking way. We had that deep connection, she and I, like no one else. Yes, she thought I was an asshole most of the time, and yes, that connection was because of the people I'd murdered while I was possessed, but it was something.

It was fucked up, but it was something for me to hang on to. It was mine.

She'd been mine.

Now she had that with Rome. No, she had a fuck of a lot more than that.

She had no idea she was the reason I'd never taken that last step. And she'd never know the reason I'd stepped back from the ledge yesterday and used a knife on my skin to work through my pain instead was because I knew I'd see her that night.

That was the reason I'd still be here tomorrow morning, and not on the bottom of that fucking cliff, because I'd see her tonight as well. So yeah, I'd spent the night going through my pictures of her. Anything to still feel connected to her and to stop the images of her and Rome together from invading my head.

The door to the rooms out back opened and shut. Not the private dens below ground, but the rooms in the back of the main clubhouse, where the hounds hooked up with humans and others they didn't want knowing about their inner sanctum. I looked up as a hound walked out, a female wrapped around him, her long blond hair a mess around her shoulders. They were making out as he carried her toward the exit on the other side of the room.

I recognized the hound's boots, the chrome skulls on the sides, like his bike. Rome. I sucked in a breath, and my fox lost his shit, charging forward, snarling and growling. I barely kept my seat.

I felt Relic's gaze slide to me, hearing the growl rumble from deep in my chest.

There it was, right the fuck in front of me. Rome and Jasmine. Something I'd never wanted to see. Fuck no. I wanted to scratch my fucking eyes out. She lifted her head and laughed.

I froze.

Not Jasmine.

Some other female. Human, not witch.

I stood so fast, my chair scraped behind me and fell over. He was fucking around on her? He had her, he had Jasmine, and he was fucking some random chick instead? *What the actual fuck.* That piece of shit! If Jaz were mine, if she wanted *me*, if I wasn't so fucked in the head, I'd never let her go. No other females would exist. Hell, they already didn't, not in any real way, and she wasn't even mine.

I slammed my mug on the table.

"Yo." Relic frowned. "What's up?"

I ignored him and started across the main room as Rome walked his female toward the door. I didn't know what I was going to do—no, fuck that, I knew exactly what I was going to do. I was going to slice the tendons in the backs of his legs, and as soon as he was down, I was going to kick the fuck out of him until he was unconscious. He leaned in and kissed the female again—

The door opened before they reached it—and Jasmine walked in. *Fuck.* I walked faster to get to her, waited for the pain to hit her eyes, the betrayal.

She smiled. "Hey, Rome. Hey, Brandy." Then she carried on past like she didn't give a fuck that the male she loved, her mate, was stepping out on her.

I slammed on the brakes, stopping in my tracks.

She didn't care.

Because they weren't together.

She'd lied to me. My fucking legs almost buckled underneath me, and I switched directions without thinking, going after her. She'd just finished punching in the security code for the dens, and I came up behind her and opened the door, making her jump. She spun round, eyes wide.

"Jesus, Ren. You gave me a fright," she accused and scowled up at me.

"You lied to me." Her head jerked back. "You said you and Rome were together, that you were mates," I said, firing my own accusation at her.

Her brows shot up. "No, I didn't."

"Yeah, you did."

"No, Ren, I didn't. Think back to our conversation. You made assumptions. I didn't confirm or deny anything. That's not lying, that's omitting information, because it's none of your damn business."

"You've come here the last two nights, you said—"

"I said nothing like that at all. I spent most of last night doing research on past soul disappearances at home, and the night before that I met with Councilor Trotman."

"Trotman?" No, she hadn't said she was coming here, had she? I'd thought up the absolute worst scenario and made it truth.

"Shit, I wasn't supposed to tell anyone he helped me," she muttered.

I dragged in a deep breath because my lungs burned from holding it. My hands were shaking, and there was a feeling in my gut I hadn't experienced before in my life, a feeling I couldn't have, not about this female. Not her. My gaze moved over her, her beautiful, perfect face, those full lips, those wide green eyes. Her sweet little body that I'd seen bare, twice now. My gaze lifted, and there were two butterflies on her hair.

I'd never wanted to kiss anyone more in my life.

And she was right. She'd implied, but she'd never confirmed it. "I saw him with Brandy, and I almost—"

"You almost what?"

"I thought he was stepping out on you, that he was gonna hurt you."

"And that's your business how?"

I was breathing hard, trying to think, to find the right fucking words. But I didn't know what to say, what the hell I was doing. Still, when she spun away, yanked the door open, and strode through, I followed her, down the stairs and into the tunnels.

She stopped and spun on me again. "What, Ren? What do you want?"

"You implied...and I thought...I thought..." The words flew from me, and I choked them back.

"You thought what?"

That I'd lost you.

We stared at each other. I was breathing hard, as if I'd been running all fucking day, and without my say-so, my gaze dipped to her perfect lips.

They parted, and she drew in a startled breath. "Ren."

The door opened and Rome and Relic started down the stairs, shattering the moment. I took an abrupt step back, as if Jasmine were my worst nightmare and not every one of my wildest dreams. But then my possessive instincts went haywire again as Rome drew closer, and I grabbed her arm and towed her down the hall, away from them, and into the room I kept here, where I stayed sometimes, shutting the door behind us.

She looked around, her gaze going to the bed, the small dresser with clothes I kept here as well. "What's going on?"

What the fuck was I doing? Why had I dragged her into my

room and shut her in? *Because you want her to yourself. You want to shut her in here with you and never let her leave.*

"Ren." She licked her lips, and I was fucking mesmerized. "My power, when I use it like I am with you…it can be confusing, can make people feel things that aren't—"

"Have you talked to Chaos?"

She frowned at my sudden change of subject, but I couldn't hear her tell me what I was feeling wasn't real. I couldn't. Convincing her it was the truth was pointless. I couldn't have her, no matter how much I wished otherwise, I wasn't fit for any kind of real relationship, especially not one with her, because Jasmine deserved everything, and I had nothing to offer her.

"No, not yet. I don't want to hassle Wills with this. I know Warrick and Chaos's relationship isn't the best but was hoping to catch Warrick today, see if he could put me in contact with the knight."

"I'll call him. Chaos is a friend. Let me set this up for you." I stared her down, because I knew how stubborn she was, and I wasn't taking no for an answer for this next bit. "And I'll take you to the asylum."

Her lips parted. "No. You don't need to do that."

"You need help, yes? I can help. Your familiars aren't useful in this instance. You need protection. Plus, I owe you." I crossed my arms so I didn't reach for her. I wanted her arms around me again. It was agony, but I craved it. After only a few sessions with her, I craved her touch, when touch had been something I couldn't stand, still couldn't stand from anyone but her.

"You're already repaying me by hunting down Agatheena's feral."

"And I'll be doing this as well," I said, making sure I left no room for argument.

"You won't take no for an answer, will you?"

"No." I held her gaze. "If you go alone…or with anyone else, I won't be happy, Jasmine."

She blinked up at me, and I could see her fighting her temper. She wasn't a fan of my tone or what I'd just said, but she also knew I wasn't backing down. "If you insist." She blew out a breath and crossed her arms. "Thank you, I guess."

Jasmine

"So, like, how safe are we here?" I asked as we walked past demon businesses, clothing shops, bars, and cafes, while passing actual demons on the street. Their gazes followed us, their eyes giving them away, something otherworldly shining through.

Ren's hand was suddenly on my lower back as he scanned the street. "No one's going to hurt you, Jaz, because if they try, I'll gut them right here in the street."

I looked up at him, and my mouth went dry. He meant it. He looked like he had in the forest when we left Agatheena's, right before he killed all those demons. "But we have safe passage to the asylum, yes?"

"Chaos cleared it. We'll be fine."

This part of the city was where demons who followed the rules lived. The Knights of Hell monitored them and had a close relationship with their leader, a demon named Rune, a male chosen by Lucifer to keep all those living in this city in line.

"What do you think Rune's like? I mean, he's in charge of all the demons here, so he has to be kind of terrifying, right?" I rubbed my arms, goose bumps lifting all over them.

Ren ran the tips of his fingers down my spine, then back up, like he was trying to offer comfort but didn't want to touch me fully. "It'll be fine."

It just made me feel even jumpier, setting my nerve endings off into little spasms and making it hard to focus. After what he said during our first session together, I knew Ren avoided touch. I'd seen females on his lap, their hands on him, but now that I thought about it, he always moved their hands away, with a forced laugh or a movement that would dislodge them, and unless he was really drunk, he kept his hands to himself.

Knowing that now, I could look back and recognize the discomfort on his face during those times. Is that why he drank so much? The fact that he'd touched me in the forest to make me feel safe and the way he was touching me now, trying to comfort me despite how uncomfortable it had to be making him, said just how much I hadn't been hiding my fear either time.

"I'm glad you're here," I said, wanting him to know how much I appreciated him, despite my resistance.

He was still scanning the street. "If you came here without me, Jaz, I would've followed you, anyway, only I would've been pissed."

My gaze shot up to him. "Are you serious?"

"Deadly."

"You would've followed me?"

"Yes."

He was still looking everywhere but at me, scanning our surroundings for trouble. "Why?"

"Because you're not the shy little female I first met. You've got all this attitude, venom when you feel like spitting it, but you don't have one single thing to back all of that up with."

"Yes, I do."

"Jasmine, you don't."

"Relic and Mags taught me some moves."

His lips actually curled.

"What?" I bit out.

"A few moves won't do shit against a rabid demon," he said, glancing my way before going back to searching the surrounding streets.

"Are you saying I'm weak?"

"No." His fingers did another swipe down my spine, making me shiver. "I'm saying your attitude could get you in trouble, and I'm going to make sure that's not going to happen."

I was getting more pissed by the minute. "First, I'm not an idiot. I would never do anything I thought was truly dangerous. And second, you can't watch me every minute of every day, so how will you know if I'm doing something you deem dangerous or not."

"I won't, but I can discourage it."

"How?"

"A good spanking is excellent for a quick attitude adjustment." As soon as the words left his mouth, he kind of froze.

My mouth dropped open. "Spanking?"

I expected him to back down, to apologize, instead he turned my way, the gold flecks in his eyes brighter. "Yes, a good spanking works wonders."

My mouth opened, closed, then my face heated, and I knew it must be glowing bright red, a mix of outrage and, goddess, excitement. "You wouldn't."

"Try me."

"You don't get to tell me what to do," I said, sounding like a sullen teenager, but I was dumbfounded, and angry, and highly turned on, which was confusing as hell.

"There it is," Ren said, pointing at something, as if the conversation we were having wasn't anything out of the ordinary.

I turned to look, and dread washed everything else away. "Jesus." I'd tried to imagine a nearly two-hundred-year-old insane asylum, but even my imagination hadn't conjured anything like this. It was as if they'd plucked the building from old England and dropped it in the middle of Roxburgh. It'd been called Sunnydale back in the day, but there was nothing sunny about this place. The stone walls were dark with a slick moss, the windows topped with pointed arches like a cathedral. It was massive. I couldn't even guess how many rooms this place had.

We walked through the gate and into a large garden area at the front where I assumed patients would've been allowed out to sit on fine days, and made our way toward the wide heavy, wooden doors. This place had been decommissioned in the early 1980s, and I couldn't imagine how awful it must have been in this place for its residents.

I stumbled back when I felt the press of several disturbed souls.

"Jaz?" Ren asked as the sound of sliding metal on metal reached us through the door.

"There are restless spirits here, a lot of them." I could feel them, but thanks to my sigils, they were kept at a distance.

"You gonna be okay? We can leave?" His hand, still on my lower back, gripped my shirt, fisting it as if he wanted to tear me away from here.

"I'll be okay," I said. "I just wasn't expecting it."

The door opened, and Ren straightened. His arm slid around me, and he pulled me back, shocking the hell out of me. He was touching me again.

"Who the fuck are you?" the demon at the door said, head up, scenting the air.

I opened my mouth to speak, but Ren got there first. "We're here to see Rune."

"He's busy, and you'd be wise to get the fuck off his territory. He's not a fan of shifters."

I shook myself out of my stupor and pulled out of Ren's hold. "Chaos organized this meeting with Rune. He's expecting us."

"Name?" the demon snapped.

Ren said our names, and the demon pulled out his phone, tapped the screen, put it to his ear, then barked out a few words I didn't really understand before he shoved it back in his pocket. "Let's go."

He strode back inside, and we followed.

A shudder instantly rolled through me as we walked across the threshold. This place was worse than I thought. The old linoleum was stained and cracked, everything was cold and stark, and the smell was indescribable. Like hospital, but mixed with a whole lot of other things that turned my stomach. As we passed doors, I could feel the emotional echoes of the people who'd lived here. I shuddered again, and when the press of the spirits trapped here pushed harder, causing icy tendrils to slide over my shoulders and down my back, my hand shot out and I grabbed Ren's.

His fingers flexed around mine, and his gaze sliced down to me.

"I'm sorry," I said and quickly pulled my hand away.

"This way," the demon said, rounding a corner and heading toward an ancient-looking elevator.

Ren said nothing as he took my hand again, holding it firmly. My heart raced, and I couldn't look at him. How many times had I imagined doing this? Holding his hand like this. But in my wildest dreams we'd been walking on the beach or down the street, not through an asylum filled with demons and tortured souls.

The demon hit the up arrow. "Top floor," he said. "Don't wander around. We won't be responsible for what happens if you go somewhere you shouldn't."

"No worries there," I said as the doors slid open and Ren led me inside.

He hit the button for the top floor, and the doors slid closed again. "You doing okay?" he asked.

"Yeah, I'm fine. Sorry, I'm just feeling a lot here, and it kind of freaks me out." I loosened my hand around his, attempting to let his hand go. "I'm okay now."

He looked up at the numbers ticking over as we climbed higher but kept his fingers firmly around mine, not letting me go. The elevator bounced to a stop. "I've got you, Jaz, okay?" The doors slid open.

I didn't know what to say. I was feeling seriously breathless and a little dizzy from everything I was feeling, from Ren holding my hand, from the spirits here and the emotional echoes bombarding me from the past. "Thanks," I said. It was all I could get out.

We stepped into a small foyer. There was only one door we could go through, so we walked up to it, and I knocked.

The sound of heavy footfalls echoed through the door, and I had to stop myself from taking several steps back the closer they got. Ren moved so he was standing mostly in front of me, his grip on my hand tightening.

Finally, the door swung open, and if I hadn't already been bracing for some kind of impact, I would've jerked back and fallen on my ass.

A demon filled the door, towering over me. I looked up into his otherworldly eyes, a color between yellow and green. Power oozed from him, heavy and thick, and made my belly tremble.

"Jasmine," he said, his voice resonating through me.

"Uh...um, yes, that's me." I needed to pull it together. This guy was a pal of Lucifer's for fuck's sake. Showing weakness to a male like this was a really bad idea.

He stepped back, opening his door wider, his pale, terrifying gaze sliding over me. "Come in, lovely." His gaze slid to Ren. "You can wait out here, fox."

"Where my female goes, I go," Ren bit out. *His female?*

My gaze shot to Ren. He was pissed.

"Yours, is she?" Rune said.

"Yeah," Ren snarled. "And she doesn't leave my side."

Rune dipped his head, his face close to my neck, and he breathed in deep, then made a rough sound. Ren jerked me back with a growl. Rune grinned, flashing a set of fangs very much like a vampire, even though that wasn't what he was. "I don't smell you, fox." He looked down at me. "You smell like innocence and fear. An intoxicating combination."

My face went up in flames, humiliation filling me. My gaze darted to Ren and back up to Rune. "I don't care who you are, you don't get to scent me. Ever. Understand?"

"Jasmine," Ren said low, tightening his hold on me.

Rune grinned wider, a long, vibrating rumble rolling from his chest. "Oh, lovely, yes. I like you very much."

"The feeling is not mutual. I find you kind of sleazy, actually," I bit out, letting my humiliation run my mouth, then slammed it shut. *Fuck.*

"You're brave as well, little witch," he said. "Thankfully, for you, I like that as well."

"How about you take a fucking step back," Ren snarled.

Rune looked up. "You're starting to annoy me, fox."

I needed to get it together and this meeting back on track before Ren started a fight. "Chaos brokered this meeting for a reason. Can we stop all this...weirdness, and get down to it?"

Rune chuckled. "Yeah, lovely, let's get down to business."

Ren growled again.

The massive demon stepped away from me. "It's your lucky day," he said to Ren. "As delicious as she smells, I don't fuck with virgins."

Oh my goddess. NO. He did not just out me like that. My humiliation flamed higher as I followed him into what was obviously his apartment.

I didn't look at Ren as I took in my surroundings. Rune had made the top floor into one huge studio space. There were lots of windows, and it felt very different from the rest of the building.

"It used to be a rooftop garden. They walled it in sometime in the 1950s," Rune said as if he could read my mind. "So, lovely, little Jasmine, what is it you want from me?"

"Access to your library."

His brow arched. "Why?"

"Death is missing souls."

"And I should care, why?"

"He isn't the only one. Lucifer's missing some as well. Ask him if you don't believe me."

Rune studied me for several long seconds. "And you think you can find them?"

"I have to, my sister's depending on it."

He straightened. "All right, lovely, you want access, I'll give you access."

Relief flooded me. "Thank you—"

"But you have to do something for me in return."

Ren grabbed my hand again. "She's not doing a damned thing for you."

"Yes, she is. Or she'll leave here empty-handed."

Chapter Fifteen

Ren

"WHAT DO you want me to do?" Jaz asked Rune.

I fucking hated this asshole.

"You're a medium, yes, lovely?"

"Yes."

He nodded. "You feel the souls here?"

"I do."

"I need you to get rid of one of them. He's surpassed malevolent and taken a turn into violent poltergeist territory. I need him gone. He sticks to the fourth floor, a space I need and haven't been able to use since we moved in here."

"No fucking way," I growled. "Not happening."

Jasmine placed her hand on my forearm, silencing me with a single touch. "This is what I do. This is part of my job."

"Good," Rune said. "Get rid of him and you'll have free rein over the library." His lips curled up. "Any time, day or night, you're welcome to stop by."

Jaz blushed. "I appreciate it." She looked around his apartment. "Do you have a room I could use?"

"You don't have your things with you, for protection," I said, trying to stop her from doing this.

"My bag's in the car. I have what I need in it. Could you get it for me?" she asked, then turned back to Rune. "I need somewhere private to prepare."

"Bathroom?"

"Perfect."

"I'm not leaving you here on your own," I said, staring down the demon eyeing her like a juicy fucking steak. Despite what he said, he wanted her.

"He's friends with Chaos. He's not going to hurt me," Jaz said.

"Yeah," Rune said with that fucking smirk still on his lips. "Me and Chaos are buds, she's safe with me. There's a lock on the bathroom door if you're worried."

Chaos was not this asshole's bestie. I knew that much.

"Please, Ren. I need to do this."

Fuck. "When you're locked in the bathroom, I'll go get your bag." As if a lock could actually stop this fucker.

"Do you have a robe I could use? And some gauze would be good as well," she asked Rune.

My hackles shot up.

"Gauze is under the sink. But no robe. Would one of my shirts work?"

"Thanks. Yep, that'll work."

No. No fucking way. "Use my shirt." I'd walk around shirtless, I didn't give a fuck. For some reason my fox would not tolerate another male's scent on her. Neither of us could.

"It'll be easier with something that opens at the front. It's fine."

Rune grabbed a shirt from the back of a chair and handed it to her, his eyes dancing when he looked my way. He'd worn it. He was purposely giving her a shirt covered in his scent. I stared him down, struggling to breathe through my rage.

"Ren?"

My gaze sliced to Jaz.

"My bag."

"Lock yourself in the bathroom," I said again, and she hustled to the room Rune pointed to and shut herself in. I heard the lock engage a moment later. I turned back to the demon. "You touch her and I'll fucking kill you."

"Big talk for a little fox." He flashed his teeth. "You have no idea what I'm capable of."

"I don't care. You hurt her. I will find a way to end you." I strode out the door.

The smell of Jasmine's blood hit me as we got into the elevator. It was mixed with Rune's scent, and my already hostile fox lost his mind. "You're bleeding." I grabbed the front of the shirt she was wearing, about to yank it open.

She gripped it tighter at the front, her eyes widening. "Ren," she snapped.

I spun on Rune who leaned against the elevator wall. "What the fuck did you do to her."

"He did nothing. I did it to myself," Jaz said, bringing my attention back to her.

"What?" There was too much danger here, too many unknowns, and my protective instincts were off the charts. Add in whatever the fuck this was, and I was close to losing it completely. That's when I spotted the blood soaking through the white shirt she had around her body, at her stomach, her upper arms. "What the fuck did you do, Jasmine?" I growled.

She frowned at me. "A poltergeist of this strength requires extra measures. Protection glyphs."

"You carved them into your skin?" I said in disbelief.

"They're not deep, and it's nothing Else's balm can't heal. I've done this before several times."

"You carved up your own skin," I said, my breathing weird, heavy. She should never do that. Never suffer that. She was perfect and clean and good. Only monsters like me carved up their own skin, only those who deserved it. "That's not right. You shouldn't...you shouldn't do that."

She studied me. "You've seen Willow cut herself hundreds of times."

Jasmine looked genuinely puzzled, and I realized how I sounded. Like an overprotective mate. I needed to calm the fuck down. Being here with all these demons was fucking with me, that's all this was. "I just saw the blood and reacted. Sorry."

Rune chuckled behind me, and it was hard, but I ignored the asshole.

The elevator stopped with a ding, but the doors didn't open.

"We rigged it this way. Didn't want anyone on the fourth floor who wasn't supposed to be there," Rune said. "Whenever you're ready, lovely, say the word and I'll open the doors."

"Oh, I thought there'd be somewhere I could..." Her face darkened.

She'd mixed up some of her oil in the apartment, which meant she needed to strip off and cover herself in it like she did when she was with me. I'd take that fucking demon's eyes out before I let him see her like that.

She removed her sigil necklace and cuffs and put them in her bag. "I'm going to need you both to turn around, please, gentlemen. I need some privacy."

Rune arched a brow but did as she asked. "So what am I missing out on?"

I turned my back as well but kept him in my periphery. If he so much as peeked, I'd kill him.

"I need to cover myself in the oil I made upstairs, so the spirit can't possess me," she said as the scent of the oil intensified in the small space. Which meant it was warming against her skin.

Rune groaned. "So you're telling me, you're behind me, naked, and rubbing oil all over your body?"

"Yes."

He made a purring sound. "All glistening and slippery?"

"Um..."

"You're positive I can't watch?"

I snarled.

"Positive."

Rune chuckled again.

"Right, all done."

"What if you get into trouble?" I said, fear a gnarled knot in my gut.

"I won't," she said.

"I'm not shutting this door after you," I said, close to snatching her up and getting the fuck out of there.

I heard her rummaging around. "Fine, but I'm putting down a salt line, it's mixed with cemetery dirt so it's pretty potent. You'll be safe behind it. If the spirit does try to get to you, and the line thins, leave before it breaks. I'll follow when the job's done."

"Not leaving you behind, Jaz. Not fucking happening."

"Open the door," she said without answering me. The doors slid open. "And, Rune, please get Ren out of here if you have to."

I snarled again.

❧

Jasmine

I stared into the corridor and tried to keep my breathing even. Unlike the other parts of the building I'd seen, this floor had been left untouched. There was grime on the floor and walls, doors hanging off hinges. The hall was lined with several gurneys, worn leather straps dangling down their sides. I took another step and hissed when I stepped on broken glass.

"Jaz?" Ren called.

"Just some glass on the floor," I called back and kept moving.

I hadn't told Ren quite how dangerous this was. I'd dealt with poltergeists before, but never alone, always with Zinny. I knew what I was doing, though, and it wasn't like I had any other choice. We had no leads. The feral was still on the loose and, who knows, he might have scented Ren and left the area. Even if Ren found him, Agatheena might never give me the information I needed. I didn't know how long I had before Zinnia was trapped in Limbo for good, and the demon library might actually have some answers.

A crash came from the other end of the hall, and I headed toward it, whispering the spell I'd need to send the soul where he belonged, letting it build and slowly swirl around me. I needed the magic to grow in strength, to gain momentum, especially since it was just me.

I peered through the window in the next door. There were papers scattered around the room. An office. Pushing the door open, I cautiously walked in. The emotional energy in the room was dark, sadistic. Whoever had used this office had saturated it in their ill intent, in their cruelty and the pleasure they took from it. There was an overturned filing cabinet, a hole in the wall where it once stood. Files spilled out from the obvious hiding place. I picked one up, flinching in horror when I saw what was inside.

The pictures were old, in black and white, and they turned my stomach. What was documented here was not just images but written in careful detail was pure, unmistakable evil. Torture. The other files I picked up were the same. This creep had worked here, was charged with looking after the patients in his care, and instead he'd abused them, running secret experiments on them, torturing them over and over again.

Another crash came from out in the hall. I dropped the files and walked back out, glaring back toward the elevator when I saw Ren and Rune both watching me. Ren's face was contorted with fear, and Rune's was utterly unreadable. I turned away and carried on. If I wasn't quietly freaking out, perhaps I'd be embarrassed that I was naked again. But right then that was the last thing on my mind. I walked to the next door. It was stainless steel, no window this time. The emotions coming from that room lifted the hair on my arms and sent icy claws down my spine.

I increased the pace and volume of my spell. "What is evil must not walk among the living. Hell, take this soul so dark, remove it from the mortal realm, never to return." The poltergeist was behind that door. I felt him. He was excited. He knew I was coming, and he wanted to hurt me. Gripping my knife tighter, I flicked out the blade and sliced the final glyphs into my forearms.

Ren's snarl echoed down the corridor, but I didn't dare break concentration and look his way.

I let the blood slide down my arms and onto my feet, letting it strengthen my powers as the spell swirled faster and faster within me. My hair whipped around my shoulders from the force of it, and I lifted my arms and cried it out again, then aimed my hands at the door. It flew open, crashing into the wall, and I walked in.

The poltergeist stood beside a gurney and smiled wide when he saw me. There was some kind of contraption that sent ice through my veins on one side and an electrotherapy machine beside that. There was also a table covered in knives and other things he used to cut his patients. A hand drill for the lobotomies he performed on them while they were still awake, and another table with horrifying things he'd obviously used only on his female patients, in his "study" of the reproductive systems. All of it without consent or anesthesia or pain relief of any kind.

"Welcome," he said. "Please climb onto the table."

I stared him down, repeating my spell again and again, louder, until I was screaming it, my hair flying around me.

His twisted features contorted further, and he flew at me. I stumbled back but didn't stop my chant, didn't slow. He roared when he realized I was protected and he couldn't possess me.

Hadeon was going to be pissed I was calling on him so soon. "Hell, take back this soul so dark, remove it from the mortal realm, never to return," I cried, over and over again.

Light and heat swirled beneath the ghost, the ground jarring with a boom before Hadeon appeared. He snarled and spun to me, then paused and slowly turned back to my poltergeist who was now frozen in place. "Well, now, aren't you a piece of shit," Hadeon said to the ghost, then he grabbed the evil fucker by the throat and dragged him screaming to Hell.

I collapsed against the wall. He was gone. It was done. Shoving the door open, I walked out into the corridor.

I didn't have time to brace before they came at me.

Souls, his victims, so many of them. They came at me all at once, the ferocity of their anguish hitting in a torrent. They didn't want to harm me. They didn't want to hurt anyone. They were terrified, and that terror was so great, so overwhelming, there was no stopping what was about to happen, something that hadn't happened for a very long time.

I lifted my gaze to Ren, but I couldn't warn him. There was no time to explain. He saw the look on my face and started running toward me.

Everything went black.

Ren

I sprinted down the corridor, dropping to the floor beside Jasmine. Her body was limp, her face without any sign of life. I knew that look, I saw it every day. "No," I snarled. "Jasmine!" I pressed my fingers to her throat. Nothing. Not even a weak pulse. "No. No no no. Don't go, butterfly. Don't you fucking dare leave me."

I scooped her up in my arms and ran for the elevator. "Call a healer. She's unresponsive."

Rune stared down at her, and his head tilted to the side.

"Fucking call someone," I roared, clutching her to me and slamming my hand on the button for the ground floor. I pressed my ear to her chest. This couldn't be happening. Her heart wasn't beating. She wasn't breathing. She couldn't be dead. Jasmine couldn't be dead.

I looked up at Rune, snarling when he touched her forehead.

He shook his head. "She's not dead."

"She's not breathing. Her pulse—"

"Have you ever heard of catalepsy?"

"What? No, what the fuck are you talking about? She needs a healer. Now."

Something swirled in Rune's yellow-green eyes. "She's not dead. Her condition, whatever this is, is similar to catalepsy in humans. Something back there triggered it, but she will wake up." He hit the button for the top floor, and as soon as we hit the ground level, the doors closed again and we were on our way back up.

When the door opened again, I followed Rune back into his apartment, Jasmine's lifeless body clutched to me. "Are you sure?"

"Her mind's still active, as if she's in a dreamlike state. I'd get nothing if she was dead."

I sat on the couch and brushed her hair back from her face. "Wake up, butterfly. Open your eyes for me. Come back to me, baby." My fox whimpered and clawed at my subconscious before releasing a mournful howl, calling to her, trying to get her to reply, not understanding what was happening.

I don't know how long I sat there, holding her to me, begging her to come back to me. Light dimmed and night fell. I forgot

Rune was even there until the lights switched on. I looked up as he disappeared into the bathroom, shutting the door. The shower came on a minute later.

She'd been out for hours. What if he was wrong? What if she was gone? My heart shredded in my chest.

I looked back down, and Jasmine blinked up at me. Her wide green eyes unfocused, confused. "Ren?"

I released a shuddering breath. "Christ, Jasmine." I crushed her to me. "I thought you were dead. I thought you were fucking dead."

"I'm okay," she said croakily.

"What the hell happened back there?" She licked her dry lips, and I had the strong urge to crush my mouth to hers.

"I-it hasn't happened for a long time. I thought I'd be okay—"

The bathroom door opened, and Rune walked out in pants, no shirt, flashing his inked and branded chest, grinning when he saw Jasmine awake. "You're back, lovely."

"Glad to see you're not distraught over my possible death," she said to him, trying to straighten in my arms.

Which was when I realized she was naked against me with only Rune's shirt covering her nakedness. I tugged it down to make sure it covered her ass.

Rune grinned. "The fox was distraught enough for the both of us."

Her gaze darted back to me. "I'm sorry, you must have been..." She chewed her lip. "I'm sorry," she said again.

"You're okay. That's all that matters. How are you feeling?"

She sat up, and I was forced to let her go. She stood and I held out my hands to catch her if she fell, but she seemed sturdy on her feet.

"I'm fine. There are never any lasting effects." She tightened the shirt around her oil-slicked and cut-up body. "I'll just grab a quick shower, then you can show me the library?" she said to Rune.

"I take it that means our poltergeist's gone?"

Her expression hardened. "Yes, to Hell, where he belongs." Then she strode to the bathroom. "I'll be quick." Then she shut the door.

I stared after her. I was shaking. She'd recovered, but I sure as fuck hadn't. I'd never forget the way it felt to hold Jasmine's lifeless body in my arms.

How the fuck was I going to go back to normal after this? Be alone with her again tonight, let her touch me, wrap her arms around me?

How was I going to ignore this feeling inside me, the fucked-up voice inside my head, god, roaring through my skull, telling me that Jasmine was mine.

Mine.

Chapter Sixteen

Jasmine

REN LAY STILL as I bent over him, tattooing the finishing touches to one of his sigils. His abs clenched. Jesus, his stomach was roped with muscle. My fingers accidentally brushed his side, over the scar there, and he shuddered. I was trying to make as little contact as possible, but it was hard. I repeated my spell, holding his skin taut, and inked the flick at the bottom. I may not be an actual tattoo artist like Rome, but I was an artist, and I was going to make sure the sigils I'd inked on Ren looked good.

"You sure you're okay?" Ren asked for about the tenth time since we started.

"I'm okay, Ren, honestly. It's like nothing happened." After I woke, Rune had shown me the library. It hadn't been nearly as impressive as I'd imagined—I thought he might be holding out on me, honestly—definitely not as vast as ours, but he had let me take a bunch of books on loan, and I'd be poring through them as soon as I got home. I needed a freaking breakthrough like now. If I had to exorcise a hundred twisted poltergeists, I would if it ensured Zinnia came home.

"For you, maybe," he said, and it was obvious he'd said it through gritted teeth.

I moved to the next spot, just below his belly button. "I am sorry I scared you. I wasn't prepared for all those souls. I've never felt anything like it." His abs tightened again under my hand as I started the next sigil, and I tried not to notice that this time, he wasn't hard. Not that I wanted him to be, right?

Of course not.

But my head was basically hovering over his junk, which meant last time hadn't been about me at all. He'd explained why he'd reacted that way, but still...at the time I'd wanted it to be about me, that he'd wanted me. It was stupid. It shouldn't make me feel less, or unattractive, but it kind of did, even though I knew wanting me, especially when I held him, healed him, was a twisted side effect of my magic. And so was the possessive way he'd been acting, the protectiveness. He was confused, and the sooner this was over and done with, the better for both of us. Being this close to him wasn't good for me, was messing with me, even though I knew the truth.

I glanced up. His eyes were squeezed closed, the fingers of both hands in tight fists, and color slashed his cheeks.

"Is it hurting?" As soon as I spoke, goose bumps lifted across his stomach, right where my breath had brushed his scarred skin.

"I'm good," he said, not looking at me.

"Ren?"

"Yeah?"

"You look in pain."

His nostrils flared. "I'm good, Jaz."

"I don't believe you. Look at me," I said.

His chest expanded, then his eyes opened, dipping down and hitting me. His gaze was dark with bursts of gold flecks, swirling, intense. The fox was back. "I'm good, Jasmine. Not in pain." He made sure to hold my gaze and not look at my nakedness when he said that.

A swooshing sensation dipped low in my belly, and I had to drag my eyes from his. "Good." When I looked back down, there were more goose bumps—he also wasn't soft anymore. Nope, he was hard as hell.

He'd looked at me, and he'd gotten hard.

My face heated when I realized that's why he'd been concentrating so hard. I was about to ink a sigil on the base of his dick. He'd been trying to stay in control, now he'd lost it completely. *Shit.*

It had nothing to do with me, being touched was overwhelming him, he just wasn't used to it, that's all. He was a guy with a healthy sexual appetite. I was a naked female smeared in oil. Even if I was a mess, bruised from my fall with cuts that were still red and raw, I was bent over his dick. Of course he'd get hard.

I could be anyone.

I thought I'd lost you.

He'd said it when I woke up. I'd been unconscious before that, but I'd heard his voice off and on. I was pretty sure he'd called me butterfly, his voice rough and filled with fear. I tried not to think about it and focused on finishing the sigil.

Now for the next one. My face grew even hotter. "I just need to, um...your jeans."

He lifted his ass and pushed them down like he had when I did his back. "Enough?"

"Yep," I said way too brightly, trying to cover my embarrassment. The thick base of his cock was right there, the denim forcing it to angle down, which had to hurt in his current state. "I'll try to be quick."

He grunted.

I glanced back up and he had his eyes closed again, his arms crossed over his chest. "Just two more," I said and started on the next one just above his dick. I outlined it, then carefully filled it in, wiping away the ink as I went. I finished it in record time, then paused to load up with ink and gather my courage.

"Okay, last one. Ready?"

He grunted again, his breathing shaky as I leaned over him and started spelling. I pressed my needle to the base of his dick. A thick vein ran down the middle, and it was getting in my way. "Sorry, I just have to..." I inwardly cringed as I used the thumb of my other hand to kind of press on it, moving it as I worked. "There's a...a vein and I need a smooth, um..."

"Don't talk, Jasmine," he growled out. "Do not fucking talk."

Now he was *pissed* at me? "So sorry if my voice offends you—"

"Not offended, Jaz. Your warm breath on my cock is the problem."

"Oh." I slammed my mouth shut, my cheeks so hot now my freaking eyes watered. Somehow I managed to recite the spell, while trying not to breathe on him too much, as I worked the tattoo gun. It wasn't easy, not when I was fighting the instinct to push his jeans down farther. Not when I wanted to shove them all the way down and let his cock spring free to ease my curiosity. He smelled of soap and musk and the forest. My nipples tightened, and I bit my lip and did my best to stop the pervy direction of my thoughts and get this done.

"The outline's done," I said and used my cloth to wipe away the extra ink.

A shiver rolled through Ren, and my gaze shot up to him again.

"Finish it, Jaz," he bit out.

"Right."

"And don't fucking talk."

Oops. I forgot. I changed my needle so I could fill in the outline and dipped it in the ink spiked with my potion. I pressed it to the silky skin of his cock, and he shuddered again. I wanted to ask if he was okay, but I bit my lip and stopped myself. I had to keep wiping away the extra ink so I could see what I was doing, and every time I did, he jerked.

On the next swipe, he growled low. Tingles lifted across my scalp and down my arms.

Holy shit, he was really hard now. It had to hurt, having it forced down like that, not to mention my needle working over it. Shame burned through me when I was forced to squeeze my legs together to ease the intense throb there.

I finally did the last little bit, quickly swiped away the ink, then straightened. "All done."

His arms were still locked over his chest, and he was breathing in and out shakily, as if he were trying to slow it down.

"You okay?" I asked.

"That all of them?" he said instead of answering.

Most likely because it was a stupid freaking question. He wasn't okay. How could he be? This whole situation was fucked up to the extreme. "Just the two on your neck, and then we're finished."

He nodded, reached down, and cursed as he yanked up his jeans. "I'm fucking sorry, Jaz. You shouldn't have to deal with that shit. I thought I had it under control, but you're fucking beautiful, and you were touching me, and you're naked, not that I'm looking," he quickly said. "But I know you are, and every one of your breaths against my skin felt...and I...and your hands on me, and fuck...I'm making it worse."

You're fucking beautiful.

My stupid, hopeful heart sped faster. Ren thought I was beautiful? "It's okay," I said. "You don't need to explain. If you could just sit up. We'll get the last two done."

He rubbed his hands over his face and nodded.

Ren

. . .

She moved up beside me, and I could feel the warmth radiating from her bare skin against my side. She wasn't touching me, but it was as if she were pressed against me so damn tight, her warmth soaking right through me.

Dammit, I'd had my dick under control until she'd made me look at her. The only place I could look was her eyes, and as soon as I had them locked on mine, my cock had stiffened. I wanted to reach down and squeeze it, badly. It felt like it was going to be torn off shoved down the leg of my jeans the way it was. But there was no way in hell I was going to adjust it in front of her. She had to think I was the biggest fucking pervert.

This was when Edward's voice would usually invade my mind and tell me I was making her skin crawl just being this close to her, but it never came—and I realized it hadn't for a while now. And then the heat of Jasmine's skin seemed to intensify, and all my attention was back on her.

I tried not to look, and I didn't, but when she leaned forward, pressing the needle to the side of my throat, I could see the flash of color from the tattoo on her chest in my peripheral vision, the way her soft tits swayed as she moved. I sucked in another fortifying breath and closed my eyes. I tried to zone out as she did the first one, but the fox could smell her blood still, and I could still remember the way she felt in my arms, the fear, the roar of *mine* through my head. She swiped the ink away and more goose bumps lifted across my skin.

"One final sigil to go, then I'll get out of your way. You won't have to see me again for a week." Her warm breath brushed my skin once more, and it took everything in me not to shiver again.

I hated the thought of not seeing her again for another week. Yes, doing this with her was torture, but it was...it felt good as well. She thought I was a manwhore and an asshole, and more than likely a pervert at this point, but being this close to her, just the two of us— Christ, these past several days had done more for me than anything else had since I was possessed.

The thought of not seeing her tomorrow night? I hated it. Yeah, I might see her at the clubhouse, or when I was hanging out with Willow, but it wouldn't be the same, I wouldn't have her to myself, and I knew every day until I could be here in my living room with her again, just the two of us, would feel like a fucking eternity.

She moved to my other side, dipping her needle in the ink, then got started. I closed my eyes and tried to focus on anything but the feel of her fingers curled around the back of my neck. Her thumb pressed to my skin like she had the base of my cock, but this time to hold the skin taut, not to press down a bulging fucking vein because blood was pumping hard and fast to my engorged cock—and still was with her so near.

Minutes ticked by. "I just need to fill it in."

Her soft voice had tingles dancing all over me. Then she was back at it, filling in the final sigil, whispering her spell. The soft sound of her voice repeating the words over and over again was a torment, Heaven and Hell all rolled into one. I needed her to stop for my own fucking sanity, but I thought I'd die if she did. I'd hated touch for so long after what happened, and now I was addicted to it, to Jasmine's touch. Only hers.

The longer she worked, the closer to the end we got and the more I dreaded its arrival.

"All done," she finally said, still in that soft voice.

Her hand was curled around my throat as she wiped the excess ink from the final sigil. "You suit them, you know. They look really good."

"Yeah?" I turned to her and realized my mistake too late.

Our eyes locked, our faces, *our mouths*, so close, and every one of her soft breaths now brushed my lips instead of my throat. Our gazes held. She blinked, her soft green gaze bright and startlingly beautiful. A scent reached me—arousal. Jaz was turned on, pussy wet.

Fuck. I gasped in a breath that only made it worse. I looked away and quickly stood.

She stood as well, and like last time, she grabbed my shirt, pulling it on. Her head was dipped. "We need to do your healing, then I'll leave you to the rest of your night."

How the fuck was I going to survive it? "Sounds good."

Not looking at me, she stepped into me, wrapping her arms around my waist. She hadn't cleaned up and changed first, like she usually did, and with how thin my shirt was, I felt every one of her curves pressed against me, soft and warm. Her power slid through me, gentle but persistent. I kept my hands at my sides, fingers fisted so fucking tight my knuckles felt close to splitting. She murmured her words of encouragement, like last time, but I was lost in the feel of her, of her power, a jumble of thoughts and sensations, in her addictive scent.

The emotions swirling inside me were drawn away, her power sliding through my body as if she was stroking me, soothing me from the inside out. I sucked in breath after breath as it was all taken from me. For a short time, those awful feelings were gone.

The euphoria built, slow and steady, and I started to shake.

"Ren?"

Her voice washed over me, and I stared down at her. My arms were locked around her small waist now. I didn't remember doing it, but I was holding her tight to me. *Let her go.* I couldn't fucking do it; like the last two times, I couldn't let her go. My gaze dipped to her luscious mouth. So pretty. So fucking inviting.

She blinked up at me and licked her lips. "Ren?"

I swallowed hard. "Yeah?"

"When you thought I was with Rome, that we were seeing each other, you didn't like it, did you?"

I gritted my teeth. We couldn't go there. I couldn't tell her how I was feeling. I didn't fucking understand it, not really, and nothing could ever happen between us, nothing beyond this. I'd only hurt her, and I'd run off the edge of that fucking cliff before I ever did that. But still, my arms remained locked around her, not letting her get away, holding her to me.

"And when you thought I was dead…"

"I can't talk about that," I choked out. "I can't fucking think about it, not yet—"

She reached up, cupping my jaw, and shook her head like she was shaking something loose. "What you're feeling, it's okay. You don't…you don't want me. I know it's the magic."

No. It was her. It was Jasmine. "Don't," I rasped, but at the same time, I leaned into her touch. "Don't stop."

"Ren," she whispered, breathing harder.

Her gaze dipped to my mouth and back up.

She wanted to kiss me too. She wanted *me*. I could fucking smell it.

I couldn't make myself release her. I couldn't turn away. I needed to taste her again. Just one more time. Just once more before this ended, before she left me without her for a whole fucking week.

My fox pricked up his ears and edged closer. I was trapped by her warmth. It radiated from her body, her eyes, her soul. Jasmine was pure warmth, and I was drawn closer like I was in the grip of hypothermia and she was the only thing that could save me.

"Please," I finally rasped, pleading with her. I wanted to taste her again so badly, but I was in control this time, and I needed her to want it as well. I needed her to kiss me.

"Please what?"

"Kiss me, Jasmine. I need you to kiss me."

"Ren—"

"Please."

Trembling, she slid her arms around my neck. She licked her lips, her gaze searching mine, then finally she lifted to her toes, and

I dipped my head closer to hers, her lips a mere breath away, waiting, desperate for her to close the distance between us.

Her cheeks were deep scarlet, so sweet and shy and beautiful, then she finally pressed her mouth to mine.

My mind went blank. There was nothing, no one, just her and me and the taste, the feel of her mouth on mine. I tried to stay still, to keep my hands to myself, but I snapped. Every moment I'd spent with her had slowly worn me thin. I was at breaking point, and knowing this was the last time, the last kiss, I broke in half—no, I fucking splintered apart.

My arm hooked her around her waist tighter, the other delving into her long blond hair as I hoisted her higher, the shirt she'd put on slid up, and my hand met hot and slippery bare skin. I groaned against her lips and opened my mouth over hers, kissing her deeper. Her sweet, little tongue tangled with mine, the urgent sounds she made driving me fucking wild. "You taste so fucking good, butterfly," I rasped against her lips. She hooked her legs around my waist, her bare pussy grinding on my hard cock through my jeans, and I hissed and quickly reached down to adjust my hard-on.

The side of my hand slid across her slippery flesh, and I almost came in my jeans. She ground down harder. "Touch me...please."

If I touched her pussy, I'd throw her on the couch and fuck her. This felt so fucking right, but it wasn't right. She was all but naked, and this was moving too fucking fast. Her fingers were in my hair, her mouth so hot and sweet and perfect.

I wanted her so bad I shook, but I couldn't do this.

Images of blood and gore flashed through my mind, on my hands, hands that were sliding over Jasmine's body, hands that were tainted and wrong and evil.

Someone knocked on the door, and I pulled away, panting.

Jasmine froze, blinking up at me.

"Ren, it's Mom!"

"Shit!" Jasmine cried and flew out of my arms. She snatched

up her clothes and ran from the room. The bathroom door slammed a second later. I didn't need to worry about having an erection in front of my mother. It deflated all on its own at the realization of what I'd just let happen, again. But this time, I'd let shit get out of hand. I quickly grabbed a shirt from the clean laundry I'd dumped on the chair, yanked it on, then strode to the door and opened it.

"Mom, hey."

She beamed at me like she always did when she first saw me and, like always, that look was quickly followed by concern.

"Have you been eating enough, honey?"

"Yeah, of course."

"How about sleeping? If you don't get enough sleep—"

"I've been sleeping. I'm okay." She worried, but she was usually more subtle.

She bit her lip and nodded, her eyes glossy. What was going on here?

Then it clicked into place. Tomorrow was the anniversary of what happened to me. I wasn't the only one who dreaded this time of year.

She looked past me to the candles, the salt, the string and herbs set out on the mat, and frowned. "What's going on, Renny?" Her gaze flew to my throat, to the sigils she could see there. "Ren?"

"Everything's fine. I promise."

"Hi, Mrs. Macanroy," Jasmine said, walking into the room.

Mom's gaze slid to Jaz, and she beamed. "Oh, Jasmine! I assumed it was Wills here. It's so nice to see you. How've you been, honey?"

Jaz smiled, her cheeks still pink, her mouth darker and swollen from our kiss. A yearning filled me, and I wanted to yank her back into my arms and finish what we'd started. I wanted to claim her, bite her, mark her. I felt dizzy and overheated. My skin was clammy and my fucking gut ached.

Ours.

My fox didn't say much, but his voice echoed through my mind now.

Only ours.

I froze. *No.* He couldn't mean what I thought he did.

Claim mate. Bite. Mark.

My lungs seized and my heart slammed with force against the back of my ribs.

"Oh, am I interrupting, is this...is this a date?" A smile so wide it hurt to look at covered my mother's face.

"No," I said quickly, not wanting to get her hopes up, and locking my fucking knees so I didn't fall on my ass as what my fox said rang through my skull. "Jasmine was just doing some ink for me."

The concern was back. "Are you okay?"

"They're just simple sigils," Jasmine said. "For general well-being," she added.

Mom frowned, then looked up at me and forced a smile. "Well, that's good."

"So did you need something, Ma?" I asked when she stood there, the worry taking over again.

"I thought tonight was the night we were going over the plans for the renovations. If you're busy, maybe we can do it tomorrow? It'll have to be early, though. I have an appointment with the designer at lunchtime."

I'd forgotten our plans completely, but if she left me here with Jasmine now, I wasn't sure what I'd do. Either fuck her, or tell her to leave and hurt her, and I wasn't sure which would win out right then. "It's all good. If we don't do it now, we won't get a chance in the morning." Mom didn't need my help with this, but she liked to include me since my parents insisted it was my business as well. Tonight's visit wasn't really about that, though. No, it was about the three-year anniversary of her son being possessed and going on a killing spree, and her needing to be close to me, to reassure herself I was okay.

Jasmine quickly moved around the living room, grabbing her things, still blushing like crazy, and I shoved my hands in my pockets so I didn't reach for her when she walked over to us. She smiled at Mom. "Nice to see you again, Mrs. Macanroy."

"Call me Sally, honey," Mom said and walked into the living room and began unloading color samples and bits of fabric onto the couch.

Jasmine smiled up at me. "I'll leave you to it."

I nodded, my throat so fucking tight I wasn't sure how I was managing to still talk. "Jaz…"

She shook her head and smiled brighter, her eyes lit up and filled with happiness. "I'm fine. You hang with your mom. We'll talk later, okay?"

I nodded.

Her gaze darted to my mother, who wasn't paying us any attention, organizing everything and laying more stuff out on the coffee table, then back to me. She lifted to her toes, curled her fingers around the side of my throat, pulled me down, and pressed a quick kiss to my lips, making my heart thump hard. She dropped back down, grinned wider, then spun away and ran up the stairs and onto the street.

My fox whined, then growled, and the urge to run after her, to grab her and drag her back was so intense, I took a step after her.

"Renny, what do you think?" Mom said.

I slammed on the brakes and forced myself to shut the door.

And every step I took, taking me farther away from her, the more my fox lost his shit.

Fuck.

Chapter Seventeen

Jasmine

MR. JENKINS HELD my hand tighter than I thought possible, seeing as how frail he was. A tear slid down his weathered cheek, and he shook his head. "My granddaughter told me to make this appointment months ago, but I was a skeptic and an old fool." He smiled and another tear streaked down his face. "That was my Nelly, no if, ands, or buts about it. No one knows what you just told me, only her and I."

I squeezed his hand in return. I worked with a lot of humans, they made up eighty percent of my business, and I loved that I could give them this peace of mind. A message from a loved one to ease their fears and their hearts. "I'm so glad I could help you today," I said softly. "Nelly loves you so much, I can see it radiating from her." She'd crossed over two years ago, ascending straight to Heaven. I'd tapped into her energy as soon as Mr. Jenkins walked in.

Tell him he has to stop sitting in that living room and get out of the house and enjoy himself. Tell him to use the money in our holiday account and go on the cruise we always planned.

Her voice echoed through my mind, her features soft, but her tone no-nonsense. I chuckled. "She wants you to get out of the house and enjoy yourself. She said you're to use the money in your holiday savings account and go on that cruise the two of you planned to go on."

His lips quivered and more tears fell. Often in situations like this, the tears weren't sad ones, but came from relief, from the confirmation that their loved ones were okay. Add to that the intense emotions that came from truly knowing there was something more after death, that death wasn't an end, that it was just moving to the next part of your journey...it was a lot to take in. Mr. Jenkins was feeling all of that now. He also missed his wife terribly.

To have that kind of love—

Tender new shoots of hope grew, unfurling inside me. Ren felt something for me, he did. This time, it felt different. He'd had more control. He'd kissed me because he wanted to last night, not because of my power, I was sure of it.

If his mother hadn't arrived when she did, I didn't think we would have stopped at kissing. I'd tried to convince myself the way he looked at me all the time was nothing. I told myself it was something else, because how could it actually be what I desperately wanted it to be? He'd never made a move.

For so long, he'd coped with what happened to him through alcohol, by giving himself to any female who wanted him. By not caring about himself.

But he'd changed. The fake smiles were coming less often. He'd actually laughed, and yes, he was also moodier, more aggressive—jealous—and no, they weren't great emotions, but they were something other than indifference, and that had to be a good thing. He was allowing himself to feel whatever it was he was feeling, and maybe that included the way he felt about me?

I thought about our kiss, the way he'd said my name. The way he'd growled against my lips. My toes curled in my shoes. I'd never experienced anything like that in my life.

I ended the session with Mr. Jenkins, giving him a tight hug, pouring my healing powers into him, wrapping them around the part of him that looked back fondly on his time with his wife, and smoothed the jagged edges. He'd stifled it, all his energy going to his pain, so I worked to heal it, to revive that part of him, and bring it renewed life.

Mr. Jenkins left, and I took one of the books I'd borrowed from Rune's library from my bag to look through while I waited for my next client. I hadn't found anything useful yet, but there had to be something. Please, goddess, let there be something.

As I turned the pages, my anxiety surged, that I couldn't do this, that I'd fail Zinnia.

My next client arrived, and she'd just sat down when my phone chimed. I excused myself and quickly checked who it was. My knees actually went weak when I saw Ren's name on the screen.

Can you come by tonight?

Maybe some would play it cool, leave him hanging for an hour or so, but I wasn't cool. Why would I wait? This was the male I was in love with, with every fiber of my being.

Still, I managed to find some self-control and instead of writing back and saying, *OMG! Can you believe we freaking kissed last night? It was the best kiss I've ever had. I love you so much I think I might die.*

I went with: *Sure thing. What time?*

Ren: *I finish work at six. Any time after then*

Again I reined it in and replied with a very cool: *See you then*

I scanned our messages, nearly vibrating with excitement and happiness. It was happening. It was actually happening between us.

I shoved my phone away and went back to my client. Somehow, I had to get through the rest of my appointments without self-combusting.

The day went way too slow, but at five fifteen I was blowing out my candles and packing everything away. I grabbed my bag, stuffing my demon book back in, locked up the small room I rented for work, and took the narrow stairs to the street. I waved to Beth in the shop below through the window of her flower shop and headed to my car.

My phone beeped as I climbed in, and I slid it from my back pocket so fast I almost dropped it. Not Ren this time. It was a number I didn't recognize.

Have you thought anymore about dinner?

Xavier, it had to be. I wasn't the kind of person to string someone along, not that I'd been in the position to string anyone along before, but still. There was only one person I wanted to have dinner with.

Sorry, Xavier, I'm kind of seeing someone. It's new.

His reply came a minute later.

My loss. If I think of anything to help you with your missing souls, I'll be in touch.

Me: *Thank you.*

Brushing my hands over my hips and smoothing out the fabric of my dress, I tried to steady my nerves when I headed for Ren's place. The sun had set, and I could see lights shining from inside. Taking a steadying breath and gripping the bottle of wine I'd swiped from the cupboard, I walked up to the door and knocked.

I could see his shadow moving behind the door's frosted glass. He stilled for a moment, hovering there. My smile slipped a little when he didn't instantly open up. I stared at his silhouette, and he was obviously staring at mine. Was he going to leave me standing out here? Cold dread washed through my veins, and I gripped my bottle of wine tighter.

Please. Please open it. Please let me in.

He moved suddenly, and the door swung open.

His gaze sliced down my front, hit the wine in my hand, then came back up. His gaze stayed on mine a moment, then he looked away and opened the door wider. "Come in, Jaz."

The rest of the good feelings that I'd been floating on all day splintered at his tone, at the look on his face. Something was wrong. *No. You're imagining it. Stay positive. Everything's fine.* That kiss meant something to him as well, it did.

We walked to the couch, and he motioned for me to sit. "We should talk."

No. A voice in my head screamed. *NO. Please no.* I stupidly ignored that, too, not ready to believe what every cell in my body was telling me, not ready to let the energy rolling off Ren to penetrate.

"Have you had any trouble now that the sigils are all done? Felt any souls around you at all?" I asked, stalling, desperate to not have this conversation.

He shook his head. "Everything's stopped, like you said it would. Thank you for that, Jaz, truly." He shoved his fingers through his hair. "But that's not why I asked you over."

I held up the bottle of wine. "Would you like a glass?" I stood and headed for the small kitchen. Ren watched me as I took down two glasses, my hands shaking. I opened his kitchen drawers, searching for a corkscrew, but there wasn't one.

Ren strode over and slipped the bottle from my hands, setting it aside. "Jasmine, we need to talk—"

I spun on him. "No, we don't."

A look crossed his face, telling me he'd rather be anywhere but here.

A sane person would take the hint and retreat, would try and save face. I didn't feel sane in that moment. Far from it. "Don't do this. Please." The last was whispered, pleading.

He looked pained, awkward. "You're…god, so beautiful, Jaz, so fucking gorgeous, and sweet, and funny and fierce. I care about you, I do, but what happened last night—"

"Was perfect. Was the only thing that's felt right in a really long time," I said, throwing my heart on the floor in front of him, begging him to pick it up, to take it and keep it for his own.

"I wanted you last night, I did, badly," he said roughly. "But this can't happen between us."

I was breathing hard, shaking. "Why?"

"You know why. I'm not fit for any kind of a relationship."

"But this is different, we'd be different. I could help you, we'd be good for each other," I said, close to begging.

"Butterfly," he said gently. "I'm sorry."

I grabbed the edge of the counter so I didn't collapse on the floor right alongside my bleeding heart. "You want me and not just last night. You want me now. I know you do. Why are you pretending there isn't something between us?" *Something huge. Something real.* "Why are you lying?"

The muscles in his arms tightened. "Any male would be lucky to be with you, Jaz, and I mean that, but it's not going to be me."

I closed the space between us. My guard had shattered when he'd kissed me last night. There was no throwing it back up now. I felt as if he were tearing me limb from limb. This couldn't be happening. I loved him. Goddess, so much. I fisted his shirt at his stomach, pressing in close, and looked up at him. "I want you and you want me," I said, fighting the sob crawling up my throat. "Tell me, tell me you want me too. Stop lying and tell me."

Ren winced, actually winced. Pity filling his eyes. "Don't make this any harder—"

"Say it. Tell me you don't want me."

"Jazzy."

"Say it!"

He sucked in a breath, his nostrils flaring. "I don't. Not the way you want me. I'm sorry. I'm really sorry, Jasmine. I'm not capable of that, of having a...a relationship with anyone, not anymore. I never should have—"

I shoved away from him, shaking my head, his words wounding me more than anything else ever had, and in a way I knew I'd never recover from.

I looked up at him and fought down the tears. I'd already humiliated myself enough in front of this male. I straightened my spine, my hands to his chest, and looked him in the eyes. I was about to say, *If you send me away now, you will lose me forever. Do you understand? If you don't fight for me now, I promise you, there will never be an us. Never.* But my power reached out instinctively, moving through him, and I felt his torment, and just how broken he was. I knew it already, of course. He was emotionally scarred to an extent that no amount of work on his own would heal him.

He needed help. And I was the only one who could do it.

What I was doing right now, it wasn't fair, not to him, and not to myself. He needed me to help him heal, not beg him to love me like some pathetic fool. Not make everything he was already suffering so much harder. Goddess, I was so fucking selfish. I knew what he'd been through, and still all I was thinking about was myself, what I wanted, what I needed. I loved him too much to do this to him.

I shook my head and choked down my pain. "You must think I'm a desperate idiot. Goddess, I'm so sorry." I forced a laugh and took a step back. "No, you're right, of course. This"—I motioned between us—"would be a horrible idea."

He searched my gaze, and his jaw tightened. "Jasmine—"

"It's fine, Ren. Honestly. I lost my head there for a moment." My heart felt as if it had been mangled in my chest, but I forced a deprecating grin. "I thought we could have some fun, but mixing business with pleasure is never a good idea, right? Can we just forget this happened?"

His gaze searched mine, then he nodded. "If that's what you want."

"It is. Right, I have to take off, but I'll be in touch so we can sort out a time for your next session."

He stood impossibly still, watching me closely. "Okay."

I walked around him and strode blindly toward the door, my heart hammering in my chest. I walked through the door and up the stairs as calmly as I could, hoping he didn't see how hard I was shaking, then as soon as I reached the top and was out of sight, I ran, like I could outrun what had just happened.

Whatever hope I'd had, had turned black, had shriveled and died. It was bitter and cold and so wrong I wanted to claw at my skin, at the center of my chest and the organ pounding so desperately there. It still called for him, still demanded I go back, even now.

Chapter Eighteen

Ren

I strode out onto the street and watched Jasmine run like hell away from me. She'd tried to backtrack, to pretend she didn't care, that she'd only come for some fun, but she was lying.

My heart was pounding like it was trying to liberate itself from my chest.

Fuck, when I answered the door—the look on her face, the hope, the excitement. Everything she felt for me had been right there, open and real and so fucking raw.

And I'd smothered it, killed it.

I'd hurt her.

Oh fuck.

I bent at the waist, gripping my thighs, and dry heaved. Everything inside me was rebelling against what I'd just done. My fox was losing his shit, shredding the ground beneath his paws, howling in pain.

She was ours, our mate, and I'd rejected her. I pushed her away.

A weak, tainted piece of shit like you has no right touching a female like that. Edward's voice echoed through my mind. My broken mind bringing him back as if he'd never left.

Images of the newspaper article I'd seen this morning, crumpled up and tossed on the floor of my father's office, flashed through my mind. A piece written about the families of the victims, *my victims*, three years later. Their faces...how they felt about their loved one's killer still on the loose...

My skin crawled.

Letting her go was the right thing to do.

I had to move. I couldn't stand here, and I couldn't go back into my place. Not when all I could see now was Jasmine standing there, so beautiful, eyes filled with pain, not when her scent had filled every inch like she'd always been there. I strode down the street and through the field, then into the forest. I didn't dare shift, not right then, not when we both wanted to go after Jasmine so badly. If I let animal instincts take over, my fox would take us straight to her.

Christ, the pain in her eyes was all I could see. I could feel it. Her pain had felt like a kick to the backs of the knees. It'd taken everything in me to stand fucking upright in the face of all that pain. I should never have kissed her, touched her. I should have fucking resisted. I could tell myself that, but it'd been impossible. I'd been drawn to her so completely that resisting wasn't an option, and now I'd made everything so much worse.

A demon snarled up ahead, and I pulled the knife from my boot and kept running. It stepped out in front of me, and I attacked, taking out all the pent-up agony and rage I was feeling. I sliced and sliced, a sound coming from me that could only be described as a disturbed wail before I finally removed his head. After that I heard no more demons as I ran toward my cliff.

The demons in these forests knew me well. I'd lived alongside them for long enough. They knew what I could do, and they'd learned to stay the fuck away from me. The sound of rushing water echoed ahead, and I pumped my arms harder, sprinting faster. It'd be better for Jasmine, for everyone if I was gone. If I dove off the edge of that cliff. I gasped for breath, struggling to process what just happened back in my kitchen, what I'd just done.

Oh fuck.

What had I done?

What I had to. I was stained with blood. A monster.

A monster who was still torturing the innocent people he'd killed, their souls unable to rest because of me, because of how fucked in the head I was. A monster who hurt everyone around him.

You're a weak, pathetic coward, Edward's voice snarled. I punched the side of my head and roared. "Shut up!"

He wasn't there. He was gone. That was my own voice.

And it was right.

I ran and ran until sweat poured off me, until the cliff finally came into view. I dug my heels in deeper, my breath puffing in and out faster. I looked straight ahead, focusing on the night sky, and raced for the edge.

Almost there. It was almost over—

A heavy weight slammed into my side, knocking me back several yards from the edge. I spun with a snarl, and came face to face with a giant hellhound. Warrick.

No one was stopping me. I jumped back up and sprinted toward my goal a second time, but he moved quickly, tossing me away from the edge again.

I stood, panting hard. "Get the fuck out of my way!" I roared.

Warrick shifted, his golden eyes burning into me. "Not letting you kill yourself. You're not doing that to Willow and Violet. And you're not doing it to me, to your brothers."

"Why the fuck are you here? Just go."

"We stopped by the house just as you took off. Your scent, brother...it's not right. What happened?"

We?

Willow stepped forward, out of the shadows, her gaze locking on mine before she strode right for me.

"Don't," I bit out.

She ignored me and kept coming, wrapping her arms around me. I didn't want her comfort, couldn't take it. I pulled her arms from around me, stumbling back, and tore my shirt from my chest, hands shaking, and went for the tree. I pulled out the knife and made the first slice. It was the only thing that would stop me from losing it completely in that moment. The relief was instant.

"Ren," Willow cried out and tried to run to me.

Warrick snagged her around the waist and hauled her into his arms. "Let him."

"What? No!" She struggled, but Warrick held her tight.

"He needs it."

He knew, somehow Warrick knew. I recited the positions of each slice like a mantra, remembering each slice I'd made in an innocent person, shaking, bleeding. My shame, my brokenness on display in all its horror for Willow to see. Something I'd never wanted. Something I would have done anything to prevent. But I couldn't stop. It was the only way to ease this fucking awful feeling inside me, the only way.

When I finished, blood slid down my body, pooling at my feet.

Willow's sobs filled the night, while Warrick held her upright, holding her tight in his arms.

I thought I'd already hit the lowest I could. I thought I'd been there. I'd been so fucking far from it.

"Why?" Willow whispered.

I looked over at her, the numbness setting in. "It's the only thing...that makes it okay."

"Makes what okay?"

"Living."

Chapter Nineteen

Jasmine

I CHECKED MY PHONE AGAIN. Still no reply from Mom. It was the middle of the night, but I was still awake, the awful feeling in my gut wouldn't go, not after what happened with Ren.

Paris was five hours ahead, it'd be early morning there, but still I hoped she'd answer. I needed my mom, for once I needed her, but as usual she was never available, not for me, and not for Zinny.

We'd never been enough. I tried to tell myself different, but it was the truth. She'd taught me a lesson, and I'd been too stupid to learn from it.

Words mean nothing, actions speak the loudest.

Mom told us she loved us, but she left us behind, and she barely called. She'd forgotten both my and Zinny's birthdays last year. Ren had shown me he didn't want me, that he wasn't interested in me, by being with a constant stream of females right in front of me, never giving my feelings one single thought—because I was so far off his radar, I was on another planet to him.

He'd shown me, time and again, and I'd ignored it, desperate for him to love me. I'd known he'd only kissed me, touched me, because of my magic, because his emotions had been thrown into chaos. And yet I'd convinced myself we had something real.

And I'd forced him to say it.

Tell me you don't want me.

I don't. Not the way you want me. I'm sorry. I'm really sorry, Jasmine.

It was more than I could bear, this pain. Even when there'd been no cause for it, I'd had hope. That's what love did, it lied to you. It turned you into a blind fool, the unrequited kind anyway. Deep inside, in the part of me I'd tried to ignore, I'd allowed myself to imagine us together, because anything else felt so wrong.

Voices drifted up from downstairs.

Willow's voice, and she sounded upset.

A muffled sob came next, and I shoved the covers off, rushed out to the hall, and started down.

"Oh goddess," Aunt Daisy said, cradling Violet close. "I thought he was doing better."

There was a low rumbling voice. Warrick.

I stopped on the stairs, not wanting to intrude, and because I knew instantly who they were talking about.

"So did I," Willow said, and she sounded defeated, heartbroken. "Warrick stopped him, but if we hadn't followed him, he would've done it. He would've...jumped off that cliff."

I gripped the banister, my heart seizing in my chest.

"How many times has he almost jumped off that fucking cliff and I had no idea?" Willow said. "I should have been with him, especially today—"

"Today?" Daisy asked.

"It's the anniversary of when he was possessed, the first day Edward forced him to kill. There was this...this big fucking write-up in the *Roxburgh Times*, interviews with the grieving families, the faces of all the victims, a *serial killer still on the loose* angle.

When I saw it, I rushed to Ren's, but he'd already taken off." She made a strangled sound. "Goddess, Mom, he cut himself, he...he mutilates himself..."

"He's been doing that a while," Warrick said. "Those scars, he never lets them fully heal."

Daisy sobbed.

I went back up the stairs feeling sick to my stomach. I hadn't realized what date it was. I'd been worrying about myself, about my feelings, when Ren had been suffering. I could help him heal, but this would never end for him, it would never go away.

Ren was broken, and he needed me. But I couldn't give him that at the expense of my own sanity. I wouldn't let him keep suffering, but if I didn't do something to stop this pain in my chest, I wouldn't be any use to him.

I'd been desperately trying to heal myself, to smooth away the jagged edges of my own pain, but the wounds were too vast, too deep. They were scars now, thick and raw and there was no healing them.

He needed me, but I couldn't do it, not like this. Not when I couldn't breathe, couldn't walk and talk and live in a world where he was while I loved him, knowing he didn't love me back.

This had to be over.

It had to end.

I wouldn't let Ren hurt himself anymore.

I loved him too much for that.

I stared up at the brownstone, the vintage lantern above the door making its shiny black surface gleam.

All I could think about as I sped here in my car was the face of the female who'd walked out of that door the last time I was here. The peace, the joy, the *relief* that flowed from her.

I wanted that. I needed it. I needed to be free of this pain. I couldn't take it another moment. I wasn't strong enough to help Ren as long as this agony was inside me. I wanted it gone. I wanted this feeling inside me gone. For good. And the only way to do that was by putting up a thick, impenetrable wall and blocking it off, suffocating it. Killing it. For Ren's sake, and mine.

I jogged up the stairs and knocked before I could change my mind. I was on a pain Ferris wheel, and this was the only way of getting off that ride and staying off it for good.

The door opened and Xavier stared down at me, a frown lowering his brows. "Jasmine? You've been crying. Is everything all right?"

I barely realized I was crying, no, sobbing. My throat hurt and my eyelids were tight and puffy. Goddess, this was humiliating. "I need your help in a…a professional capacity," I said, my voice shaky and broken when I was trying so hard for it to come out strong.

"Come inside, let me make you some tea and we can talk."

I shook my head. "I don't want to talk, I want this"—I pounded my fist to the center of my chest—"gone. I want it gone."

Placing his hand on the small of my back, he steered me inside and into the same room where I'd met with him the last time I was here. He sat me down and crouched in front of me. "What, Jasmine? What do you want gone?"

My lips quivered, and I squeezed my eyes closed, trying to catch my breath when another sob was right there. I felt weak and pathetic, but that small bit of hope, that kiss, it crumbled the wall I'd built to protect myself and there was no getting it back up. I needed someone else to do it for me. I needed Xavier to do it for me. I grabbed his hand in both of mine, my eyes locked on his steady, cool gaze. "I'm in love with a male who will never love me back, and I want you to take it away, Xavier. Please, can you lock it away?"

His gaze didn't falter, but he didn't say anything either. He just stared into my eyes. Again, I felt drawn in, held in place, like he was looking inside me. I let him. I opened myself up and let him see it, all of it.

Finally, he asked, "You're positive there's no hope?"

"None. I've endured this...this feeling for so long. I've watched him with other females. Seen him try to drink his own pain away. He doesn't...he doesn't want me...he..."

Say it. Tell me you don't want me.

I don't. Not the way you want me.

His words echoed through my skull again, and I bit my lip to hold in an agonized cry. My throat was raw from fighting it. He didn't want me, but he did need me. After what I heard Willow say, I had to put him first, over my own pain. Mine was nothing to his. This was the only way. I wouldn't let Ren take his own life. Nothing was more important than that. "He doesn't want me. He told me. Please, will you help me."

Xavier stood and slid his hands in his pockets. "You understand how this works? If I do this, it can't be undone."

"I understand," I rasped. "Does that mean you'll do it?"

He studied me for several long seconds, then nodded. "If this is what you truly want, who am I to deny you."

I dragged in a breath, it felt like the first one since I ran from Ren's house. "I don't have any money with me, but I'm good for it. Whatever your price—"

"No payment." He held out his hand. "Come."

I took it and let him lead me from the room and down a wide hall. He opened a door at the end and flicked on a light, then carried on down a set of steep stairs and along to another door. He opened it and led me into a large room. This was the basement, but it didn't feel like one. The lighting was warm and the walls were emerald green. Shelves covered in books took up most of the wall space and, getting a closer look, I saw they weren't the kinds of books found in your average library. These were old, and I felt the whisper of power flowing from them. Magic. There were several globes and an old-school blackboard with symbols drawn in chalk, variations of the same one.

He led me to the edge of the room, then moved a chair to the side before he rolled the mat back, revealing the hardwood floor. There were intricate symbols painted on the wood in white, laid out in a hexagon. Symbols I'd never seen or used before, not in my family or coven and not in any books in our library.

"What are these," I asked, looking up at him.

He looked down at them as well, his head tilted to the side as if he hadn't really looked at them in a long time, not with fresh eyes. "They're symbols I created, well, modified. They help to boost my blocking gift and enhance my ability to pinpoint with absolute accuracy the location of the particular emotion that I need to seal off."

"They're beautiful," I said, telling him the truth. To do this, to create these, Xavier saw things in a way a lot of people didn't, couldn't.

His lips lifted on one side in a small smile, but those intense lavender eyes stayed the same, cool and unaffected. "Thank you. They took me a very long time to perfect."

I motioned to the blackboard. "Are those others you're working on?"

"Yes." He frowned at the chalk drawings. "I'm getting close, but they still need work." He turned back to me. "Please, take a seat."

He motioned to the chair he'd just moved and I did as he said, a flurry of nerves making my legs shake. I sat and watched as he strode to the other side of the room and proceeded to remove his jacket, followed by his shirt. He folded each carefully and placed them on a desk. He toed off his shoes and removed his socks, then turned to me. His pale, hairless chest was rigid with muscle, and the same symbols on the floor were tattooed on his chest and stomach in the same arrangement in red ink.

My heart hammered harder, but I made myself stay where I was. I had to do this for Ren, and for me. I was no good to him in my current state. I couldn't help him while I was hanging on to such intense feelings for him. He didn't deserve my anger. He'd done nothing wrong. I'd pumped him full of magic, had filled him with so many emotions he'd avoided in so long, and it had made him feel something that wasn't real. It had confused him. He never would've kissed me otherwise.

"What happens now?" I asked.

Xavier stepped into the hexagon. "Now, I take your pain away."

I wanted that, so badly. "What will it feel like?"

"It won't be painful, if that's what you're asking. You may feel a little pressure while I build the walls, some get a mild headache afterward, but only for a short time, and nothing more than that." He lowered himself to the floor and crossed his legs. "I need to go into what looks like a trance while I find the source of your distress. Right now, while you're feeling it so acutely, it shouldn't be difficult, but it helps if you think about the source of your pain —in this case, the male you love. It'll broadcast the location of those emotions louder for me."

"Okay." That wouldn't be hard. Ren was the only thing in my head in that moment.

Xavier closed his eyes and rested his hands on his knees.

I did what he asked and let it all tumble through me. The cemetery several years ago, legs shaking as I walked over to give him his message. That instant connection snapping into place between us because of it. Watching him with other females when he finally stopped living in the forest and came home. Our fight, the one where I called him names, letting my own hurt feelings control me. The kisses, the way he'd held me to him so tight, making him laugh in the forest. The look on his face when I arrived at his place tonight. The way he'd looked at me when he told me he didn't want me.

My heart clutched in my chest as if it were happening all over again, and I fought the sob trying to crawl up my throat—

A pressure in my head had me sucking in a startled breath. No, it wasn't painful, but it was weird. Xavier was in my head, shuffling through my emotions. I breathed through it, through the odd sensations and the pain of my unrequited love for Ren.

I stayed focused on him, replaying that last kiss over and over in my mind, the look on his face, the things he'd said, and until this moment, the emotional pain had only grown more acute with every replay. I let it play out in my head, and again, and again, and each time, it grew less painful. With each run-through, I stopped feeling what I had during those encounters, the emotions becoming muted, and the physicality of it becoming more pronounced.

Until finally—that's all there was left.

The pressure in my head eased, and I felt Xavier withdraw.

I breathed slow and easy, searching for it, for Ren, for my love for him, but it was—gone. All of it. There was nothing there. I thought about him and felt nothing but sympathy for his predicament. There was still attraction, but no emotional connection.

No pain.

It was gone. I was free.

I wasn't in love with Ren anymore.

Chapter Twenty

Ren

THE FERAL HAD MOVED DEEPER into the forest. I kicked a pile of bones and searched the area around me. I'd been out here every night for almost a week.

I hadn't seen Jasmine since I hurt her and she ran from me. She was due to come back to heal me the day after tomorrow. But there was no way she was coming back, not now. Not after what I did.

I headed back the way I came. I'd been avoiding any place I thought Jaz might be, and it was fucking killing me. She was my mate. I knew that now with every part of me. She was mine, and I fucking craved her—her voice, her warmth, her touch, her mouth. Now that I'd had those things, being deprived of them was a new kind of torture.

I couldn't be the male she deserved, though. It didn't matter how much I wanted her, I was no good for her, no good for anyone. But I could do this. I could help find these souls and make sure Zinnia came home. For Jasmine.

It took another thirty minutes, but I finally reached Agatheena's cottage. Smoke drifted from the chimney, the door firmly closed. I couldn't walk up and knock, so I did the only thing I could, I called her name. I was no doubt attracting every demon in the forest, but I didn't care, this was fucking important.

Several minutes later, the door finally opened and Agatheena walked out. "You trying to get killed, fox?" she said as she started down the steps.

"I need to talk to you."

She rolled her eyes as she slowly made her way toward me. "Figured that much out for myself."

A demon burst from the trees behind me and I spun, flinging my blade and burying it in the demon's neck. I stalked over, hacked off his head, dusted the ashes from my hands, and walked back.

Agatheena watched me with that shrewd gaze. "You kill the feral yet?"

"You know I haven't." The witch knew every damn thing.

"Then not sure why you're hanging around my front gate caterwauling," she said, looking at me like she was sizing me up for her pot.

"I give you my word, I will kill it. I'll kill anything you want me to, just give me the information Jasmine needs now."

"Manners are free and yet you seem to have forgotten how to use yours," she said.

I ground my teeth. "Please."

She eyed me, then shrugged. "Fine." She pulled a vial from her pocket and tossed it to me through the barrier between us. "Your blood, fill it. Not risking you going back on your word."

I sliced my arm and filled the vial, pushed the stopper in, and tossed it to her. "I won't go back on my word."

She put it in her pocket and tilted her head, looking at me in a way that I didn't like, not at all. "Taking this information to her won't earn you forgiveness, you realize that?"

I wanted to tell her to mind her own damn business, that she didn't know what she was talking about, but she saw right through me. "I don't expect forgiveness. I just want to help her."

"That's good, because you're too late."

My fox's ears pricked at the eerie note to her voice, the look that shifted through her eyes. "What's that supposed to mean?"

She shrugged a bony shoulder, her eyes flashing red, her demon side coming through. "Only that you missed your chance."

The old witch was fucking with me and enjoying it.

She pointed to a glass jar hanging off the tree. There was a small piece of folded paper inside it that hadn't been there before. "There's your information. Get that feral taken care of." Then she turned and headed back up the path.

I stared after her, my heart in my throat. *You're too late.* Those words echoed through my mind and kept on doing so as I took the piece of paper from the jar, shoved it in my pocket, and headed for home.

❦

This was the last place I wanted to be.

The line to get into The Vault had been down the street. Thankfully I knew the bouncers, and they'd let me through. I'd been trying to find Jasmine, to give her the message from Agatheena, but she wasn't home or at the clubhouse. Warrick said some of the hounds had come here, Iris, Mags, and Rose as well. Jasmine would be with them.

It didn't happen often, but there was a band playing tonight. The vampire cover band played older music and were a favorite around the city, which meant the place was packed. I worked my way through the crowd, but it wasn't hard to find who I was looking for. The hounds stood head and shoulders above everyone else. There were a lot of pack members from Silver Claw here as well. Bram stood to the side, talking with Ronan and Draven.

Bram's three brothers, Payne, Rook, and Talon, were with them as well.

The band was playing, so I knew exactly where I'd find Jasmine. I searched the dance floor. She and Rose with their pale blond hair made it easy to find them in the crowd. They were at the edge, so Iris, Mags, and Rose could stay close to their mates.

The song ended and I started toward them. Jaz had turned and was talking to Rome and Relic, a huge smile on her face.

"Hey, Roxburgh, you wanna get *Close to Me*?" the singer called out.

The crowd cheered as they started playing The Cure song. Jasmine did a little jump and grabbed Rome's hand. The big male grinned down at her and shook his head. I could see him mouth, "I don't dance, Jazzy," from here.

A growl tore from my chest. I didn't want her near Rome. No fucking way.

You threw her away.

Because I didn't have any other choice. That didn't change the way I felt, though.

She danced anyway, right in front of Rome, still holding his hand, moving around him while he stood there with a fucking huge grin on his face. Jaz laughed and sang and moved between Rome and Relic as if they were living, breathing fucking poles for her to swing around.

My fox wanted to break free, and my claws pressed against the tips of my fingers. Before I could reach them, Bram's brother Talon was there. He took her hand and led her out onto the floor, the cocky crow pulling her into his arms, laughing and dancing with her, with my Jasmine.

Mine.

I planted my feet to the floor, not knowing what the fuck to do. I wanted to kill him, tear him limb from limb, but I'd given that right up. I'd given her up, and there was no going back, so I watched them, rooted to the spot, not sure what the fuck to do, feeling like I was dying inside.

I may have given her up, but I needed her to look at me. Selfishly, I still needed that from her. I wanted her eyes on me. I missed it, craved it. I needed it. I'd been without it for almost a week.

As he spun her around, her gaze finally found me. Usually, I'd see a change in her. A multitude of emotions would flash through her beautiful eyes, because she'd felt the pull toward me like I had toward her. But this time, there was nothing. Her gaze skittered over me like I was anyone else. There was none of the hurt or disappointment I'd seen before she left my place a week ago.

There was just...nothing.

Jasmine

Talon laughed when I spun around him. All I was feeling in that moment was happiness, a release, blowing off some steam after a week of reading from the demon library, of combing Nightscape for any reports of unusual spiritual activity, of driving around aimlessly and walking the city with my sigils off hoping they'd just pop out and show themselves, and coming up with absolutely nothing—and that sense of freedom, just for a couple of hours, didn't change when I spotted Ren across the room. The pain didn't come. The feeling of wanting him so bad it was like an open wound was gone.

He was just Ren.

My cousin's emotionally scarred familiar. Someone I'd known for a long time. A male I cared about the same way I cared about Roman or Relic. I wanted to help him, the same way I would anyone who came to me suffering and in need of my brand of healing.

I'd been avoiding him this week, afraid that when I finally saw him it would all come rushing back. But it didn't. The constant longing, the awful pit in my stomach was gone.

Throwing up my arms, I tilted my head back and sang at the top of my lungs, the relief pouring from me.

The song ended, and when the next started, everyone rushed toward the stage. It was a crowd favorite. I'd seen the band play before with Mags a couple months ago. The lead singer was hot, and when he sang this song, everyone went wild. I was pushed back, and Talon stopped me from falling, catching me with an arm around my middle.

Iris and Rose had moved back as well, standing with their mates. Mags was scowling beside me, trying to see. Then Bram was there, grabbing her and lifting her onto his shoulders. I looked up, jealous, she'd have a perfect vantage point from up there.

Talon bumped my arm, then motioned at himself and pointed upward. I grinned and nodded. He gripped my hips and tossed me onto his shoulders as well. Mags laughed and grabbed my hand, right as the drums kicked in and everyone started losing their minds. The crowd was singing and jumping around, and I danced on Talon's shoulders, belting out the lyrics at the top of my lungs. The room was so hot, and I noticed several of the wolves had taken their shirts off, dancing in their bras. I had on a sports bra that looked more like a top. Screw it. I tugged my shirt over my head.

Talon held up his hand. I gave it to him, and he tucked it in the waistband of his jeans.

Tomorrow, I'd get back to my search, but tonight, I'd take this small reprieve from the constant worry over the missing souls, and Death, and bring my sister home.

Mags looked over at me, grinned, and pulled up her top. Bram reached up and grabbed the bottom of it, yanking it back down. I cackled, and she scowled and tried again. Next minute, Mags was pulled down, tossed over Bram's shoulder, and his hand came down on her ass as he carried her toward one of the dark corners. No doubt to make out.

I wanted to make out with someone too. I glanced down at Talon's tattooed hand on my knee. He was hot. There was no doubt about it. He had intense black eyes and a wickedness about him that was incredibly appealing.

The song ended, and I looked down again, surprised to see Ren was standing in front of him. I hadn't even seen him come over. I always used to know where he was if he was in the same room. Right now, his face was all twisted up and he looked pissed off. I couldn't see all of Talon's face, but I thought he might be smiling.

I tapped his hand, and he looked up. I motioned for him to put me down. He gripped my waist and lifted me from his shoulders, then hooked his arm around my neck.

I looked between him and Ren. "What's going on?"

"Can we talk?" Ren said, his eyes blazing.

I glanced at Talon. He winked.

"Does it have to be now?" I kind of wanted to kiss Talon. He was cute, something I hadn't really noticed before. I mean, I'd noticed, I just hadn't cared.

"Yeah, it has to be now." Ren grabbed my hand, yanked my shirt from Talon's waistband, and towed me across the floor to an empty table in the corner.

"What's going on?" I asked.

He thrust my top at me, and I blinked down at it.

"Put it on, Jaz. There are creeps all over this fucking club staring at your tits," he growled out.

"What?" I looked around. "No they're not, and my tits are covered."

"Believe me, they're looking."

I took my top back, but I didn't put it on. It was hot and there were people wearing a lot less than me. "I don't know what this is about, but I'm here with my friends. I've had a shitty fucking week, and I need this. If this isn't important, I'm going to head back." I took a step away from him, but he grabbed my wrist, stopping me. "What is it, Ren? Jesus."

"I spoke with Agatheena. She gave me the info you need."

I stilled. "She just gave it to you?"

"I swore I'd get the feral. She took some of my blood, deal done. I was going to kill it anyway. No big deal," he said, his gaze dipping below my chin, and his lips peeled back in a snarl before they slid back up.

His words weren't matching the expression on his face. He was wound tight and pissed off. The veins in his forearms and biceps were bulging, and his eyes were nearly glowing.

"Well, can I have it?" I said, starting to worry that my healing wasn't working. He should be starting to feel it, a change in his emotional well-being, but if anything he seemed more tense than usual. Ren had a lot of healing to do, though, and sometimes the process made people act out of the norm.

"It's back at my place." His gaze locked on mine.

"Oh, well, I'll just get it tomorrow when I come by for your healing session." I glanced back at the dance floor when the next song started. I loved this song.

"So you're still coming over tomorrow, then? I wasn't sure after...what happened."

He studied me, and I gave him a measured smile. "I'll be there. I haven't been at home crying over a broken heart, I promise." Not anymore. If my heart was broken, I had no knowledge of it, not anymore, and that's the way I liked it.

"I hurt you," he said. "And I feel fucking shitty about it, about how I handled everything."

"Don't worry about it. I'm completely over it."

"I don't believe you," he said, looking even more pissed.

I frowned. Now I was getting pissed off. "Well, believe it."

"The way you're acting...the way you're looking at me like I don't exist..." he said, stepping closer. "The way you're throwing yourself at Talon, taking your top off in front of all these males? Are you trying to make me jealous? Is that what this is?"

I stared at him in disbelief. "You didn't want me, Ren, and that's fine because I can tell you with one hundred percent honesty..." I held his gaze. "I don't want you, either, not anymore." He flinched, and I felt bad, but I ignored it and carried on. "I care about you. You're Willow's familiar, you're a friend, but I promise you, that's all you are to me. You definitely haven't influenced my actions tonight. I just want to enjoy myself."

He looked, goddess, lost. I gentled my voice. "I want to help you, Ren, more than you know, but you need to get a handle on your emotions. I know it's confusing, the type of healing we're doing. It can make you think or feel conflicting things. You wouldn't be the first client I've treated that started to feel, I don't know, possessive over me or whatever. Or imagine some kind of deeper connection. The fact we've known each other a long time, only makes it more confusing."

"That's not what's happening here," he said.

"If you say so." Of course that's what was happening here. He was behaving like some protective older brother. "How much have you had to drink?"

He planted his hands on his hips. "Nothing. I'm not drunk, Jasmine."

"I'm sorry if you're struggling at the moment. Maybe you should be with Willow right now?"

His brows shot up. "What? I'm fine."

I smiled. "Okay, well, that's really good. I'm going to head back. You have a good night. I'll see you tomorrow," I said and walked away.

He was acting this way for the same reason he'd kissed me during our sessions: he was going through a massive emotional upheaval. He would get past it. With more healing, he'd get well again.

He just needed time.

Chapter Twenty-One

Ren

I OPENED the door and Jaz stood there, her bag over her shoulder and a barely there smile curving her lips. Her hair was down and tousled in a way I wanted to sink my fingers into, and she was wearing makeup, more than she usually did, her gorgeous green eyes surrounded by charcoal and her full lips deep red. "Hey, Ren," she said and walked in.

"Hey." I studied her, still surprised she actually showed up, but she seemed...fine. More than fine. And when she turned to me, her gaze was warm but nothing more. There was no anger or sadness. She looked at me like I could be any one of her clients. Something unpleasant curled its fingers in my gut. Something was seriously off. "Are you okay?"

Her features rearranged into surprise. "Of course." She waved me forward. "Because your sigils are done and we're only working on your emotional healing today, we won't need any warding. Let me just quickly change out the crystals, it'll keep the souls calm, then we can get started."

"Sounds good." I watched as she rushed around, picking up the crystals she left last time and packing them in her bag. I couldn't take my fucking eyes off her. She took out a small pouch with new ones and walked around laying them out while spelling, muttering the words under her breath.

When she was done, she walked over to me and tilted her head back. "You ready to get started?"

"Yeah, sure." Was I ready for her to wrap her arms around me? No, I fucking wasn't. I'd craved it, wanted her hands on me all week, and now that I knew Jasmine was supposed to be mine, I wasn't sure I could do this and let her go again afterward. How could I do this and not kiss her? I hadn't been able to resist the other times, but I had to. The reasons we couldn't be together hadn't changed.

"Cool. Let's do this, then I'll be out of your way," she said.

I didn't want her out of my way. I couldn't have her, but I needed her close. I needed her. Jesus, this was hard, confusing. What did I do with these conflicting emotions? "You don't need to rush off," I said. I wasn't trying to give her mixed signals, but I was feeling fucking desperate.

"I actually do. I've got somewhere I need to be." She pulled her phone from her pocket and checked it. "In half an hour as a matter of fact." She slid off the light coat she was wearing and draped it over the back of the couch.

I let my gaze leave her beautiful face and slide down the rest of her body. My mouth went dry and my hands immediately curled into fists. She was wearing a black dress, one that clung to her body and every one of her sweet curves. A couple of silver necklaces rested on the mounds of her soft breasts, and she wore silver bracelets that jangled as she moved. Her legs were bare, and she was wearing lace-up boots with a chunky heel. Add the hair and the makeup and she looked edgy and sexy as fuck.

The grip in my gut turned into jealous fury. "Hot date?" I said, and somehow I kept all that I was feeling out of my voice, or at least I hoped I did.

She glanced up at me, and her cheeks had turned pink. "Something like that."

My fox lost his mind, and I grabbed the back of the couch to stop myself from leaping over it, pinning her to the wall, and demanding she tell me who. I wanted to tear the fucker to pieces, whoever he was. I couldn't stop myself asking, "Rome?"

Her brows shot up, then she chuckled as if I wasn't over here internally having a rage seizure. "Roman and I are friends, nothing more. You know that. He's like...a brother." Her cheeks darkened further. "I was a dick for giving you the impression that there was ever anything more between us." She shook her head. "So no, not Rome."

"Then who?" I asked, because I had to know.

She chuckled again and tucked her hair behind her ear. "No one you know. I'm nervous enough, let's talk about something else. Like Agatheena's message, for example. I'm desperate to know if she has something that can actually help."

There was not one thing I would rather talk about than who this male was and where I could find him alone later tonight so I could fuck him up. Because this wasn't fucking happening.

I was the stupid fucking asshole who'd rejected her, though. I didn't get to decide who she dated.

"Right, yeah, of course." I shoved my hands in my pockets because my hands were shaking like hell from rage and regret and this awful feeling that I'd made a terrible mistake. "It's just one word. I don't know what it means, never seen it before, so I'm guessing it's a clue. I'll give it to you after we...do the healing."

"She's not making it easy, then? Yeah, she definitely didn't like me," Jaz said, then rounded the couch and took the last few steps until we were almost touching, but not quite.

I shook harder, and there was no hiding it.

"You okay?" There was concern in her eyes.

The shy, longing looks she always gave me, that I'd told myself were something else, were gone. Feelings I only now realized she'd had for me, because she'd felt what I had, that connection, one mate recognizing the other. Or at least she had. Apparently, I'd destroyed anything she'd felt for me completely. And no, I wasn't okay. "Yeah, this healing thing, it's intense, that's all."

She nodded. "I know." Then she wrapped her arms around me, pressing her soft, warm body the length of mine. Her face to my chest. Warmth immediately flowed from her into me, but it felt different. Everything was different. Before, I'd felt as if she were part of me, somehow. Now there was a distance between us, and I hated it.

"It's okay, Ren. Everything's going to be okay," she said, her voice soft, soothing.

Still, that distance persisted. I shook harder, a restless feeling, an ache in the center of my chest burrowing deeper. Something was missing.

"I've got you," she said.

Again, without realizing I was going to do it, my arms curled around her in return, and I held her tight, desperate for what was gone, whatever it was that was missing.

"That's good, Ren, let it fill you," she murmured.

I squeezed my eyes closed and wished this was how it could be, that she could be mine, that I wasn't this broken mess—

Something shattered inside me.

She stilled. "Ren?"

"Yeah?" I choked out.

Jaz rubbed my back. "You're hurting, I can feel it. There's a...a new scar."

She was the new scar, and it felt so big, it eclipsed everything else. Another rush of warmth washed through me, and my legs almost fucking buckled. "All good, Jaz. Guess when old shit heals, new shit comes up."

"I guess," she said, sounding unconvinced.

The euphoria hit, and it took everything I had not to bury my face against her throat and fill my lungs with her scent—to take her gorgeous face in my hands and kiss her breathless.

The time passed way too fast, then she was counting down the last ten seconds and I had to force myself to loosen my hold on her, to release her when her arms finally fell away, letting me go.

Like always, she gave me space to feel what I was feeling after the intensity of a session, only this time what I was feeling was something completely different. "Jaz, are you all right?" I asked, when I saw her dab at her eyes, her hands trembling slightly. She soothed my pain, and I made her cry.

She smiled and nodded. "Yeah, all good."

The urge to pull her close and comfort her grew fiercer. "I'll go grab the note," I said and quickly walked away before I did something I shouldn't, then took the few moments in my room to try to get my shit together.

When I strode back out, she was in her coat, ready to leave. I didn't want her to go, though. I wanted her to stay. I handed her the note.

"Thanks." She opened it and frowned down at it. "Halcapio." She looked back up at me. "What does that even mean?"

"No idea."

She blew out a frustrated breath. "Cool, thanks for nothing, Agatheena. I'll show Mags, maybe she's heard it before." She shoved the note in her pocket and smiled up at me. "You're making great progress. I hope you know that. I don't know how much you feel yet, but I saw it during the session. Your original wounds are looking so much better." She frowned. "This new one that appeared—"

"The new one doesn't have anything to do with what happened. I don't want it gone. I want to keep it." I never wanted the sting of giving up Jasmine gone. Never.

"Are you sure about that?"

"Positive."

She nodded, her gaze searching my face like a doctor would their patient. "Right, well..." She aimed her thumb over her shoulder. "I need to head off. If I don't see you before then, I'll see you in a week's time."

"If you find out what the note means, let me know, yeah?"

"Sure thing," she said, then walked out.

I gripped the back of the couch to stop myself from following her, because if I saw her with someone else right now, I would kill them.

I would end them right in front of her, and there'd be no coming back from that.

Jasmine

Xavier sipped his whisky, his very nice lips tilting up on one side. "So, any luck finding your souls?"

"Unfortunately, no."

He sat back. "I'm sorry to hear that."

"Not as sorry as me." I thought about them constantly, so much so, I'd started dreaming about them, about finding them, about Zinnia stuck in Limbo forever, about her calling my name.

He inclined his head. "I can see how much that distresses you. Let's change the subject to more pleasant things? How was your dessert?"

I smiled at his attempt to make me feel better. "Amazing. I've never had anything like it." Xavier was handsome and extremely charming. He was an intelligent guy, well read. Interesting. He also could wear the hell out of a suit. I really liked talking to him. I wasn't nervous around him, which was surprising. I was shy by nature, yes, that had improved over the last few years, but going on a date? I should be a sweaty, blushing mess.

"This is one of my favorite restaurants," he said. "I really wanted to share it with you."

I sipped my wine. "I'm glad you did." I studied his features, his contained expression. "So why did you ask me out?"

His brow arched. "You don't know?"

I shook my head and smiled. "Nope. Only you know that. I'm a medium not a physic."

"Well, let me enlighten you, then, Jasmine. First, you are stunningly beautiful. Honestly, after you left the first time you turned up on my door, I wasn't able to forget about you."

Okay, now I was blushing. "That's...really nice of you to say."

He chuckled. "I tell you I think you're astoundingly hot and you think I'm being nice?"

"It's nice to hear it," I said and had trouble holding his gaze all of a sudden. "You're not too bad yourself."

"I'm glad you think so."

His voice had grown deep, husky. I wasn't sure I was ready for what I heard in his voice, but I didn't hate it. "And you're not put off knowing that I was in love with someone else?"

He leaned forward, resting his elbow on the table. "No, because it's gone. This male who held your heart has been banished from it. Which means there's now room for you to fall in love with someone else."

This male was smooth. He knew all the right things to say. That wasn't necessarily a bad thing, but I hadn't been around too many males this well adjusted or controlled. All the males around me, besides Arthur, tended to be volatile. "I'm not sure I'm in the market for love just yet," I said and tried not to fidget under his direct stare.

"No one goes out looking for love. It finds us whether we're expecting it or not." He grinned, and I got a flash of fangs. "That's what I'm told anyway."

"You've never been in love?"

He took a sip of his drink, then shook his head. "No, I never have."

"I'm sorry."

"I'm surprised you feel that way, even after the pain you suffered?" His gaze dipped to my mouth and back up. "And don't be sorry. Everything happens for a reason, yes? My time will come if it's meant to."

"I hope that's true. I like to believe we're not all wandering around like idiots, making the same stupid mistakes over and over again."

His grin widened. "It's a nice thought."

"As for love. Yes, my feelings were unrequited, and I may not feel it anymore, but I haven't forgotten the storm that would whip up inside me whenever I saw him. The excitement, the stupid, useless hope." I screwed up my face. "I guess deep down I'm a romantic...or a sadist."

He chuckled again, and his head tilted to the side. "And have you seen him since?"

"Yes."

"What did you feel?"

"It was gone. The storm had passed completely. I care about his well-being, but that's all. No more excitement, no hope for more. No pain thinking about him with someone else." I'd felt none of that earlier when I went to his house. It was an odd feeling. Was I relieved? Absolutely. But there was a small part of me that missed it.

"I'm glad," he said. "I hated seeing you in so much pain."

An hour later we were sitting in Xavier's car outside my aunt's house. "I had a great time tonight, Jasmine. I'd love to see you again sometime."

"I did too." And I meant it. "And I'd like that."

His deep lavender eyes dipped to my mouth before he reached out and gently cupped the side of my face, leaning in. Did I want him to kiss me? There was no reason to stop him, right? I leaned in as well, and his lips brushed mine softly before he lifted his head.

"I'll be in touch," he said.

I opened the car door and got out. "Night, Xavier."

"Good night, Jasmine."

I shut the door, and he drove away. My fingers lifted to my mouth and I stared after his car as it turned the corner. He'd kissed me. I tried to decide how I felt. I mean, it was...nice.

A scrape came from my right, and I spun around. Ren stood there. He was in gray track pants and running shoes. His shirt was off and tucked into the waistband of his pants. His eyes glowed gold from the shadows, the moonlight highlighting his muscles that were glistening with sweat. Before, seeing him like that would have had my knees trembling. Now? Well, that hadn't really changed. Ren was still beautiful. There was no denying it. But it was just lust, nothing else.

He was panting. "Good date?"

"Yeah, it was."

He planted his hands on his hips. "That was him, the car that just drove away? Xavier, Ronan's friend?"

"Yep."

"You seeing him again?" he asked.

"Probably, yeah."

His chest expanded sharply and a growl rolled out. "He touched you."

"If he did or didn't, is my business," I said, because he couldn't keep doing this, playing the overprotective big brother or whatever this was.

"I can smell him on you, Jaz. He put his hands on you." He took a step closer.

My pulse sped up. "I'm not sure why it matters to you?"

"I'm just making sure it's what you wanted?"

His gaze glowed brighter. His behavior was starting to piss me off. This was why I'd been so confused, this was why there was always this stupid bit of hope I couldn't shake. I hadn't been able to see it clearly before, so blinded by my feelings for him, but I saw it now. "That's not your place. You don't need to look out for me. I have plenty of people doing that already."

"Jaz." He took another step closer, his voice impossibly rough. "Last week, what I said... I hope you're not seeing this guy because—"

"He's not some rebound from you, if that's what you're implying. You don't need to worry about my feelings. Yes, I care about you, I do, but not like that. I want you happy and healthy, but I'm not harboring any secret hope of you one day becoming my boyfriend." *Not anymore.* "I'm over it, Ren. Like completely. I don't need to be another thing you feel guilty about, okay? Don't think about it anymore, please. I'm not."

His head dipped, his abs flexing with every panted breath he took. "You're completely over it," he said under his breath. "Right."

"I'm just gonna head inside. I still have some books to go through from the demon library. I've been searching for some reference to what halcapio means."

He nodded. "I'll help."

I blinked up at him. "You don't have somewhere else you'd rather be?"

"No. Not in the mood to drink, and I'm too wired to sleep. May as well do something productive."

There was no real reason to say no. And if the answer was in one of those books, we'd find it faster with two of us. "Okay, sure."

He followed me inside, tugging his shirt on before we walked into the house, and headed to the kitchen. Stanley was sitting on the counter when we walked in and grinned at me when he saw Ren.

"I'll leave you to it," he said and winked before he walked out.

I put the kettle on and pulled down two mugs. "Tea? Coffee? Cocoa?"

"Coffee, black, thanks."

I made the drinks and put them on the table. "I'll just get changed and grab the books. Be back in a sec."

"Where are they?"

"Up in my room. I'll show you."

He followed me upstairs. I'd taken Rose's old room when I moved in. It had its own bathroom and was one of the bigger bedrooms. We walked in and I pointed to two stacked piles on the floor next to my desk and art supplies. Ren grabbed an armful and headed downstairs. I grabbed a pair of yoga pants and a hooded sweatshirt and went into the bathroom. I bumped the door with my hip and dumped my clothes on the counter, then quickly washed my face, took off my boots, and stripped off my dress.

"That all of them?" Ren asked, his voice close.

I spun around and he was standing there, staring at me. I thought I'd bumped the door closed, but there was a decent gap.

He bolted from the room.

My face heated. I mean, he'd seen me naked more times than I'd like to think about, but it didn't matter. I was in my underwear, pretty pink lace bra and panties. Did he think I'd been hoping Xavier would see me like this tonight? I hadn't, I just liked nice underwear. *Why do you care what Ren thinks?* I quickly got changed and headed back downstairs.

"I didn't mean to look," he said when I walked in.

"It's not like you haven't seen it all before." I was trying to make light of things but it just made everything more awkward.

I sat and pulled the first book off the stack, and Ren grabbed the next.

We read in companionable silence for several hours, and more than once I'd been so absorbed I'd forgotten he was even there. Ren had made us another coffee and a snack, and we discussed some of the weird things we found. It was nice actually. I would've found this impossible before, concentrating on reading with him right there. I would've been hyper focused on him. Not anymore.

Several hours and three cups of coffee later, I finally found something. I scanned the page, then looked up at Ren. "I've got it."

"What does it say?" He got up and moved around beside me, scanning the page I'd been reading over my shoulder, then straightened. "Fuck. That can't be good."

No, it most definitely was not.

Chapter Twenty-Two

Ren

RUNE SAT back on his leather couch, shirtless, trousers undone, and sipped his morning coffee. A female rushed out of his bathroom. She darted glances his way, but Rune was staring at Jasmine in a way I did not fucking like.

The other female scooped up her shoes and headed for the door.

Rune's gaze slid from Jasmine and the pile of books we'd returned and focused on his retreating companion. "What are you forgetting, Kelsey?"

She stopped and turned back. He said nothing, just waited. She rushed back to him, and he reached up, fisted the back of her hair, and pulled her down for a hard kiss. The female whimpered. I glanced at Jaz, and she was bright red.

My little female couldn't hide how she was feeling. She never could. I'd just forced myself to ignore it, until now. Now that she didn't seem to care in the least about me anymore.

She's not yours.

I'd decimated any feelings she'd had for me a week ago, which was seriously bad timing, since I wanted her now more than ever. Now that I felt the changes inside me, the way her healing was pulling me from the shadows and into the light. No, I'd never recover from what that monster made me do, I'd never forget, but I didn't feel as if I were drowning, suffocating in a sea of horror and despair anymore. I could fucking breathe again.

I hadn't been to my cliff since the night I hurt her and Willow and Warrick followed me there. I hadn't thought about going there or the difference in the way I'd been feeling, until last night when I sat with Jaz poring over books and managed a whole twenty minutes without remembering. Without seeing blood on my hands, or hearing the sound of agonized screams. Something had definitely shifted inside me, and it was because of Jasmine.

She licked her lower lip, and I wanted to pull her to me and kiss her. I wanted to beg her to let me kiss her the way Rune was devouring the female wriggling on his lap.

Jaz shifted, her gaze darting to me, then away.

Rune finally let her go. "Back in bed," he said low, gritty.

The female rushed to do as he said, and the massive demon turned back to Jaz, now with an obvious fucking hard-on. "Care to join, little witch?"

I barely choked back my snarl.

"I'll pass, but thank you for your kind offer," she said with a humorless smile and a good dose of sarcasm.

"I promise you'll like it," he drawled.

"And I promise I'll slit your fucking throat if you say shit like that to her again," I growled out.

Jaz spun to me, a frown on her pretty face. The three mourning cloaks that had been sitting on her shoulders, fluttered around her head, giving her away. I'd pissed her off. Again. "Maybe you should wait downstairs," she said to me.

That wasn't happening. "I'm not leaving you with him."

"You've interrupted my morning," Rune said. "If you're not going to join in, then get to the fucking point."

"Halcapio," Jaz said. "Defined in the demon physiology book I borrowed from your library as one who consumes living souls for subsistence. What can you tell us about soul eaters?"

His silver gaze narrowed. "Why?"

The book hadn't given a huge amount of information, just a few lines. "Because we think that's what's happened to the ones we're missing," I said.

"Impossible. There are no Drar here," Rune said.

"That you know of."

His silver eyes flashed red. "I would know."

"Would you?" Jaz said. "There's no chance one could have slipped through?"

He stood, sliding his hands into his pockets and paced away. If there was a soul eater, also known as a Drar'toth demon, then that wouldn't be good for Rune. Lucifer was his boss, he was missing souls as well, and it was going on right under Rune's nose.

He turned back. "I'll put some feelers out."

"What can you tell us about the Drar'toth?" Jaz asked. "Are they humanoid in appearance?"

"Yes. They're also a solitary breed. Live alone. They're always hungry. Food doesn't satisfy, but they gorge on it between souls, trying to satiate their hunger. They run hot, something they bask in when they're in Hell, but not here. Hellfire and the sun or artificial heating are not the same. They have trouble regulating their temperature here."

"So they'll be sweaty and drinking and eating a lot?" I asked.

"Yes."

"And the souls, what happens to them? Is there a way to free them or are they lost forever?"

"You can free them, or what's left of them, by killing the soul eater, but they're not easy to catch or kill. They absorb knowledge from the souls they devour. So they know how to blend in among humans, and depending on the souls they ate, they can be deadly and highly intelligent."

Great.

"You'll let me know if you find them before us?" Jaz asked.

He studied her for several long seconds. "If there is a Drar in this city, it's probably best you leave it to me, little witch."

My fox's hackles lifted, and his lips peeled back with a snarl. Jaz's gaze sliced to me when the sound crawled up my throat. We didn't like the demon implying we couldn't protect our female.

"I can't just sit back and do nothing," she said.

"You won't have to," I said. "I'll be with you."

"You think you're capable of taking on a Drar'toth, fox?" Rune said.

I grinned. "I'm capable of a lot of things, demon." Grabbing Jaz's hand, I tugged her from her seat and led her from the apartment and toward the elevator.

We got in and her hand slipped from mine. I wanted to snatch it back, so fucking badly.

"So you still want to help me?" she asked, studying me.

"Yes." No fucking way would I let her do this alone. I couldn't let her even if I wanted to, which I did not.

"You don't have to, you know? I can ask Rome or one of the other hounds." She chewed her lip. "Look, things got complicated between us for a minute there, but you don't owe me anything, Ren." She looked up at me, unflinching, nothing but sincerity in her eyes. "I shouldn't have let things go as far as they did. I'm sorry for that, really I am. Please, don't blame yourself."

Now she was acting like she'd somehow taken advantage of me? "I want to help you. It has nothing to do with what happened between us." *Don't say it.* I couldn't hold it in, though. "I know I said some things to make you believe otherwise, but I did want to kiss you, Jaz, badly."

She didn't believe me. I could tell by the look in her eyes.

The doors slid open. "You're confused," she said, striding out and down the corridor. "The intensity of our sessions has been messing with you. Like I told you, you're not the first person I've worked with to feel things that aren't there. One client begged me to go out with him repeatedly, another followed me for a couple weeks, positive I was the love of his life, then it wore off and they moved on."

She'd had a fucking stalker? I fought down the urge to find these males and choke them out. Barely containing my rage, I kept pace beside her and pushed the main door open. We walked out into the crisp autumn morning air. I needed to shut the fuck up, but I couldn't. There'd been this shift inside me. Now that I could see more clearly, I felt...different, more in control. "I'm not confused," I said. "I knew exactly what I was doing. Yes, your powers broke through to the part of me that'd been holding me back. But those feelings had always been there. Whatever you think happened between us, you need to know I wanted it as well."

She stopped and turned, blinking up at me. "You said you didn't want me, and you meant it."

"I was scared of the way I felt about you. I should never have said that, I should never have—"

"Whatever you're about to say, don't." She shook her head. "You only think you felt something for me, and you're wrong. You've suffered for so long, Ren. I've helped you get relief from that pain, that's all this is. You're misinterpreting gratitude for something else." She shook her head. "I don't think you should help me with this."

I bit back a growl. If I kept pushing, she'd back away completely and get someone else to help. "Okay, maybe I am a little confused," I said, lying. I wasn't fucking confused. Jasmine was mine, but she wasn't ready to hear it. "Let's just...put all of that stuff aside for now, yeah? Zinnia getting home is the most important thing. So let me help you."

❧

Jasmine

I eyed him. Before my visit with Xavier, I would've jumped on the things he'd just said. I would've believed every word and not seen the truth. It was nothing more than transference; he was associating all the good things he felt during our sessions with me just like my other confused clients. It wasn't *me* he wanted, it was the way my powers made him feel. He hadn't been interested in me before we started his healing and now, suddenly, he thought he was. It seemed clear to me.

I should tell him no, but I could tell by the look on his face, no matter what I said, he was determined to help. "Fine. But if you make googly eyes at me, you're done."

He grinned. "No googly eyes. I can manage that."

We strode down the street, passing demons like this was totally normal. It was hard to compare these demons with the ones who lived in the forest. On the outside at least, they seemed like an entirely different species.

Ren unlocked the hearse, and we got in. The engine rumbled to life, and the three butterflies on my head fluttered down to rest on the back of my hands. They were sending warmth and love through me, a lot of it, as if they were trying to comfort me. I wasn't sure why. I didn't need comforting. It was like they were seeing something I couldn't.

"I'm okay," I said to them as their wings rose and fell slowly. There was another rush of love. "I promise." I looked up and Ren was watching me. "They're comforting me for some reason."

"Yeah?" he said as he pulled out onto the street. "Why?"

I shook my head. "No idea. I'm assuming it's from being around all those demons." I lifted my hand, and they crawled back onto my hair. "So where do we think a soul eater would hang out?"

"How many all-you-can-eat restaurants are there in the city?" Ren asked. "Cheap ones. If you spend all your time eating, drinking, and overheating, it can't be easy holding down a job."

I grinned and pulled out my phone to search for all-you-can-eat places nearby. "I'm going to go out on a limb and assume he'd hang near demon territory. It'd just be instinct, right?"

"Makes sense."

"Joe's All-You-Can-Eat Home Fry is just a couple blocks away."

We walked into the restaurant a short time later. It did not smell great. It was dark and dingy and the decor didn't look like it'd been updated since 1982. "Hungry?" I said to Ren when he screwed up his face.

His lips twitched. "Tempting, but I'll pass."

The wall by the entrance was covered in pictures. Joe's Home Fry Challenge was written in block letters and tacked above pictures of customers with plates scattered across their table. All but one of them looked ready to barf.

We checked the rest of the place out, but I wasn't sure what we were doing here. How this would help? The demon wasn't just going to wave us over and show himself, even if he was, by some miracle, here at this precise moment. But it wasn't like we had anything else to go on.

We walked into Jumbo Jim's Seafood Bizarre twenty minutes later. "Joe, now Jim, who's next?" This place wasn't much better, but it at least looked clean and was definitely busier.

"Johnny. Has to be," Ren said and grinned.

I wish he'd stop grinning at me all the time. I mean, I was happy he was happy. But it gave me a weird feeling. Thankfully, that feeling was not swoony and lovey-dovey, that was impossible. It was something else, and I didn't like that either.

"Jim's got his own wall of people trying to give themselves a heart attack," he said, motioning to the wall above the bread and condiments table. Jim's Gut Buster Showdown.

I scanned the pictures. "Same green-around-the-gills expressions."

"Except this guy," Ren said. "He looks pretty happy with himself."

I took a closer look. "That guy was on Joe's wall as well. Everyone else looked ready to toss their cookies, except him. He has more empty plates than any of them. The dude looks like he won the lottery and is ready to go back for more."

Ren leaned in to take a closer look. "Definitely looks like he's enjoying himself."

It was probably nothing, but I snapped a picture, anyway.

We didn't linger long and headed to the next place. Sapphire Cabaret.

"A strip club?" Ren asked when we headed for the main door.

"Yep, but a lot of the reviews mention their buffet. Apparently it's cheap for all you can eat and the food is good." I smiled at the doorman as I walked in and Ren grabbed my hand, surprising me. "What are you doing?"

He was scanning the room, jaw tight. "This place is full of horny humans. You need to stay close."

I tried to pull my hand free, but he gripped it tighter.

"Ren, it's fine."

"Humor me."

The grip he had on me, it wasn't like I had any other choice.

Sapphire's had their own all-you-can-eat challenge, only here you got to eat off one of their dancers, and yep, they had pictures as well. "There he is again." The plain-looking male sat at a table, face shiny, a naked female lying in front of him, covered in grease and what looked like gravy and a few dregs of mashed potato. There was a green bean under one of her naked boobs. I pulled out my phone and compared pictures to make sure I was looking at the same guy. "That's definitely him." He was average build, average looks, the type of guy who'd blend in easily with a crowd. I scanned the picture again, then looked back up at the one on the wall. "Huh."

"What?"

"Same date. Look." I showed Ren the picture I'd taken. It had January 12 written under the photo and so did the one on the wall here. "This guy stuffed himself full at Jim's, then came here and did it again."

"Dude's got a serious appetite," Ren said before tightening his grip on my hand and leading me to the bar. He waved over the barman.

"What can I get you?"

He held his hand out for my phone and aimed the picture at the guy. "We're looking for someone. There's a picture on your wall. Does he come here often? Do you know his name?"

The guy leaned against the bar. "Might know his name, but I'm finding it hard to remember just now."

Ren growled, yanked his wallet from his back pocket, and pulled out a couple bills, sliding them over. "How's your memory now?"

The guy grinned. "What do you know, it's all coming back to me." He pocketed the money. "Guy's name's Frank, don't know his surname. He comes here every Thursday night without fail. Sweaty guy. Freaks some of the girls out, but he pays well. Sits by the air-conditioning vent near the buffet table and stays there for a few hours, eating until he's stuffed, then leaves."

"You know anything else about him? How to contact him?" I asked.

"Nope. Now you want a drink or what?"

Ren shook his head and turned to me. "Think we might've found our guy."

"We'll have to come back tomorrow."

"Looks that way." The next song began and a female walked out in a thong and started dancing around a pole. "Let's get the hell out of here."

I laughed at how uncomfortable he seemed. "You don't want to stay for the show?"

"Not even if you paid me," he muttered.

"Hey, sweet thing, how about a private dance," a male voice said before someone grabbed my hips and pulled me into them. My back met a hard, round belly and a sweaty, fleshy arm came around me as he ground his dick into my ass.

Before I had a chance to even try to get away, Ren's fist shot out, throat-punching the other male. The guy's arm fell away, and he hit the ground a second later. With a snarl, teeth bared, Ren kicked the gasping human in the ribs, then grabbed my hand and towed me from the room.

"You could've killed him," I said as we walked out onto the street.

"I don't give a fuck. No one touches you, Jasmine. No one. Understand?" His chest shook with violent breaths.

I blinked up at him, confused and seriously unsettled. I got that he was protecting me, but what he'd just said, the way he'd said it... This was getting out of hand. "You need to calm down," I said when his gaze kept sliding back to the door we'd just walked through, as if he wanted to go back in there and finish what he started. "He was just some creep. It's over. Done."

"I want to go back in there and break his neck," Ren growled. "I want to make him fucking bleed." He paced away and back.

I grabbed his hand. "We need to go." He looked on the verge of giving in and doing what he'd just said.

He didn't budge, like he hadn't heard me. "What he did, the way he...rubbed against you?" A look of disgust covered his face. "I should cut his fucking dick off. I should gut him and watch him bleed out. I should—"

"Ren. Breathe." I grabbed his face to get his attention, because he was still looking at that door with murder in his eyes. "Ren," I said with more force. His gaze slid to me, and his eyes flashed.

"Let's go, okay? We need to go. Someone might've called the police. We need to get out of here."

His fierce gaze dipped to my lips. "Jaz." He swallowed, his Adam's apple sliding up and down. "Butterfly," he said roughly.

I tried to step back, but his fingers thrust into my hair, then his mouth crashed down on mine.

Chapter Twenty-Three

Ren

OH FUCK.

Yes, this is what I needed. Jaz's warm curves pressed to mine, her soft lips. She was all I wanted, all I needed. I was so in love with this female. So insanely in love with her, I couldn't think straight.

I'd been in love with her for a long time, but I hadn't allowed myself to feel it, to recognize it. I hadn't believed I deserved it. That male had touched her and I'd seen red and everything fucking snapped into place.

Edward had possessed me, poisoned me with his evil, broken me, but Jasmine was putting me back together, piece by jagged piece.

I groaned against her mouth—

Then I realized she was utterly stiff in my arms. Her lips were pressed tightly together. I tried to coax her to kiss me back, but she kept her mouth firmly closed.

My fox growled, the sound vibrating in my chest. She shoved at me, hard, and that was when I realized it wasn't the first time.

I loosened my grip on her, and she yanked her mouth from mine. "No, Ren," she bit out. "Let me the hell go."

Oh fuck. "I'm sorry, I thought—"

"That I'd want you to kiss me? Making out with the first female you see when you're struggling to deal with your emotions isn't working for you anymore, Ren. I thought you were starting to see that." She stepped back. "Jesus." She dragged the back of her hand across her mouth as if my kiss disgusted her. "Let's just get the hell out of here."

My heart smashed against my ribs. "I'm sorry," I said, feeling fucking wrecked. Looking at the coldness in her eyes was a slap in the face. My fox whined, confused. Why didn't our mate want us anymore? Why wouldn't she look at us like she used to? I wanted to snatch her back in my arms and kiss her until the female I knew came back. Because Jasmine had never looked at me like that, not as long as I'd known her.

That warmth was completely gone when she looked at me now. A couple weeks ago, she'd wanted me. Now. She didn't.

"I'll take you home."

She strode off ahead to the hearse.

You missed your chance.

Agatheena's words echoed through my head.

I'd fucked up so badly. I'd truly lost her.

A piece of shit like you never deserved a female like that, the voice in my head hissed, Edward's voice. Self-loathing filled me. He was gone, but echoes of his evil, his poison remained.

We drove in silence, because I didn't know what the hell to say.

When we stopped outside the house and Jasmine got out, I felt her pulling away even more.

There had to be something I could do to fix this.

And I knew who had the answers.

Panting, I stood over the feral's body and called to Agatheena. He'd put up a serious fight, I was bloody and battered, but the job was done. She wanted proof, I had her proof. I just hoped she gave me some answers as well. After I'd dropped Jaz home, I'd come out hunting.

Agatheena knew what was going on with Jasmine, why she'd changed. Something was seriously wrong and I needed her to tell me. The small but fierce witch appeared on her porch, squinting down at me. "He still warm?"

"Yes."

She waved a hand. "Good. Bring him here."

The low hum of her magic vanished. She'd dropped the ward so I could pass. Grabbing the feral's hind legs again, I dragged him down the path to the cottage.

"Around the back to my shed," she said, coming down the stairs to lead the way.

I followed her along the side of the house and around the back. She waved her hand again, and the door to the small shed flung open. I followed her in, and lamps on the walls ignited, lighting the space. There were hunks of meat already dangling from meat hooks. I wasn't sure what kind, but there was a bloody pile of clothes in the corner.

"Hang him there," she said. "Upside down."

With a grunt, I lifted the massive feral wolf, forcing the hook through flesh, and stepped back. The witch shuffled up, took a vicious-looking knife from the wooden bench beside her, kicked a bucket under the feral wolf shifter, and slashed his throat. Blood immediately spilled from the deep slice.

She walked back out and I followed her, the door slamming behind us.

"I'll be in touch if I need you for anything else," she said, dismissing me.

"I need to ask you a question, something you said about Jasmine."

She climbed the stairs to her cottage and turned back, eyes narrowed. "And what was it I said, fox?"

"That I'd missed my chance, that I was too late. Why did you say that? You know something, don't you?" I was trying to keep the desperation out of my voice and failing badly.

"I know many things that you don't."

I ground my teeth. "Jasmine's changed. I want to know why."

"You sure about that?"

"Yes, I'm sure. Fucking tell me."

"You may regret asking for the truth, fox. The truth isn't always easy to swallow."

I swallowed down my snarl. "Tell me. Christ, she used to look at me like, like—"

"Like she was in love with you?"

My breath shuddered. "Yes." My hands shook at what I saw in her eyes. "And now, when she looks at me, there's—"

"Nothing?"

"Yes."

"It's simple, fox. Jasmine has been in love with you since the first time she met you. She continued to love you, even while she was forced to watch you drown your pain in booze and other females, knowing there was nothing she could do, knowing that you'd never be hers. After you rejected her, her pain was unbearable. It hurt so much, she knew the only way she could help you heal was to let that love go. So she did. She let you go the only way she knew how."

I was going to be fucking sick. "She let me go? What does that even mean?"

"It means she doesn't love you, not anymore." Her eyes flashed red. "Unrequited love's a bitch, fox, but I think you're finding that out for yourself."

Then I was airborne, Agatheena's magic snapping around me,

gripping me powerfully before dragging me back down the path and launching me out of her property. I landed hard on the ground as her cottage door slammed shut.

I stood there, breathing hard, feeling sick to my fucking stomach.

Jasmine had let me go.

It was late afternoon when I got back, but instead of going inside my place, I felt a pull in a different direction, as if something had wrapped around me. The hum of magic. Jaz. I knew it was her, and I doubted she even knew she was doing it.

It grew in waves that took my fucking breath way.

Waves of distress.

I spun around and ran in the direction she was pulling me —the field down from my house where she spent a lot of time. As I hit the edge, I spotted her. She was on her knees, her body bent forward, her hands out in front of her, and she was sobbing. I ran for her, scanning the field, looking for the danger.

As I got closer, I slowed down and sucked in a breath. "Jaz?"

She looked up at me, eyes red, cheeks wet with her tears. "Who would do this?" she sobbed. "W-who. Why?"

In her cupped hands were several butterflies, the mourning cloaks she always had with her, and others. At least fifty, all dead, lay lifeless around her. *Fuck.* "What happened?"

"They were poisoned. S-someone came here and used p-poison on them."

I crouched beside her, not sure what to do but desperate to comfort her. "Why don't you put them down, Jaz. Let me get you home."

She shook her head. "No, I have to bury them. I'm not leaving them like this. They loved me, Ren. They loved me so much. They loved me like no one else ever has. And now they're gone. Someone hurt them."

"Tell me what to do to help, and I'll do it," I said, feeling fucking helpless. I wanted to pull her into my arms, but she wouldn't want that from me. She was my mate, and I couldn't even comfort her when she was in pain.

She looked up at me, and the agony in her eyes cut so fucking deep. "A box. I need a box."

"Okay. Don't move, I'll be right back." I sprinted home and grabbed the shoebox still sitting in my room from the new running shoes I'd bought and grabbed a spade from the small garden shed we had behind the main building, then rushed back.

Jasmine was where I left her, tears still running down her face. She was talking to her little dead familiars, her pain so acute I felt it as if it were my own, burrowing into my chest.

I placed the box down beside her and opened the lid. The tissue was still inside, and I quickly smoothed it out.

Jaz gently placed the butterflies in her hands on the bottom, then carefully picked up one closest to her off the ground.

"Can I help?"

She nodded.

I watched how she did it and tried to be just as careful as her. When the bottom was covered, I folded over another layer of tissue and we slowly collected the rest, until we had them all. She placed the lid on and picked it up. I followed her across the field, and she pointed to a spot by an oak tree. I dug the hole she needed, and she placed the shoebox inside and covered it with dirt, then she placed her hand on top and closed her eyes.

When she looked up at me a minute later, her lip was quivering, but there was anger in her eyes now as well. "I won't let anyone else hurt them."

I swallowed hard, struggling with seeing her like this and not sure what the fuck to do. "What do you have in mind?"

"I'm warding the field," she said and strode to the edge.

I went after her. "You can't do that, Jaz. This place belongs to someone else, you ward it and things will get messy." No one knew who owned it, but it'd never been fenced and no one had ever seemed interested in building on it. Which meant anyone could wander onto it. But it was still someone else's property.

Another tear streaked down her face. "What if they come back, what if—"

"If they come back tonight, I'll stop them," I said. "I'll stay there. I'll make sure they're safe."

She blinked up at me, her eyes like glittering emeralds. "You'd do that?"

I tucked her hair behind her ear. "Of course." Usually when I touched her, she'd shiver or her eyes would get this soft, dazed look in them. Now there was only gratitude there, pain, but nothing else, not for me, not anymore. Agatheena was right.

Then she collapsed, her grief too much. I scooped her up before she could hit the ground and pulled her into my chest. I pressed my lips to the top of her head. "I've got you, butterfly. Let it out. Let the pain out."

She sobbed against my shoulder, and I felt the turmoil and pain rolling off her, slicing through me. That the mother would do this to her, give her familiars like this, so fragile and unable to live a long life, that Jasmine would love with her whole heart only to get it broken over and over again was cruel. It was fucking torture, and I hated that fucking evil bitch for it.

I carried her down the street, and she clung to me the whole way, sobbing against my chest. There was no reason for anyone to spray pesticides in that field. Unless whoever owned it was finally going to do something with the place, and they'd used some kind of weed killer to clear the field? That was the most likely scenario. I needed to find out who owned that land. This couldn't happen again. I wouldn't let it.

When we reached the house, the front door opened and Else limped out, her face etched with worry. "Is she hurt?"

I shook my head. "Someone used poison in her field."

Else made a pained sound. I didn't need to explain, she knew what that would mean for Jaz's tiny familiars.

"Take her up to her room. I'll get one of my calming elixirs," she said and headed to her and Magnolia's workroom.

I carried on upstairs to Jaz's bedroom and looked at the bed. I didn't want to put her down. I wanted to keep her in my arms, but I promised to guard her field. I doubted anyone was coming back, but I wouldn't let her down again. If it gave her peace of mind, I'd fucking stay there every night.

Pressing a kiss to the top of her head, because I fucking had to, I laid her on the quilt. She curled in on herself, and all I wanted to do was get onto that bed with her and hold her in my arms. Else walked in, and I crouched down in front of Jasmine. "I'll make sure no more of your familiars are hurt, Jaz. I promise."

She stared blindly ahead, lost deep in her pain.

Else moved in, and I forced myself to step back, to turn and leave.

It was getting harder and harder every day.

What the fuck was I going to do?

Chapter Twenty-Four

Jasmine

"How you doing?" Mags said, easing the bedroom door open.

I looked up from my phone. Xavier had texted, asking me out again, but I wasn't sure I wanted to. No, I knew I didn't. He was a nice guy, handsome, but I just wasn't feeling it. I was also still feeing emotionally drained and fragile after yesterday. I'd spent the night with my magic focused inward, healing the wounds yesterday had left me with. It'd taken hours. A wound that deep needed a lot of work and still wasn't completely healed, that kind of pain never was, but it was at least bearable. Even so, I definitely wasn't in the mood to be around anyone who wasn't family. "I should be used to the pain of losing them by now, but it never gets any easier. And yesterday, what happened...with so many of them at once..." I swallowed the lump forming in my throat.

It was early morning and I was sitting on the end of the bed. I needed to get up and get my shit together. Tonight we were going after a soul-eating demon, and right now I was struggling to work up the energy to go downstairs and eat breakfast. Magnolia climbed up beside me. "I can't imagine what it's like for you. Why the hell did the mother do that?" She shook her head. "It's fucking cruel." Her gaze went to the comma butterfly on my hand. "And who's this?"

"He was at my window this morning. Like the mourning cloak, his species can handle the cooler weather a lot better than some." I looked up at my cousin. "Somehow, he found me."

"He's beautiful," Mags said, her gaze searching mine. "Else said Ren brought you home?"

"Yeah." He'd carried me the entire way.

"He's at your field now, you know. He's been there all night."

Warmth curled in my belly. "He said he would, but I didn't think he'd..." What did I think? "That was nice of him."

Mags smiled gently. "You think he's just doing it to be kind? He obviously cares about you, Jazzy, a lot. You don't stay up all night in a field for just anyone."

"We're friends," I said, and I guessed that was true now.

"You sure it's not more than that?" she said, studying me closely.

"It's really not more than that," I said.

"If I had a friend who looked at me the way Ren looks at you, Bram would gut him." Her eyes danced, her lips curling deeper. "You like him, Jaz, I know you do. You've had a thing for Ren for forever. This is a good thing, right?"

I hadn't planned to tell anyone what'd happened between Ren and me, but this was Mags. She loved me and Ren, and if she got involved now, thinking she was helping, things could get seriously messy. "We kissed," I said to her. "Several times. I made it clear I wanted more, he made it clear he didn't. Yes, he's protective of me right now, attentive, and despite what he says...and does, things that might suggest he feels otherwise, it's not what you think, it's my power making him act this way, not me. You know I've had other clients misinterpret their feelings toward me. He's started healing, and his emotions are all over the place. He didn't want me before we started, and once I'm done and everything calms down, whatever it is he thinks he's feeling will fade away, just like it did with the others."

She blinked several times. "You hooked up," she shrieked. "And you're only telling me now?"

"It's over, I didn't see any reason to—"

"Well, you were wrong. You hook up with someone, *with Ren*, the male you have been freaking in love with for years, you tell your favorite fucking cousin."

I thought I'd kept my feelings a secret, obviously not. "How I felt doesn't matter. It's over. I'm fine."

"You're fine? *You're fine.* Bullshit." She rubbed her temples. "You two have been circling each other for fucking years. You convinced yourself it was one-sided, but it's not. The longing fucking looks across the room, the yard, the cemetery, the forest, you name a location and you two have eye-fucked. It wasn't missed by me, or anyone, honestly. Whatever he said to you when he pulled back, he was lying. He's scared, guilty, doesn't think he's worthy, insert all the negative self-talk here, and it's on repeat in that male's head. He told Bram he's tainted, that he can't get the blood off his hands no matter how hard he scrubs them. You know, you've seen his emotional damage. But one thing I do know without a shadow of a doubt? He cares about you, a lot. He's just scared shitless."

She was wrong. "It's my power," I said again, almost desperately.

"It's not. I know he's done a fucking terrible job of showing you. The alcohol and the females certainly didn't help, and if any other male did that, then laid a hand on you, I'd chop it off. I'd tell you he was a player and to run for the hills, but this isn't just some male, this is Ren. My sister's sweet, loving, protective familiar. A male we've known since he was fourteen. He was drowning, the booze and the one-night stands were a coping mechanism. A crutch. He hasn't been to the clubhouse to party since you started working on him, you know that, right?"

I shook my head. "No, you're wrong." A sick feeling twisted in my belly.

"I'm not. Jaz, I'm not wrong—"

"It's too late," I said, cutting her off. I couldn't hear another word. She was wrong. Ren didn't want me. He didn't.

"It's not. It's never too late."

"It is." I held her eyes. "I did something. Something to lock them away."

She stilled. "Lock what away?"

"My feelings for him. I don't...I don't love him, not anymore, and I never will again."

Mags flinched. "You didn't."

"It hurt, Mags, so much. He told me...he said...he said he didn't want me. It was unbearable, but he needed me. He needed me to help him heal, and I couldn't do that with all that pain. So I let him go so I could be what he needed."

"Jasmine...what the hell have you done?" She gripped my shoulders.

"He was hurting himself, over and over again. He tried to take his own life. I couldn't let him do that, I couldn't."

"How did you do it?"

"The how doesn't matter. It's done."

A tear streaked down Mags's face. "And there's no way to reverse it?"

"No."

She pulled me into her arms and hugged me tight. She said no more, because there was nothing else to be said.

I stared at the wall, that feeling in my stomach, the twist, gripped tight. I didn't know what it was. I shouldn't feel anything when it came to Ren. Certainly not regret or sadness over what I did. The love I had for him was gone, right? How could I be sad over something I didn't want, that I wasn't capable of wanting anymore?

I couldn't stomach breakfast and headed down the road to the field instead. My new friend sat on my shoulder, fluttering his wings gently as I walked. It was midmorning, Ren would be at work now and I wanted to check the damage. If I'd lost others through the night, they'd need to be taken care of.

"You stay on my shoulder, sweet boy," I said, and he fluttered his wings.

He may not be able to understand my words, but he could read my emotions, and I knew he'd stay where he was until my apprehension, my fear over what I'd see was gone.

I walked through the old fence and stopped in my tracks. Ren sat under my favorite tree. There was a wild fox and two tiny cubs beside him. He was murmuring low, and the mother came closer, bringing her cubs with her. She butted her nose against his hand.

"Hey, mama," he said as she took something from his fingers. "That's a good girl."

His gentle, husky tone gave me familiar flutters low in my belly.

I tried not to freak out. It was fine. He was a good-looking male, that hadn't changed just because Xavier had walled in my feelings for him, and he was being kind to animals. I could appreciate both of those things. He'd never stopped being attractive to me. I still *liked* him, I still thought he was...hot, I just wasn't *in love* with him.

He glanced up and something shifted in his eyes before a highly attractive smile curled his lips. The fox spotted me, too, and loped off into the trees, her cubs following. Ren stood. "Hey."

"You're still here." I walked over to him.

"I said I'd keep them safe," he said, searching my face. "How you doing, Jaz?"

A zip of electricity shot through my belly, then slipped lower. Not good, not at all. "Thank you, for doing this. Knowing you were here last night, it helped a lot. And I'll be okay."

"I'm glad.

"So what species is your new friend?" he asked, motioning to my shoulder.

"He's a comma butterfly, smaller than the mourning cloaks but, sadly, he'll only be around for a couple more weeks, a little longer if I'm lucky, then he'll go off to hibernate." Sympathy filled his pretty eyes, and I looked away. "Usually I can handle their loss a lot better. Yesterday was...a shock. It wasn't the end of their life cycle. Someone had cut it short."

"I spent the night doing research on my phone. I know who owns the field. I'll make sure no one comes back and sprays poison here."

"How?" I scanned the wide field. When the street was subdivided, this large field had been bought but never developed. It bordered the forest and now felt like it was part of it.

He crossed his muscled arms. "I'll talk to him."

"You'll talk to him?"

His lips quirked up on one side. "I can be persuasive."

He was smiling more. Did he realize that? And they weren't fake smiles clouded by shadows, they reached his eyes. "You think just talking to him will work?"

"Trust me. In the meantime, I called Ronan. He's on his way. He's gonna block the trees they sleep in. By the time he's finished, whoever sprayed poison won't be able to see them. It'll be like they're not there."

I smiled, huge, and had to fight the sudden urge to throw my arms around him. "Thank you, Ren. Seriously. Thank you so much."

His gaze fell to my lips, and he pulled in a shaky breath. "Anything for you, butterfly."

There went those damn zaps in my belly again, accompanied by a warm, soft feeling in the center of my chest. It was gratitude, that's all. He was being kind, and I appreciated it. One friend appreciating another. Then why the hell was I blushing? I hadn't blushed around him since before I went to Xavier for help.

"So what time are we going to the Sapphire tonight? I mean, if you still want to help me." Had Xavier messed up somehow? Had he, like, left a crack in one of the walls he'd built or something, because there were feelings, definite feelings starting to brew inside me. Not the same as before, nowhere near what they were before, but there was something there.

"I'll come by around nine and pick you up."

I stuffed those feelings down deep. "Sounds good."

Chapter Twenty-Five

Jasmine

THE SAPPHIRE CABARET was a lot busier than it had been the night before. There was a group of guys here for a bachelor party and several other groups of guys in suits dotted around the room, while big burly males stood by the doors, scanning the crowd and making sure no one misbehaved.

"Stay close," Ren said as we headed for a booth across from the all-you-can-eat buffet, putting a whole room between us and it.

I slid in first, and Ren followed.

No one was eating, but going by the steaming hot food, the buffet had just been replenished.

"He'll be here soon," Ren said.

My gaze slid to the door. "Get it while it's hot."

"Exactly."

A female stopped by the table and took our drink orders.

Ren's body was pressed to my side, and it made my belly feel kind of weird, so I shuffled over an inch. "So I did some more research, and Drar'toth demons can make a soul last months."

"How's that possible?"

"They ingest them, but feed off the souls slowly until there's nothing left."

"This guy has to be leaving corpses all over the city. Why haven't the knights taken him out?" he said, looking down at me, studying my face intently. "This demon, he's dangerous, Jaz. We see him, you stay back, okay?"

"I have no desire to get close to him," I said, ignoring the look in his eyes. I saw real fear there, fear for me. "And as for why the knights haven't taken him out? Maybe he hasn't been here long. There's no way they would've given a Drar permission to live here, they're far too dangerous. He had to have escaped Hell another way. This guy has adapted quickly, takes only what he needs, gorging on human food between souls, and the bodies he leaves would appear unharmed. No fang or claw marks, no blood and gore, just a body. Nothing to alert the knights that something was up."

Another female stopped by the table. She leaned over it. "You want a dance, handsome?"

She was eyeing Ren, and I gripped the table, alarmed when the green-eyed monster stirred and lifted her head. There was no way I was jealous. Impossible. Who Ren let dance all over him made no difference to me.

Ren barely glanced her way. "No, thanks."

"What about your girlfriend?" she said, leaning further over the table, her gaze coming to me.

"I'm not his girlfriend," I said, far too loudly, and Ren stilled beside me. "No dance, thank you."

She shrugged and strode away, then thankfully the drinks arrived because my face had flushed hot as my mind raced. I sipped my drink and purposely didn't look at Ren. I could feel his eyes on me, and I wanted to squirm. He was studying me as if he were trying to see inside me. Could he see the way I was internally freaking out? I really hoped not.

"There's a guy at the buffet," Ren said. "He just handed a wad of cash to the barman we spoke to yesterday. He went straight to the table to load up his plate."

A guy in a shiny gray suit was leaning over the table, piling spoon after spoon of mac 'n' cheese onto his plate. "How much money?" I asked.

"A lot more than you'd pay for one meal."

"This must be Frank." When the pasta was piled dangerously high on his plate, he added four rolls on top and hustled to a table, sat down, and proceeded to eat, or more, devour everything on it, almost in an uncontrollable frenzy.

"That shit's definitely not human," Ren said.

"Nope. I guess a lot of places would bar someone who showed up all the time and consumed more food than should be humanly possible. They wouldn't make any money out of it." His face was greasy, and he had what looked like sores around his lips. His hair was slicked back and his dark eyes darted around the room as he scooped up mouthful after mouthful of food with a shaky hand. There were food stains on the lapels of his jacket and on his white shirt, I could see them even from here, and given the way the dancers screwed up their faces and avoided him, I had to assume he didn't smell that great either.

"Frank obviously likes it here if he's willing to pay extra instead of hitting another spot," Ren said, curling his fingers around his glass.

We watched as the guy glanced up at one of the dancers between mouthfuls, his spoon actually pausing for the first time as he watched her move around the room. "He has a thing for one of the females."

Ren followed my gaze. "I think we've found our demon."

For the next three hours, we watched as he all but cleared the buffet table, basically all on his own, then sat back to nurse a drink while he watched his favorite dancer work the room, give lap dances, then perform on stage. No other female seemed to catch his attention.

He watched her as she headed for a door in the back, then got up and followed—until one of the bouncers cut him off, shaking his head.

The demon's face turned red, but he strode back across the floor and out the main doors.

"Let's go," Ren said, grabbing my hand.

We walked out onto the street. Frank hadn't gotten far. He was standing at the edge of the building, beside an alleyway, waiting. He slipped back into the shadows when someone appeared at the entrance.

It was the dancer he'd been watching. She was in street clothes and sneakers, her shift obviously done for the night. She looked around, then strode down the street. Frank followed, and we followed Frank.

"What's he going to do?" I said as we kept pace. "What if he hurts her?"

"I won't let him," Ren said.

Shit.

The dancer turned a corner ahead of us, and the demon rushed after her. We had to stay back so he didn't see us, and when we rounded the corner, the dancer was at the door of an apartment building. She walked in, the door closing behind her. "Where is he?"

"He can't have just disappeared."

The apartment building was on a corner, and we rushed across the street and down the other side of the building. Nothing. He wasn't there either. "Where the hell did he go?"

A noise came from above us, and I glanced up and grabbed Ren's arm. He looked down at me and I pointed up. Ren tilted his head back. "What the fuck?" he mouthed.

The demon was on a fire escape, two floors up. He was peering through a window, his pants around his ankles, his hand moving fast as he jerked off.

"We need to stop him," I whispered.

Ren pulled me aside, into a shallow alcove in the wall, where the streetlights didn't reach. "After tonight, she won't ever have to worry about the asshole again. But I can't take him out yet. We need to follow him. After what you said about his feeding habits, we need to make sure he doesn't have anyone locked up somewhere."

Ren was going to kill him; it was the only way to free the souls the demon devoured. Still, the idea terrified me. Frank groaned low above us. I cringed.

"So um...have you had any more trouble at your place? Are the souls still quiet?" I whispered, trying to ignore what Frank was doing. I also needed to know. I felt them with him, but they were different, so much calmer. Even more than I would have expected.

"No more cold patches or touches," he said and moved closer. "Thanks to you."

"I'm really glad I could help," I said.

"I've been um...meditating, like you said, and Rose gave me the name of a counselor." He looked uncomfortable. "She offered online sessions, and I've done a few."

I blinked up at him through the shadows. "You did?"

"Yeah," he said low. "I want to let the guilt go, Jaz. I want to help the souls move on." His throat worked. "And I don't...I don't want to feel this way anymore. I don't want this awful fucking jagged rock right here." He pressed his closed fist to the center of his chest.

I wanted that for him, too, above anything else. "I'm proud of you." I smiled up at him. "I want that for you as well, you don't know how much."

"I wouldn't even be able to take those small steps if it wasn't for you, for all the ways you've helped me."

"Seeing that pain leave your eyes, seeing you smile again..." My voice was husky with emotion. Locking away a part of myself didn't feel like much of a sacrifice knowing this was the outcome. I wouldn't have been able to continue to do my job properly if I'd been nursing my shattered heart. "It's all I wanted."

His eyes softened, and he moved another inch closer—

A groan reached us and I looked up as Frank orgasmed. Something I could have gone my entire life never seeing or hearing. He quickly pulled up his pants, and Ren curled an arm around my waist, pulling me deeper into the alcove. Frank jumped to the ground, something no human could do without injury, and headed off down the street.

"Let's go," Ren said against my ear, making me shiver, then taking my hand again, and we followed after him.

Ren

"This is recon only," I said to Jasmine, who had a seriously determined look on her face. "Once we find where he's bunking down, you need to leave."

Then I'd do what needed to be done. No fucking way was I letting her get close to this monster.

She's already with a monster. That's why she stopped loving you. She knows what you truly are, sees it when she tries to heal you, and it disgusts her. Edward's voice in my head piped up, trying to drag me back down, to destroy all the work Jasmine had done, the work I'd done. I forced his voice out of my head. I couldn't let him win.

She doesn't love you, not anymore. Agatheena's voice joined in, echoing through my mind.

"I don't like that idea," she said. "Not one bit. Who knows what that creep's capable of."

My fox bristled. Did she think we weren't strong enough to protect her? "But I know what I'm capable of," I said, and my voice was rough as hell.

"I know you're strong, Ren, and I know you can fight, but this guy is a demon. He literally just jumped two stories to the ground like it was nothing."

Her hand, so small and soft and warm in mine, was another reminder of how breakable she was. "I know I'm a fox, not a hound like Rome, but I can protect you just as good as he could." My words came out a snarl.

She blinked at me. "I know that."

What the fuck was I doing? Talking myself up like I'd ever be good enough for her. Did I really think that would change her mind? That she'd suddenly want me again? I didn't want her to change her mind, right? It was a good thing she didn't want me anymore, that she didn't love me, and I needed to remind myself of that when I was with her and every instinct in me roared to make her ours.

Love wasn't a cure. I could love her, and she could love me, but that didn't change the fact that I would never be the male I was before. Yes, I was doing a lot better, but my mind was still broken, and my soul would forever be scarred. I wasn't what she needed, mate or not. "Sorry, I'm on edge. You're right, we don't know what he's capable of, which is why I want you far away from him when I take him out."

"It's okay. I get it," she said. "He's taking the next street."

He disappeared, turning ahead of us. I kept hold of Jasmine's hand and walked quickly after him as quietly as we could. But it wasn't a street he'd turned down, it was an alley, and something groaned from the shadows. "Stay behind me."

I took a step into the darkness, and glowing red eyes opened from the depths, locking on to me. Frank was looming over a human, a homeless male going by the makeshift shelter he was slumped beside.

"He's feeding," Jaz said, her voice shaking.

Frank dropped the other male, leapt across the alley, and scrambled up the side of the wall like fucking Spider-Man. We ran to the human male on the ground, his face was gray, the life washed from him, already gone. "It's too late."

"We can't let him get away," Jaz said, looking up to the top of the building.

"He'll need to come back down." I leaned in and scented the dead male's shoulder where Frank had gripped him. It was hard with the scent of unwashed human trying to overpower it, which was probably why Frank chose the target he had, but it was still fresh enough that I could pick it up. "I need to shift. I'll be able to pick up his scent easier."

Jaz nodded as I quickly stripped and handed her my clothes. "Stay close, my fox is quick, and once he catches Frank's scent, he'll take off. If you lose me, get somewhere safe and call Bram and Mags."

She nodded.

Her eyes widened as I shifted, my joints popping, bone and muscle reshaping. I was big for a fox, bigger than any in the wild. If anyone saw me, hopefully they'd assume I was a dog. I expected him to take off instantly, but instead, my fox nudged Jaz, pressing his snout into her palm. She gave him what he wanted, running her hand down his back.

I gave him a mental nudge, and he finally trotted to the dead male, scented him, then turned, and nose to the ground trotted from the alley and down the street. Jaz jogged along beside us. The streets were quiet, but they weren't empty. My fox ignored the looks he was getting, though, focused on finding our target. He turned another corner and slowed, scenting a small area more thoroughly. His ears pricked up, and I felt the spike of adrenaline rush through him.

He had the demon's scent.

He took off, and I heard Jaz's feet on the pavement as she ran after us. I wanted her to leave, to go somewhere safe, to stay back. But she didn't, she stayed with us, and though my fox was constantly aware of Jasmine, he was also focused on finding his target, of showing Jaz how clever he was.

He carried on through a parking lot behind a tire shop. There were old tires in the back, stacked up, and he sniffed around them until he picked up the scent, then took off again. A brick building loomed behind it, every single window in the abandoned building had been broken, the walls graffitied. The demon was inside.

I shifted, and Jasmine handed me my clothes. I pulled them on quickly. "You need to go. You're not coming inside."

"You need me," she said and pointed to the brick wall in front of us. "That symbol isn't just graffiti, it's an alarm, it'll let him know you're coming, and that one"—she pointed to another—"that one will cause sickness if you pass, stomach pain, violent shakes, vomiting. I can neutralize them, but there could be more inside."

I ground my teeth. "I don't like this."

"I'll stay back." Her gaze held mine. "I trust you to protect me."

Fuck. "You need to stay behind me at all times."

"I will."

She strode to the symbols Frank had spray-painted on the wall, pulled her knife from her pocket, and sliced her palm. I hissed, the scent of her blood setting my fox off. The scent of her blood fucked with both of us. He snarled, searching for danger. I did my best to calm him, to reassure him our mate was okay, but he was pacing and on edge.

I wanted to snatch up her hand and stop the bleeding immediately but forced myself to stand back while she spelled under her breath, then pressed her blood-soaked palm against the demon symbols. It sizzled, acrid smoke drifting from her. Jaz tensed but didn't make a sound, then she moved to the next and did the same.

When she was done, she curled her hand against herself. I strode over and took her wrist, lifting it.

"It's nothing."

I ignored her and carefully uncurled her fingers. Her skin was blistered and raw. "You're burned. We need to dress this." My fox howled, hating she was injured, that we'd let her hurt herself.

"I'll take care of it when I get home, besides, there could be more inside," she said.

The thought of her doing that again made me want to snatch her off her feet and carry her away from here. But Frank had seen us back there. He knew what Jaz looked like, and I wasn't leaving until he was nothing but ash.

"If shit gets dicey, you run, okay? Get the fuck out of here as fast as you can."

"I will."

The way her gaze darted from mine, I was pretty sure she was lying. *Fuck*. "Let's go. Keep your hand on my back so I know where you are at all times."

She nodded and, on quiet feet, I led her into the dark building. There were massive old machines filling the enormous space. The place smelled metallic, of oil, and broken glass crunched underfoot as we crossed the concrete floor.

We made our way carefully, and were nearly to the other side, when Jaz fisted my shirt and tugged, stopping me. I looked at her over my shoulder, and she pointed to the floor at the end of one of the machines. It was nearly impossible to see in this light, but it was there. A symbol.

Jaz quickly lowered herself to the floor and rolled under the machine, the scent of her blood came next, then the hiss of her flesh and that same acrid scent. She rolled back out and slid under the one beside it, another hiss, more of that scent. I felt helpless, following her as she checked the rest of the machines.

I knew she was in pain. I felt her distress. The connection between us that I realized had always been there felt different now, somehow stronger, but also muted in a way that didn't feel...right.

She finally rolled out from under the last machine, and I took her good hand and helped her up, unable to stop myself from pulling her into my side. I needed to touch her, to feel her close. I pressed my mouth to the top of her head. "Okay?" I whispered.

She nodded. Another fucking lie. She trembled, and the palm of her hand looked as if she'd dipped it in fucking boiling oil. The fact she wasn't crying in pain spoke of her strength and determination, two things I already knew about this female.

I placed her good hand against my side, needing to know she was with me, and moved to the doorway in front of us. I peered into the darkness, listening. My fox pricked his ears. Nothing but silence came from the shadows.

Sliding my knife free, I stepped through, Jasmine right behind me.

It was a small room, an old office perhaps, but nothing else. I pulled out my phone and used the flashlight. No other doorways, no exit.

"Are you sure he came this way?" Jaz whispered.

I nodded and walked to an old storage shelf. "His scent is stronger in here." He definitely came into this room. I shone my phone at the floor. There were marks in the dust from the narrow wheels under it.

I turned off the light, shoved my phone in my pocket, and reached for the shelf but Jaz stopped me with a hand to my bicep, pointing to the other side. Another fucking symbol.

I clenched my teeth. I couldn't watch her go through that again, but she was already whispering her spell. She pressed her blood-covered and blistered hand to the symbol and pain etched her beautiful face, her skin leaching of all color. She shook from it, and I moved in behind her and wrapped my arms around her, wishing I could absorb the pain, take it from her. Smoke rose, the sizzle and scent of her burning flesh reaching my nose. But she didn't pull away, she finished her spell, breaking its dark magic before finally dropping her hand and collapsing against me.

I turned her to face me, and tears glistened on her cheeks. I brushed them away. My mate was crying, my precious female was burned, in pain, and I couldn't do anything to ease it. "I'm sorry," I choked out. Useless words, and not just for her physical pain, but for the pain I'd caused her over the years while I'd been lost in my own. Blind, dumb, deaf to everything. So focused on getting through one more day, just one, that I hadn't seen anything around me, or anyone.

She wiped her face on her shirt and smiled crookedly at me, cracking my chest down the middle.

"I'll live," she said, her lower lip quivering.

I gripped the back of her head and pressed a kiss to the top of her hair, knowing that's all she'd let me do, all I'd let myself do, but still needing that contact so fucking badly. "You ready?"

She nodded. "Yeah, the pain's subsided some."

That was her third lie of the night. The pain was still there in her gorgeous eyes, but I nodded and eased the shelf forward. More darkness greeted us behind it, but there was a flicker of light in the distance, lower than the level we were on. The basement.

"Stairs," I said against her ear and placed her hand on my back again before slowly, carefully, making my way down. I wanted to leave her up here, but if he doubled back and found her alone—no, I couldn't leave her alone in this place.

As we reached the bottom, music drifted out of a room to the side. There were shelves and other clutter down here, and we slipped into the room. The sound of Frank humming along to the music reached us. I peered through one of the shelves.

He was doing a weird fucking little dance as he stripped off his clothes. He tossed his jacket aside, then his shirt, before shucking his pants. His skin was sweaty, more scabs like the ones around his mouth at his joints. He straightened with a groan of relief, and Jaz grabbed my arm, her nails digging in.

Holy fuck. His greasy skin writhed. Souls moving beneath it. Hands stretched his flesh, fingers splayed, faces, mouths open in silent screams. They were trapped inside him. He spun in a slow circle, swiveling his hips, singing along with the song playing.

I took Jaz's hand, placed it on one of the shelves, and mouthed *stay here*. She nodded.

My best bet was taking this fucker by surprise. He strutted about, still dancing, singing, swinging his flaccid dick around like he was hot shit. No doubt on a high after just feeding.

He dance-walked farther away. The humming stopped, there was a clang, like pots and pans being moved around. He couldn't still be hungry.

I eased closer, saw a flash of naked skin, then it was gone. A crash came from behind me, a shelf toppling over. *Fuck.* He knew we were here. I sprinted for Jasmine, but it was too late.

Frank had his arms locked around her, his scabbed, sweaty face pressed against hers, grinning wide.

"You hurt her, you die screaming," I snarled, taking a step closer. My heart was in my throat. I knew I loved her, but right then I realized my whole fucking world was in that soul-sucking demon's arms.

"Imagine, if you will," the demon said in a weird voice that resonated through the room. "Her sweet, juicy, vibrant soul writhing beneath my skin. Imagine it screaming in agony as I feed off her slowly, piece by delicious piece, until there's nothing left of her. Until every last trace of your female ceases to exist."

Jasmine's lips were moving, spelling, and the demon hissed and slapped his hand over her mouth, then opened his. Jasmine's muffled scream came next. He was devouring her soul.

I ran at him but hit an invisible barrier. He grinned and pointed up. There was a symbol painted on the ceiling right above him. Some kind of protection or barrier.

Jaz flailed in his arms, trying to get away while I lost my mind, slamming into the invisible wall over and over again. Frank howled suddenly. Jasmine had her knife buried in his thigh, and with a cry, she dragged it up, slicing his leg wide open.

The demon's arms fell away from her with a howl, and he stumbled back. As soon as he stepped a toe over the symbol, the barrier dropped, and I pounced. I yanked him away from Jasmine and unceremoniously started hacking at the piece of shit. He rebounded fast, though, punching me in the ribs with the force of a wrecking ball.

My ribs shattered, and he knocked the knife from my hand. I wrestled him to the ground, hissing when he sunk his teeth into my arm. He was incredibly strong and fast. Jasmine dove on his back, her little knife plunging into his back over and over again.

Fuck. I slammed both hands against his ears, and he screamed as I plowed my fist into his face. Snatching my knife from the ground, I slashed his throat. Blood sprayed me, and ignoring his gurgled screams, I sawed through his thick skin and hardened bone.

Finally, his head gave, rolling with a thud to the floor. A second later he turned to ash.

Jasmine landed on top of me, ash on her face, and in her hair. Then the screams of dozens of trapped souls burst into the air, a frenzy of fear and pain, and Jaz curled around me, holding on tight.

I wrapped my arms around her. "You're okay," I said against her hair. "I've got you." Words she'd said to me, to make me feel safe when I'd been so fucking lost.

One by one, the souls' mournful screams came to a stop.

We couldn't see them, but the reapers must be here, taking the missing souls where they were always meant to go, reestablishing balance.

Jasmine gave me all her weight, and I rubbed her back. "Jaz?"

Nothing.

I lifted her head. She wasn't breathing, and every bit of life had drained from her face completely. "Jasmine!"

Chapter Twenty-Six

Ren

I CARRIED Jasmine to her room, thankful everyone was in bed. It was close to morning, but I had no idea what the time was.

Laying Jaz on the bed, I shut us in and crawled up beside her and pulled her against me, holding her tight.

This was the same thing that happened at the demon compound, this wasn't what it looked like, what it felt like, I knew it, I felt her...fuck, her life force inside me. My fox howled inside me, calling for her to wake up. Jasmine was going to be okay. She wasn't leaving me. I just had to hold on, hold on to her.

I lay there holding her lifeless body as time ticked by, until the sounds of the family waking, going down to the kitchen for breakfast, drifted up from downstairs. They didn't know we were here, and I wasn't getting off this bed to tell them, not until Jasmine woke up.

She'd been out for hours last time, but this was definitely longer.

"This is the second time you've done this to me, butterfly. Made me think I lost you." I pressed my face into her shoulder and breathed in her scent, curling around her more tightly. She felt cold. Fuck, she was so cold. I tugged the quilt at the end of the bed over her. "That's enough now, Jaz. You can wake up now, baby." I shook her a little as panic filled me. "Wake the fuck up, Jasmine. Wake up now."

Not a sound, no movement, nothing. The gaping hole in my stomach and behind my ribs was unbearable. Living without her wasn't an option.

She's okay, I reminded myself for the millionth fucking time.

Because Jasmine was here, her life force, right there in the center of my chest, burning bright.

I rolled her to her back and cupped her beautiful face. Her skin was pale, had lost all color, all life. I didn't know how long this thing could last, but I was seriously starting to freak out. "Jaz, please, I need you to come back to me." I pressed a kiss to her forehead, her cheek. "Come on, butterfly, wake up." My eyes stung, and my chest felt as if there was a boulder on it. "Come back to me, Jazzy."

There was a tapping at the window. The curtains were still open and early morning sun filtered through, backlighting tiny flappy wings. Butterflies, so many of them, trying to get in, to get to her. I got off the bed and opened the window. Maybe they could reach her when nothing else could. They flew to her instantly, a multitude of color surrounding her, covering her, pouring their love into her, calling her back.

A witch needed her familiar. They needed each other. If anyone could get through to her, they could. I dragged a chair to the side of the bed and sat, taking her hand in mine, and then I prayed. I prayed to the goddess to bring her back to me.

Her hand jolted in mine. My head shot up.

She blinked several times, and the butterflies covering her all took flight, fluttering and dancing above her. "Ren?"

My eyes closed and I bent my head over her hand again, pressing my mouth to her skin, feeling it warming beneath my lips. Her other hand brushed the back of my head.

"Ren?"

Relief pumped through me with such force, I shook. Her fingers flexed against mine, and I lifted my head.

"W-we did it, didn't we? We freed the souls. It's over," she said, a small smile curling her lips.

I nodded and released a shuddering breath. "For a minute there..." I tried to calm my pounding heart. "I thought...I thought I might lose you."

"I'm sorry... I—"

"I love you," I choked out, unable to hold in those words another day, another moment. "I'm in love with you, Jasmine."

She stared at me, her eyes wide, then she started to shake her head.

"Don't tell me I'm wrong or that it's because you've been helping me and I'm confused. I know what I'm feeling. I fucking know. You are mine. You're fucking mine, Jasmine." There were a lot of reasons why I should keep this to myself, that I should let her go, but I needed her. I'd tried to fight it, but I couldn't do it anymore. Living without her wasn't an option. It just wasn't. And whether she would admit it or not, she needed me as well.

Her lower lip quivered. "I don't...I can't—"

"You loved me, you did." I held her tighter. "I'll make you love me again."

"You can't," she said, her voice filled with anguish. "You can't fix it. I don't..." Her throat worked. "I care about you, so much. You're my friend, but I can't...I can't love you the way you want me to."

Why the fuck was she saying this? My fox paced, confused. He didn't know why our mate didn't want us. He wanted us to take her home to our den. He wanted to claim her, bite her, mark her.

She was ours, but she was denying us. "I know I hurt you, but I'll fix it. I can fix it."

Her fingers curled around mine. "You did nothing wrong. It's me. It was me. I wish it was different, Ren, I do, but I can never love you—"

The door flew open and Mags rushed in. "I got here as fast as I could. I had to deliver the souls. I was there, you were on the floor...thank the goddess you're okay."

Mags ran to Jaz, and I stepped back, retreating. Shaking so fucking hard my legs felt unsteady under me. She couldn't mean that, but she did. I saw it in her eyes. I felt it. I fucking felt it through the bond she was denying.

She could never love me.

She didn't want us.

Jasmine

Ren walked out the door, and I stared after him, utterly frozen.

"Jazzy?"

"Ren said he loves me," I whispered as my tiny familiars settled around me.

Magnolia stared down at me, her eyes wide, filled with things I didn't want to see right then. "Oh, Jaz."

"He can't mean it. He can't," I said, trying to convince myself I hadn't seen the truth of his feelings shining at me in his gorgeous eyes.

"I think he meant it," Mags said gently and sat in the chair Ren had just been in.

"What have I done?" I choked.

"There's definitely nothing you can do—"

I shook my head. Xavier said it couldn't be undone, more than once. He told me to make sure it was what I wanted. I never in a million years thought Ren would ever fall in love with me. It had been an impossibility in my mind.

Mags sat forward. "And you really don't feel anything for him, nothing?"

"Nothing like before. I want him to be happy. I recognize how handsome he is, I'm still...attracted to him." I'd tried to ignore it, but that was something that had never stopped, even after what Xavier did. "I like him, a lot, but I don't love him. It's just not there anymore. It's gone." My love for Ren was trapped behind impenetrable walls, and there was no busting them down.

Mags grabbed my hand, her gaze filled with sympathy. "I'm so sorry."

"He'll get over me, he will, and then all this...it'll just be a bad memory."

Magnolia nodded, but she didn't look convinced.

She left, and I got out of bed and stared out the window. As I did, something rose up inside me, a strange feeling, a yearning that I couldn't decipher, that I didn't understand. It reminded me of when I was a child and Mom would send us here during school holidays while she took off on another adventure.

And even though I'd loved it here, and my family, I'd missed Mom terribly.

I felt homesick, I just didn't know what I was homesick for.

Chapter Twenty-Seven

Ren

My fox whined and pawed at the ground. He'd been doing it all day. He wanted us to go back to our mate, to bring her home where we could keep her safe. He didn't understand why she didn't feel the bond, and neither the fuck did I.

I'd never heard of it happening before. When a fox found his mate, when that lightning struck, there was no mistaking it. The male felt it first, yes. But as the bond grew in strength, his female felt it, too, and Jasmine was my female. I knew it with everything in me, but still she was indifferent.

Agatheena's words slammed into my skull.

"It's simple, fox. Jasmine has been in love with you since the first time she met you. She continued to love you, even while she was forced to watch you drown your pain in booze and other females, knowing there was nothing she could do, knowing that you'd never be hers. After you rejected her, her pain was unbearable. It hurt so much, she

knew the only way she could help you heal was to let that love go. So she did. She let you go the only way she knew how."

What the fuck did that even mean? How did you just let it go?

My muscles ached to run, to run to my cliff; my palm itched to grip my knife to ease the throb of my scars, something I hadn't felt for a while thanks to Jasmine, but I'd been fighting it back all day. I didn't want it back. I didn't fucking want it.

I paced across the room. Going there now would undo all the work Jaz had done. All the work I'd done. I needed to stay strong, to keep my head.

I wasn't giving up on her, I couldn't.

Someone knocked at the door. It was late, and I strode to it, hoping it was Jaz on the other side, but knowing it wouldn't be.

Bram stood there. "You got a minute?"

"Is it Jaz? Is she okay?"

He studied me. "She's fine. Can I come in?"

"Not really in the mood for company, brother," I said, shutting the door and following him into the living room.

"I know," Bram said. "But you got me, anyway."

"Mags told you what happened?"

He nodded. "Just got back from a job or I would've been here earlier."

There was only one reason Bram was here, he was worried what I might do. "I'm alright," I said. Was I convincing him or me? "You don't need to babysit me. Yeah, my mate just told me she didn't fucking want me, but I don't plan on swan diving off the edge of a cliff, not tonight anyway. I'm not giving up that easily."

"Mate?" Bram straightened. "She's your mate?"

I rubbed my hands over my face. "Yeah. I didn't know, not until she started helping me. Deep down, somewhere, I know I did, and that's why I stayed away from her, because I couldn't fucking bear to be near her as tainted and fucked up as I am, and because I was afraid. I'm still fucked up, and I'm still afraid I'll fuck things up and hurt her, but I want her more than anything. I need her. She's everything. She's—"

"I know. I know how you feel," Bram said. "I know what she means to you. I had no idea she was your mate, though. Does she know?"

I shook my head. "She doesn't want me. She doesn't feel it."

Bram shoved his fingers through his hair. "There's a reason for that."

I gripped the back of the couch. "What did she do?"

His jaw worked as if he were wrestling with something.

I knew this male well. We'd grown up together. Something seriously fucked up was going on. "What the hell is it? Tell me."

"If I'd known what this was, between you and Jaz, I would have spoken up sooner."

I had no idea what he was going to say, but my friend was a male of few words, and he didn't get involved in shit if it didn't involve Magnolia. For him to speak up now meant it was something serious, something he couldn't ignore. My fingers dug deeper into the couch, and my fox paced.

"I know what it's like to be in love with someone and think there's no hope. I didn't think it was my place to tell you after Mags found out, if I'd known—"

"Fucking tell me, Bram."

"She went to someone, I don't know who, someone with powers and asked for help."

"What kind of help?"

"Help with her heartbreak, over you, and they did something to her...to stop her loving you, Ren. That's why she doesn't feel it, she can't."

I struggled to fucking breathe. I'd hurt her that much, so much she'd done something to break free from me, to cut me out of her like a piece of rot. I didn't blame her after the way I ignored her, flaunted other females in front of her—rejected her.

Fuck. She'd been living in pain as long as I had and I hadn't seen it, so caught up in my own.

Maybe I should walk away, leave her alone, let her be happy without me. But she was ours, our mate, and I couldn't let her go.

I grabbed my keys and strode out the door. Bram shut it after us and strode down the street with me. It was late, Jaz would be asleep, but I couldn't wait.

"What are you gonna do?" Bram asked as he kept pace beside me.

"Fucked if I know, but she's mine. I can't just walk away. There has to be a way to fix this." The alternative was too fucking awful to consider.

We walked around the back of the house.

Bram clapped me on the back before heading for his tree house, and Mags, in the backyard, and I used my key to get into the house. It was silent. Everyone was asleep. Walking into Jaz's bedroom in the middle of the night was probably a terrible idea, but it was as if I were being pulled to her by an invisible force. My mate was here. Where she was, I needed to be, whether she felt it as well or not.

I took the stairs and stood outside her closed door, my breathing shaky as fuck, my gut a sack of jagged fucking rocks. But I needed to hear her say it. I needed the truth. I gripped the door handle and eased it open. The curtains were open, the moon casting shadows across the walls, the tree outside the window making them sway.

Jasmine was sitting up in bed, her knees drawn up, her arms wrapped around them, her eyes wide and on me. I didn't say anything, shutting the door behind me, and stared back at her across the room. She was utterly breathtaking. Her blond hair was a sexy mess around her face, her tattooed arms bare. She bit her lower lip, and her eyes drifted shut for a moment before opening again, except now they glistened with tears.

"You know, don't you?" she whispered. "You know what I did?"

I took a step closer. "That you loved me, and now you don't? That you had someone destroy what you felt for me because I hurt you so much that you couldn't bear the pain another moment?"

"You didn't know you were hurting me," she choked out.

"You didn't tell me."

"I thought it was the best thing for both of us. It hurt to be around you, but I wanted to help you. You needed that from me, more than anything else. I didn't think...you said you didn't want me, and I believed you." She bit her lip again. "I never thought—"

"That I'd fall in love with you? That after you helped me and I could see clearly again through all the blood and pain and horror, that I'd finally see you? That I'd see my mate?"

She jolted, her entire body rocking back. "What?"

"You really didn't know?" I stepped closer. "Christ, Jaz, that new wound that opened up inside me, while you were healing me? That was you. That was wanting you so fucking badly, but forcing myself to give you up when that was the last thing I wanted to do. That was giving up my mate."

She stared at me wide-eyed through the shadows.

"You are my mate, Jasmine. My female. My reason for breathing. You've been my reason for a long fucking time, even before I knew. It was your eyes I saw when I stood at the edge of a cliff and imagined stepping off, it was your eyes that pulled me back, time and time again. I just didn't know why, not until you wrapped your arms around me and everything clicked into place. The truth. What we are to each other."

She was trembling so hard I could see it even through the shadows. "I didn't know."

I closed the space between us, unable to stay away from her another moment. "I know I hurt you. I fucked up, but please, butterfly, fix this. I need you, Jaz. I fucking need you."

Tears streaked down her face. "I c-can't. I wish I could, but it can't be fixed." She sobbed. "I'm so sorry. I'm so sorry I did this to us. I'm so s-sorry—"

"Who did it?"

"It won't change anything."

"I'll make them fix this, I'll—"

"You can't."

"This can't be it."

"I'm sorry," she said again.

This couldn't be happening. It couldn't be true. My world had narrowed to her. Without her I was nothing. Something snapped inside me. I grabbed her shoulders. "Love me back," I demanded, pleaded. "Please, butterfly. Please love me back."

"I can't," she sobbed.

I held the side of her face with one hand and curled my fingers around the side of her throat with the other. "You're mine. You're fucking mine, Jasmine. I won't let you go. I'll make you love me again. No matter how long it takes." I brought my mouth down on hers, needing her taste more than anything else on this planet.

She fisted my shirt, but she didn't push me away. "I'm sorry," she said against my lips. Our panted breaths mingled, then she tugged me closer and kissed me back. "I'm sorry," she said again, then lay back, taking me with her.

Trembling, I covered her, kissing her deeper, harder. I should get the fuck up and leave, but I couldn't do it. My mate was kissing me, touching me, and I was lost, completely fucking lost. Her hands slid down between us, tugging at my belt, sliding down the zipper, then her hand was on me. I groaned into her mouth.

She wriggled, tugging off her panties, then her thighs were hugging my hips. The head of my cock brushed over hot slick flesh, and I tried to lift my head, but she hooked her arms around my neck and pressed her forehead to mine. "It's okay," she rasped and lifted her hips.

I slipped inside her, just the tip, and I shook harder. "Jasmine?"

"It's okay," she said again.

I was too fucking weak to resist. My mate might not love me, but she wanted me. Her pussy was primed for me. I pushed forward, and her nails dug into my back with a cry. "Yes," she whimpered. "Please."

Mouths still touching, breathing each other's air, I slid deeper, unable to hold back. "Oh fuck," I groaned. She was so fucking tight and wet and impossibly hot.

Her hips lifted again, taking me deeper, her nails scoring my back, and I couldn't restrain myself. I started to move. We shook and rocked against each other, and I pinned her down more firmly with my body, lifted my knee for better purchase, and slid deeper. She cried out against my lips, her pussy squeezing me so damn tight, fluttering and clenching around me. "You feel so good, Jaz. So fucking perfect."

Her feet locked behind my back, and she strained against me, arching. Her mouth opened, and I covered it with mine, smothering her screams as she came for me fast, trembling. Her pussy gripped me fucking tighter, and I finally had her under me. There was no holding back, no finding an ounce of control in that moment. I thrust into her, utterly lost but somehow finding the strength to pull out at the last moment and grind my cock between our bodies, coming on her stomach instead of inside her like I desperately wanted to.

We lay there panting, still clinging to each other. Both of us were still dressed, our clothes damp with sweat and stuck to our skin. I kissed her neck, her jaw, and looked down at her beautiful face. She stared back at me, and there was a guarded look in her eyes that I fucking hated. "This isn't...I didn't come here for this, I—"

"It's okay," she said again, her fingers brushing my jaw. "It felt right. Please, don't question it."

"What happens now?"

She shook her head against the pillow. "I don't know." Her gaze searched mine. "I wish this changed things..."

She trailed off because it didn't, not for her. I was so in love with her my heart felt as if it might burst, but nothing had changed for her. Not one thing.

"I wanted to...to give you this before I leave," she said, staring at my chin.

It was like she'd punched me in the stomach. "Leave?" I grabbed her chin and shook her. "A pity fuck before you leave me? That's what that was?"

"No, it wasn't like that. I wanted you. I never really stopped wanting you that way, even after..."

"Even after you took what was mine and cut it out of you? Even after you stole our future from us and tossed it away. And now you're going to bail. Leave me here like I don't exist?" I snarled. "Find someone else you can love? Is that it?"

She pushed at my chest, and I had no choice but to get off her even though it was the last thing I wanted to do. I stood, stuffed myself back in my jeans, and did them up. Jasmine sat up, returning to the position she'd been in when I walked in here. Knees up, her arms wrapped around them. I could smell us, our come, the tinge of blood because my mate was a virgin until a few minutes ago, and instead of tending to her like my fox and I both wanted to do fucking desperately, she was pushing us away.

"I did that, and I'll own it," she said. "But I truly thought you'd never love me back. I never would have done what I did otherwise. I'm leaving for you, to make it easier on you. I don't want to hurt you, Ren. You've been hurt enough already. You should be with someone who can love you like you deserve."

I was breathing hard, my blood pumping through me so fucking fast I felt dizzy. "Let me make one thing perfectly clear. I'm not giving up on you, on us. Not fucking ever. You leave me, I will follow you. I will always follow you."

Then I turned and walked out the door, before I snatched her from that bed and kept her anyway.

Chapter Twenty-Eight

Jasmine

"I HATE SEEING you like this, Jazzy girl," Stanley said from his spot at the end of my bed.

I dragged my hand across my face, wiping away my stupid tears. "I hurt him, Stan, so badly. I never wanted that. I did it because I loved him, because I didn't want to hurt him, and I did it anyway."

He dropped down to an elbow, lying across the mattress. "You didn't know he was your mate. It's not your fault, sweets." Sympathy filled his eyes. "And that male was so closed off, there was no way you could've known."

There was an ache between my thighs, reminding me of what I did with Ren. I'd wanted him. I'd never stopped wanting him that way, but all I'd done was make it worse. I'd meant it to be a good-bye, I guess. But giving myself to him like I did had been selfish, and I'd made everything worse.

"Do you like him?" Stan asked.

"Yes, of course."

He smirked. "You obviously think he's hot."

My face heated. "Obviously."

"Maybe you don't need to love him to be with him, not at first? You're mates, that connection has its own magic. That bond can break spells and fight evil, it can bring people back to life and heal wounds...it can even break down barriers. I don't know much about foxes or how they mate, I assume by marking? Do you know for sure that mating properly won't change things between you? This Xavier guy blocked your love for Ren, but does that mean you can't fall in love with him all over again? Plenty of people have mated first and fallen in love later. Not everyone knows their intended mates for years before they're thrown in their path. Iris and Draven are a perfect example of that."

I blinked over at Stan, my heart doing a giant thump in my chest. "I...don't know."

"Well, before you pull up stakes and leave us all in the dust, don't you think you should find out?"

I chewed my lip. "You think he'll want to try?"

He gave me a look like I was a complete idiot. "Uh...yeah. You're all he's thinking about, Jaz, I promise you that." He tilted his head to the side. "I know you don't feel it anymore, but do you remember how it felt to be in love with him?"

Pain sliced through me. "Yes. It hurt like hell."

"Then maybe this is a good thing? Maybe it's a way to start fresh." He climbed off the bed. "I'll let you mull that over, and I'm gonna go check on my girl. I can hear her singing in her workroom. You know I love it when she does that." He winked and walked through the door, heading down to be close to Else.

If there was ever proof of how strong the mating bond was, all I had to do was look at Stan. He'd stayed by Else's side for over fifty years.

I shoved back the covers and strode to the shower. The mating bond *was* a powerful thing. Maybe this could work. Maybe all hope wasn't lost. I wanted him still, I cared about him a lot. That was a good start, right? I didn't want to live my life without my mate, and I didn't want Ren to either, to suffer because of what I did. I had to at least try.

﹩

Asking Ren if he wanted to try to make this thing between us work wasn't something you did over the phone, but when I came by the funeral home, there'd been a whole lot of cars parked out front. Someone was having a viewing or a service, which meant Ren would be busy.

I'd gone back to the house, and with no missing souls to hunt, I'd had the whole day to think about what I'd say when I saw Ren. I still wasn't sure how to approach this. The only thing I could do was just lay it all out and see what he thought, but the nerves in my belly were off the charts.

When I finally walked back to his place, it was getting dark. He would've finished work a few hours ago. I'd wanted to come sooner, but Aunt Daisy needed some help at the cemetery harvesting.

My nerves were insane by the time I knocked on Ren's door, but nothing but silence came from inside. I walked back up the stairs.

"Looking for Ren?" Mr. Macanroy was walking out of the funeral home. He was tall and lean with the same russet-colored hair as Ren.

"I am, yeah. Do you know when he'll be back?"

He slid his hands in his pockets. "He went for a run a while ago, but I'm sure he'll be back soon."

"Oh, okay. I'll come back."

"I was actually hoping I'd see you, Jasmine," he said, stopping me. "I've been wanting to thank you for what you've been doing for Ren. He's changed so much...we're seeing glimpses, more than glimpses of our boy, the way he was before..." His amber eyes, so like Ren's, softened. "Just seeing him smile again...thank you, Jasmine."

"I'm glad I could help, but it wasn't just me. He did the work."

He pressed a key into my hand. "Go in and wait for him. He won't mind."

"No, I shouldn't—"

"It's fine." He gave my hand a squeeze and left.

I stood there for a minute, not sure what to do, but then a fat, cold raindrop landed on my cheek, then another and another, then the sky opened up. I ran down the stairs to his front door, unlocked it, and rushed inside.

Ren's scent filled the space, and I unconsciously breathed deep. I loved the way he smelled. It instantly made me think about him pressed against me, his weight, the sounds he'd made. I shivered. It'd been good, really good. Who was I kidding, it was amazing. I had no idea it'd be like that, that connection, that chemistry. That had to count for something, right?

I walked deeper into the living room and stood there, not sure what to do with myself. Yes, I'd been here a lot lately, but I didn't want to invade his privacy. In the end, I sat on the couch.

I tried to busy myself by flicking through Nightscape, but I hadn't slept after Ren left my room the night before, and as hard as I tried to stay awake, it didn't take long for the tiredness to take over. I resisted, but something about being here, and Ren's scent, being around his things, had me struggling to keep my eyes open.

I startled awake when something cold hit my arm.

I looked up.

Ren stood over me, hair wet, water dripping down his bare chest. He was wearing jeans that he must have just pulled on because they were dry, unlike the rest of him. He stared down at me, his chest heaving.

"You're, ah...your dad let me in," I said, suddenly feeling awkward and shy.

"I see that," he said, glancing at the key on the coffee table.

"I was going to wait outside, but then it, uh..." My gaze dipped without my say-so, taking in his wet, bare chest, and for some reason seeing all the sigils on him, the ones I'd tattooed on his skin, had my skin flushing hot. "Started raining."

"You can come here whenever you want, Jaz." His gaze moved over me, and his nostrils flared. "My mate can come and go as she pleases."

My mouth went dry. The way he was looking at me, the intensity, was something I'd never seen before. He looked wild, on edge, like he was holding himself back.

"We're not mated yet," I said, and it came out a husky whisper.

He quirked a brow. "Yet?"

I licked my dry lips, still trying to decide the best way to word this. "Last night, after you left—"

"After I left you last night, I came here and tried not to tear the walls down, then when nothing else would work, I sat where you are now and looked through all the pictures I have of you on my phone, taken when you weren't looking, some when you were. I've got a whole file of you, Jasmine, that I look at when I need to calm the storm inside me. Pictures, because the real thing was out of my reach. I had that, needed that, needed you, and somehow I didn't work out what you were to me until it was too fucking late."

He had pictures of me? I forced myself to focus on what I needed to say, but it wasn't easy, not after what he'd just confessed, and not with the way he was staring down at me. "You were right, the things you said before you left."

"Which things, Jaz?" Gold flecks burst through amber, his fox swirled in his eyes, staring out at me.

"When I did what I did, I took something from you as well." I was finding it hard to breathe normally. "No, I didn't know what we were to each other then, but I do now, and I'd like to try to fix it. I don't know if it's possible," I rushed out, "but a friend of mine reminded me how powerful the mating bond is, and that anything's possible between mates."

His stomach muscles clenched, and the veins in his forearms bulged. "What are you saying, Jasmine? You want us to mate?"

"Um...that was suggested, but I don't think we should go that far, if...if it doesn't work, I don't want you tied to me and suffering."

"If what doesn't work? I'm still not sure what you're suggesting, butterfly?"

My belly went all zippy and flippy-floppy when he called me butterfly. "That we stay...close, that we try to develop the mating bond. You feel it. Maybe I'll start to as well and—"

"You'll fall in love with me again?"

"Yeah. Maybe."

He leaned forward, gripping the cushion above me with one hand and the arm of the couch with the other. "How close are we talking, Jaz?"

"Well, um..."

He leaned in more. "This close?"

I nodded.

"How about this close?" he said and came closer still, his mouth hovering above mine.

I nodded again as electricity shot through me.

"Closer?" he said with a whole lot of growl in his voice.

"Yes—"

His mouth slammed down on mine, and he hooked a muscled arm around my waist, hauling me off the couch. I wrapped my arms around his shoulders, my legs around his waist. This was dangerous, so damn risky. If this went wrong, if it didn't work, I could hurt Ren all over again, badly. But I owed it to him, to both of us, to try. I had to at least try. I may not be able to feel the love

I'd had for him before, but I still remembered the wild fantasies, the dreams I'd had, the images I'd played through my mind over and over of the two of us together.

I wanted him, I wanted this to work. I wanted to love him again, but this time without any of the pain and sadness. I wanted to know what it was to love him without holding anything back. I wanted to love him this time, knowing he loved me in return.

His tongue delved into my mouth, and he carried me through the living room and down the hall into his bedroom. He lowered me toward the mattress.

"Not here," I blurted as everything seized inside me. "Not where you brought..." *All the others. Not where I saw you with Bree through the window.*

He hitched me higher, and the bedside drawer opened and closed, then he was striding back into the hall. He opened the next door. It was a small room with a set of weights in the corner and a couch against the wall. He sucked on my mouth, there was no other word for it, like he couldn't get enough of me, then stood me on my feet. He quickly tossed the couch cushions aside and pulled on a nylon strap, unfolding the bed. Then he grabbed a couple duvets from the closet behind him and tossed them on the foldout. He turned back to me, grabbed me before I knew what he was going to do, and tossed me on top of it.

"Better?" he asked.

"Yes."

"Good." Then he was on top of me, kissing me again, deep and insistent. I thrust my fingers through his damp hair, wanting more. Goddess, the male could kiss. Not that I'd kissed a lot of guys, but none of them had come anywhere close to this.

He did the mouth-sucking thing again and lifted his head, staring down at me. "How you feeling after last night, baby? You sore?"

My face went hot again. "A little achy, but it's not so bad now."

His jaw clenched. "I should have been more careful. I should have looked after you when we were done."

But I'd ruined things, and he'd left.

"It's fine. I'm fine."

He shook his head. "It's not. But I'm going to look after you now, Jazzy. You trust me, don't you?"

I did. I'd seen all of him. I'd wrapped my arms around him and seen every part of his soul, the pain, the anger, the scars, and the crippling guilt. But not one part of him was bad. Ren was a good male, so incredibly good. Under all those awful shadows crowding him, surrounding his soul, was a warm, gentle light. His true nature, the sweet fox I'd known as a kid. "Yes, I trust you."

His gorgeous eyes seemed to grow brighter, and an animalistic sound rumbled through his chest. He gripped the bottom of my shirt and lifted it over my head. "I'm gonna take care of you, so good. So fucking good, butterfly." My bra came off next, and he lowered himself down on top of me, kissing me sweet and gentle this time. "You're so beautiful, so fucking perfect," he said as he trailed kisses along my jaw. "So warm. Every part of you. I just want to take care of you, protect you." He kissed along my jaw. "I want to give you everything you need, make you feel good. I want all of it, Jaz, all of you."

He wasn't holding anything back. Ren was laying it all out for me, and it was exhilarating and terrifying. I would have done almost anything to hear those words from him a few weeks ago. And I won't lie, it felt nice, really nice to hear them even now. I could almost believe the feeling welling up inside me, but what I was feeling was a memory. Those feelings were gone, and I'd be doing us both a disservice by believing the lie my brain was trying to tell me.

You didn't just fall in love that easy. It wasn't going to be so simple. Wanting it and actually having it were two very different things. This was lust and affection for a male I'd known since I was just a kid, that's all I was feeling in this moment.

He sucked my nipple into his mouth, and I arched beneath him, a groan leaving me as I gripped his hair tighter. Ren wasn't in a hurry, he licked and sucked and toyed with me.

"Wanted to do this for so long," he said, holding my other breast in a firm grip. "Night after night, you naked in my house. Fucking torture, Jaz. Having you wrapped around me, kissing you, holding you, then letting you leave?" He tilted his head back and held my eyes as he licked the taut peak. "I fucking hated it. More than once I had to stop myself from following you, from snatching you up and carrying you back to our den."

I shivered at the way his voice had grown more gravelly, like his fox was blended with it. He kept his eyes on me as he spread my thighs. I shivered again when his hands slid to my sensitive inner thighs. His thumbs moved in circles over my jeans, up and down but not high enough, not where the ache had deepened and I was so damn slick. He kissed between my breasts, over the tattoo there, then down, sucking kisses over my feverish skin until he reached the waistband of my jeans.

I was panting now, squirming. He held my eyes as he popped the button and dragged down the zipper, a question in his eyes. I nodded. Yes, I wanted whatever he wanted to do to me. Badly.

I lifted my hips, and he dragged my jeans down my legs and tossed them on the floor, then his hand, fingers splayed, slid up my thigh and rested on the top of my pussy. He licked his lips and, over my panties, dragged his thumb along my slit.

"So fucking wet, butterfly. Jesus." He watched what he was doing as he pressed his thumb deeper, adding more pressure, grinding it against me. I whimpered, and he looked back up at me. "You don't even know how long I've been wanting to taste you. I hurt this sweet pussy last night, and now I'm going to worship it."

Oh fuck. I was close to combusting. I watched as he hooked his finger around the fabric plastered against my aching flesh and dragged it aside.

"Fuck," he groaned. "Fucking look at you," he said, his voice a low growl. He leaned in, his eyes lifting to mine, and he tasted me, a soft lick that had me trembling.

His tongue was hot against my swollen, slick flesh and I couldn't take my eyes off him. His had drifted closed, and he did it again, his muffled groan filling the room. He gripped the sides of my underwear and tugged them down my legs and tossed them aside, then he was back. He gripped my legs, his hot, rough-skinned hands roaming my inner thighs, squeezing and holding me wide as he lapped at me again.

"Fuck, baby."

"Ren..."

His mouth covered my pussy then, his lids fluttering as he tasted every inch of me, a look of bliss on his stunningly handsome face. I wanted to watch, but I couldn't hold myself up any longer, not when he sucked on my clit and gently slipped one of his thick fingers inside me. My ass lifted, arching against his mouth, wanting more, needing more.

But he kept the same pace, building the sensations in slow, steady waves that made me gasp and rock my hips, lost to the pleasure building inside me.

"You gonna come all over my hand, butterfly?"

I whimpered again. "Y-yes."

"Yeah, you fucking are," he growled.

He slid in another finger and increased his pace, finger-fucking me deeper. "Shit...ahhh..."

"I wanna feel my mate's pussy squeezing my fingers. Give it to me, Jasmine. Give it to me now."

I screamed and rocked uncontrollably against his hand as I came all over his fingers like he told me to. When I collapsed back, panting and trembling, he climbed off the bed and shucked his jeans. His long, thick cock jutted from his muscled body, and he curled his fingers around it, stroking slowly as he came back to me, between my spread thighs.

"Need to fuck you now, baby. Need it so fucking badly," he choked out.

"Please," I said, my voice husky from my screams.

He grabbed something off the floor, a condom. He tore the foil and rolled it on. I couldn't believe I was doing this, that we were doing this. It could all go so fucking badly, but I wanted him. My desperation to feel him inside me again surpassed everything else.

He covered my body with his, his skin so scalding hot. I wrapped myself around him instantly, wanting him as close as he could get to me. His kiss was hungry, urgent, and I returned it with the same. Maybe this would be enough, maybe I didn't need to love him. I liked him, cared about him, wanted him beyond all reason, craved him. Maybe that could be enough.

And then I couldn't think anymore because he reached between us, taking his cock in hand, and rubbed against my slick opening.

"Tell me if you want me to stop," he said. "If you're too tender."

I nodded, but that wasn't going to happen. I felt empty in a way I never had before. Emptier than the night before in my room.

He pushed inside, just the head, and I dug my nails into his shoulders. The stretch a little sore but mostly magnificent.

"Okay?" he asked, staring down at me.

I nodded again, and he gave me more, forcing a wanton groan from me. There was that dull ache, but the pleasure far outweighed it. I spread my thighs wider, my hands sliding down to his ass, and I lifted my hips.

He growled and rocked, filling me with every inch of him. I looked down between us, and he did the same, and we both watched as he slid out, then thrust back in. The sigil I inked on the base of his cock disappeared inside me, and something about that was so incredibly hot. Ren growled.

"Oh fuck," I rasped. "More."

He hooked an arm under my hips, the other delving into my hair, this thumb sliding along my jaw. He held my eyes as he slid out and thrust back in. My lips parted, noises coming from me I'd never made before, unable to hold any of it back with his eyes locked on mine. They silently demanded I hold nothing back, that I give him everything I was capable of giving him, and I had no choice but to obey.

His mouth took mine, swallowing my cries and feeding me his groans and growls as he fucked me harder, faster. It didn't take long before he had me gasping, my next orgasm rushing up on me. My inner muscles clamped down on him, and he lifted his head, still sucking at my lips, tasting my tongue while he watched me lose it completely. When my pussy gripped him again, he started fucking me faster, and I flew to pieces, crying out and shaking under him as I came again.

"That's it, baby. Fuck. That's it," he growled.

A moment later he throbbed inside me, his entire body shaking, his muscles jumping as he pounded into me, coming with me. Sharp canines extended from his top jaw, and the sight, the thought of them puncturing my flesh, of him marking me, just made me come harder.

I knew he wanted to do it, his fox shone from his eyes as he ground into me, as he trailed the sharp points along my shoulder and shook even harder, from holding himself back, from fighting the instinct roaring inside him telling him to do it.

"I'll never get enough of you," Ren rasped against my ear. "Not fucking ever, butterfly."

Chapter Twenty-Nine

Ren

I GASPED, my hips thrusting forward, pushing deeper into my precious female's mouth. Water sprayed my back and dotted her face as she looked up at me, eyes hot as she sucked me hard.

We'd spent the last week staying close. Really fucking close.

I hadn't let her spend a night away from me since I found her here. I'd had her in every room of the house except my bedroom. But I had plans to make her comfortable in there, and I was starting on that when she left for work this morning.

I cupped her gorgeous face, sliding my thumb around her stretched lips. Nothing had ever felt this good. Everything we did together was the best I'd ever had. Fuck knows how I'd resisted biting her, marking her, mating her, like I was desperate to.

"Fuck," I groaned when she cupped my balls and massaged. Her other hand moved between her thighs, rubbing her clit, getting off on sucking me. The sigil she'd inked on my cock close to her lips but not making it into her mouth. "You close, baby?"

She whimpered and nodded. Her eyes were wide, and as she stared up at me, I hated that I still saw the distance there, the disconnect, but I did. She wanted me, got hot for me, she *cared* about me, but when her lids fluttered, closing for several seconds, then opened again, I got hit with a sadness in those green eyes, fuck, an apology. Because she knew exactly what I saw, what I searched for every time her eyes met mine.

I didn't want that from her. Shit, I couldn't look into her eyes and see that. I fucking hated it. I didn't want pity, never from her. I shifted, about to pull out. I didn't want it like this.

But then she swirled her tongue around the head of my cock and sucked it down deep with another whimper. I wasn't prepared, and the needy sound sent me over the edge. She knew I was about to come, and like the other times she'd taken me in her mouth this week, she gripped my hips and didn't let me retreat, letting me come down her throat.

Panting, I pulled out of her mouth, hooked her under the arms, and pressed her against the wall. Swiping her hand from between her legs, I thrust two fingers inside her. "If I see pity in your eyes when we're getting each other off again, butterfly, I'm gonna spank your sexy ass until it's bright red."

At my growled words, she cried out, coming hard for me. Her hips rocked against my fingers until she was done, then she fell against me, wrapping her arms around my shoulders. I held her up, kissing the top of her head, then straightened and tilted her head back so I could kiss her swollen, sweet-as-fuck lips. "You hear what I said? Don't want you thinking about anything but how good you feel when we're together. That's it, nothing else."

She wrapped her arms tighter around me, her head to my chest. "I wasn't thinking about anything else." She was lying. She might not be able to feel the mating bond between us, but I did. Yeah, it was muted because of the block, but what she was feeling still flowed to me.

"I love you," I said. I couldn't hold it in, it had to come out.

I'd said it every day, and I'd keep saying it. One day soon, she'd say it back. I believed that. I had to believe that. Then I squeezed her ass and swatted it, making her laugh, taking the tension away when the seconds stretched out and I knew today wouldn't be that day.

I'd asked her again who fucked with her mind, but she wouldn't tell me who blocked her love for me, like she knew that as soon as she did, I'd go after them and tear them apart. I'd make them fix it even if they died trying. She was right. No one should be able to fuck with people's emotions that way, even if she had asked for it.

We got out of the shower and I hooked a towel around my hips and grabbed the other before Jaz could so I could dry her off. We may not be officially mated, but my fox didn't care. We needed to take care of her. Bathe her, feed her, protect her, and make her come as many times as she could handle, and today when she left for work, we'd make sure our den was perfect for her as well. We'd make sure my room was completely different, that she was the only female to see what was in it, touched the things in it—new paint on the walls, new bed, new bedding. New bedside tables and two new dressers were arriving this afternoon as well, one for Jaz. And I was going to put the bed on the opposite wall so the room looked nothing like it did now.

"So you'll be gone all day?" I asked as I rubbed the towel over her shoulders and arms. My gaze slid to her mouth. God, her mouth was addictive. I wanted to kiss her all the fucking time.

"Yeah, I have a busy schedule. A couple new clients as well, and things always take longer with newbies." A smile curled her lips. "You know I can dry myself."

"Where's the fun in that?" Jesus, I wanted her again. I wrestled my need into submission. It wasn't easy.

I finished drying her, which was more torture for me than her because everywhere I trailed the towel, I wanted to taste her skin afterward. She smelled different now. My scent was all over her, and both my fox and I loved that as well. It filled me with pride, made me feel fucking ten feet tall

She headed to the small room we'd been sleeping in, and I followed, pulling on a pair of jeans, then hovered at the door, watching her dress. "You want anything in particular for dinner?" I asked, eating up every smooth, inked inch of her.

She glanced up at me. "Mags wants to hang out. Have a girls' night, so I'll stay at home tonight."

I gripped the doorframe tighter, and my claws punched through the tips of my fingers. "Will I see you tomorrow?"

She seemed distracted and nodded absently as she tugged on her boots, then proceeded to gather all her things that had accumulated over the last week, stuffing them in her bag so there'd be nothing left of her except her scent. I didn't like it. My fox clawed at the ground, growling his displeasure, but there was nothing I could do. If I pushed her, she'd retreat. She was already scared she'd hurt me, that if this didn't work, she'd have to leave and it'd fuck me up. She was right, of course, but I couldn't let her know that.

We'd had a healing session last night, and I knew she'd seen how big my feelings were for her. She hadn't said anything, but she'd been quiet afterward, at least until I'd tugged her ass to the edge of the couch, yanked down her panties, and ate her pussy until she screamed out my name.

Some might call what I did avoidance, but they'd be wrong. I just didn't want her getting in her own head about us.

She hitched her bag over her shoulder, and the little comma butterfly that'd been hanging around her lately fluttered around her head as she tilted it back to look up at me. "I better take off."

I nodded as I gripped the side of her neck and used my thumb under her chin to keep her head tilted back, then I bent down and kissed her, hard and deep, before hooking her around the waist and holding her close so her body was pressed to mine, branding her with my scent as best as I could. While she was away from me, I wanted everyone to know she was taken. I couldn't mate her, so this was the next best thing.

I lifted my head a little and gave her another small kiss, then another, then forced myself to step back when what I wanted to do was toss her on the foldout and fuck her over and over again until she loved me back.

Her face was pink and her lips were puffy again. "Fuck," I said low.

"What?" She licked her lips.

I groaned. "I'm two seconds away from tossing you back on the bed, butterfly."

She grinned, pressed a kiss to my bare chest, patted it, then stepped around me. I followed her to the door, trailing her like a sad fucking pup. She opened the door and looked back at me.

Her smile softened. "You know...you're the best male I've ever known," she said.

I didn't know what to say. There was this look in her eyes I couldn't read.

"I just...I wanted you to know that," she added, then she flashed me another smile and walked out, closing the door behind her.

Jasmine

I stared up at the house, so tall and forbidding. The look on Ren's face, the tone of his voice when he told me he loved me again this morning and I couldn't return the sentiment was branded on my mind. I was hurting him, and I couldn't do it anymore.

I took the steps and knocked, wrapping my arms around myself, feeling chilled even though it was warm today.

The door swung open. "Hey," I said, like an idiot, not entirely sure of the reception I'd get.

Xavier tilted his head to the side. "This is an unexpected surprise."

"Sorry to just show up at your door like this." I hadn't fully decided I was going to come here until I walked out of Ren's place this morning. But despite what Xavier said, that this couldn't be undone, I had to try. He was my only hope.

"Do you want to come in?"

"Please."

He stepped back, and I walked inside.

He motioned to the living room, and we took our seats. Sitting back, he crossed his legs and sighed, a look on his face that said he was far from happy. "I assume this isn't a social call?"

I'd offended him when I turned him down, obviously. "About what happened between us. It wasn't you—"

"No, then what was it?" he asked, and his voice was colder than I'd ever heard it. "You're just not a fan of money and power? You don't like presents or being treated like a princess? Or being flown all around the world? I could have given you anything you wanted, Jasmine. Anything."

This whole arrogant routine was new. "I'm sorry if I hurt you—"

"You didn't hurt me. You wasted my time." He tapped the arm of his chair impatiently. "And now you're here wanting something else from me, yes?"

I shifted in my seat, guilt filling me. "I'll pay you whatever you want."

"And what is it you want, little witch?" He sat forward, eyes narrowed. "What made you come here this morning, reeking of another male, an animal no less, mouth still swollen from...well, it's not hard to guess. What made you think you could walk in here and ask anything of me after you led me on, then brushed me aside like nothing?"

I didn't want to be here. Everything inside me was telling me to get the hell out of this house, but he was the only person who could help me, if it was even possible at all. He said it wasn't, that he couldn't reverse what he did, but I had to try. "I really do like you, Xavier. There just wasn't...a spark between us, you have to know that. You had to feel that as well. And I...I think I know the reason for that. Ren, the male I came to you about, well, it turns out, he's my mate, and what I did...it was a terrible mistake."

"The fates may have selected you for him, but that doesn't mean their choice was correct."

"It was, Xavier, I know it was the right choice. I need to know, is it possible...if I spend time with him, if I try to strengthen the bond between us, can I fall in love with him again?"

"That's what you've been doing? Why you smell of him?"

"Yes." I didn't like the way he was looking at me. He looked angry.

"No," he said without flinching. "Even if you mated with him, let him mark you, nothing would change. You can like him very much." His brow arched. "You can lust after him, but I think you worked that out for yourself. But no, there can never be love, not for him."

Oh goddess. "There has to be a way to reverse this. Please, Xavier. Please, there has to be something you can do—"

"I've always believed people should stick to their convictions." His gaze slid away, his jaw pulsing like he was grinding his teeth. "I told you what would happen. I told you it would never be undone, and now you're here begging me to undo it." His face was stone, but something had shifted in his eyes. "You disappoint me, Jasmine. I thought you were different than the rest. I thought you were a female of your word. But you're just like all the others, like her, aren't you?"

Would never be undone. He didn't say *couldn't*. Not this time. "Who are you talking about? I'm like who?"

He stood suddenly and paced away. "You truly want the

barriers removed, despite all the pain your love for this male caused you?" he said, his back to me.

"Yes."

He paused. His hands were balled into fists, his knuckles white under the strain. "Is love truly worth it, the risk of all that pain, do you think?"

"Yes, absolutely. I didn't think he could ever love me back, but I was wrong. When it's real, Xavier, when it's returned, there's nothing else like it," I said, ready to fall at his feet and beg him to help me. "Is there anything you can do? Anything?"

"When your sister and Ronan found each other...I was surprised," he said, ignoring my question. "A male such as me with a female, not to just sate a base need but because he held affection for her. Because he...loved her." He shook his head. "I didn't think it was possible. Not after all he'd been through. If he can find that, then a male like me, a male capable of those kinds of emotions should be able to as well, shouldn't he?"

"Yes." I stood and moved closer to him. "I absolutely believe there is someone out there for all of us, Xavier."

His gaze sharpened, filling with a determination that had me taking a step back. "Doing what I'm about to ask of you is...going against my own convictions. Convictions I've lived by for almost all of my life, but I've been contemplating it for some time. Then I met you and began thinking more seriously about it, about what my life would be if only I'd allow myself to truly experience it. To move forward, though, I need someone like you to help me. If I do as you ask, you will do something for me?"

"You can do it? You can remove the barrier?" Hope fired through me.

His lavender eyes were so dark now they looked black. "Not easily, and at a great cost to me. Are you willing to pay a great cost in return?"

"What do you want me to do?" I'd do anything to be with Ren, to give him all of me. I was desperate. This week with him had been one of the best of my life, but every day he told me he loved me was like a slice to my soul. I was hurting him, not being able to give him that in return, and it was killing me.

"I have walls of my own. Walls I built as a child, some to protect myself." His gaze hardened. "Some my mother forced me to build. They limit me, restrict me. They stop me from being the male I was born to be, from finding the happiness I find I now crave. Whether that's a female of my own, or something else entirely, I'll never know if I stay as I am. I want the walls gone, but to break them would be dangerous, without help." He stared me down. "Which is where you come in. I need you to use your healing abilities on me to repair the damage done by..." His jaw pulsed. "By my mother, and the wounds breaking the walls down would leave, and in return, I'll remove the walls I built for you."

There was no need to think about it. I wanted that part of me back. I wanted my love for Ren back. "I'll do it. I'll help you."

"How long will it take? To get me through the worst of it?" he asked.

"I won't know until I see the damage," I said, not willing to give him any time frames. Depending on what he had locked away, it could take months of coming here to work with him. "It could take some time."

He took several steps closer. "Can we speed up the process with more intensive, more frequent sessions."

"It's possible, but I wouldn't advise it. That kind of healing shouldn't be rushed—"

"But it can be done?"

"Well...yes, I suppose."

He cupped the side of my face, and when I tried to jerk back, his other hand shot up and grabbed the other side of my head, holding it firmly between his hands.

I tried to pull away again. "What are you doing?"

"Ensuring you don't renege on our deal. You will stay here until it's done."

"No...I can't do that." I tried to pull away again, to fight him off, but he wouldn't let me go. Pain burst through my head, and it felt as if my entire body was thrust to the side.

"Yes, you will."

Everything went dark.

Chapter Thirty

Ren

I DRAGGED the old mattress from my bedroom and carried it outside, then hitched the new one up from the back of the hearse and carried it inside and to my room.

The paint was dry. I'd had a fan heater blowing in here all night. The blue walls had been replaced with a deep sage-green color, the closest I could find to Jasmine's eyes. I loved it. Tearing off the plastic, I tossed the mattress on the bed frame I'd pushed to the opposite wall, and the two new dressers I'd ordered had arrived earlier. I'd put one where the bed used to be and the other by the door. I'd also grabbed some new curtains from the store. I didn't know about that kind of shit, but the gray ones the shop assistant told me to get looked pretty good.

The dryer beeped; the new sheets and duvet cover were dry. They'd smelled too chemically straight out of the bag, and my fox hadn't liked it. I didn't know what time Jaz was coming over, but I wanted everything perfect when she did. I wanted her to walk in here and feel like she'd stepped into a brand-new room. Ours. No trace of anyone else. Honestly, I couldn't even remember anyone else. Those drunk nights, burying my pain in whoever wanted me, had dissolved into nothing, into a bad dream long forgotten, replaced by Jasmine.

I grabbed all the trash from the new bedding and scooped up the mattress plastic from the hall, then carried them out to the dumpster. After one final look around the room to make sure everything was perfect, I got started on dinner. I'd been without her an entire night and never wanted to spend another one away from her again. Jaz never said she'd be here in time to eat, but I liked feeding her. She always seemed to get hungry around midnight as well, usually after I'd made her come and she'd napped for a little while. She'd get up and stand in front of the fridge in one of my shirts and pick at whatever she could find. I fucking loved watching her eat before she came back to bed, then fell asleep, sated and full. It eased my fox and me both.

I had a chicken in the oven and was chopping tomatoes for the salad when my phone beeped. Wiping my hands, I grabbed it from my pocket.

Jaz. My stomach instantly tightened, my heart fucking swelling in my chest. How the fuck had I not seen exactly who she was the minute I laid eyes on her? It felt impossible that I hadn't known.

I quickly tapped the message open.

Butterfly: I'm sorry, Ren, but this thing between us just isn't working out. I'm leaving. It's the best for both of us. You'll see. Please don't come looking for me.

I blinked down at those words, scanning them over and over again, as if they'd reshape and reform into something else. But they didn't. *This thing between us just isn't working out.* I read it again, and again, trying to get it to make sense, because everything inside me said it didn't.

But it was right there. She'd typed out the words, her nails tapping against the screen like they did when she sent a text. Nails that had scored my skin, fingers that had glided over my body, thrust into my hair and held me to her as if she were afraid I'd pull away.

I thought about yesterday morning, the way she'd looked up at me in the shower. The look in her eyes that had been a blade in the chest, that distance, that look of pity. Affection, not love.

I grabbed the edge of the counter when my legs fucking buckled beneath me.

Jaz had left.

She was gone.

Still, I sprinted from the house and out onto the street and didn't stop until I ran into the house and up to her bedroom. I shoved open drawers. Her stuff, it was still there. It was all still there. I fisted my hair. What the fuck was going on?

"Ren?" Mags stood at the door, sympathy in her eyes. "She messaged you?"

"This doesn't make sense, all her stuff—"

"She asked me to pack everything up, that she'd come for it sometime soon."

"When?"

She shook her head. "She didn't say. I'm sorry...goddess, Ren, I'm so fucking sorry."

The door opened and Willow walked in. Violet was asleep in her car seat, and she handed the seat and Violet to Mags, then strode toward me. I stumbled back. I couldn't do it. Willow was my witch, my best friend, I was her familiar, but I couldn't do this. If I let her comfort me, if I let this pain inside me take hold, I'd fucking shatter all over again—and this time there would be no coming back from it.

Willow stopped and held up her hands as if she were trying to soothe a wild animal about to bolt, and I realized my claws had punched through the ends of my fingers, that my canines were extended, and with every one of my panted breaths, my fox's growls resonated through my chest so loudly I wasn't sure I could speak, even if I had the words.

"Jaz just needs some time. Give her some time. You two have been pushing things pretty hard this week. She's just spooked, that's all," Willow said and took another step closer. "The bond between mates is stronger than anything. Block or not, she'll come back. I know she will."

Willow was wrong. Whoever it was who created the block inside her, had a power stronger than the mating bond. My mate fleeing from me and asking me not to look for her was proof of that.

Fur sprouted across my chest and stomach, my thighs. My fox was taking over. The last time he managed to do that was after Edward's evil spirit was exorcised from my body and the knowledge of what I'd done had been too much.

My fox dulled the pain. He didn't understand complex emotions and was all about instinct. He was the reason I'd survived as long as I had without Jasmine's healing touch.

He snarled and exploded forward, taking over my body and making it his, and I surrendered to it, letting him.

"Ren!" Willow called.

But we were already at the bottom of the stairs and out the door, flying along the street toward the forest.

You are the best male I've ever known. I just...I wanted you to know that.

She'd said those words to me before she left yesterday, and I'd been too stupid to realize she was saying goodbye.

Jasmine

My head throbbed as I blinked into the darkness. Where the hell was I?

The last thing I remembered was talking to Xavier.

He'd grabbed me, held my head, then everything went dark—

I quickly sat up. I was still in his house. Still in the living room where I'd been talking to him. There was no sign of Xavier now, and dim light filtered in through the large windows, the night filled with stars. Had he taken the walls down in my mind, is that why I'd passed out? But I didn't feel any different. I stumbled to my feet and walked out of the room. The lights were on in the foyer. I looked at the clock on the side table. It was after ten. Ren would be worried. He'd be wondering where I was.

I rushed to the door, every instinct in me screaming to get the hell away from here as fast as I could. I gripped the door handle and yanked the door open—

A scream tore from me, and I stumbled back.

Nothing.

I was looking out at nothing.

No stairs, no path, no houses. No street. There was only darkness.

Nothingness.

"I wouldn't walk out there if I were you. You might never make it back."

I spun around. Xavier was walking toward me. He looked wrong, as if I were looking at him through heat waves on a hot summer day. He kept coming, then stepped through the strange distorted-looking air, stopping in front of me.

"What the hell is this?" I said, backing away from him, putting more space between us.

He slid his hands in his pockets. "You're in my world now, Jasmine. And in my world, no one can see or hear you, and you can't leave it unless I allow it. This is where you'll remain until you finish the work you're here to do."

"What the hell are you talking about?"

"I told you when you first came to see me that I wasn't an explorer of realms, that I preferred it here. Well, I created my own realm. It's exactly like my home in every way, except no one can ever find it."

Ronan could create alternate realms—their home was in one—and apparently so could Xavier. "You don't need to keep me here. I promise I'll help you. I'll come back as many times as you need. I will. But I can't stay here. I have people who love me. My family" —*Ren*—"will be worried about me. They'll come looking for me."

He stared at me, his eyes terrifying in their utter lack of empathy. "They won't find you. No one can until I choose it."

"What about Ronan?"

"Why would he ever come looking for you here? Ronan thinks that when he developed his emotions, he became like me. He thinks my emotions have always been as developed as his now are. He also sees me as a friend. He'd never think I could do anything like this."

His words slid over me like ice. "*Thinks* you've developed emotions?"

"I'm good at imitating them. Although I'm not completely without them. I was, after all, raised by my human mother. I'm definitely not a victim of my specie's defect, losing them completely through maternal abandonment. No, my lack of emotion is due to my own actions. I omitted the extent of the blocks I've created in my mind, which is why letting you leave isn't an option. If we start and you decide not to come back, there is a chance I could lose my mind all together."

"I wouldn't do that."

"I can't risk it," he said simply and without sympathy. "We'll begin in the morning." Then he strode away through the quivering wall between realms, leaving me there and ignoring my screams to let me out.

Chapter Thirty-One

Ren

My apartment felt cold.

I quickly chugged back my coffee and dumped the mug in the sink. I'd only been gone a couple days, but it felt as if all traces of life in this place had faded to nothing. I got back from Philly late last night, but it'd been a fucking waste of time. I thought she might have gone home. She and Zinnia still owned a house there, but Jaz hadn't been back, and none of her friends there had seen or heard from her.

Shoving my feet in my boots, I grabbed my keys and walked out, got in the hearse and headed down to Daisy's, parked and walked into the house. Everyone was already here, and they'd all been searching for Jasmine frantically.

Iris looked up when I walked in, her familiar, Nia, at her side. "You look exhausted."

I didn't need sleep, couldn't sleep, not until Jasmine was home. "Any news?"

She shook her head.

Warrick leaned against the wall, Draven and Ronan there as well. Bram stood behind Mags.

"Nothing," Rose said. "None of us have heard from her since she asked us not to contact her for a while."

The last two weeks, I'd called and texted her repeatedly, and she hadn't picked up or replied, not once, which I guess should be expected if she was trying to get away from me, but then why had she asked her cousins to give her space? For the first few days she'd written them back, even if her replies had been stilted and distant. But for the last week there'd been no word from her at all. Wanting space or not, that wasn't Jasmine. She put others first, always.

I shook my head. "No, fuck this, she wouldn't do that shit, not to any of you."

I'd tried to trace her phone and so had Bram's brother, the male was good with that kind of thing, but not even he could find her.

She'd vanished completely.

"Zinnia's due back in less than a week," Mags said. "She wouldn't miss that, she'd be here."

Jasmine always spent the days before organizing something for her sister—a party, a girls' night...fucking something—then she'd wait for her to walk out of the forest. She wouldn't miss that. The fact she wasn't here now, planning her sister's homecoming, said more to me than anything else could. No matter what she thought about me, she wouldn't ignore everyone else, and she wouldn't miss the opportunity to make a fuss over her sister coming home.

Iris stiffened. "You think something else is going on?"

"None of this feels right," Rose said, her face going pale. "But I just assumed..." Her gaze slid to me.

They'd all thought the same thing, that she was staying the hell away from me, that she needed time to herself to heal.

"No, you're right. This isn't about her needing space, she wouldn't let us worry like this. Something's seriously wrong,"

Mags said. "I think someone or something is stopping her from contacting us."

Daisy grabbed Art's hand. "Who would do that?"

"Fuck." Willow stood. "And she definitely said nothing during your sessions, anything, some kind of clue of where she could be?"

I shoved my fingers through my hair. "If she had, I would've said."

"Shit, I know," she said, her hands shaking. "I'm just...fuck."

I glanced at Mags. She nodded. They needed to know everything.

"There's something you don't know," Mags said. "She wasn't just looking for those missing souls because she wanted to help Zinny, she was searching because when they were at Limbo's gate, Death demanded Jasmine find them, he said if she didn't, there was a risk Zinnia could be stuck there."

"Goddamn it," Else said.

"She knew there was nothing anyone else could do, so she kept it to herself. Only me, Bram, and Ren knew about it. We did what we could to help."

"While she was looking, she talked to some powerful people," I said. "And I just have this feeling..."

"You think someone she talked to did something?" Willow said, the horror in her voice, on her face, almost sending me over the edge.

"I don't know." I didn't know fucking anything and I was on the verge of losing my fucking mind. The mating bond, the connection between us had been growing and strengthening by the day when she'd been here, but now? "She's still alive, I feel it, but it's...the connection's muted." Similar to the last time she passed out, but so fucking faint now it terrified me. I clung to it, like I had that night in her bedroom. It was my lifeline, because if I could still feel it, no matter how faint, it meant she was still alive. She was still breathing—she was still with me.

Bram nodded, the other males in the room nodded, grunted,

obviously knowing what I was describing from having mates of their own. It didn't matter that we weren't officially mated, I'd spent enough time with her, holding her, kissing her, inside her, that we were connected on a deeper level.

"Family's everything to her," Daisy said, lips quivering. "She wouldn't just leave...oh goddess."

No, she wouldn't; not even to escape me. If she could come home, she would have, I was positive of that.

"We're still hunting for her," Warrick said. "And we won't stop until she's home."

The hounds were born trackers, with abilities that went beyond using scent to find their target, and so far, they'd had no luck either.

"I know we assumed she was concealing herself, but I think wherever she is, there's some kind of power masking her," Willow said.

"I think you're right," Mags said and stood. "Me and Bram will head to Agatheena's. She might be able to help us."

The witch boasted that she knew everything; I only hoped she felt compelled to prove it, because Jasmine was in trouble. I knew it down to my bones.

"We need to widen our search," Iris said.

Draven nodded. "I'll get the pack to search the forest. If she's in there, we'll find her."

"And I'm gonna hunt down every person she's been in contact with over the last couple of weeks," I said.

"Everyone keep in contact," Willow said.

I nodded and walked out.

I would find her. I would bring her home.

I stared down the street at the massive brownstone. My second stop. Zara Harris, the female Jaz and Rome had met with, assured me she hadn't seen Jasmine since the day they stopped by her place. She seemed believable enough, but I didn't trust anyone.

I'd spent the last two days going through Jasmine's client list from the last couple weeks. It was easy enough for Talon to hack her online booking system. I'd tracked every one of them down, but no one had set off any major alarm bells.

I focused back on the house. I'd been here for several hours now, watching. I'd met Xavier several times. We'd briefly spoken, once at Ronan's place, but other than that, I knew nothing about the dhampir—except, of course, that the fucker had been interested in Jasmine and had taken her out on a date. That he'd kissed her. The steering wheel groaned as I gripped it tighter. I didn't know much about Xavier's powers, so I'd called Ronan to get any info he had on the male. He said Xavier was private, he'd never told Ronan what he could do, but it was known in their circles that he could travel through metaphysical planes, but Ronan wasn't sure if he could create his own. Ronan and his sister, Luna, were both extremely powerful. Ronan could block entire streets, could create entire realms that existed inside another, and could move around completely undetected, which meant, Xavier could be capable of fucking anything. He also ran a business from his home, but Ronan didn't know what that business entailed, again, because the male was private.

I scanned the front windows. I didn't fucking trust him, and not just because he wanted Jasmine. I just, I didn't like the guy.

A female rushed along the street, and I sat up straighter when she took the stairs to Xavier's front door and knocked. She seemed jittery, nervous, her hands shaking. When no one answered the door, she checked her watch, then knocked again, harder this time.

It was coming up nightfall, and there were lights on in a couple of the front rooms. I'd assumed he was home.

Her shoulders slumped when there was still no answer. She turned, about to leave when the door was wrenched open. Xavier stood there, rumpled, a harried look on his face.

I couldn't hear what they were saying, but the female looked upset. Finally, he shook his head, and shut the door. She covered her face with her hands, shoulders jolting with her sobs.

Grabbing a small pack of travel tissues from the glovebox, I shoved the car door open and jogged along the street and through Xavier's front gate.

The female looked up and sniffed. "If you're here for an appointment, don't bother, he just cancelled mine."

I held out the tissues. "Are you okay?"

"No." She took the one and used it to dab at her eyes. "I was really hoping to get this over with today."

"Yeah, me too," I lied. "I can't believe he's cancelled."

Fresh tears slid down her cheeks. "God, I'm a mess. Do you have a broken heart as well?" She flushed and bit her lip. "Sorry, I shouldn't have asked that."

I stilled. "No, it's fine. And yeah...I do." I forced myself to appear calm, instead of grabbing her and demanding to know what the fuck she was talking about. "So do you know how it works?"

She shook her head. "Not really. I found out about him through a friend of a friend. I just know it works. I never knew blocking someone's emotions was possible." Her face fell. "God, I just want it over with, you know?"

I nodded, my heart fucking racing.

Blocking emotions.

"Anyway, thanks for the tissue," she said and scurried past, heading down the street.

My fingers curled into fists. It was Xavier. He was the one who'd locked away Jasmine's love for me, who'd fucked with her mind.

I took the stairs and banged on the door, fighting down my rage. When Xavier didn't answer straightaway, I banged again, harder.

The door was yanked open when I pounded on it a third time

and the male filled the doorway, the scent of lemon floor cleaner and bleach drifting out behind him, as if he'd doused the place in that shit. His gaze hit me, and something shifted through his deep lavender eyes. "What do you want?"

My fox's hackles lifted instantly. We really didn't fucking like this male. I wanted to barrel past him, to barge into his house and call for Jasmine. I wrestled my anger and fear down. "You're a friend of Ronan's. I'm Ren, his sister in-law's familiar." I held his gaze, not letting him look away from me. "Their cousin Jasmine's my mate."

He blinked several times, rapidly, but otherwise didn't move, didn't react. "Okay," he said. "And I will repeat. What do you want?"

"Can I come in?"

"No. Say what you're here for, then leave. I'm busy."

I wanted to grab him by the throat and fling him aside. "You know Jasmine."

"Yes, I do." His head tilted to the side. "We dated."

"You had one date, and then she realized she just wasn't that into you...since she already had a mate, something she didn't recognize because you'd locked away her ability to feel it."

"I blocked the pain your rejection and neglect caused, at her request," he said.

"And then you swooped in and tried to take her for yourself."

"Is that why you're here? To stake some kind of claim? Because you're wasting your time. Jasmine turned me down when I asked her out again. Jealousy is unnecessary."

I wanted to plow my fist into the asshole's smug face. "The reason I'm here is because she's missing, and she hasn't answered any of my calls or texts."

"Unsurprising, since she feels nothing for you."

It took all my strength not to stagger back a step. I ignored his verbal strike. "Are you sure you haven't seen her?"

"Are you suggesting I've somehow lost all cognitive recognition?"

"No, I'm suggesting that you're hiding or withholding something from me for some reason, and I strongly suggest that if you have seen or heard from my mate, you tell me right the fuck now."

"I assure you, I have not. And if I had, the decision to contact you or anyone, for that matter, would entirely be hers."

Then he shut the door in my face.

Every instinct in me roared to get inside, that he was hiding something. I felt for the buzz of magic, something I was more than familiar with, but there was nothing, and no wards either. I'd seen a human security system, though, a panel inside by the door, an alarm. I strode back to the hearse and got in.

Then I pulled my phone from my pocket and hit Willow's number.

"Any news?" she said before I could say a word.

Wills had been struggling with Jaz's disappearance, all her family had. But Willow had Violet to think of, and she was limited to how much time or how far she could go searching.

"No news. But I've got this...shit, it's more of a gut feeling than anything else. It's probably nothing, but I...I can't seem to let it go..."

"Jasmine's your mate. Your instincts are invaluable. Listen to them. Do you need me to come to you?"

"No, I'm on my way to you now. I need your help with something."

"I'll be waiting."

I disconnected and started the hearse. I just needed to pick something up from Willow, then I was coming straight back.

Xavier had to leave sometime.

Jasmine

. . .

The door to the basement room opened again and Xavier walked back in, the strain of our session today was still etched on his face.

"Who was at the door?" He'd left me in this room several hours ago. I was just thankful he'd kept me here in the "real world" for a little while instead of his metaphysical, monstrous one. He'd showered and changed, but that was the only difference I saw in him since he left to see who was banging on the door.

"A couple clients. I sent them away. Let's get back to work."

I didn't want to. I didn't want to delve into Xavier's pain again, not yet. It was too much, too awful, but when the session was over for the day, he'd put me back where no one could see or hear me—and where monsters hid in dark hallways.

The small comma butterfly fluttered over to me now and landed on my shoulder, offering me comfort. The little guy had tracked me here before Xavier trapped me in this house, and somehow he found me. I'd been feeding him water and overripe fruit from the food Xavier had given me.

"Ready?" Xavier said.

There was real fear in his eyes. "Yes." He was seriously struggling but determined to do this no matter the cost to him, or me.

The first barrier he dropped was two weeks ago, during our first session. It had been intense, to put it mildly. The emotions had been so strong, they'd almost knocked me over.

He obviously needed time to recover, but he insisted on doing this as fast as possible. I wanted this over as well, so I could go home to my family, to Zinnia who would be home in a matter of days—to Ren. But that meant my magic was almost constantly drained, leaving me weak, and fucking defenseless.

Xavier was a desperate male, emotionally unstable, confused and conflicted, and right now he was capable of anything.

I wrapped my arms around his waist and had to stop myself from shuddering. I didn't want to touch him, be near him—I didn't want to be anywhere near what was inside this male. Something lurked deep, something that sent ice down my spine, and I'd been getting closer to it with every wall he dropped.

But I had no choice, so I poured my powers into him. It flowed through every part of him, seeking out the biggest wounds. Xavier had lived in this house all his life, and he'd compartmentalized his emotions like an internal replica of his home. He'd locked unwanted emotional responses in different "rooms" of his mental house. There were blind spots and rooms I couldn't even get close to, and behind those thick barriers, Xavier was still the little boy he'd been when he'd built them. So vulnerable, so scared, and so incredibly sad.

Within moments, I was shaking. The emotions of the little boy were agonizing, and tears immediately sprang to my eyes. "Do it," I rasped.

He shuddered a moment before his arms wrapped around me, and he dropped the walls, exposing another emotional wound.

I whimpered and held him tighter. "You're a good boy, Xavier. Y-you did nothing wrong. You didn't deserve to be punished."

He gasped, and his arms tightened around me, so tight it was painful.

"You didn't deserve it," I said again.

He made an inhuman sound, like a wounded animal, and I braced. His nails elongated, digging into my sides through my shirt, making me cry out.

Another wall dropped.

Oh goddess. It was bad. I thought I'd find abuse or neglect, but what I found was something else entirely.

A longing for blood, for death, a need to hurt and torture, flooded me. Pushing back against my powers was the desire to kill, so strong inside him, it was like riding a raging tide.

This was Xavier. This was his true self. Evil in its purest form flowed from him into me. I cried out again, trying desperately to heal the wounds he'd exposed, but terror made it impossible to do what I needed to. This was what his mother had forced him to wall in—the sadistic monster that he truly was—to protect herself and those around him.

He was panting, and the way he hissed, the strange sounds he made, I knew his fangs had extended.

"Yes," he snarled. "Fuck."

I tried to push away, but he held me with inhuman strength. His fangs scraped along my shoulder, tearing the fabric. "No!" I screamed. "Don't...p-please."

A dark chuckle rumbled through him, then he struck. His fangs pushed through the flesh at my throat and agony fired through me. It hurt, oh goddess, it hurt worse than anything I'd ever endured. A dhampir's bite, like a vampire's, could give pleasure or pain. He chose this, he chose pain.

If this was the end, I was glad he chose the latter. I'd take pain over pleasure from this monster every single day if I had to endure it. The last time I experienced pleasure was with Ren, and that's how I wanted it.

He pulled more deeply from my vein, and I tried to scream, but the sounds wouldn't come. My vision blurred and my head spun, my limbs growing heavy and weak.

He pulled his fangs from my throat suddenly, his tongue rasping across my flesh. "You want to feel the love you have for your mate again, witch?" He pressed his mouth to my ear. "Then I'll give it to you."

I did. I wanted to feel my love for Ren again, so badly I ached, but the damage the block coming down would create would be vast. I'd seen it in Xavier, and I wasn't strong enough to heal myself, not like this. But I didn't care. If I was going to die, I wanted to do it loving my mate.

"Are you afraid of the pain?" He tilted my head back and stared down at me. My blood smeared his lips. His lavender eyes were black now that he'd fed.

I shook my head.

He brushed my hair away from my face. "Liar. I can hear your heart beating. It hurts, but you can heal yourself, Jasmine. I know you can. I've watched you do it."

He'd watched me?

"You look confused. Let me enlighten you. When I was trying to discover if you could help me, I decided to do an experiment, to see if you could use your gift on yourself. So when you were tucked up in your bed, I went to your favorite field, the one you often go to, the one you told me about on our date, where your tiny familiars live, and I poisoned them."

I whimpered, and a tear streaked down my face. He'd done it. He'd killed them. Even when the walls inside him had been intact, locking the monster in, the evil had seeped out of him.

"You're such a pretty little thing, even more so when you cry. I had planned to free you after you healed me, but now I think not." His head tilted to the side. "I finally know my own mind, Jasmine." He tapped the side of his head. "It's all in here now, just how it was before Mother forced me to lock it away, back again in glorious vivid color, down to the minutest detail." He grinned, flashing his sharp fangs. "And I know exactly what I want to do with you. Should I tell you?"

I wanted to pull away, to shake my head, but I'd lost too much blood, all I could do was lie helpless in his arms.

"I want to make you suffer in every way it's possible to make a being suffer, for no other reason than the pleasure it will give me. I want to feed from you until you are close to death. I want to fuck every hole in your emaciated body, torture you to the edge of death, then bring you back from the brink, and do it all over again."

I managed a pathetic jerk in his arms.

"Are you game, little witch?"

"N-no. Please, please let me go." I knew begging was pointless, he probably enjoyed it, I'd seen inside him, but my will to live didn't give a fuck about common sense.

He made a tutting sound and gripped the sides of my head. "Being trapped here will hurt all the more while you're missing your mate, won't it, Jasmine?"

His power pulsed inside my head, seeking out the walls he'd created, and a moment later—they crashed. An emotional wound tore open inside me, and I screamed.

My body jerked to the side, and he tossed me back into the alternate reality he'd created, still in the same room inside his house —but where no one could ever find me.

Chapter Thirty-Two

Ren

X AVIER JOGGED down the stairs at the front of his house, got in his car, and sped off.

I watched the car until it turned at the end of the street and disappeared from view. The house was dark, no movement coming from inside. He'd turned off all the lights when he left, which I hoped meant he planned on being gone a while or, better yet, all night.

Xavier said he didn't know where Jasmine was, but there was something about him that set my fox off, something inside me that told me I needed to be here. I sure as hell didn't trust that male. Staying tucked in the shadows, I pulled my phone from my pocket and hit Willow's number.

"You there?" she said.

"Yeah, and I've got my opening. Still not feeling any magic. There definitely aren't any wards, just the security system."

"Piece of cake," she said.

Tugging the hood of my sweatshirt up, I ran across the street. I hadn't told Willow the address or whose house I was breaking into because she'd be here in a heartbeat. Yes, she could look after herself, but being her familiar meant her safety was my priority. It didn't matter that she didn't need my protection, that she never really had, but that instinct never went away, and she knew better than to force me to divide my protective instincts between her and Jasmine. If my female was in there, worrying about them both could cause me to make a mistake.

"Cakewalk," I said, my heart beating faster as a surge of anticipation, of urgency filled me.

"Now I want cake," she said.

"When don't you?"

"Good point. You sure the house's empty?"

"It's empty." I'd been watching the place for hours, and no one else had come in or out until now.

"Okay, this is just your straightforward, run-of-the-mill B and E. Don't loiter. Don't fuck around in one room too long. Keep your ears pricked. You need to be scenting constantly—"

"I got this, Wills." Her fear for me was bleeding down the line.

She was quiet a beat. "I know you do."

I rushed up the steps. "I'm at the door," I said low, scanning the street.

"You know what to do," she said.

Yeah, I did. I picked the lock easily, then shut the door behind me. No sounds, no movement greeted me. I quickly got out the vial, popped the cork, poured Willow's blood onto my palm in an X, then hovered it above the security panel. "Ready."

The hum of magic from Wills's blood was instant. She recited the spell, and I repeated it. As soon as I finished, the small red light flashing on the panel died.

"It worked." We'd never tried anything like this. We'd heard of it being done, the witch–familiar connection acting like a kind of conduit. Familiars were often sent in by their witches to do tasks for them, especially animal familiars, since they could go places undetected, but we'd never tried.

She sighed in relief. "Thank fuck. Let me know when you're out."

We disconnected, and I shoved my phone away and walked deeper into the house. If he knew something about Jasmine that he wasn't telling me, I'd find it. My fox's ears were up, listening for any sign of life in the big, old house. I sniffed the air, searching for her scent, but I wasn't getting anything, not under a layer of floor cleaner and bleach. No one used that much of the stuff unless they were trying to mask something—or someone.

I headed for the stairs. I'd start at the top and work my way down.

I wasn't leaving until I'd searched every single room in this house.

&.

Jasmine

I wrapped my arms around my knees tighter, shivering, my muscles seizing as waves of agony radiated through me. If I didn't die from the emotional wound Xavier had torn open when he released my feelings for Ren, then he'd make me suffer when he came back.

There was no escape from this world he'd created.

In this realm, it was as if I were in his mind. The rooms where he'd locked away the most vulnerable parts of himself in his psyche, where he kept his deepest fears, were locked here as well. He had walls so thick in his mind I couldn't get through, but here, in this realm, those rooms were guarded by monsters, dark shadows with sharp teeth and claws.

I didn't know if he knew they existed. I had to assume he

avoided those places here the same way he did in his mind. The house was big enough that he'd never have to go to those rooms, in this realm or the one he occupied.

A creak came from outside the door. I stilled.

Oh goddess, he was back.

I dragged my upper body off the floor and somehow struggled to my feet. The handle rattled, followed by the sound of metal on metal, the handle turning again—the lock clicked.

I stumbled back several steps, fear, adrenaline spiking so high black dots danced across my eyes.

The door swung open and the light flicked on.

Ren.

I ran to him.

Ren

I walked deeper into the basement room. The walls were covered in bookshelves. Old books by the looks. The guy liked globes, and there was a blackboard with chalk drawings on it. Symbols of some kind. A mat had been rolled back and there was a sigil configuration on the floor.

I stayed clear of whatever that was painted on the floor and pulled out my phone, taking pictures of it and the blackboard. I'd never seen anything like them. I took a few more of the room, then shoved the phone back in my pocket. Striding to the desk, I searched the drawers, then moved to the shelves. There was nothing here. Nothing that would lead me to Jasmine, anyway. Why the fuck was my gut telling me this was where I should be?

The urgency tightened in my chest. "Jasmine?" Her name fell from my lips, desperation making me say it again, louder this time, then again—until I was roaring her name, not caring who the fuck heard me.

ॐ

Jasmine

A sob escaped as Ren lost it, calling my name until his voice was raw.

I lifted my hands to his face, but they went right through, like he was a ghost. "I'm here. I'm right here."

He looked straight ahead, looking through me. His chest heaved as he stared unseeing right at me. "Where the fuck are you, butterfly?" he choked. "I need you to come home to me."

With the walls inside me gone, the love I felt for him flowed through me and straight to him. "I'm here!" I cried out again, willing him to see me.

With a curse, he turned away, walking out the door. I ran after him, out into the hall, trying to make him see me, hear me. He shut the door after him, locking it again. His head tilted, and he listened for a moment, the house still utterly silent, then he kept walking. I ran in front of him—and he walked right through me.

"Ren! Look at me." He stood by the security panel, pulling a vial from his pocket. "Please, Ren."

He smeared blood in an X on his hand and lifted it, hovering over the keypad, then muttered a spell. The light above it began flashing again.

"No...no, don't leave. Don't leave me here."

He looked back, looking through me again, then yanked the door open.

"Ren! Don't leave me!"

He walked out and shut the door behind him.

I banged on it with all my strength, but he didn't hear me, he didn't come back. I ran to the window and watched as he tugged up the hood of his sweatshirt and strode away.

My legs gave out. I sat there in a heap on the floor, not sure for how long, staring into the darkness, fighting the monsters in my own mind, the ones telling me that there was no way out, that I should just give up. Fighting the still gaping wound inside me that Xavier had made, too weak to repair it.

No.

Ren would come back. He would. He'd find me. I had to believe that.

I just had to stay alive.

The nudge of a soul reached me. It didn't mean me any harm, but it was persistent.

Pushing myself to my feet, I took off my necklace and cuffs and placed them on a small table. A woman appeared in front of me. She was tall, her dark hair streaked with gray and pulled back in an elegant bun. She was wringing her hands, fear in her eyes.

I knew who she was instantly. "You're Xavier's mother."

She nodded and moved back, waving her hand for me to follow. Not all ghosts could verbally communicate, some could only show me things. I followed her up the stairs to the second floor, to the room at the end of the hall. It was locked. She pointed above it, and I reached up and found the key above the doorframe.

She walked through the door, and I quickly unlocked it and followed.

The room was feminine, adorned with lots of mauve and pink. This was one of the rooms Xavier avoided in his mind, a room he never went to in the real world or here in the one he'd created. I walked deeper into the bedroom and tripped on something. I looked down and bit back my cry. A skull, an old one by the looks. Feeling sick to my stomach, I got down on my knees and looked under the bed. Several bodies, clothing hanging off their bones, were stuffed under it. Xavier's mother nudged me, and I got up and followed her to what had once been her dressing room. It was large, dust- and cobweb-covered clothes hanging off the racks.

And on the floor were more bodies.

So many.

I stepped over the remains of humans and animals. Dead bodies that had been left where they fell to rot, their bones and clothing all that remained of them.

Images flashed through my mind: Xavier's mother showing me what happened here, what Xavier was, what he did. All of it. Everything channeled through me like a horror movie.

I grabbed for the wall, sick to my stomach.

These were Xavier's kills. Before his mother forced him to lock away his sadistic cravings, this was where he brought his victims. It would have been so easy. One moment they would have been in his home, the next, hidden by his power, confused, alone.

Until a little boy with black curly hair and wide lavender eyes found them. A little boy who looked sweet and innocent but was anything but. He'd lead them to this room. His mother's room, a replica of it at least, that he'd created and used as a dumping ground in his own special playground.

More images flashed through my mind; his mother was trying to help me. Showing me where I needed to go.

"Thank you," I said.

He avoided this room, but I wasn't safe in here. There was only one place he wouldn't be able to find me. I had caught a glimpse of it during one of our sessions.

Xavier had a complete blind spot—his conscience—and it'd been walled off so thoroughly in his mind that he had none to speak of, which was why he'd spent most of his life mimicking others and their emotional responses. He hadn't liked the way his mother made him feel when he did bad things, so he'd made sure he didn't feel it anymore. He'd locked it in the attic of his psyche, before he'd even created this secret realm he'd trapped me in. After he'd locked that part of himself away, the true monster he was came to being. Over the years, he seemed to have forgotten about the attic. I doubted he even thought about it at all when he'd created this alternate realm. The biggest risk was that it might not exist here at all, but I had to try.

To get to it, though, I'd have to pass the monsters he had guarding the top floor and the other rooms he kept walled off.

His mother turned toward the door, then back to me, panic in her eyes.

Xavier was home.

The sound of a car door closing outside jolted me into action.

I had two choices: stay here and endure Xavier's torture and hope I survived long enough for Ren to find me, or somehow get past the hall of monsters on the top floor and make it to the attic, if it even existed here at all, and hope Xavier couldn't find me.

The door opened and closed downstairs.

Adrenaline spiked, giving me the surge of strength I needed. Xavier's mother waved toward the door urgently.

"Thank you," I said to her again, then spun away, out of the room, taking the next two flights of stairs as fast and quietly as I could.

I looked up to the fourth-floor landing. The darkness up there was dense, suffocating. My magic might've been all but drained, but I was a witch, a Thornheart, and I sure as hell wasn't weak.

I thought about Zinnia, about Willow, and Mags, about Rose and Iris, and Daisy and Else. All of them warriors in their own way. I may not know how to fight these monsters physically, but I was clever and resourceful.

I rushed back down to the third floor. I didn't have much time. Xavier would be going down to the basement to check on me soon. Flinging doors open, I searched until I found what I needed. Then I rushed back up the stairs.

It was now or never.

When I reached the fourth-floor landing, I held up the candles I'd found in one of the bedrooms and drew on my weakened magic, whispering the spell to light them. Fire flared. The candles were thick, real beeswax, and they cast a decent pool of light around me.

A scuttling sound came from just ahead, followed by claws being dragged along the wood paneling lining the hall. I was still weak, my legs unsteady, something the fear and adrenaline pumping through me wasn't helping. This was a long shot, but in fairy stories, dark equaled bad, and light, good. No, the world wasn't that black and white, but to a child, that was truth, that was why Xavier had monsters protecting the most vulnerable parts of his mind in darkness.

An adult might have created locks, steel walls, or buried them deep underground. But Xavier had been a child when he created the barriers in his mind and this alternate realm in his house—somewhere he could be himself, where he could do the terrible things he craved before his mother found out what he was.

And what was a child scared of? Monsters, under the bed, hiding in the shadows waiting to pounce.

"Jasmine!" Xavier bellowed downstairs.

Fuck.

I took a step forward into the dark hallway, holding one of the candles behind me and one in front, so I was surrounded by a ring of soft light. Oh goddess. I could hear the monsters moving around me, surrounding me. I held the candles higher and stifled my scream.

One of them slithered in front of me, the light from the candle casting shadows on its hideous face. Its pupils blew wide from the light, and it hissed, lifting a bony arm to protect its eyes.

"Get back," I said. "Let me pass."

It didn't move. Jagged teeth filled its wide mouth, its eyes huge in its gaunt face. I could feel another close behind me, could hear it breathing, could smell its sour breath. The one in front of me lifted a dirty claw-tipped finger, arm outstretched. It breached the light around me—

With a shriek and a hiss, he scuttled back.

I was right. Light hurt them, scared them. I took another step forward, chancing a quick look behind me. The others were gathering closer, but stayed back after seeing what happened to their friend. As I advanced, the one in front moved back.

Something swiped at my ankle, slicing flesh, and I bit my lips to stop from crying out.

I needed more light. I lifted one candle high and lowered the second. I could feel blood trickling down my leg. There was another quick swipe on the other side, where the shadows were thicker. I kicked out and made contact with something. It growled and snapped its teeth. I couldn't let go of the candles, and I had to walk carefully. If the flames went out, I was screwed. So far they hadn't figured that part out, and I was praying to the mother that they didn't.

I was close to the end of the hall, where I assumed the attic stairs would be—if there were any at all. The monster in front jerked forward, teeth flashing. I waved my candle at it, and it slithered back out of the light. Something stood against the wall ahead. A ladder. It was misshapen and narrow, but it led up to a manhole in the ceiling.

The monster in front of me slid to the side to escape the light, joining the monsters behind me. I turned so my back was to the ladder. Almost there.

When I finally bumped into the wall, I carefully placed the candles on the floor so the light formed a wide circle around me. "Stay the hell back," I said and gripped the ladder with a hand behind me, stepping onto the first rung backward. It was awkward, but I wasn't giving them my back, not yet.

One of them swiped at me with a snarl, still staying clear of the ring of light. The candle flame wavered perilously. His black, red-rimmed eyes watched it do this, and he waved his massive clawed hand at it again. It disappeared for a moment, then flared back to life.

The monster looked at me, and I was positive it smiled.

Fuck.

He swiped at it again and the flame went out, dousing one side of the ladder in shadow. I spun and scrambled up the narrow rungs, screaming when it was wrenched to the side beneath me. I didn't look down and shoved open the attic door above me. It swung open as the ladder was wrenched from the wall. I grabbed the lip of the opening just in time, dangling and kicking my legs as the monsters below jumped for me, their claws scratching, gouging, their growls and hisses deafening.

With a cry, I dug my toes into the holes left from where the ladder had been attached to the wall and hauled myself up. Then with the last of my strength, I lifted the trapdoor that was lying on the attic floor and slammed it shut after me and shoved the steel bolt across.

Silence filled the room.

I spun around, searching the small space. Dim light came through the only window. I was above the peaked roof at the very top of the house, a tiny little attic room all on its own. It didn't seem to be connected to the rest of the house. I could make out a large wooden trunk against the wall and bed in the corner with an upturned crate beside it. A wooden truck with chipped blue paint sat on top, and there was a stack of papers inside the crate and crayons scattered around it. I grabbed the papers.

Xavier had drawn these when he was a child. His mother had shown me images of him up here. I looked through the pictures, and my stomach turned over. Drawings of death, red crayon spurting from a stick-figure cat's stomach. Decapitated people.

Monsters like the ones in the hall.

I'd been right. They were a creation of his child's mind, then manifested in the realm he'd created. But this room felt different. The hum of Xavier's power was gone. The air didn't move like heat waves rising from scorching sand. If I was right, and he'd blocked this room from his mind completely, then he definitely might not know this attic was here anymore. And if he didn't know it was here, perhaps I'd left his realm? Could this tiny little blind spot in his psyche be safe?

The bolt in the trapdoor rattled, a low growl echoing from below.

Or not.

Fuck.

I rushed across the room to the wooden trunk and heaved and shoved and finally got it on top of the door. I had no idea if that would hold, but it was all I could do.

I straightened and turned.

Then it hit me. There was *light*. It was dim, yes, but light all the same.

I rushed to the window and looked out. No blackness. No nothing. It was still before dawn, but the street, the houses, they were all there, but there was also no getting down from here, not when I was four stories above ground.

I was out of Xavier's prison, but now I was in another one. If I had time to regain my strength and my magic, there was a lot I could do, but flying or telepathy wasn't one of them. "Goddamn it."

Something moved beside me, and I spun around. The comma butterfly had found his way to me. His orange wings fluttered madly. I felt his love, his relief at finding me again. He'd been with me a while now, and he wouldn't have much time left before he needed to find a place to hibernate or he'd grow weak and die. He'd already been with me longer than should be possible. I held out my hand, and he landed on my palm.

"Hello, my little friend. I'm so glad you're here." He may not understand the words, but he understood the feelings that went with them. What I was about to attempt was a long shot, but it was all I had. He'd been with me when I was with Ren; he knew what I felt when I was around him. I thought of Ren now, letting those feelings flow from me—of course what I felt now was so much bigger, so much more, but the vibrations would be the same. "Bring him to me," I said. "Find him." It would take him at least a day to make it home, maybe longer.

His little wings fluttered again, and he lifted off my hand.

"Thank you," I whispered and watched as he flew through a broken panel in the louvered air vent above the window and disappeared—hopefully, to make the long journey back to Ren.

All I could do now was wait and hope like hell that he understood what I wanted him to do.

That he had enough fight left in him to get to Ren and bring him to me.

Chapter Thirty-Three

Ren

THE CEMETERY WAS quiet and oppressively dark even though we were only a few hours from dawn.

Willow, Iris, Rose, Mags, Daisy, and Else all stood in a circle. They'd been like that now for most of the night. They were calling on their ancestors, asking for help, for anything that could lead them to Jasmine.

Else was shaking, losing strength. She couldn't do this for much longer, and going by the desperation in their voices as they chanted, and the pain on their faces now, they weren't getting the answers they wanted.

I strode away. If I didn't move, I'd fucking roar, or tear something to pieces. They didn't need to see me like that. I'd caused that family more than enough worry over the years. Jasmine was their family, but she was my mate, and I needed to bring her home.

Another day had passed, though, with no news. The hounds, the wolves, Agatheena, they all had nothing. I burst into a run, needing to burn off the rage, the fear inside that I'd never find her, that she was lost to me forever. She'd put me back together, and whether she wanted me or not, I would bring her back. Somehow, I would find her.

Chest heaving, I stopped and paced back and forth, only realizing in the moment that I'd come to Jaz's field. I dropped my ass under her favorite tree, for no other reason than she'd been here. I pulled out my phone and worked my way through every picture I had of her, and fuck it hurt. I ached for her. Her absence was a crater in my chest. Squeezing the phone tight, I closed my eyes and again prayed to the mother. I wasn't a witch, but if anyone could help, it was her. She didn't answer, of course, she never did.

My breath burst from my lungs when something flowed in the center of my chest.

Jasmine.

What the fuck? I narrowed my focus to where I felt her, where the mating bond pulsed inside me steadily.

It flared again. I didn't fucking move, didn't breathe—

It happened a third time.

I shot to my feet. That feeling, it wasn't muted, not anymore. She was using magic to reach out to me, she had to be. "Fuck. Fuck!" My female needed me, was calling me, I was sure of it, and I had no fucking clue where to look. I paced, my body primed to run, but I had nowhere to go. I made myself breathe. *Think.*

I swiped my phone open again and scrolled through the pictures I'd taken at Xavier's house. That fucking house. There was something about it, something off. My instincts still told me that's where I needed to be. I hadn't looked at the pictures since I got back yesterday. Now I searched each one, enlarging them, studying every inch, looking for something...fucking anything.

I zoomed in on the next one. I'd taken it in the basement room. What the fuck was that?

Something tickled my cheek. I swiped at it and tried to make the image bigger. Was that? There was a shadow, a shadow that looked—

I zoomed in again. The unmistakable outline of a cheek came into focus, a chin, lips. I knew those lips, that chin, I'd run my fingers over that cheek. It was faint, ghostly, like looking at a faded reflection in a pane of glass.

Jasmine.

But not a ghost, because I felt her. She was alive.

Something brushed my cheek again. I tore my gaze from the screen. A small butterfly darted and dived around my face. What the hell? It was dark, butterflies weren't out at night. It fluttered and swooped around me, not stopping. It was the same kind of butterfly that had been with Jasmine the last time I'd seen her. I was sure of it. It was darting away, then coming back, then darting away and coming back, like it...like it wanted me to follow.

My heart pounded harder in my chest. Was this really what I thought it was? Could Jaz have sent one of her little familiars to find me?

The butterfly darted around me again, flying away, then coming back. I held out my hand, and it landed. "I know where we're going." I cradled the butterfly in my hands and ran for my place and the hearse. She was in that fucking house. He was keeping her there and using his powers to hold her prisoner. That had to be it.

I jumped in the hearse, and the butterfly stayed on my hand as I started the engine and roared out onto the street. I needed to keep my cool or I'd wreck the fucking car. *Fucking focus.* I was getting her out of that house, and if I had to kill that fucker to break her free, I'd do it.

If he'd hurt her...

I gripped the steering wheel tighter.

Then I'd draw on all the twisted fucking shit Edward had forced me to do when he'd possessed me. I'd risk it all, even my sanity, and I'd get her back.

I'd make him bleed.

I'd make him scream.

And I wouldn't stop until I had my mate home safe.

The drive to the house felt like an eternity. I had no plan, but I knew I couldn't just storm in there like I wanted to. If I did that, he could vanish with Jasmine. He could take her away, hide her behind another of his blocks, and I'd never find her.

Parking the hearse a block away, I got out, pulled on my hooded sweatshirt, and followed the little butterfly to the house. Sticking to the shadows, I stood across the street. All the lights were on, and my fox tensed, tilting his head to the side, listening.

Xavier was raging. The butterfly danced around my face, trying to get me to follow. I ducked low and sprinted across the street and down the side of the house. Peering through the window, through the lace curtains into the living room, I spotted him. Xavier's face was red with fury, and he was screaming Jasmine's name. He paced away, then back, then called for her again. His hands and chin were stained with blood. My claws punched through the ends of my fingers, my canines descending.

I told myself she was okay...because she had to be. If she wasn't, he wouldn't be raging like he was.

He couldn't find her. Somewhere, somehow, she was hiding from him in his own house.

I forced myself from the window and let the butterfly guide me. He darted up, flying higher until I lost sight of him in the darkness. *Fuck.* I strained, trying to see. The clouds parted, and light from the nearing dawn cast a dull light across the side of the house. There. He was swooping and swerving, struggling, then he rounded the corner back to the front of the house. I eased around the corner, looking up in time to see him disappear through the vents above a single window at the very top, in the small peaked tower in the middle of the roof.

Something moved behind the window.

A shadow.

Jasmine.

It had to be. She was in there. I knew it with everything in me.

The bond between us bloomed then, so big and bright and beautiful.

I ran around to the side of the house, searching for a way to get up there. I couldn't go inside and risk him trapping me as well, or finding her. These old Victorians usually had a way to escape in case of fire.

Around the back, there was a narrow steel ladder attached to the side of the house above the porch. Jumping, I grabbed the edge of the porch roof and swung up, then walked as quietly as I could across the roof. The ladder was rusted, neglected. I gave it a strong tug and, thankfully, it held. I scrambled up the next three stories as fast and as quietly as I could, not wanting to linger on the old thing.

My fox retreated, not a fan of heights, but he didn't go too far. He was as desperate to get to our female as I was. Everything inside screamed for me to run to her, but I couldn't. I had to balance carefully on the ridge to make my way to the front of the house.

When I finally reached it, I crouched down, gripped the edge of the roof and dropped over the side, planting my feet on the window ledge.

The window opened, and I swung into the room, landing with a thud on the wooden floor. My hand went to my knife as my eyes adjusted to the darkness.

Then I saw her.

Jasmine stood several feet away, staring back at me, eyes wide. "You found me," she rasped, her lips quivering.

Then she ran at me.

Jasmine

. . .

My body collided with Ren. One of his arms locked around my waist, and the other went to the back of my head. He dropped his face to the side of my throat and breathed deep, scenting me, his fox rumbling in his chest when he exhaled.

"Thank fuck," he growled, his muscles trembling.

I fisted his shirt, holding him to me, afraid to let him go, afraid this wasn't real and he wasn't actually here. Tears stung my eyes, then spilled over.

Ren slid his fingers under my chin, tilting my head back. His gaze searched mine, then a shuddering breath fell from between his lips and I knew he saw the truth of what I felt for him shining back. He saw my love for him burning bright.

"Butterfly," he said hoarsely, then his mouth was on mine, kissing me with a hunger and desperation, so sweet and fierce that my heart ached. His big hands held my face, breath puffing from his nose, our lips fused. He dug his fingers into my hair, kissing across my cheek, along my jaw. "You're okay," he rasped. "You're okay, baby." He said it over and over, I knew to reassure himself as much as me. Finally, he lifted his head. "We need to leave."

Taking my hand, he started toward the window. Rain tapped against the roof. I tried to limp after him as another gush of blood trickled down my leg, a cry falling from my lips.

"You're bleeding," he said and crouched beside me before carefully taking my foot in his hands. He hissed as he studied my sliced-up feet and ankles, the gouges along my calves. Fury rolled off him. "Xavier did this?"

I shook my head and motioned to the trapdoor. "No, his monsters."

"Demons? There are demons in this house?"

As if I'd called to them, their roars echoed from below, the trunk lifting an inch off the ground before crashing back down. I jumped, my nerves shot from an entire day and night of listening to them.

Ren pulled his knife free, growling.

"Not demons. Creations of Xavier's mind. They've been here since he was a child. His mother's spirit came to me, she showed me everything. This was where she put him when he did…" I shuddered. "Terrible things. He's a sadistic monster, Ren, and his mother was afraid of him. Eventually, she made him lock away that part of himself. This house, at least the alternate reality he created within it, is exactly how he's compartmentalized his emotions. All the rooms on the top floor are where he's locked away the things he doesn't want to deal with. It's all up here, and up until a couple days ago, so was his bloodlust and desire to inflict pain."

"He released it?"

"Yes. That's why he had me here, to help him heal the wound left when he dropped each internal wall. When I wasn't healing him, he threw me into the realm he'd manifested as a child, a duplicate of his house."

Ren frowned. "But Xavier's raging downstairs looking for you. Why can't he find you up here?"

"Because he locked away all memory of this room and the pain it represented when he was a child. It's a blind spot to him, which is why it doesn't exist within his invisible realm. This room is outside of it, and why you were able to find me."

"Jesus."

"Up until yesterday, when he released his true nature, he hadn't tried to hurt me, but as soon as he let that wall drop, he changed…and I, I knew I had to find a place to hide."

"I'm going to fucking kill him. Right after I get you out of this place." His fingers trembled as he gently cupped the side of my throat. "There's no way you can climb out of here like this, though. And I won't risk carrying you, not while the roof is wet and slippery."

"And the moment we go through there"—I motioned to the

trapdoor in the floor—"we're back in Xavier's fucked-up little world with the monsters he created." More roars and growls came from below. "They only exist in his realm. They shouldn't be able to pass through into this one, but I didn't want to risk it. They're afraid of light, it hurts them, but there's nothing up here we can use, and I left my candles at the bottom of the ladder."

His eyes blazed, his chest expanding with his rough breath. "You could've been killed."

"But I wasn't."

He strode to the trapdoor and the trunk on top, about to shove it aside. "Wait here."

I grabbed his arm. "I'm not even sure they can be killed."

He shoved his fingers through his hair. "I want you out of this place right the fuck now." He checked his front pockets, then the back. "My phone. Fuck. In my rush, I left it in the hearse." He looked up at me. "If the only way to get you out of this room is through the house. I'm not leaving you here, not even for a moment. We'll use the daylight to our advantage."

"But if we go through the house, we'll still be stuck back in Xavier's hidden realm."

He flashed me a grin. "Xavier knows you're here somewhere, but he sure as fuck won't be expecting me."

The idea of Ren taking on Xavier terrified me, but I also knew what Ren could do. My pulse raced. "It's almost dawn."

The gold of his eyes glowed in the dim light. "There's just enough time to tend your wounds." He cupped my chin, running his thumb across my lips. "Then I'm getting you out of here and taking you home."

Chapter Thirty-Four

Ren

I SCOOPED Jaz up and carried her to the bed in the corner of the room, crouching down in front of her. Blood still seeped from some of the deep scratches. Her wounds badly needed dressing. What they really needed was one of Else's or Mags's balms, but for now I would do what I could to keep them clean.

I checked my knife strapped to my thigh. The monsters below us were scratching and crashing into the trapdoor, making the trunk jump, desperate to get to Jasmine. And it was only a matter of time before Xavier remembered this place with all the shit he'd done to his head the last two weeks. Jasmine wasn't safe. I reached back and tugged off my shirt, then used my knife to cut it into strips.

"You'll get cold without your shirt," Jaz said, as always worrying about everyone else before herself.

"I'm good, baby. I run hot." I grinned at her, trying to remove the worry from her eyes. "Pretty sure you already know that. Woke

354

up every night you were at my place with these ice blocks you call feet tangled with mine."

Her lips curled up and some pink hit her pale cheeks. "Fine, you got me there."

I carefully wrapped a strip of my shirt around her calf, another around her ankle, then her foot, tucking it under. "Not too tight?" She shook her head and watched as I did the same with the other foot. "That's all I can do for now." And I fucking hated it. Every one of my instincts demanded I get her to safety and have her wounds properly tended, then find her food and feed her. I couldn't do any of those things.

The shadow on her face vanished as the sun finally rose higher, light glinting off her blond hair.

It was time.

§

Jasmine

"Stay behind me," Ren said as he gripped the iron ring that would open the trapdoor. "If things go wrong, you run back here and lock yourself in, okay?"

"Okay," I lied, because he needed to hear it.

"You're lying," he said, eyes narrowing, seeing right through me.

I cupped his jaw, leaned in, and kissed his gorgeous lips. "If something goes wrong," I said against them, then lifted my head, "there's no fucking way I'm leaving my mate and running to safety."

His eyes flared, a rumbling sound coming from his chest. "Say it again."

"My mate," I whispered.

His eyes drifted shut for a moment and he breathed deep for several seconds before they opened again. "That's right." He took my chin in his fingers. "Mine." He flashed his teeth. "So how the fuck did I not know how stubborn you are? It's literally a trait of every female in your family."

I grinned. "Thank you."

His gaze went to my mouth, and his eyes darkened. "I will protect you, Jaz, and sometimes you might not like the way I do it, but you're mine, and you come first always, even if me doing what is necessary fucks you off." His gaze dropped to my smiling lips. "And even if you're being cute."

I planted my hands on my hips. "Are you saying you'll make me do what you want?"

"I'm saying, if shit goes wrong, even if I'm bleeding out, I will pick you up and throw you back up here whether you like it or not."

My cousins had shared how possessive mated males could be, and no, he hadn't marked me yet and made it official, but that didn't seem to matter. Going by the arrogant line of Ren's jaw and the steel in his eyes, he wasn't joking. I also knew arguing would only make him more determined. For now, while he was like this, I needed to tell him what he wanted to hear when it came to this stuff and work around it. That sounded better than lie to his face, but he was out of his mind if he thought I'd hide up here while he bled out. "And I'm the stubborn one?"

He grunted.

Yep, he'd gone full cavemen. "We'll cross that bridge if we get to it."

"Jasmine," he growled.

"Fine," I lied.

He growled again and shook his head, because yes, he knew exactly when I was feeding him a bunch of crap. "Stay behind me," he said again and opened the trapdoor.

The snarl of monsters reached us before we saw them, followed by their shrieks and the sounds of them scuttling back as the morning light from the attic flooded the section of hall below us. Ren gripped the lip and swung down, then motioned for me to follow. Snarls echoed around us, the monsters now hiding in the shadows, watching, waiting for an opening, for a chance to get to us.

I did the same as Ren, dropping down, and he caught me, placing me carefully on my feet. I searched for the candles, but they were gone. *Shit.*

Ren spun suddenly and kicked the door closest to us open, more light flooded in from the room, forcing the monsters to retreat and allowing us to move forward. He kicked open door after door, flooding the hall with more and more light. Until we were almost at the end. Ren kicked the last door open, but there wasn't enough light to reach the stairs, and definitely enough distance for the monsters to pounce.

I yanked off my sweater. "Stand back."

"What are you doing?"

"Creating light." I held my sweater out in front of me and whispered the spell to create fire. My sweater ignited, and spinning it like a lasso over my head, I grabbed Ren's arm and made a break for the stairwell. The monsters shrieked and swiped at us but dove for the darkness, pressing themselves into the corner.

As soon as we hit the landing, their growls and howls stopped, and I tossed my burning sweater on the floor.

Ren stomped the fire out. "Nice work." He hooked me around the waist and kissed me. "Now you need to hide, and I'll deal with Xavier."

"If you call for him, he'll have warning. I need to be the one to get his attention."

"Not fucking using you as bait, Jasmine."

"Yes, you are." He shook his head, and I wrapped my arms around his waist and tilted my head back, looking up at him. "You won't let anything happen to me. It's our best chance and you know it." His fox flared in his eyes, he was about to tell me no. "I'm doing it, Ren." I didn't have an inner animal, but like he said, I was a Thornheart and stubborn as hell, and I made sure he saw that in my eyes.

He cursed. "You don't get anywhere near him. You call him and you get the fuck back and leave the rest to me."

"I can do that."

He grabbed my hand again, and we crept down the stairs. The closer to the bottom we got, the louder Xavier's ranting became. There was a crash, and he roared. When we hit the bottom of the stairs, Ren motioned to the living room, and we slipped along the wall and rushed in.

Xavier lay on the floor outside the realm he'd created. He was shirtless, sweating and shaking, obviously struggling badly with his new exposed emotions now that he'd been left to live with them for a full day and night, and desperate for me to heal him.

Ren stood behind the wall beside the door to the living room. Grabbing my arm, he pulled me to him and kissed me. "I love you," he said, staring into my eyes, like he had so many times, knowing I couldn't say it back, and not knowing if I ever could.

Cupping his whiskered jaw, I held his gaze in return. "I love you, too."

He sucked in a sharp breath.

I smiled up at him, gave his hand a squeeze, and stepped into the doorway, staring out at Xavier's distorted figure. "Looking for me?"

His head lifted, and with a growl, he shot to his feet. Shaking, he strode straight for me, moving from one realm to the next as if it were nothing. His fangs had elongated, his features inhuman with pain and also hunger. "You've been a very naughty little witch, Jasmine, hiding from me," he said panting.

"I know it's crazy, but the idea of letting you torture me to the point of death only to bring me back from the brink and start all over again wasn't really something I was in a hurry to experience," I said.

He stopped, his lavender eyes so pale and bright and full of twisted rage that I wanted to step back, retreat. "You shouldn't be able to hide from me, not in my own world. I searched everywhere for you. Tell me where you were?"

He took a step forward, and I took one back into the living room so I was even with Ren. I could see a tiny bit of apprehension in Xavier's eyes. He didn't know how I'd evaded him, and he was obviously afraid if he came at me, I might vanish again. "You have blind spots, Xavier. Places in your mind you've walled off. Did you know your mind is just like this..." I held my arms out. "Like your home. And the emotions you're afraid of, you've walled off so thoroughly that the rooms are blind spots. Spots that are completely outside this hidden world of yours."

"You escaped?" he asked, his eyes narrowing, then shook his head. "You think I'm fucking stupid? If that were true, you wouldn't be here."

"When you were a little boy, you did lots of bad things, didn't you? Things that scared your mother."

He stilled, completely, unnaturally.

"You scared her, disgusted her so much that she'd lock you in a room to escape you."

"No," he snarled. "You're wrong."

"You made up monsters, hideous creatures that you imagined protecting you, monsters that would kill anyone who tried to stop you from doing the sadistic things you loved to do."

"I don't know what the fuck you're talking about."

"I can show you, if you want me to. They're on the fourth floor, Xavier. They've been up there a very long time."

He was breathing heavily.

"Do you ever go up to the fourth floor, Xavier?"

He frowned. "No."

"Did you even search for me up there?"

His chest heaved and he started to shake, confusion, rage twisting his face.

No. He hadn't. "Why? Why do you think that is?" I needed contact usually to work my magic, but I reached out for him now and slid the tendrils of my power around him, not enough he'd notice but enough to press at the wall in his mind, the wall he'd locked all those memories behind.

He shook his head. He didn't have an answer. He didn't know why he avoided the fourth floor, and now the memories were pressing against that wall while I pushed with my magic from the other side.

"You were a bad boy, Xavier, and that's where bad boys go."

He roared and charged me.

I stumbled back as he ran at me, and Ren exploded from his hiding spot, knocking him to the ground. He went at Xavier like a wild beast, his fists connecting with the dhampir over and over again.

Xavier was taken by surprise, and blood spilled from his nose and ran down his chin. He roared and swung back, missing, then tried to shove Ren off. But Ren wouldn't be moved. They rolled across the floor, Xavier's mouth open, fangs extended, trying to bite and tear at Ren, who shoved him away. Xavier jumped to his feet and staggered. Ren pulled his knife free and charged the other male.

Xavier's eyes flared bright purple, and he threw a hand up. Ren was thrown out, outside the barrier of Xavier's realm. Still in the same room, but not here. Not with me anymore.

"Run, Jasmine!" he roared, unable to see or hear me but knowing I could still hear him.

Through the distorted air, I watched him spin away and run for the front door. I knew exactly where he was going—to the attic, to get back in.

I retreated and sprinted out the door, agony shooting up my

legs. The sound of Xavier pounding after me echoed on the wooden floorboards, his gait off. He was injured.

I ran up the stairs, using the railing to pull myself along, leaving a trail of blood as I went. He was closing in on me, so close.

"Jasmine!" he roared. "Come back here."

I hit the fourth-floor landing and backed up as far as I dared to the shadows and the snarling monsters. Their growls rose higher as they moved closer. Xavier swung around the corner, his face contorted. He slowed when he saw me standing there.

A snarl came from behind me, and his gaze sliced from me to the shadows behind me.

"Do you recognize them, Xavier? Your monsters?" I said, trapped between them.

"I don't…" He shook his head. "What are they doing here?"

"You put them here. I can help you remember," I said, pressing deeper into the wall when he took a step closer. I reached out with my magic, letting it build and grow. I'd had the night to recover, and I was close to full power.

Xavier moved closer still, and the monsters' frenzied snarls grew in volume when they saw him. They wanted him, wanted to get to him. Xavier had created them, then he'd abandoned them here, and they were angry.

Xavier grabbed for me, and I knew it was coming. I latched on to him, wrapping my arms around him with all my strength, pouring my power into him, aiming it all at the attic wall in his mind. He groaned from the force of it, grabbing for the wall to hold himself up. My magic had finally had the chance to recover and he was momentarily weakened by the force of it.

I knew the moment it won out, when he stopped trying to shove me away and wrapped his arms around me instead, so tight I thought he might actually crush me.

He groaned again, then struck, burying his fangs in my throat. I screamed, but I didn't let go. I needed to stop him, and the only way to do that was to break down every one of his emotional walls —before he drained me completely.

I cried out again and slammed the last of my magic into him, and it was like dominoes. As soon as the thickest wall in his mind came down, the rest followed, crashing down one by one, opening wound after wound, wounds I would not be healing.

He screamed and pulled away from me, his fangs tearing my flesh as he did. I fell back, pressing my hand to my throat. Xavier stumbled to the side, gripping his head, and that was close enough.

A black leathery-clawed hand grabbed his shoulder and yanked him into the darkness.

Xavier screamed, a bloodcurdling death rattle that sent ice down my spine.

The world shifted, the distortion that had surrounded me vanished. The realm Xavier created dying along with him.

Then Ren burst from the hall and gathered me up in his arms. "Butterfly," he choked, pressing his hand to the wound at my throat.

It was finally over.

Then those words took on an entire new meaning, because Ren was alone. I realized for the first time in three years, there were no souls with him.

He'd finally let go of his guilt.

"They're gone," I choked out.

"What?"

"You freed them, the souls, you did it. They're gone, Ren. You set them free."

Chapter Thirty-Five

Ren

"I'M OKAY," Jasmine said again.

As soon as we'd gotten out of Xavier's realm, the hounds had picked up her scent. By the time we got to my place, everyone was here. My small apartment was overcrowded with Jasmine's family, our family.

Daisy grabbed her again, hugging her so tight Jaz squeaked. Else had cleaned out her wounds, and dressed them, including the one at her throat. Watching Jaz in more pain had been fucking hard to bear, but none of us knew what kind of shit was on those monsters' claws. Her wounds would need to be closely monitored and Else had given us strict instructions before she slathered Jaz in balms, while Mags had given her spoonful after spoonful of potions and tonics.

I watched her now, a tired smile on her face, and my fucking heart clenched.

She loved me.

Jasmine loved me.

And right now, my female was exhausted, especially after losing so much fucking blood, but there was no way she'd say so. No, that's what I was for.

I pushed away from the wall. "Time to go, everyone. Jaz needs her rest."

Else turned to me. "I'm not leaving. She needs looking after."

"Love you, Else, but I'm kicking you out. All of you. I can take care of my mate."

Bram chuckled low beside me, and Mags nudged him to be quiet.

Daisy beamed. "Yes, we should go. Ren's got this."

Draven, Warrick, and Ronan collected their mates, and Relic and Rome said their goodbyes. Daisy and Art and Mags and Bram followed, and Else left last after giving me a list of instructions.

"I'll call if we need you," I said to her and pulled her in for a hug.

She wrapped her arms around me in return and nodded, then lifted her head and held my face in her hands. "Take care of each other," she said, then left.

I closed the door, and turned to Jaz.

She was watching me, a small smile on her lips. "You can take care of your mate, huh?"

"Yeah, I can," I said and strode over to her, scooping her up in my arms. "Doesn't matter that we haven't made it official, butter-fly, it's a done deal." I carried her down the hall and into our room. She froze in my arms, twisting to take everything in.

"Everything's new." I pressed my nose to the side of her throat and breathed in her scent. "We wanted our female to have a den that was all hers."

"I can't believe you did all this," she said, then she shook her head. "No, I can believe it."

Leaning forward, I carefully eased her to her back on the bed. "I'd do anything for my beautiful, precious female. Anything."

"I know."

I tugged off my shirt and climbed into the bed with her and we stared at each other through the dim light. "The block he used to lock away what you felt for me…" I rasped. I knew the truth, I could see it in her eyes, she'd said the words. But I needed to hear her say it again. "It's really gone, isn't it, butterfly? You…you love me again?" My voice sounded as desperate as I felt, and I didn't give a fuck. Jasmine knew me like no one else, she'd seen every part of me, I didn't have to pretend to be anyone else but the male I was with her.

She cupped the side of my face. "The block's gone," she said, her voice a husky whisper. "And everything I felt for you is back, and it's so big and so wild and, goddess, all consuming." Her eyes danced and glistened. "I'm so desperately in love with you, Ren, it's kinda ridiculous. And somehow, I love you even more now than before, when I thought that was impossible." She traced my lips with her thumb. "Does that answer your question?"

"Yeah," I said, my fox rumbling his approval through my chest. My heart pounded. "And in case you were in any doubt? I'm so fucking in love with you, Jasmine Thornheart, I don't know what to do with myself. I've loved you a long time, even before I allowed myself to see it. You're the reason I'm still here. You're the reason I woke up and chose to live one more day. It was your eyes in my head, your face, your voice, that pulled me back from the ledge every time I stood there. You are literally my reason to walk this earth, and I promise I will never, ever hurt you again."

A shuddery breath fell from her lips, then she thrust her fingers into my hair and pulled me to her, kissing me fiercely. She tasted fucking perfect, like autumn and home.

Her fingers dug into my flesh, her movements restless against me. She grabbed at the front of my jeans, trying to tug them open, and I took her hands and lifted them, shaking my head. "Butterfly, you're still too weak from blood loss—"

"I don't care, I want you."

"Baby—"

"I need you, Ren. Please," she choked out.

And I needed her. No way was I strong enough to stop this with her looking at me like that, with that tremble of need in her voice. "Okay, but first, I make you come."

She growled under her breath.

Christ, she was cute. Fucking shaking, I slid my hand down the front of her pj shorts. Else and Daisy had helped her shower and change before they sorted her wounds when we got here. "You'll get me, but not until I've tasted you." Her hips lifted, her panted breaths prickling goose bumps across my shoulders and down my arms, my stomach muscles were so fucking tight they were close to cramping.

She wriggled her hands free and weakly tried to shove her shorts down for me.

I grabbed her wrists again and held them more firmly. I wanted her hands on me badly, but just the warmth of her touch was enough to snap my control. Touch was still overwhelming at times, but not in a bad way, not with Jasmine. I shook my head and chuckled when she growled again. "You're injured, butterfly. You have to promise you'll stay still and not hurt yourself, or we can't do this."

"I'll stay still," she said in that same breathy, husky voice, and my cock throbbed harder. "Now, take my damn shorts off."

I grinned. "As you wish." I carefully peeled them down her legs, stopping at her knees.

"Ren," she gritted out.

"Can't get them any lower than that without hurting you or messing with the bandages." Else said Jasmine had to be extremely careful for the next two days, no bumping them or fucking with the dressings. I slid my hand up the side of her pj top, over her ribs. Goose bumps lifted across her skin, and her stomach trembled. "But I can work with you like this. Trust me."

She wrapped her arms around my neck, looking into my eyes. "I do, with every part of me."

I kissed her again deeply, then fucking shaking, I curled my hand around one of her breasts, squeezing. I played with her nipple as my tongue slid over hers, kissing her over and over again, small sips of her perfect lips, then devouring her with the full force of my hunger.

The scent of her pussy was driving me to madness. Trailing kisses across her jaw and down her throat, I sucked her tender flesh, marking her skin, and as I slid my hand down her belly, her legs parted as far as they could, which wasn't far. Her hips rolled, and I growled, fighting with my hunger for her, barely stopping myself from tearing the shorts from her body completely.

I gave her what she wanted, what I needed. I covered her slick pussy with my hand and slid my middle finger along her slit, pressing deep. She whimpered, and I circled her tight opening, teasing us both before gliding higher. She gripped my forearms, her nails digging in. Her lids were heavy, her lips swollen and parted, and when she bit the lower one and rolled her hips against my hand, I almost came in my fucking jeans.

"You close already, baby?"

"Yeah."

I jerked her top up with my other hand and yanked down the cups of her bra, then sucked a tight little nipple into my mouth as I slid two fingers deep inside her. Jaz fisted my hair with a cry. I fucked her with my fingers, while I worked her clit with my thumb. She tightened around me, and I lifted my head to watch.

She sucked in a breath, then screamed.

Oh fuck. Her pussy felt so good clamping down on my fingers. She was so fucking gorgeous straining for me, her beautiful eyes dazed and heavy with desire. When she quieted, I kissed her again while I tugged my jeans open and shoved them off, my cock was so hard I couldn't take it any longer.

"Roll to your side, baby," I said, helping her so her gorgeous round ass was aimed at me. I wanted to slide inside her so badly, but I wanted her taste on my tongue as well. Getting off the bed, I kneeled beside it, gripped her ass, spreading her, and dragged my tongue along her pussy from behind, groaning.

She pushed back against me, wanting more, and I gave it to her. I wanted to spread her legs wide so badly, but I wouldn't risk jostling her and hurting her, and I doubted she had the strength right then to do much more than lie there and let me pleasure her, which was more than fine with me. I sucked and licked her until she was dripping and rocking and begging me to fuck her.

I had decent self-control, but not now, and never with Jasmine. She destroyed me with a fucking look, broke me down with a plea. I was hers to command. I wanted to worship her for the rest of our lives.

She sobbed. "Please, Ren. Please."

"Shhh, butterfly, I'm gonna take care of you." I got up on the bed, and she tried to roll to her back, but I stopped her, keeping her on her side. She watched as I fisted my cock, then gripping one of her ass cheeks, I held her wide and slid the head through the center of her soaking pussy lips. "In this position, it's gonna feel like too much at first, so I'm gonna need to take it slow."

She bit her lip and nodded, her cheeks dark, her chest rising and falling fast.

I tilted my hips forward, the head sliding in. Her hand shot back, and she grabbed my thigh, her nails digging in. I leaned over her, holding the side of her face. She looked up at me, a sob falling from her lips as I slid in another inch. I gritted my teeth, holding myself back when all I wanted to do was thrust inside her to the root and claim her, bite her.

"Okay?" My voice was nothing but a growl.

"Y-yeah."

"Not too much?" I slid in another inch, then back.

She whimpered, and her eyes fucking dazed. "Yes, but I...I like it. Oh goddess...please. I want it."

She was killing me. "You want more, mate, I'll give it to you. You want your male to claim you, don't you, Jasmine?" I snarled, snapping the words, animal instinct taking over. "You want your male to make you his."

"Yes, do it. Make me yours."

There was no stopping me now, now that I had her in my arms, now that I was finally back inside her, now that she loved me again. I slid in deep, planting myself fully inside her, and she turned from me, crying out. I needed to see her face when I claimed her, so I gripped her chin so she couldn't look away, making her look at me, then I started moving, unable to go easy or slow.

I fucked her deep, hard. I wasn't going to last long, no fucking way. Not when she was everything, fucking everything to us and we were finally going to make her ours. We were going to mark her, and love her, and take care of her for the rest of our lives.

I slid my hand lower, curling my fingers around her throat, and leaned in, dragging my nose along her jaw to her ear, breathing her in, scenting my mate, a scent that was already branded on my soul. A scent I would recognize for the rest of my life, a scent that would lead me to her in the next so I'd make her mine all over again. "Gonna give you my mark, butterfly." I slammed into her with a grunt, a growl quickly following as I kissed my way down her throat.

One of her hands curled around the back of my head, holding me to her, as if I'd ever pull away, then her other hand took one of mine, linking out fingers. I kissed and sucked the skin between her neck and shoulder and my teeth sharpened, my canines extending. My fox threw his head back and howled his approval as I bit down on her flesh.

Jasmine screamed, her pussy clutched me so fucking tight, over and over, as she came for me, and with a snarl, I came with her.

I slammed into her, the taste of her pussy and her blood on my tongue filling my senses. I owned every part of her and she owned me.

I finally slowed my thrusts and gently licked and kissed the mark I'd given her, and Jasmine shivered. When I lifted my head again, she brought my mouth to hers, kissing me.

"You taste that, Jasmine Thornheart?" I said against her lips. "That's mine," I growled. "All mine."

Then I got into bed beside her, wrapped her in my arms and held my mate while she drifted off to sleep.

Chapter Thirty-Six

Ren

Jasmine walked into the living room, and I studied the way she moved. It'd taken her a week to regain her strength after Xavier almost drained her of blood and nearly another two weeks for the wounds on her legs and feet to heal, but the scars were still there. Fading, but still fucking there. I forced down the out-of-control feeling inside me that came with that memory, along with the desperate desire to go back in time, drag Xavier from that shadowed hall, and finish him myself.

I studied Jaz again. My mate was stubborn and incredibly strong, add in the fact she never complained and had that caring and loving nature of hers, always choosing to put others first, which meant she often forgot to take care of herself. Good thing she had me to do that now.

"You sure you're okay going for a walk?" I asked her again.

Her lips curled up. "Yes, Ren, I'm sure I can handle a short walk. You seriously need to chill."

"Well, that's not happening. I will never be *chill* when it comes to your health and safety," I said, and my fox added some growl to my voice, making sure our mate knew we were in accord on this matter.

She grabbed my hand and towed me through the door and up the stairs to the street. "Both of you can relax. I'm more than fine. And if you think you have a hope in hell of stopping me from going to my field, you're completely crackers."

"Crackers, huh?"

Her smile brightened, lighting up her eyes. She'd been desperate to get out among her butterflies for the last week, but I'd not been ready to let her out of my sight. I still wasn't. "We've been mates for nearly three weeks. When does this newly mated, crazy protective streak start to calm down again?"

"Calm down?" I laughed, it was low and gritty and seriously dark.

Jaz's brows shot up. "Mags said you guys go a little loopy and a lot caveman when you first mate, but then—"

"But then nothing, butterfly. Every day that you're mine, the need to protect you grows fiercer, right along with the bond between us." I grinned. "That isn't gonna change, so you'll just have to put up with me fussing over you."

She stopped and wrapped her arms around my middle, smiling up at me. "I think I can handle it."

"I'm glad to hear it."

"I feel pretty protective over you as well," she said. "Bree better steer clear of me for a while."

My stomach sank. "You know you have nothing to worry about. Those other females, they're not... Fuck, Jaz, I don't remember any of it. That part of my life, it doesn't exist anymore—"

She pressed her finger to my lips, silencing me. "I know. I don't feel threatened. I trust you completely. But I also don't like the thought of you with anyone else." She grinned. "Sadly, you didn't come to me a sweet little virgin, and this mate thing isn't only making *you* loopy, so prepare for your female to stake her claim on you whenever the urge strikes."

"Yeah? And how do you plan on doing that?" I said, knowing where she was coming from, because even though Rome was just her friend, I still wanted to tear the male apart whenever they were in the same room.

She slid her arms from around me, took my hand, and started walking again. "Well, I thought I'd keep it simple. Making out with you *a lot* will probably do the trick."

"Most definitely. At every opportunity."

Her laugh was light, beautiful. "That was my plan."

We walked through the gates of the field, and every part of her lit up. I'd been waiting to tell her something for a while, and now was the perfect time. She laughed and spun around as butterflies surrounded her, landing on her. Her breath hitched as her little familiars showered her with love and affection, and she gave them the same in return.

"I've missed you," she said, then sat in the middle of the field, her arms outstretched, talking to them, her pleasure and joy infectious.

I watched her, couldn't take my fucking eyes off her. She was the most exquisite creature I'd ever laid eyes on. She was everything I'd ever dared hope for and never thought I'd get.

Jasmine was my salvation. She'd saved me, by loving me. She saved the souls who'd been trapped with me. She'd helped me to finally set them free.

When she looked back at me, I walked over and sat on the ground beside her. "They missed you, and they didn't even know you until now."

"Yes," she said. "And it's the same for me."

"I get it. When I finally let you in, it was like a part of me I didn't even know was missing was returned to its rightful place."

She moved, and her little familiars took flight, fluttering above her as she climbed onto my lap, straddling me. Her arms slid around my neck. "You're the love of my life, Ren."

"And you, butterfly, are mine." She kissed me, and I held her tight and kissed her back. "I thought maybe we could have our mating ceremony here, what do you think?" I asked when we came up for air.

Her cheeks grew pink with delight. "I mean, it'd be perfect. This is one of my most favorite places, but wouldn't we have to get permission from the owner?"

"I'm asking her now."

Her chin jerked back, and a cute little frown shifted her features. "What?"

"The field's yours, Jaz."

"What?" she said again, her brows shooting up.

"I thought perhaps we could build a house here. Over there." I pointed to a spot on the other side of the field. "We won't disturb your butterflies over there or the other insects and animals who live here, what do you think?"

"You bought this field?" she whispered.

"Yeah."

"When?"

"After I found you here sobbing, after..." I didn't finish that sentence. Neither of us wanted to think about that time, or who did it. "I wanted to be able to protect it for you."

A tear streaked down her cheek. "Thank you." She kissed me again, then peppered more all over my face.

I swiped away her happy tears and grinned. "Is that a yes?"

She laughed. "That is most definitely a yes." One of her hands cupped my face, the other gripped the side of my neck, right over the sigils she'd inked there. "Thank you for trusting me with your heart, Ren," she whispered. "I promise I'll protect it with everything I have."

I cupped her beautiful face in return. "Thank you for trusting me with yours, butterfly, and I promise you, if anyone tries to hurt it, or take you from me again, I will burn their world to the ground until there's nothing left but ash."

Epilogue

Jasmine

Four months later

MUSIC DRIFTED THROUGH THE HOUSE, along with the sounds of my family's laughter. The house had been built in record time, mainly because it was small, but it was truly everything I'd hoped for. We'd planned it carefully, neither one of us had wanted to disturb the little ecosystem here, and there was room to expand when the time came.

Which meant the house was quirky and unique and I adored it. Bram and his brothers had helped Ren build it, since they had experience, they'd all built their own homes, and Bram's tree house behind my aunt's place was exactly the style I wanted.

"Sit down, those ankles are looking kind of puffy," Mags said to Iris.

"They are not," Iris said and looked down, then cursed when she couldn't see over her round belly. She was only five and a half months along, but with twins on the way, she was well and truly showing.

She lifted a leg out in front of her. "They're fine."

"They're not," Wills said from her spot on her mate's lap.

"I'll sit when I want to sit," Iris said, a stubborn look on her face.

My cousin had been struggling with the whole taking-it-easy part of her pregnancy. Draven strode over, picked her up, and set her on the couch. Then he sat beside her so he could pull one of her feet into his lap. "Time to rest those cute, puffy little ankles," he said.

"Draven," she growled. "I want to dance, not sit here like an invalid." Nia trotted over and rested her head on Iris's belly.

"Rest now, and you can dance later," he said and started massaging.

Her eyes rolled back, but she kept the stubborn look on her face. "Fine. But only for a little while." She ran her fingers through Nia's soft fur.

Draven grinned but was wise enough to turn away so she didn't see him.

Mags stood with Bram, his arm draped around her shoulders. She was telling him something and he was smiling. Rose was standing in front of Ronan, his arms were around her waist, and they were talking to Art and Aunt Daisy, who was holding a sleeping Violet. Else and Connor were sitting on the couch sampling the finger foods, and Stan stood behind her with an amused look on his face, listening to her tell some story that had Connor bark out a laugh.

My gaze slid to Zinnia. She stood alone, staring out the window. She had to return to Limbo in a few days and she was trying to hide it, but I knew she was scared. We'd found the missing souls, but we were still running out of time. In five months, I turned twenty-one. If we didn't find a way to get Zinnia out of her deal with Death by then, I'd lose her. She'd be trapped in Limbo with him forever.

Ren's arms slid around me from behind, his chin resting on

my shoulder. "We'll find a way," he said, reading my mind. "The females in this family can overcome anything." He kissed my neck. "We're proof of that."

I covered his hands with mine, linking our fingers. "I know, but it feels...it feels like I'm already losing her."

"Whatever happens, you'll never lose her. Your sister won't go down easy. She'll always find a way back to you."

Ren was right, but Death wasn't just some demon or monster that could be slain. He was a god, and in his eyes, Zinnia was his. He'd never back down. He'd never let her go.

The music was turned up, and Mags grabbed Zinnia's hand, dragging her into the middle of the room. Wills joined her, and Draven lifted Iris to her feet because there was no stopping her. Else and Daisy joined in as well.

I turned in my mate's arms and kissed him. "I love you, Ren. And I love our home."

He grinned down at me. "I love you, too, butterfly. Now get out there so I can watch my mate dance."

I laughed and spun away, running to dance surrounded by my family.

Right now, we were all safe, and we were together.

I was going to hold on to that for as long as I could.

Zinnia

I whispered the words and stood back as the boulders shifted, rolling and reshaping into a tall, wide arch.

I'd said my goodbyes last night, and I didn't have it in me to do it again this morning. Jaz would be pissed when she woke and found me gone, but she'd understand.

Leaving her always sucked, but knowing she'd found her mate, that she was loved and protected, definitely helped while I was away.

A wolf howled in the distance. Ash. I knew her howl, and she said she'd be on patrol this morning. She'd no doubt picked up my scent. Throwing back my head, I howled in reply, giving it my best shot, anyway. Others in her pack joined in. Their howls of farewell, lifting goose bumps across my skin.

I shivered and turned towards the gate; if I loitered out here too long, Death would come for me, and that was the last thing I wanted. I wasn't ready to see him, not yet.

Hitching my pack, I stepped through the gate and onto the path of skulls—

"Zinny!"

I spun around. Jaz stood there, Ren at her side, a bloody knife in his hand, and a grin on his face. My brother-in-law had left a trail of demon ash to get her to me.

My stubborn sister lifted her hand, and I smiled, not wanting her to see my pain or fear, and lifted my hand as well.

"I love y—"

The gate shut, vanishing in front of me, cutting my baby sister off, and locking me in Limbo.

I forced myself to turn away, from everyone I loved, and start walking. The path to Death's home was long and winding, but as long as you didn't veer off it, avoiding the dark forest either side, it was safe.

As I walked, I rebuilt my defenses, shutting everything down, my fears, my sadness, my rage—still, I wasn't prepared for the terrifying awe when I rounded the last bend. I never was.

The huge black, stone castle, jutting up from the ground always managed to steal my breath and make my knees tremble.

I walked up its wide steps, to the massive arched doors that swung open for me.

"Mistress, we've been anticipating your arrival," Egon said.

I smiled. "Hey, Egon." When I first met the male, I'd gone for my knife. Thankfully, he hadn't taken offence. Egon was a horned demon. His skin was leathery and deep green. His eyes were scarlet and he had pointed, shiny black horns.

"Your room is ready, Mistress," he said.

"Thanks. I'll head straight up."

"Would you like me to bring you a small repast? Dinner is still some hours away."

I shook my head. "No, thank you. I think I'll just unpack."

He dipped his head. "As you wish." Then his scarlet eyes met mine. "The master requests you to seek him out after you have settled."

"I'm not sure why he always insists I do that, he knows exactly when I get here." Egon said nothing, just waited for me to give him the answer he needed. "But yes, I'll find him."

Relief filled his eyes, and something else that set me on edge before he rushed off.

I headed up the wide, black staircase to the second floor and wall sconces lit the way, making the stone gleam. My chamber was almost at the end of the hall. Mors slept in the room beside mine. I'd never been inside, but I imagined it as some kind of twisted, torture chamber, full of things that would make your stomach churn.

I dumped my bag on my bed and all I wanted to do was get under the covers, close my eyes, and sleep for the next month. But if I didn't go find Death now, he'd come looking for me, a dark shadow, in robes that moved like they were a living, breathing thing, those blue eyes glowing from beneath its hood, full of anger.

If he was here at the castle, he was either with his brother, Somnus, or in his study. Still, I knocked on his bedroom door first. When there was no reply, I took the stairs to the next level. Somnus's bedroom door was closed. If Mors was with him, the door would be open. The study it was.

The heavy wooden door was open when I reached it, a fire

crackling from within, causing light to dance across the wall. The clink of ice told me he was inside. Power flowed to me then, wrapping around me, pulling me forward, telling me he knew I was there. The fear that always came when I was with him, filled me now and there was no stopping it. I let him draw me into the room—

Then froze, a gasp forced out of me before I could stop it.

Death stood in front of the fire, a tumbler in a tattooed hand.

But there was no robe.

I'd been coming here for a year and a half, and I'd never seen him without it.

He was shirtless, in only a pair of black trousers. His body was hairless, what I could see of it, anyway, from his tattooed skull to his waist. In between the ink, his skin was pale, and he was lean and cut with muscle. His head was dipped, looking into his drink as he swirled it. I still couldn't see his face.

"You came," he said, his voice rolling over me like thunder.

Words he said every single time. It took me several attempts to reply. I was having trouble catching my breath. "L-like I had a choice," I said, like I always did, but this time my voice shook.

He carefully placed his glass on the mantel, and turned to me, firelight dancing across his features.

I took an abrupt step back. Mors was...terrifying, his features etched by violence, and carved by death—and so utterly beautiful, it was hard to look at him.

His face was free of ink and he had a prominent nose, high cheekbones, a strong jaw, and sensual, dark crimson lips.

"Your robe?" I rasped.

"I no longer require it," he said, shaking me to my core with that terror-filled voice.

"You don't need it?" What the hell was that supposed to mean? I wanted it back. This, seeing him like this, it was too much. Way too much.

He shook his head, eyes boring into me. "I'll see you for dinner, consort. Make sure you're there on time."

I barely suppressed my shiver.

The way he said it, made it sound like I was the main course.

THANK YOU!

Thank you so much for reading
Jasmine and Ren's story! I hope you loved it!

Zinnia and Deaths's book is next in
A BOND IN FLAMES

Also by Sherilee Gray

Blood Moon Brides:

Blood Moon Bound

The Thornheart Trials:

A Curse in Darkness

A Vow of Ruin

A Trial by Blood

An Oath at Midnight

A Promise of Ashes

A Bond in Flames

Knights of Hell:

Knight's Seduction

Knight's Redemption

Knight's Salvation

Demon's Temptation

Knight's Dominion

Knight's Absolution

Knight's Retribution

Rocktown Ink:

Beg For You

Sin For You

Meant For you

Bad For You

All For You

Just for You

The Smith Brothers:

Mountain Man

Wild Man

Solitary Man

Lawless Kings:

Shattered King

Broken Rebel

Beautiful Killer

Ruthless Protector

Glorious Sinner

Merciless King

Boosted Hearts:

Swerve

Spin

Slide

Spark

Axle Alley Vipers:

Crashed

Revved

Wrecked

Black Hills Pack:

Lone Wolf's Captive

A Wolf's Deception

Stand Alone Novels:

Breaking Him

About the Author

Sherilee Gray is a kiwi girl and lives in beautiful New Zealand with her husband and their two children. When she isn't writing sexy contemporary or paranormal romance, searching for her next alpha hero on Pinterest, or fueling her voracious book addiction, she can be found dreaming of far off places with a mug of tea in one hand and a bar of chocolate in the other.

To find out about new releases, giveaways, events and other cool stuff, sign up for my newsletter!

www.sherileegray.com

www.ingramcontent.com/pod-product-compliance
Lightning Source LLC
Chambersburg PA
CBHW031835310726
48972CB00005B/1290